THE
GOD FIELD

Norman Kinch

The God Field© 2018 by Norman Kinch.

Cover design by Tané Kinch

Printed by Amazon Kindle
April 2018

ISBN:9781980457558

For Kathy, Vergi, Tané and Sinan

Chapter 1

"You're a complete fuck up!" Sian said calmly, with purposeful venom. "You can't show feeling…you can't show *love*."

Peter had just had an argument with his wife over his perceived indifference to the elegant gown she had tried on in readiness for an important function they were due to attend later that day.

"Can you please dress up smartly, just for today? After all, this is the biggest occasion of your academic life!" Sian said in a condescending tone.

He had hoped that she would refrain from verbally attacking him that day, for he was about to receive one of the most distinguished prizes in physics-the Feynman Medal. The award is given once every four years to an individual who has made an outstanding contribution to theoretical physics and is held in great prestige by the scientific community. Peter was due to receive the accolade in Queens Hall in Cambridge.

To please his wife, he dressed in his best attire when they later set off. It was the morning of Saturday 15 October 2011.

They avoided the soulless M5 motorway and drove instead along the slower route of winding country lanes, which suited the battered elegance of his cherished navy blue 1974 MG roadster. The leisurely pace of the journey and the refreshing beauty of the countryside seemed to have a calming effect on his wife, who never once reproached him on the journey; if anything, she was quite nice to him. Peter thought this might be because she held a begrudging pride in his receiving the honor. They were to meet up with their two children, Julia and Stephen, both in their early twenties, who had travelled up by train the day before to take in the sites of this historic university city. Peter had not seen them in some time and the thought of meeting them again filled his heart with a warm glow, which to some extent offset the hurt inflicted from Sian's embittered heart.

However, he was more troubled by a new theory he had developed. Its implications were so profound that they shook him to the very core of his being, for if true, would quite simply be the most revelatory knowledge to come to humankind. This was because his research had led him, reluctantly, into the realms of the *divine*. He had hypothesised the existence of a strange Mystery Field, (which he later called the God Field), that seems to be intricately involved in the creation all living and non-living things. Astoundingly, his latest test results in Manchester University seemed to verify its existence. This confirmation meant he had to venture, with the utmost resistance, into an area where very few physicists would dare to tread-into considering the possibility of a universe designed by a *God*.

If his fellow scientists found out about the `Godly` pathway he had taken, his reputation would be burnt at the scientific altar like the heretics of the past. He would then, no doubt, follow the fate of the brilliant, but unorthodox cosmologist, Fred Hoyle. His status took a rapid nose dive when he dared to question the accepted scientific dogma of the Big Bang and later postulated that life on Earth was seeded from outer space by viruses hitching a ride on board stray comets. Therefore, Peter understandably kept quiet about his new idea.

But no matter how hard he tried to blank his discovery out of his mind, it kept on eating away at his soul like a pack of wild dogs relentlessly pursuing a hapless wildebeest over vast distances of the African savanna. His theory appeared to have developed a bizarre life of its own and seemed to cry out to him, `Look at me some more and uncover my deeper secret. ` He felt an inner compulsion to determine what this might be. However, he feared that if he did so, he might be drawn into a deluded mission like the mad young Irishman he met in his local pub a few weeks previously. The wild-eyed man, convinced that he was a reincarnation of King Arthur, believed that Peter was one of his Knights and their destiny was to seek the Holy Grail together. His crazy behavior and verbally aggressive manner unnerved Peter, who had to flee to another pub to escape.

As they drove through the tranquil countryside, he couldn't help but dwell upon the God inferences of the Mystery Field. He still wouldn't allow himself to accept his findings which seemed to prove that some form of mysterious intelligence was involved in creating the universe. If anything, his psyche felt even more muddled and isolated than before. Trust `God, ` he mused to himself, to one day give you something so wonderful and the next to make you pay a heavy price for `His` gift.

Nothing, however, prepared him for what happened next. As they approached the town of Bishop Stortford, Peter suddenly slammed his foot on the brakes, sending them both hurtling forwards, causing him to bash his forehead on the steering wheel. When he lifted his head, he yelled out to his wife, "Sian! Look at those leaves over there!" The car had come to a stop a few feet from a twisting column of autumnal leaves in the middle of the road ahead of them. The spinning `structure` soon reached heights of over eighty feet. Although it looked like a tornado, it made no sound. He felt compelled to leave the car and walk towards it. His wife's protestations of "please don't go near that thing," made little difference, as he approached this strange phenomenon. By now, the swirling edifice had gained an incredible intensity. Fearless, he reached out his fingers to touch the vortex. Its energy consumed him. It was as if gentle hands were caressing every cell of his body.

Then, all of a sudden, the mass of leaves stopped spinning around and fell to the ground in a huge heap around him. He collapsed into the pile, exhausted by the extraordinary experience he had somehow been entangled with. He lay motionless for several minutes until the sound of an approaching vehicle brought him back to the real world. Sian then rushed over, grabbed him by his arm and led him to the passenger seat of the car. She took the driving wheel for the remainder of the journey. They were both in a state of shock. They hardly exchanged a word with each other for the rest of the trip, both carefully avoiding talking about the strange event that had just unfolded.

This was not the first inexplicable visitation to have befallen Peter recently; several other weird events had occurred since he came up with his theory.

His first `vision` happened two years earlier in his small study in Imperial College in London, on the day of his first insight that the universe may be shaped by a mysterious underlying field, the Mystery Field. Later that day, as this `revelation` slowly embedded itself into his subconscious, he slowly drifted into a trance. He is suddenly aware that he is deep in outer space hurtling with great speed through a wormhole between two parallel universes. On entering the new universe, he finds himself in a giant cloud of gas with the most profuse glow of light emanating from its center. He felt hypnotically drawn to it like a baby to its mother. However, he felt no forces acting upon him, only a balm-like energy that left him, for this time in his life, feeling at peace with himself. Upon reaching the heart of the nebula, all was silent and still. All around him, he could see iridescent rays of light transcribing moving arcs and other lines of curvature through space, as they looped within and around each other. He was witnessing the genesis of a new star unfolding before his eyes. He reached out his arm to grasp a ray of this golden light, which spiraled around in a glowing whorl of energy. It was if God himself was creating a miniature world in the palm of his hand.

The most upsetting `supernatural` experience had happened two weeks before his Cambridge visit, whilst holidaying with his family in Mousehole, in Cornwall, where they were staying in one of the quaint former pilchard fishermen's cottages in this charming seaside village.

Early one morning, he had driven by himself to the beautiful, deserted, white sandy beach at nearby Porthcurno. It was a serene, windless dawn. The waters were calm, except for the gentle breaking of waves. Whilst looking out towards the sea he noticed the swell of the incoming waves in the distance gradually increasing in size. Before long, they reached heights of over fifteen feet, before crashing down like thunder on the beach. But there was still no wind. It was a beautiful sight, especially when the rays of the rising sunlight shone through the crest of the waves, which looked like streaming crystals of aquamarine. However, their powerful wash soon caught up with him, causing him to lose his foothold and fall fully clothed into the surf. Each subsequent wave was bigger than the last. Now fearing for his life, he somehow managed to discard his shoes and summoning up all of his energy, swam to the shore. He then ran as fast as he could towards the top of the beach. Glancing back in panic, he could see a giant wave of some seventy feet in height come hurtling down upon him. It crashed with tremendous power, twisting and turning him underwater like a helpless piece of driftwood. The great force of water swallowed him up for what seemed like an inordinate amount of time. He could barely hold his breath any longer. He thought his time was up.

He was shaken out of this dream-like regression when the wave finally tossed him indignantly onto a sand dune above the beach, like a dog spitting out a foreign piece of food. It was as if the ocean Gods had taken him into their watery realm, like an alien abductee, to analyse him and had found him wanting. They were angry that he was still in a state of emotional slavery, trapped in time by negative events from his childhood, which prevented him from growing into the adult male that he should have become.

"*Only you can save yourself!*" they seemed to be pleading with him.

When he finally snapped out of this tumult, Peter lay bereft and bedraggled on the wet sand. Eventually the chill he felt from his damp clothes stimulated him into getting up and heading for his car. He drove back to Mousehole in a daze, unable to make much sense of what had just happened to him.

As they drove onwards, Peter pondered on the meaning of these strange events. He somehow `knew` that they were in some way linked to his theory. He wondered whether his breakthrough had somehow drawn him into the underlying creative process of the Mystery Field itself. `Have I become a part of the same mysterious process which my theory implies is forming the universe? Are these experiences psychically guiding me towards addressing the deep unease within myself? ` He was not sure of the answers to these questions, but he was certain of one thing-his mind was beginning to disintegrate and lose a grip of reality. The thought of losing control of his mental faculties scared the life out of him. His discovery had now become more of a curse than a blessing.

When they approached Cambridge, his thoughts ventured to the impending award ceremony. He was apprehensive about attending and had almost cancelled his appearance at the last minute, which would have meant someone else having to except the award on his behalf. However, he decided to go in the end because he thought the occasion would be a welcome diversion from the mental confusion his theory had brought him.

Just as the car turned into a main artery road leading to the city centre, his wife finally broached the subject of the strange manifestation they had witnessed on their journey.

"Peter, what was it we saw earlier on the road?"

"I *don't know* what it was and I don't want us to ever talk about it again either," he replied in an uncharacteristically abrupt manner.

Sian parked the car in front of Queens Hall. This grand structure overlooked the River Cam, near the peculiarly designed Mathematical Bridge. She pulled up in a spot reserved especially for them as distinguished guests. She cherished such moments of special treatment, for she received so little these days from her husband.

As they entered the foyer, Peter was overwhelmed by the intense volume of sound coming from the melee of chattering guests as they snacked on elaborate canapés and sipped fine wine. He recognised several faces in the crowd and a few, on seeing him, came rushing over to congratulate him on his achievement. But the strange event of the swirling leaves came to mind and derailed him even further. He stood rigid, his mouth tongue-tied like an animal transfixed by fear. After several prompts from his wife to speak, he could only mouth disjointed and inappropriate sentences.

"Ah Mark! It is *so* nice to see you looking *so* spritely and dapper!"

"Hello, Bob-you look super!"

`Why am I talking like this, ` he thought, when he became aware of his odd way of speaking?

He then caught sight of Simon Noyce, a trusted, but morbidly shy, former colleague. Needing to connect with someone with whom he could feel at ease, Peter walked over to him and warmly shook his hand. As he did so, he was instantly connected to some dark place in Simon's soul with such a poignancy that it hurt. He had somehow tapped into his inner anguish. He sensed the guilt he had been carrying since childhood when he had accidentally pushed his best friend, Michael Mehan off a tree, paralysing his legs, making him wheelchair bound for the rest of his life. The pain of this tragic event resided in the darkest recesses of his subconscious; it made him hate himself and to withdraw from the world. Peter felt Simon's suffering so intensely that he quickly snapped his hand away and immediately left his company to talk to another former workmate, Gavin Jobs, he saw standing nearby. Simon was left alone, taken aback by Peter's unexpected `rude` behavior.

By contrast, Jobs was never one towards whom one could feel any warmth or sympathy. This was due to his cold and offish manner, which mirrored an individual with little empathy for the plight of others. However, upon meeting his eyes, Peter once again made an instant bond with the soul of another person. He felt Gavin's torment in being the unloved son compared to his good looking, affable brother, Timothy, who was the apple of his mother's eye. Gavin's response was to put on a hard facade, which acted as defense mechanism from feeling the emotional hurt of being rejected by another human being.

Unfortunately, this had the effect of making him appear unfriendly and unapproachable. In his heart, all he really wanted was to be liked, and above all loved, by someone else. Such asymmetric affection by a mother to her children often causes permanent emotional scars to those who feel neglected. Peter felt moved to put his arms around the shocked Gavin, who surprisingly did not recoil in horror, but relaxed in a way that seemed to suggest he needed a hug from another person. "Thank you, Peter," he mumbled, like a deprived child.

These experiences drained Peter of his already limited reserves of mental and physical energy. He was concerned that he could now connect with the inner suffering of certain individuals just by touching or engaging in eye contact with them. His previous `external` visions and strange experiences were disturbing enough, but he now had to contend with this new source of psychic derailment. This could only compound his distress and confuse his state of mind even more. However, whereas he had no control over the onset of his outward manifestations, he could reduce the frequency of connecting with the inner pain of other people by being mindful of evading closer intimacy with them.

Peter therefore made a conscious decision to avoid staring for any prolonged period of time into the eyes, or shaking the hands, of any of the guests for fear of being `sucked` into their souls.

Unsettlingly, he somehow knew that these new events in which he made a direct link with the inner anguish of another person, were also entwined with the unfolding properties of his theory.

Luckily, Sian, seeing that he was not himself, quickly interjected and proceeded to dominate the conversation by deflecting attention away from her confused husband. Finding his two children in the commotion also helped to calm his mind.

After a while, the Master of Ceremonies, in a booming voice, beckoned everyone to take to their seats in the cavernous adjoining auditorium. Sian and their children sat in the front row. An usher directed Peter to an ornately gilded and red upholstered seat towards the back of the stage, where several distinguished luminaries were already settled.

Peter still felt bewildered and could only dwell upon such questions as, `Why am I here? ...I do not want to be publicly recognised by my peers, many of whom I do not respect?... I know what they are like; I know their frailties and tainted histories. But, above all, I do not wish to face them because I have lost faith in our blind profession. `

He then saw another former colleague, Jake Zuchi, in the crowd, but this time he was careful not to meet his eyes when he looked back at him. He recollected how he had groveled and manipulated his way up the hallowed academic ladder of the closeted world of theoretical physics. He would quite often steal the best ideas of his research students and pass them off as his own without a smidgen of conscience. He also once, anonymously, made up some spurious allegations to malign the credibility of his main competitor for a top position in Caltech. He later felt no remorse for his subversive actions, even after being offered the position.

When he caught sight of Carlo Marcottee, a brilliant and charismatic physicist, he could only think about his compulsively lecherous pursuit of the young female students on the campus of MIT. Many were bowled over by his good looks, natural charm and renowned public reputation, (for he was often to be seen as the face fronting popular science TV programs). He would forsake his overbearing arrogance during these romantic encounters, an attribute that would have given even the pugnacious Edward Teller, of Hydrogen bomb fame, stiff competition. This made for many a successful conquest, before he would

10

eventually dump his victim when he caught sight of some fresh new young quarry. His wife, distraught by his obsessive philandering, once tried to poison him with an apple injected with cyanide, (just as Robert Oppenheimer once did to a colleague he envied in the nearby Cavendish Laboratory). For some reason, he didn't go to the police afterwards-perhaps he carried some guilt after all. His wife tragically killed herself soon afterwards. However, after only a short period of grieving, he was once again up to his dirty old seductive tricks. He was nothing more than a selfish, unscrupulous, Lothario.

Peter thought it, strange just how utterly weak of character so many of the physicist fraternity were. A brilliant mind rarely equates with a good character, he reflected soulfully to himself. There were exceptions however. One of these was Claude Rivel, who he caught sight of in the audience. Once a former colleague of his at Imperial, they rarely met now that he was based in Edinburgh, after a short spell at Manchester. They had once been good friends, although they still collaborated on several projects together. He always found him to be a genuine and honorable man. Yet Claude hated himself, no matter what personal or academic success he achieved.

Nevertheless, most of Peter's peers were a complex mixture of human strengths and weaknesses-he counted himself among these. Peter's main character defect, like Claude Rivel's, was a default mechanism for self-loathing. He felt that he did not deserve anything that was at all good. The negative thoughts that ruled his mind made him feel like a permanent failure. The truth was that he was a decent person who possessed many special qualities, most notably, an unshakable integrity and an acute sensitivity. Regrettably, he would never let himself accept these qualities to be true.

Once the assembly hall was full, the Master of Ceremonies stepped onto the podium and introduced the occasion. Several dignitaries then gave speeches in which they highlighted Peter's contributions to science, gave personal anecdotes on his life and offered glowing praise regarding his personality, (none of which he believed).

Professor Jacobs, a Nobel Prize Winning Laureate, then got up to speak. He was someone he liked and admired. When he finished, he called Peter to come forward to accept the Feynman Medal. As he approached, the audience took to their feet, gave rapturous applause and cheers which showed how well respected he was by his fellow scientists. Professor Jacobs then presented him with a crystal glass sphere with a revolving hologram of the inside of an atom with its quark and lepton particles held together by the force carrying bosons and photons. He then invited Peter to say a few words.

But as Peter held the object in his hands, it seemed to burn into his skin, making him recoil with a jolt and almost drop the precious object. `How did that happen he wondered? Glass should not burn like this as it is a very poor conductor of heat… *here we go again*, ` he reflected irritably to himself, `the Mystery Field is doing its stuff once more, on *now* of all occasions. `

As Peter stood facing the now silent crowd, he could only feel a deadness of soul within himself. He was in a kind of limbo, a ghost like state, between heaven and hell. It was as if God was still undecided about him and was wondering- `Shall I take his hand and walk by his side or shall I let him sink along with the dark mountain of fear that has been his predominant companion in life? `

However, unknown to Peter, the real God, (who was seated, invisibly, by the side of the stage), only wanted him to learn to love himself and surrender to `His` will for him. Peter, though, was the obstacle to his own salvation, for he willfully refused to hand himself over to a Higher Power.

God understood this; `He` also knew something momentous was ahead of him, which would disturb the core of his wounded soul and ultimately melt his resistance towards `Him`. This was inevitable for the Mystery Field was already set in motion.

Peter paused for a moment before starting his unprepared thankyou speech. He looked out blankly towards the distinguished assembly. A long uncomfortable silence followed. Sian feared the worst. She was worried he might not utter a word or suddenly walk off the stage and leave the building.

His eyes were then suddenly drawn towards something strange hovering underneath the grand stucco plastered auditorium ceiling. Looking up, he could see a pulsating, round shaped entity, some ten feet in diameter. Lines of tiny, flashing, yellow and crimson lights ran along the outside of its transparent membrane. It looked like some kind of incredulous creature from the ocean depths, or an amorphous organism newly arrived from outer space. It was obvious to Peter that no one else could see this `thing` except himself. It then suddenly grew in size and took the shape of a giant, see through, worm-like structure, over one hundred feet in length. Now, seemingly emboldened, it twisted and writhed its way throughout the three-dimensional space of the great hall, as if exploring its new surroundings.

`Surely, I'm imagining it… I must be going mad…but it seems so *real*. ` He said to himself.

The last thing he wanted right now was another vision. `Thank you once more, *oh fucking Lord*, ` he cursed to a God he still inwardly refused to accept.

The `creature` then disappeared as quickly as it had arrived. As it did so, minute pearls of multi-coloured lights descended like dancing fireflies upon the unsuspecting gathering beneath. The audience looked up, mystified by this beautiful shower falling upon them. On seeing their reaction, Peter triumphantly exclaimed to himself, `It is real! It is real!` He was inwardly ecstatic that the onlookers had felt the afterglow of the organism's appearance. He had not lost his mind after all-it truly had appeared.

This was the moment Peter finally let down his scientific guard and accepted the celestial nature of the Mystery Field.

`I now believe! I now believe! The Mystery Field is real…God *exists*…God *exists*,` he ecstatically said to himself.

"Come on Peter! Please start your speech," came the friendly prompt from Professor Jacobs. Peter, now feeling reassured by the shared connection of the strange `being` with the audience, which seemed to confirm the integrity of his other manifestations, collected his senses and steeled himself before saying these prophetic words.

"I am sorry, but what I am about to say may shock you…I feel am being honoured for work in a scientific field which I now find vacuous… namely our endeavours to describe the physical universe. Let me explain myself… I have discovered from my recent research that ultimately all of our theories have an emptiness inherent within them, a vast chasm of meaninglessness."

The assembly of guests, offended by his deprecating denouncement of their `hallowed` profession, shifted nervously in their seats and exchanged negative murmurings with one another. The snake-like creature then re-emerged. It looked like a giant elongated watery tube, similar to the long bubbles drawn through wire rings by street entertainers using soapy water mixed with glycerol, except that its length now stretched across the full width of the ceiling. It quickly wound its way down to float just above the heads of the distinguished gathering, as if it was eavesdropping upon their conversations. It was like a predatory phantom leviathan stealthily stalking its prey, ready to engulf its quarry-the unwary audience below. The ethereal presence was still invisible to them however.

Peter, now accepting the reality of this twisting organism, felt emboldened to carry on with his speech.

"Please let me continue." He was now about to destroy any semblance of intellectual and scientific credibility he possessed.

"The reason for this emptiness is because all of the beautiful mathematical compositions we create, lack the one thing which would help them truly vibrate with nature's heartstrings."

Peter then took in a deep breath, as he steeled himself for the earth-shattering conclusion to his address.

"We have failed to see the divine nature of existence. We have been so ensnared by our fundamentalist scientific doctrines, that we refused to examine whether the universe is created by …a God. I have now found incontrovertible proof that our universe is designed by …God!"

The audible disquiet of the shocked crowd reverberated throughout the hall.

The organism's erratic, jerky movements betrayed its unease; it seemed to be very angry about something. The apparition writhed and rolled around frantically as if wounded by their evident disapproval of Peter's denunciation of theoretical physics and his apparent belief in a God. Yet the audience still could not see it. It then vanished again but this time it released a fine watery mist over the assembly below, bathing them in a kind of baptismal blessing of reluctant forgiveness. This unexpected spray descending upon them from above, seemed to spur the gathering into taking decisive action-*to leave the room on mass*. On their way out, some shouted angry barbs of abuse towards Peter such as, "You're finished, you *God nut*" … "You fool-how could you throw it all away like that!"

"God created the universe!" Peter calmly and assuredly exclaimed, as if oblivious to the exodus, his words now muffled by the commotion.

After about five minutes, only about forty of the five hundred guests remained, most of them journalists eager to gather more sensational details for their ready-made world exclusive. They were like a pack of baying, bloodthirsty, hyenas surrounding an innocent wounded gemsbok. The remainder consisted of his family, friends and a few trusted colleagues.

As he looked down towards the few remaining guests, he felt an inner serenity; his whole body emanated grace.

"The reason for my saying these scientifically blasphemous words, is that I have found God's fingerprint permeating throughout the whole of the universe. I call this the God Field, (this was the first time he allowed himself to use this term instead of the Mystery Field). It acts by interweaving different energy fields together to enable more complex structures and ultimately life to emerge."

The gravity of his words now hit home. It was as if he had confessed his innermost secrets to a gathering of high priests and priestesses, (his fellow theoretical physicists), without the privacy of the wooden screen of a confession box in between. He was emotionally shattered. As he took faltering steps off the podium, Parthy, his gifted protégé, rushed up to help him back to his seat.

Sian was bereft with furry at his actions-she knew there was no going back from his public self-assassination, which meant his career and reputation were now in tatters. The headlines of the world's media would soon prove to be his final academic death knell.

She then called out from the front row.

"How could you! You stupid…weak man! *That's it*-it is over between us for good-expect to receive the divorce papers soon!" The verbal battering came out like the release of a blocked well that held back dirty waters.

"Shut up mum…just shut up! Now is not the time to say such cruel things! How could you talk to dad like that? I am so ashamed of you." Julia cried out angrily. Sian, embarrassed that she had been caught off guard in front of her children, chose to make a quick exit, but not before uttering these words.

"Look, you don't know dad like I do. Everything I said is true!" With that parting dagger, she left the hall, beckoning her children to follow, but they chose to stay with their father in his hour of greatest need.

His children then rushed over to him. Julia said words of comfort aimed at reaching out to his retreating soul. She still wore the `hippie-like rags` of the new age traveller she had been over the last few years, since dropping out of university, where she had studied philosophy. He felt proud of her for not compromising her dress on such an ornate occasion. Stephen was also reassuring. He could not belie the sensitive nature that lay hidden behind the finest bespoke Italian suit he wore which befitted his high-flying job in the London futures market.

Having shaken off the clambering journalists, they managed to find a moments peace in a cafe in a quiet backwater just off the city center. Parthy accompanied them.

"You old dog!" Parthy exclaimed. "I knew you were hiding something explosive, but I didn't realise it would be *thermonuclear*…Now is probably the right time to confess something to you. A few weeks ago, out of curiosity, I cheekily picked up a piece of paper, which had some equations written on it, from your waste paper bin. Please forgive me for having done this. You see, I was only naturally inquisitive as to what new theory you were working on. I carefully studied the formulas but could not comprehend their true meaning, but I did sense they hinted at a strange new energy field of some kind."

Peter responded by apologising to Parthy for not telling about his discovery earlier. He also said that he sensed Parthy was aware that he might be onto something significant, especially since the latest ghost detector tests in Manchester. But he explained he didn't want to let the cat out of the bag until he was sure of his findings, "For I had to be certain, for it appears that the cat in the box was not Schrodinger's, but *God's*."

He told them of the terrible burden his discovery had brought him, particularly as he had been an ardent disbeliever in a deity. He added that this, along with the bizarre visions and events he had experienced since his breakthrough, had pushed him close to insanity.

His children urged him to take time out and go away to somewhere peaceful for a while to recover. Julia suggested he visit a Buddhist retreat centre in Wales she had once stayed in. "Don't worry about mum, we'll take care of her," she said reassuringly. Peter made up his mind there and then to do just that. He informed them of his intention to go away that day, "To get my head right," but that he would see them all again, "in a little while."

"I knew something had been troubling you at lot lately dad," Julia revealed. Just like her to cut to the chase, he thought. "I'm proud of you for having the guts to say what you said in your speech-the God stuff I mean. I, for one, believe it to be true." Stephen did not concur with his sister in this regard because he was unsure on matters concerning the meaning of existence, especially those relating to God. He preferred the anesthetic provided through drink and strong skunk, which also temporarily helped him to forget about his concerns in working in an area of finance he found to be morally bankrupt. His inability to change career, due to the wealth and status his job gave him, was also a source of much consternation for him. Therefore, rather than discuss any weighty issues with his father, he chose instead to offer him general words of support. Peter, however, understood that his son's sensibilities were not too dissimilar to his sister's.

Both siblings put their arms around him in a show of love for their wounded father. This made Peter drop down his guard and cry. He cried inconsolably. He felt shattered like a salmon must feel after releasing its spawn in the upstream gravel beds of a fast-flowing river; completely exhausted by this moment of creation. Likewise, he felt utterly drained by his revelation of the role of a supreme supernatural energy, the God Field, in the formation of all existence.

But Peter now found himself in a strange place, one that he was loathe to be in, for he now had to accept that God exists. He had no choice but to finally abandon his position of non-belief. Although he was reluctant to leave this secure place, it meant that he could now allow himself to speculate upon why there was this ethereal `sea` underlying all of existence. Why does the God Field create order in the universe? If this source really is from God, why does `He` want structures that are more complex? Is the reason to ultimately create intelligent life, including the human race? If this was the case, why does God want this to happen? Is the real purpose of the God Field one of becoming? If so, becoming what he wondered? Is it so that intelligent, feeling beings can draw nearer to the image of God? Could the ultimate purpose of the God Field be the unfolding of its pure potential so that such beings can actually *become God?*

Discovering the answer to these questions was to prove the greatest challenge of his life. The solution, bizarrely, was to come from facing his own inner demons.

Peter now understood Einstein's assertion that God "does not place dice" and David Bohm's notion that there is a "wholeness in the implicate order," were both correct. God does indeed play dice, but they are loaded dice, for the chaotic nature of the quantum world is `sculpted` by the

God Field. The God Field initiates random events because they act as a necessary precursor to the more orderly events that follow.

He finally accepted the reality of a hidden orchestrator to all of existence, which creates all inanimate and animate structures in the universe. Such an assertion would make Richard Dawkins apoplectic with indignation.

However, having made his, albeit tortuous, discovery, Peter felt he had completed his ultimate purpose in life. Furthermore, his marriage was over and his children had grown up to be lovely, well-balanced, independent people. The universe did not need him anymore.

It was true that, like the dying salmon, his end really was imminent, but not in any literal sense, for it was to be the death of his old damaged self and the re-birth of his true nature.

Once Peter had said his goodbyes to his children and Parthy at the railway station, he walked around the city's ancient Colleges. He strayed onto several restricted college forecourts where he was sometimes challenged by vigilant porters. His mind drifted to thinking about Cambridge University's great alumni of physicists, from Newton, James Clerk Maxwell, Rutherford, J.J. Thomson, Dirac and many others. It had not been his intention to denigrate their legacy in his speech that afternoon but he now saw that it must have come over as such. They were still his heroes and their contribution to our understanding of the nature of the physical universe was still immense. But he realised that he had unconsciously used shock tactics in his speech in order to shake the gathering of distinguished physicists into seriously considering the role of a Creator in the formation of the universe

Chapter 2

Peter returned to Queens Hall late in the evening; by this time, all of the guests had left and the front car park was empty, except for his beloved little motor. He sat comfortably in the driver's seat and decided to use this undisturbed time to focus on his God Field theory once more, with the intention of unraveling the reasons for the upset it had caused him. He recalled each of the main pivotal steps in its evolution.

It was just over two and half years earlier when Peter first came up with the inspiration for his earth-shattering theory. It occurred in Imperial College in London, where he was Professor of Theoretical Physics and had previously been an undergraduate, doctorate student, research scientist and lecturer. It happened whilst he was seated by the window of a small garret room, owned by the College, situated on the top floor of a red-bricked Victorian apartment block overlooking Kensington Gardens. He preferred this to his newly refurbished, but soulless, office in the depressing Physics Department building on the main campus.

He also held his tutorials there, although the University authorities frowned upon its use for this purpose, deeming it cramped and presenting a greater fire risk. Furthermore, his students loathed the trip required to get to his dingy hovel, which involved their having to negotiate a set of rickety rear fire escape stairs. They were forbidden from taking the main entrance to the building in Kensington Gore because of objections from some of its `snooty` residents. However, their efforts were soon rewarded when they engaged in discussions there, for Peter was an inspired mentor who gave his students free reign to explore their own ideas. Also, his gift for offering perceptive feedback had the effect of teasing out from them that extra bit of insight from their imaginations which left them leaving with a warm feeling of accomplishment inside.

The view from his room over the park was both beautiful and distracting. He had wasted many hours, days, and even months gazing at this majestic scene, hoping for an insight into a fundamental problem he was working on. However, the ideas, when they eventually came, were often of the utmost originality.

Whilst looking out of this window one bright June morning in 2011, he was reflecting back to a time when his children were playing beside the Round Pond outside nearby Kensington Palace. (The Round Pond isn't really a pond as such but is more like a small lake). His children had just thrown a handful of pebbles into its waters, causing a chaotic turbulence on its surface. However, the next time they threw some into the water it coincided with the booming sound from the Rolling Stones rehearsing for a concert in the adjoining Hyde Park. The sound was so intense that it produced ripples which interacted with and harmonised those from the pebbles his children had thrown, integrating them into series of radiating, sinuous, concentric waves. Whilst contemplating upon this serene event, Peter suddenly `knew` that a mysterious field underlies and influences all others. This `eureka moment` was of such sublime splendor it gave him a rush of excitement that surpassed any of his previous scientific breakthroughs, for it seemed to relate to the underlying origins of existence.

From that moment onwards, Peter began an in-depth examination into the nature of this hidden field. His father, who was once a distinguished physicist himself, helped Peter in his endeavour. During Peter's frequent visits to him in hospital, where he lay seriously ill with cancer, they spent much of their time discussing his son's embryonic theory.

In the months that followed, Peter's carefully dissected the chief existing candidates for the so called 'Theory of Everything, ' to see if the inclusion of his Mystery Field would provide the final missing link for the elusive correct solution. As part of this process, he produced a sequence of original equations which teased out a little more of the nature of his enigmatic field. He ultimately distilled them all down to one formula of such simple austerity he found it difficult to comprehend that it related to the very process of creation itself.

His final theory was an amplification of the latest string 'Theory of Everything, ' called M theory. As in these equations, Peter attempted to unify Einstein's General Theory of Relativity of space/time(gravity), with the three major forces operating at the atomic level-electromagnetism and the strong and weak nuclear forces. He did this by introducing his 'magical' new variable, the Mystery Field, (which he later called the God Field), upon which every other is intricately dependent. At that time, he did not know what this 'phantom' factor was, nor where it came from. He only knew that it operated according to a certain set of conditions, which if met, would facilitate the formation of subatomic particles such as quarks, electrons, protons and neutrons. Furthermore, its inclusion could predict the emergence of larger structures such as stars, galaxies and even living creatures.

The unveiling of the equation and of its mysterious unknown was the greatest moment in his life. His heart sang and danced with a feeling of euphoria. In the days following his discovery, he 'floated, ' rather walked around the College, He felt like the first scientist must feel having received confirmation of intelligent life in outer space.

However, at that time, he had no awareness of the deeper spiritual implications of his theory.

Following much deep thought, Peter hypothesised the Mystery Field to be a uniform field of potential energy, which permeates the entire universe. It was everywhere and in everything; in every animal, plant, rock, star and even in empty space. The Field is also intricately embedded in the fabric of space-time, which emerged after the Big Bang and was even imprinted in the singularity from which the Big Bang came.

Peter imagined the Field to be an unseen, either-like essence, which is immersed in and interacts with the `real` world to facilitate creation. The Field emerges from a `space-less point, ` in a `time-less moment, ` across tears in the highly folded, multidimensional membranes predicted by M theory. The Mystery Field `seeds` the physical world we know of with a mysterious invisible energy, which he called Zeru, after the ancient Sumerian word for seed.

His formulations indicated that these `seeds` are string-like, (quantum field), waves which respond to underlying harmonic vibrations from the Mystery Field. The waves would cross the tears in the M theory membranes and travel along tiny quantum tunnels which unfold to link with the larger worm holes connected to our real physical world. These waves, guided by the underlying designs of the Mystery Field, would then initiate fluctuations which, by means of quantum entanglement, `create` all energy and matter. They would also `create` Dark Energy, and the Higgs Field which enables particles to have mass. A hidden potential, stemming from the Mystery Field, would always give a directionality towards greater complexity in the universe.

He realised that the physicists cherished second law of thermodynamics, in which everything in the universe eventually breaks down (entropy), is nothing more than a by-product of the main creative drive for greater complexity. In fact, it indicates that the only purpose of this `chaos` is to recycle energy and matter into more complex structures in the universe. This is why cataclysmic supernova explosions form its heavier elements. The Mystery Field would be the `architect` of such events. It would seemingly appear out of nowhere when there was the possibility for increased complexity.

However, once the ecstatic feeling from his breakthrough subsided, Peter became deeply worried, for his theory inferred that there is an invisible 'hand' creating all natural phenomena, in other words, a *God!* He had no idea that his first notion of the Field from a disturbance of ripples in the waters in the Round Pond in Kensington Gardens, would lead to implying, of all things, a Creator, for he had been a devote atheist for most of his life. The shock of discovering the potential celestial nature of existence now waged war with his entrenched non-belief system and led inexorably to the fragmentation of his personality. The strange visions and experiences, which also began at this time, only served to further tip him over the edge of reality.

The implied divine nature of his theory sent Peter in a frantic endeavour to prove that it was incorrect in some way, for this would then allow him to reject its God implications and help him to return to his safe-haven of skepticism. Therefore, he set about testing the mathematical efficacy of his theory, in a desperate search for flaws. He deconstructed and reformed its main equation and the many scaffold ones from which it was derived but could find no inconsistencies in them whatsoever. This result only served to undermine him even more.

The only consolation then left to him was the impossibility, (as he saw it), of proving the existence of the Mystery Field in the real world. After all, he inferred, it is impossible to independently measure the quantum world, where the Mystery Field mainly operated, as the very act of measurement makes the fields collapse. However, it did cross his mind that the Mystery Field might operate in a different way from normal quantum phenomena, as it is intertwined with the geometry of space/time and this might make it observable in some way. Nevertheless, he was still certain that the Mystery Field could never be detected, which meant he could carry on pretending to himself it was the product of a physicist's over active imagination.

Nevertheless, his rigorous scientific training couldn't let this go, he just had to rule out the possibility of the Mystery Field ever being observed. He therefore, obsessively, conjured up a multitude of thought experiments to flesh out the Field from its seemingly impregnable hiding place, but without success. However, it was his father who gave him a possible way forward during Peter's final visit to him in Hospital. Mustering all of his fading energy, he grabbed his son's hand and exclaimed, "Look for irregularities in the data –that is the way forward!" Sadly, he passed away later that night.

After his father's death, Peter followed his advice. He was further inspired to pursue this new path whilst reading a biography of Albert Einstein. It mentioned how he had been emboldened to question the sacrosanct doctrine of Newton's universal laws of gravitation from observations which seemed to contradict them. This ultimately led to the development of his Theories of Relativity. Peter therefore proceeded to scrutinise observational data relating to the formation of structures both great and small, from stars and galaxies, to the growth of plant stems, the development of chick embryos and the regeneration of axolotl salamander limbs.

But after several months of compulsive searching he found no significant aberrations, until it occurred to him that he may have been looking in the wrong place. He therefore shifted away from examining general sets of results to focusing on a detailed analysis of data associated with key moments in the development of life and matter. It was then that he began to uncover discordances, which implied that there might be an unseen field associated with them. He discovered that all of the structures he researched had the same anomaly. It appeared as if no scientist had thought of looking for such a common irregularity before. He could not `see` this field, but its existence was implicit, just as astronomers can infer a hidden planets presence from the way it affects the orbit of the star around which it travels. He had uncovered the first, albeit indirect evidence, that the Mystery Field actually exists.

He was astonished by this finding, which pointed to the Field being real; but his conditioned intellect just couldn't accept this truth. Surely, he thought, even if I accept its indirect existence, there is no way it could ever be seen? Peter then started a hunt to find out if there was any way of making it visible. Why he did this, knowing that it could reveal the very thing he wanted to remain concealed, only his subconscious knew. He could easily have then abandoned his Mystery Field explorations and no one would have been any the wiser, for at that moment it was still nothing more than a barren series of symbols and numbers, no matter how mathematically beautiful they were.

Peter concentrated his mind for many months on this problem but could find no way of revealing the Field. After nearly six months, he was about to give up his search when he remembered how Stephen Hawking had theorised that black holes could potentially be `seen` by the release of, (Hawking), radiation at their event horizon. Peter wondered whether some new kind of energy might be released at the point where the underlying God Field interacts with the real world. After much detailed analysis of his equations, he was stunned to discover that they did indeed predict the release of some new kind of weak radiation between the two worlds, the Mystery Field and the membranes of M theory. Although it seemed to be unlike any other known kind of energy and he was unsure how to detect it, he nevertheless could determine some of the parameters that may help him identify it.

Luckily, a `chance` event a few weeks later gave him a hint of a possible way forward. (This wasn't strictly one of chance, because God, who was seemingly always around, had a hand in this incident unfolding). Parthy, his brilliant, trusted, doctorate student, had passed onto him a science fiction novel he had enjoyed reading called *Quantum Ghosts*. Reading the book had jogged Peter's memory into recalling a revolutionary innovation in radiation detection, called Inverse Mirror Ghost Tunneling, which is meant to have an extraordinary potential in sensing even the faintest of energy fields. Perhaps it could reveal his God Field/membrane boundary emissions, he wondered?

Once he had made some speedy background research concerning the device, he called its inventor, Professor Michael Phillips, who was based in the School of Physics and Astronomy in Manchester. He asked if he could use the detector to search for the weak form of radiation his equations had predicted but gave no hint of their deeper implications. The Professor, who was very friendly, said he would be pleased to assist him. He mentioned that he was an admirer of his work and how a former colleague of his, Claude Rivel, had often spoke well of him. He pointed out that the detector was still in its prototype stage but searching for Peter's faint energy rays would help in its further fine tuning.

They agreed to work together during the approaching summer vacation. Peter invested every spare intervening moment devising an experiment they could test together.

As soon as the summer recess began, Peter travelled to Manchester. Parthy accompanied him as his assistant. He was, however, careful not to let the Professor, Parthy, or anyone else in on his discovery of the Mystery Field. It was also very unlikely that they would infer its deeper significance from the experiment they were about to start, for the radiation they were looking for was not from the Field itself but was only a remnant from interactions at its boundary with the real physical world.

Following several weeks of preparation, in which they worked closely with the Department's skeleton semester technical staff, they were ready to begin their first experiment which was designed to monitor the growth of ice crystals. They were to collect time-lapse data over several runs, each one week in length.

The detectors sensor had a series of evenly spaced quantum dots, which could sense tiny disturbances, called quantum jiggles, caused by the observed radiation. These would then excite electrons into emitting photons, which would be enhanced by the detectors cutting-edge photomultiplier to produce a fluorescent 3 D holographic image on a computer screen.

The first tests of the growing crystals produced only a faint, hazy image on the screen. However, this was soon shown to be caused by some kind of quantum interference with the sensor. Several weeks passed by and the problem could still not be resolved. It looked as if the perennial problem of impartially observing quantum phenomena, was as work. Peter was even mulling over whether to abandon the tests and return to London.

However, after three intensive weeks of further fine-tuning, the interference was cancelled out and the detector was the most sensitive it had ever been. Subsequent trails gradually revealed a constantly changing and highly folded ghost-like image that appeared to be interacting both within and around the developing ice crystals in some way. Although the images were fuzzy, faint and almost imperceptible, they appeared to be the energy he had been looking for.

Peter then compared some of the properties of the observed radiation with those predicted by his Mystery Field equation. They seemed to match. It appeared as if he had the first visual evidence that his theory may be correct. He was shocked; this wasn't the result he wanted, for it indicated that there is some form of hidden creative drive to existence. This unexpected conclusion sent him into an even deeper depression, for his unbelieving mind set wasn't ready to accept this `truth. ` Professor Phillip's, unaware of Peter's Mystery Field theory, was perplexed by Peter's underwhelming reaction to their discovery; he couldn't make any sense of it.

Following five more weeks of intensive image gathering and analysis, Professor Phillips and Peter were due to take their late summer holidays. Peter intended to carry out a much more thorough analysis of the data when he returned to Imperial after his break. They found great reward in working together and promised to meet up again soon to carry out further tests. Peter was hoping to arrange some authorised absence from Imperial in the forthcoming academic year to continue their experiments in Manchester.

The day after his return from holidaying in Italy with his family, Peter headed straight for Imperial to use its new CORE supercomputer to examine the data gathered in Manchester in more depth. He needed to process the parameters of the interactions of the radiation with the developing crystals, but this would require a lot of computing processing power and time. Luckily, there was ample available to him as the College was still relatively empty of staff and students using it, as it was over two weeks before the start of the new term.

Peter visited the computer room every day to monitor the progress of the data analysis. For several days, all that he could see were discordant wave pattern images surrounding the crystals as they grew. Out of curiosity, he translated the information into its equivalent sound impression. He then played the results via an amplifier to a loudspeaker. The noise, or rather the devastating blast, which came out, shook the computer room with such force that it shattered several of its reinforced glass windows. It was an unearthly sound. It felt like a thousand small needles piercing the brain. Everyone present held their hands over their ears and crouched down as if punched in their solar plexus. The technicians screamed at him to stop it. After scrambling over the controls of the amplifier, Peter eventually managed to switch the signal off. Peter was left feeling shaken and embarrassed. He humbly apologised for what had happened and fibbed that he had accidently set the volume to full power. No one believed him, for the sound was so extraordinary. In an attempt to diffuse the situation, he promised the computer staff that the Physics Department would pay for the damage. However, he received several strange looks from them when he later left the room.

Five days later, the data processing was complete. He knew this as soon as he saw a beautiful, moving 3D fluorescent image of intertwining, pulsating, harmonic waves which moved around and within the ice crystals. Each wave was interlaced with a series of finer vibrating, thread like, waves moving in a hypnotic dance. Once again, he converted this information into sound. However, this time he took the seemingly reckless step of plugging a pair of headphones into the computer and placing them over his ears. He knew this was a foolhardy decision after what happened previously, but he somehow sensed that the sound this time would not be harmful. He slowly increased the volume. The sound that came out was to change him forever. It was not sound as we know it. Its energy occupied him. It infiltrated his soul. It took him to a place of ultimate bliss. Peter felt as if he was listening to a secret symphony of celestial music, one that no human being had ever heard before. It was as if he was eavesdropping upon the voice of God.

Peter looked around the computer room; no one else heard the sound. However, everybody was staring at him, their faces radiant; they seemed in a state of serenity, like Peter himself. When he got up to leave, everyone else present, bizarrely, came over and hugged him warmly.

It took Peter nearly a month before he was able to look at the results once more, for the `sound` he heard that day was beyond his limited human comprehension. How could he still doubt God's existence, for he had `heard `His` voice` in that brief moment of `music` emanating from the trace memory of the developing ice crystals? Although this experience was beyond his understanding, it humbled him and made him put aside his seemingly petty calculations and thought experiments. He felt unworthy of receiving `His` voice. `Why me? ` He asked himself incredulously. When he did get around to examining the processed results of the experiment, it only confirmed what he already knew- that the radiation was the trace imprint of the unfolding properties of the Mystery Field. It proved it surrounded and permeated the crystals and was the driver of their formation.

Although he now had no choice but to finally accept the presence of the Mystery Field as an overarching and controlling `intelligent designer` of the universe, he was still unable to accept it deeper implications. His blinkered vision refused to connect the Field with a spiritual deity.

Professor Phillips thought Peter had discovered some kind of left over background radiation from the normal processes involved when a system develops. He had no inkling of its more profound significance. Parthy, though, was not so sure. He sensed that Peter was hiding something. He could see through Peter's body language and the way he articulated his words, that something was not quite right with his mentor. He knew that something big was up. Furthermore, Peter was aware of Parthy's suspicions and recognised it was only a matter of time before he would say something to him.

Peter outlined the discovery and confirmation of the new radiation, (but not the Mystery Field), to his Head of Department, who was impressed by his breakthrough. However, he was somewhat vexed that he had carried out the tests in Manchester without informing him beforehand. Nevertheless, he was keen that Peter carry out further trials and gave him two eight-week blocks to visit Manchester in the new academic year.

Three months later, Peter and Parthy were back in Manchester working with Professor Phillips again. This time they used the detector to monitor the subdivision and multiplication of yeast cells in real time. The strange time-lapse images of the energy field, once more appeared to be dynamically associated with the developing cells.

When Peter returned to Imperial, he again transferred the data to the supercomputer to compare it with his Mystery Field predictions. They matched perfectly. Just as for his previous experiment, the final dynamic 3D florescent images were of breathtaking serenity. This time, though, he was careful not to convert the results to a sound recording because he felt undeserving of `hearing` the `sound` of a God he still could not fully acknowledge.

God, who was often nearby, could not fathom how any human being would forsake listening to His `voice,` if they were given the opportunity of doing so. However, he admired Peter for his brilliant insights, as well as his genuine humility, attributes which further convinced him he was worthy of receiving `His` magical sound emanating from the God Field.

The final eight-week spell of testing in Manchester ended only three weeks before the award ceremony in Cambridge. This time Peter used the ghost image detector, (as he now liked to call it), to monitor the growth of common frog embryos suspendered in a nutrient medium. As in the previous experiments, the radiation was present. The subsequent computer analysis confirmed its involvement in the division and differentiation of the amphibian's cells. The images produced were as majestic as before. However, he still refrained from making a sound equivalent of the memory radiation.

It was approaching midnight when Peter finished churning over the development of the God Field theory in his mind. It had made little difference, for he still felt as muddled and bereft as before. Desperately needing a break from these recent tortuous events, he therefore decided to keep to his intention of `escaping ` to somewhere out of the way to recuperate.

Peter stared blankly through the dew-covered windscreen to the blurry gothic splendor of Queens Hall. He then got out of the car and took in the rawness of the autumnal night. The musty smell of fallen leaves mingled with the damp of a low-lying mist, which covered Queens Green in front of him. The surrounding Cambridge streets were eerily silent except for the intermittent shouts and disjointed noises from drunken students as they stumbled back to their digs. After a few minutes, a wind picked up which sent random flurries of fresh air over his troubled face. This helped to sooth his distressed soul.

Chapter 3

Peter then set off from Cambridge. He drove with no particular destination in mind. The dark curtain of night cast a veil over the blurry patchwork of Cambridgeshire fields. Several hours soon went by, although he had no real idea of the passage of time. Little of the outside world registered in his conscious mind with the exception of certain place name signs: Huntingdon, Kettering. Rugby, Birmingham, Telford, Shrewsbury.

Something within him had snapped since his revelation to the shocked audience earlier that day. His God Field `confession` had tipped him over the edge of despair. He felt utter hopelessness and resignation. He was a lost soul, aimlessly roaming through a world inhabited only by other lost souls.

Once Peter passed Shrewsbury, he left the main road and headed for the rolling Welsh foothills with their wooded valleys sculpted by pristine rivers. His car headlights lit up the pitch-black narrow country lanes with their ancient hedgerows, which were being buffeted by the first winds of an approaching storm. He loved this wilder landscape with its raw nakedness; it seemed to connect with some part of him which was beyond the dimensions of our pitiable existence.

It was then he became aware that his journey had not been a random one, but an inner compass needle had been guiding him towards Wales. He remembered how his daughter had suggested he stay a few days in a Buddhist retreat centre, near the town of Machynlleth in west Wales. He had been heading there *all along*. He was mystified that his aimless wandering did in fact have a purpose to it; his mind was not as divorced from itself as he had imagined. Little did he know that God had a secret hand in directing him towards this destination.

He pulled up his car into a quiet lay-by and googled `Buddhist retreat Machynlleth, ` into his mobile phone. Although the reception was poor, it eventually came up with `Ynys-hir Buddhist Retreat Centre`. The description sounded very inviting, especially its aspect which "overlooked a nature reserve, (where ospreys regularly nest), and the magical sandy estuary of the Dyfi River."

Two hours and several wrong turnings later, he finally found a sign for the Buddhist Centre. He then drove up a steep valley side and along a pebbled track where he could just make out a large building shrouded in darkness. As the little car struggled to navigate the bumpy terrain, he reflected on how well it had withstood the rough battering it had received along the Welsh country bye roads.

Although it was very late, the noise of his approaching vehicle and the automatic sensor lights disturbed someone from inside the building. A young man approached the car; Peter felt shy. In order to prevent the onset of one of his visions, he reminded himself not to make close eye contact, or touch him, or anyone else, he would meet in the Centre. `*Don't* shake his hand; *don't* look him in the eyes, ` he kept repeating to himself as he wound down the car window. However, he couldn't stop himself from examining the man's face. Luckily, he wasn't sent into one of his regressions. The man possessed strong, but also sensitive, features. Peter guessed he was in his mid-twenties. He was dressed in jeans and a tee shirt with a picture of the late, `crazy` Led Zeppelin drummer, John Bonham on its front and Mick Jagger's famous protruding tongue image on its back. Peter expected to see someone wearing a monk's robe. The young man gave him a warm greeting.

"Hello, my name is David, I'm on night duty here. Can I help you?"

Peter apologised for his late arrival and for not having booked a place beforehand. He then explained why he had come to the retreat.

"My daughter Julia once visited the Centre and suggested I stay here for a few days. To be honest with you David, I need a little time by myself to help me deal with some stressful things that have happened in my life recently." He did not explain what these were and neither did David ask him about them either.

"Certainly, Peter, you are more than welcome to stay a while… we only ask that you donate a little to the housekeeping fund and follow our basic house rules. The important ones are to respect one other and to help out a little where it is needed-in the cooking, washing up, cleaning-that kind of thing."

Judging by the way he spoke, Peter presumed that David came from a well-educated, middle-class background; he also surmised that his reside in the retreat was his way of breaking free from such an upbringing.

"Why don't you come in for a quick cup of tea and a snack-you must be tired after your long journey?" Peter willingly accepted his kind offer, as he had not eaten or drank since leaving Cambridge, having only stopped off once along the way to top up on petrol and go to the toilet.

They chatted convivially for a while. Peter was very impressed with the man's character, which seemed to belie his young years. In conversation, David touched upon the camaraderie of the residents in the Centre and contrasted it with that of his own home, "Unlike my teacher parents, who used to take out their work frustrations on each other." This seemed to add some support to Peter's supposition as to why David had sought solace in such a tranquil place.

Peter himself said very little. After they had finished their tea, David led him to a small room where Peter collapsed fully clothed onto the bed and slept a long deep sleep.

On waking up late the following morning, he lay in bed thinking about his situation. With his marriage and academic career in ruins, he sensed that something significant was about to take their place. What he did not know was that they were to be substituted with a lifesaving replacement…only God knew this.

This new life had already begun when he choose to take time out in the retreat to recuperate from the recent turbulent events in his life. However, right now, he could barely muster the energy to get up, let alone do anything at all meaningful. His heart felt detached from his brain, it was in some kind of shutdown from reality, a self-imposed strike from the world around him, a withdrawal from people and life. He was like a computer that had crashed and had all of its memory banks wiped out; likewise, he felt bereft of all of the life experiences he would need to engage in normal social communication with other people.

With his mind in such a delicate state, he dreaded meeting the other residents in the retreat. In any case, people scared him and had done so ever since he was a teenage boy. He found them to be generally predatory by nature. His life had taught him to be wary of them. In a way, he was akin to a mercat which would quickly take flight into its burrow on seeing the passing shadow of a vulture overhead. Likewise, he would shy away, through fear, from making close contact with another individual, especially when they endeavoured to connect with him on a more personal level. But why he should be afraid of meeting, the no-doubt, gentle souls in the retreat he wasn't sure. Nevertheless, he felt relief when he recalled a piece of advice David gave to him the previous night. He said Peter did not have to say much to anyone else in the Centre if he did not wish to and no one would feel offended by this. With this in mind, he got up from his bed, cleaned himself up and went downstairs to explore the house and its surroundings.

The building was a grand late Victorian country house built by a Birmingham industrialist who had made his millions from the sale of automated cotton machines. There were eighteen bedrooms on two upstairs floors and several large room spaces downstairs, the smallest of which was used as a prayer room and the largest as a study/library. At the front of the building, there was a large conservatory, which served as a refectory. It had a magnificent view over the Ynys-hir nature reserve and the Dyfi river valley.

A large former coach house was situated in the garden, which was now used as a temple. A shrine occupied the front of the room upon which lay a large golden statue of a cross-legged, young looking Buddha, surrounded on either side by scented candles. These illuminated the walls which were covered with elaborately and colourfully embroidered fabrics showing representations of different stages of the Buddha's life. A ceramic bowl of sacred water and a silvered dish containing several freshly cut winter flowers, presumably from the garden, lay on a low-lying table in front of the statue. The floor of the temple was covered in prayer mats in the shape of a lotus flower plant leaf.

The gardens were extensive and mainly planted with rose beds and sporadically distributed shrubs and trees. There was a large vegetable and fruit garden to the rear of the building, opposite the kitchen, which must have provided for most of the culinary needs of the retreat.

A prayer path wound its way through the grounds. It was intermittently lined with twelve `stations, `each with a wooden seat next to a small tree from which hung small golden bells and little bundles of flowers and plant seed head offerings of various kinds. Also hanging from each tree were copies of prayer and story scripts encased in protective plastic sleeves.

Having finished his initial exploration of the retreat, Peter decided to face up to meeting some the inhabitants of this beautiful place. However, his reticence in making the acquaintance of strangers immediately kicked in and gripped him with fear. The old negative gremlins re-surfaced in his mind and made him believe that they would automatically dislike and reject him. David, who he met at the bottom of the main stairs, sensed his trepidation and gave him a warm greeting. He took Peter to the main kitchen and introduced him to the cooks there. He then asked him if he would like to help prepare the evening meal. Peter willingly acquiesced and undertook the task of pealing, cutting and washing a huge pile of vegetables, which included the largest mound of potatoes he had ever seen. My God, he thought, these Buddhists eat enough vegetables to feed a *fucking army*-no danger of irregular bowel movement here!

When he had finished these chores, Peter offered to help with the cooking. However, he informed the others that, although he was a reasonable cook, he knew very little about cooking vegetarian food, but he was keen to learn. After some tuition on how to prepare the evening meal from a beautiful young woman called Kirsten, he set about the tasks given to him. He really enjoyed using the fresh, natural, non-meat ingredients.

David then introduced him to the other permanent residents and visitors of the retreat, an ordeal he found draining. However, he felt a sense of relief afterwards for having overcome the initial tensions he always felt when meeting someone new.

He said very little to the other diners as they gathered in the refectory later in the afternoon for their main meal of the day. The low rays of the setting sun over Cardigan Bay in the distance streamed in through the conservatory windows, its light radiating the healthy completions of the monks and their guests.

As he was leaving the dining room, after eating a delicious and hearty meal, one of the monks, perhaps sensing that meeting the other residents had been a trail for him, placed his arm around his shoulders and said.

"Don't worry about getting to know all of us straight away-there's plenty of time for that. I too, was shy when I first came here and now I feel happy all of the time! Also, remember to take regular walks around the grounds and make time for some quiet contemplation in the garden temple-you don't have to be a practicing Buddhist to go there you know; you don't even have to believe in a God!" He ended his advice with loud, uninhibited laughter, one free from our normal human constraints.

His comforting words helped to somewhat allay Peter`s fears of interacting with the other inhabitants of the sanctuary.

He later found out that the monk's name was Biko Rozen and that he was the spiritual leader of the Centre. He was in fifties and had a huge burly frame akin to that of Welsh rugby player. However, his shiny-bronzed bald head, soft golden-brown complexion and facial features, revealed his origins to be from South East Asia. He also had difficulty equating his name with someone hailing from that part of the world.

Following this initial meeting, they would often chat to each other. He initially addressed him by the name Mr Rozen, but the monk asked Peter to call him by his first name of Biko, which he later found out simply meant monk. He would soon discover that his surname name, Rozen, had particularly comic origins.

Peter did very little for the first few days; most of the time, he remained alone in his room or walked around the grounds. He was a broken man. He should have reached this place many years ago, ever since his mid-teens after which time he withdrew into himself.

However, over the following weeks, Peter slowly settled into the life of the community. He still did not talk much to the others and no one gave him any pressure for being so quiet. He relished the non-judgmental atmosphere of the retreat, for he was tired of the condemnatory world he had left behind. The mental space this gave him, helped him to slowly recover and come out of his shell. He began to take on several different tasks and especially liked the cleaning and gardening. He enjoyed undertaking these simple hardworking duties because of their routine nature and the physical exertion involved, which served as a much-needed antidote to a mind normally immersed in teasing out the fundamental laws of physics with their attendant complex mathematics. Furthermore, turning over the soil and weeding the garden gave him a connection with the earth which he found healing.

Peter found most reward, however, from walking around the prayer path. He would occasionally stop off at one of the `stations` and select a prayer or an allegory to read. On closer inspection, he noticed that each had been painstakingly and no doubt lovingly transcribed in hand written blue ink. Their borders were painted with beautiful watercolour illustrations of flowers and plant foliage, which perfectly captured their natural form and texture. A sticky label on each had the words, `*please feel free to take me,* ` written on it. Each station had a different prayer and story. However, he would always return them to their protective sleeves, reticent to keep any for himself because so much devoted effort had been invested in creating them.

He also liked sitting in silence in the temple in the grounds. However, he could not properly meditate there, for his mind continually raced with anxious thoughts. Nevertheless, he found comfort being in such a non-threatening place of peace and stillness.

Peter had banished all thought of the God Field from his mind. Furthermore, the visions and other strange experiences had stopped. This was a great relief, for he had found them to be so debilitating.

Having taken many walks along the prayer path in the following weeks, during which time he had read all of the prayers and allegories several times, he finally selected one to keep for himself. It was entitled *Revenge*. It resounded with him somehow, but he was not sure of the reason why.

Revenge

The raging river left the narrow confines of the mountain valley and languidly searched its way across a wide and fertile flood plain. It had breached its banks in several places, sending its waters radiating out like the arms of tree to lay down its rich load. On a piece of land above the flooded terrain, an embittered brother was turning over the soil with a horse drawn plough. He drilled it angrily into the thick clay soil, breaking the stride of the two horses pulling it, which had to strain with all their might to move forward. When they inevitably broke up their pace, he would lash them viscously with a long leather whip. He was indifferent to their suffering for his heart was poisoned. The tranquility of the landscape failed to permeate his troubled soul, for a deep bile dwelt within him. This had grown lately, ever since his brother had married a beautiful young woman, who was expecting their first child. He was jealous of his older brother's happiness and held a deep resentment towards him for this and the bullying he had received from him as a child.

That evening, he secretly posted an anonymous letter addressed to his brother's wife, accusing him of having an affair behind her back; it even included the false evidence of a secret love letter written to him from his `mistress. ` This broke up their marriage, for his wife could not forgive him, despite his truthful protestations of innocence. He became an alcoholic soon afterwards and died a few years later, still a comparatively young man. His covetous brother lived to be a great age but his heart was broken, for he was forever tortured by guilt for what he had done.

....

Although the story made a strong impression upon him, Peter could not see any relevance it had to his own life, for he was not by nature a jealous or vengeful person.

Peter gradually settled into the retreat and grew to like the people there and they in turn came to like him. For, contrary to his reflex mechanism for self-hatred, genuine people naturally warmed towards him, but he would never believe this to be truly the case. Although his conscious mind still felt vacant, something deep within his subconscious was stirring back to life, like the rekindling of a forgotten fire, its embers now emanating a faint glow of light in the darkness.

God, who was often there, knew that his wounded soul was taking its first tentative steps from out of the shadow place where it had been in hiding since his childhood.

One day, Peter selected a copy of another story from the prayer path, which also connected with him in some way; it was entitled *Compassion*.

Compassion

On a cold night in a dilapidated stone-built barn in a village near the Aegean coastline of Turkey, a girl was crying. She was sixteen years old. The desperation she felt was so painful that she was seriously contemplating committing suicide. She had planned in her mind to throw herself off a motorway footbridge, which linked the agricultural hinterland of foothill villages to the new area of coastal tourist development below.

Her name was Yildiz, (which meant star). She was eight months pregnant and unmarried. Her family had abandoned her because of the shame this had brought upon them. The father had disappeared because he was fearful of the fury he would inevitably receive from them. She herself had stayed because this was her home and she hoped that her mother would one day forgive her.

After she was banished from the family home, Yildiz stayed in the door-less and window-less barn. She was penniless and survived by living off the rich summer bounty of olives, nuts and all manner of fresh fruits, such as apricots and figs, which grew wild in the surrounding countryside. She drank water from a nearby well. She would occasionally raid the village gardens at night for a few hens eggs which she would boil in a saucepan over a small camping gas stove. The protein it provided was invaluable for the developing baby. However, what she missed most of all was the taste of fresh bread and coffee. One night, out of desperation, she entered the unlocked kitchen door to one of the village houses and left with a small amount of freshly baked bread and Turkish coffee. When she savoured them both later that evening, she could not remember anything having ever tasted so good.

However, as autumn was coming to an end, the supply of free wild sustenance was fast diminishing. On this chilly night, with her limited energy supplies fast diminishing, she felt as if she couldn't go on any longer. Her last thoughts before she went to sleep were of taking her life the following day. In the morning, she was woken up by the piercing call of a cockerel, which had entered the barn to confront this recent intruder to its domain. As she looked towards the main open window, she noticed that something was different. A flat piece of material protruded from its ledge. She went over to investigate and found a disposable plastic tray with green olives, vine tomatoes, goats cheese, bread and a large bottle of mountain spring water, placed neatly upon it. She quickly devoured the lot. She then returned the tray to where she first found it. This magnanimous gesture from a stranger helped to put her mind off ending her life that day.

Every morning afterwards, she would awake to discover the plastic tray replenished with fresh provisions. Sometimes a few extra luxuries, such as pine blossom honey and sun-dried tomatoes, would be included. The food and drink helped to sustain her for the remaining month of her pregnancy until she finally gave birth to a baby girl in the barn. She called the child Runa, which meant "gift of God."

Afterwards, she made a vow to herself to show compassion whenever she could and not to be overly judgmental of others. The baby's father returned a few months later and they went on to live happy and fulfilled lives together. Her mother, however, sadly never forgave her.

Yildiz never did discover who had left the lifesaving gifts for her in the barn.

....

This story moved Peter because of the way it showed the power and grace to be found in simple kind-heartedness. Although he sensed it contained a message which pertained to his own life, he was unsure what this was.

Two months after he entered the retreat, Peter felt well enough to make contact with the outside world again. During this time, his children had left repeated, but unanswered, messages of concern for his welfare on his mobile phone. He felt guilty for not having communicated with them sooner, but he had not been of sound mind. He had been in such an abject state of despair that he was incapable of summoning up the motivation to contact them. Having now steadied himself somewhat, due to the harmony he had found in the retreat, he saw that his sudden departure and lack of communication might have seemed selfish to the people that he cared about most.

His children were greatly relieved to hear his voice once more when he called them. They had a long chat in which he tried his best to allay their fears about his well-being. He told them he still needed more time to sort himself out but promised to come down to London on Christmas Eve to stay for a week or two. Peter, however, was more concerned in finding out about their welfare. After a long and friendly talk, his last words to them were, "I love you very much. Please tell mum I am sorry."

He then called his `boss` and good friend at Imperial, James Renshaw, the Head of Department, to apologise for his` disappearance` and the embarrassment his public outing of his belief in a God designed universe must have caused the College. James was greatly relieved to hear from him again and expressed genuine concern for his state of mind. However, he pointed out the precariousness of Peter's `desertion `from work and how he would not be able to protect him from the University's senior authorities for much longer.

"I will inform the Dean straight away of your phone call and of your having suffered from a nervous breakdown. But, to be honest with you, even if he is understanding, this will only buy you a little more time. Sooner or later, you will have to come back to the College to clear things up, not least `the unfortunate incident` in Cambridge. I just can't tell you how shocked and disappointed your colleagues were by this, especially the Dean, who was apoplectic with rage. I'm sorry to have to talk to you so bluntly like this, but I owe it to our friendship to be honest with you."

"I can't explain to you over the phone why I said those things in Cambridge. I did not mean to embarrass anyone, least of all the College. I really believed in what I said and I have the definitive scientific proof to back this up. Would you pass on my sincere apologies to the Dean and inform him that I need a little more time, perhaps to Christmas, to get myself together, before I return. Can you also convey these words to him, `Please consider for a moment that I may be right? '"

They ended their conversation amicably with James's assurance that he would talk to the Dean and try to get Peter some more official time off to recover. However, he was insistent upon one condition, that Peter return his phone calls, to which he reluctantly concurred.

Unexpectedly, James called Peter the following day to inform him that the Dean had made an appointment to meet him in his office at 4pm on Friday 16 December, the last day of the autumn term. Peter was surprised by the matter of fact way James relayed this information, which implied this was the last chance the Dean would give him to explain his disappearance from work and the events in Cambridge. James emphasised that prolonging his absence any further would have irrevocable consequences. His last words to him over the phone confirmed this.

"If you fail to make this appointment, then I am afraid I won't be able to defend you anymore, you'll be on your own. The Dean is *adamant* that you attend."

Peter gave James his word that he would show up for the meeting. He was somewhat shaken by his abrupt manner and the Dean's ultimatum, but he understood that his `seditious` speech at Cambridge and his subsequent `vanishing` must have put the College in a difficult position and could not be sustained for much longer.

He then went for a contemplative walk along the prayer path and selected another copy of a story that resonated with him. It was entitled *Rebirth*.

Rebirth

In a pine oak forest on a volcanic rock belt which straddles the west and east coasts of Mexico, a gently shifting breeze drifts the smoke rising from the chimney pot of a remote stone-built farmstead. It moves in diverse patterns, as if being kneaded by delicate, invisible hands. An old man opens the front door of his ancient home and heads for a nearby corrugated lean-to building, where he uses all of his accumulated strength to chop up some logs for the fire. He then goes to the well at the back of the garden to raise some water. His face is etched with ridges and furrows like that of the parched red soil of his garden, each line an epitaph to the hard life he has led as a goat herder in these hills. Yet, his life had true, for he had been a decent and honest man.

He calls over to the house for his two young grandchildren to come and help him water the vegetables and flowers in the garden; they soon come rushing enthusiastically to him. He pours some water into little children sized watering cans for them to use. As they water the plants, he tells them about the wildlife that inhabits this beautiful wilderness. He points to a huge swarm of Monarch Milkweed butterflies landing on the surrounding pine trees. He explains how they arrive in this forest in their millions after travelling through Canada and the United States. They go through several cycles of birth, death and rebirth on their migration. The children were captivated with wonder at this sight and his tale of their amazing journey.

From the doorway of the cottage, their grandmother beckons them in for breakfast; the children run over and warmly hug her before sitting down at the kitchen table to eat. They consume the food like hungry little wolves.

The old man slowly walks over to join them. Before he sits down at the table, he places some fresh logs onto the fire, which send forth multi-coloured, fluid-like flames, which flicker and illuminate the room with a dancing light.

....

Peter liked this simple tale of the old imparting their wisdom and love to the young. But he was uncertain how the tale of the butterfly's remarkable journey and life cycle, related to his own life.

Although, Peter was anxious at the thought of going back to the world he had escaped from, he understood that now was the right time for him to face up to his responsibilities. He, first of all, planned to see the Dean and resolve his situation at Imperial. He would then stay at his family home for a week or two, where he would sign the divorce papers, which his daughter said were waiting for him. However, he made up his mind not to go back to the retreat after he had sorted out his affairs, for his time there had come to a natural end. He was not sure where he would eventually head for, but he knew that it would be somewhere away from the capital.

Two weeks before his intended departure, Peter informed the people he had grown closest to in the Centre of his decision to leave. Biko and David were noticeably upset but respected his reasons for parting. They warmly invited him to come back and stay whenever he felt the need to "escape from that crazy world out there!" On the morning of the day before his departure, he took one last walk along the prayer path before sitting quietly down on a prayer mat in the temple where he looked over the copies of the three allegories he had selected for himself to keep. He had not been there for long when he heard someone noisily enter the room through the main doorway; the person had somehow got their feet caught in the doormat and stumbled in. Peter turned around to see the huge frame of Biko standing before him.

"I'm sorry to disturb you Peter, I was just about to go on my regular Wednesday walk and wondered whether you would like to join me? I thought it would be nice if we had a farewell chat before you leave tomorrow." The spiritual leader of the Centre stood by the doorway, not in his usual robes, but in a bright blue rain jacket, red bobble hat, orange jeans, walking bots and walking stick. He looked like a giant Nepalese mountain guide.

"Certainly…I'd love to," Peter replied, for he valued the opportunity to learn once more from the wisdom of this special human being.

As they walked downhill from the grand house, across the bridge by the Dyfi railway junction and onto the Ynyshir nature reserve, Biko told Peter of some personal details about himself. Their previous conversations together had mainly focused on general spiritual concerns and hardy touched upon matters of a private nature. Biko mentioned how he had not always been a monk but had wasted his teens and twenties living a life of petty theft and drug dealing on the streets of Bangkok. Eventually, he took sanctuary in a Buddhist monastery in the countryside to avoid capture from the police, who were determined to bring his crime spree to a probable fateful end. He told Peter how the monks there had given him the name Rozen, which means `Stupid Mountain, ` because of his burly figure, clumsiness and the long length of time it took him to grasp the basic tenets of Buddhism. He explained that after staying there for eight years, he was invited to help run a Zen Buddhist monastery in London where he lived for ten years before founding the present retreat which had been bequeathed by a childless descendent of the Victorian family who first built the house.

"I was one bad mother fucker!" he said to Peter. His unexpected use of such strong language, took him by surprise.

"But look Peter, I feel as if I am the one doing all of the talking. I would really like to know a bit more about yourself."

As they continued their walk along the Dyfi estuary towards its beautiful mouth in Cardigan Bay, Peter briefly outlined the key events in his life, paying particular attention in recounting recent significant events, especially the discovery of his new theory and how it had disturbed his mind ever since. He also respected and trusted Biko enough to tell him of the sexual abuse he suffered as a boy; other than his wife, he was the only other person he had ever told of this tragic time of his life.

Biko was upset, but also fascinated by what he heard. Afterwards, he remained in quiet contemplation for a while, before commenting.

"What a privilege it must be to gain a scientific insight into the workings of the Creator through your God Field theory. Your visions are also amazing; I have never known anyone to experience anything like those. I have to confess, I am little envious, for although they clearly disturbed you greatly, I wish, in a way, I had experienced them."

"Peter, do you mind telling me the prayer path stories you selected? I noticed you looking at them in the temple?" Biko asked inquisitively.

"I chose *Revenge, Compassion* and *Rebirth*."

"*Very interesting.* Are you aware that you did not choose them at random and that each was selected for a particular reason; for there is nothing that happens in the world that is purely accidental? I have a feeling that your future lies somewhere along a pathway concealed in the three stories you had selected."

He continued. "Do you know how I think the *Rebirth* story may relate to your own life? It is about how we, like the Monarch butterfly, are continually being reborn. Along its journey, a tiny egg hatches into a caterpillar, which turns into a cocoon and undergoes metamorphosis to appear as a beautiful butterfly, before arriving in the beautiful Mexican pine forests described in the story. I sense that, like the Monarch butterfly, now is the time for your rebirth. Your destiny lays in your being reborn again in your lifetime as you emerge from your shadow self. Remember, Peter, to make sure you go wherever your calling may take you, no matter how frightened you may become. However, the hardest challenge we all face is finding our true path, for many false trails will present themselves to us. Above all, don't forget that *only you can save yourself*, no one else can, not even *little old me.*" He finished these last words with loud, unbridled laughter.

God, who had been invisibly walking alongside them, also laughed with joy. He had been captivated by their conversation, especially Biko's wise words.

Biko continued, "Now that you have told me your own personal story, it is clear that you have led a deeply troubled life with a restless and undernourished soul. This is not unlike my former self. The time for you to stop running away is drawing near, just as it was for me some time ago."

"I will leave it to you to work out how the *Compassion* and *Revenge* stories relate to your own life; only you can truly understand their meaning."

On their return at dusk, Peter was so tired after their long walk that he went straight to his bedroom to sleep. Upon waking up early the following morning, he hurriedly packed his things in readiness for his departure.

He reflected upon his talk with Biko the previous day. Peter was flattered and overawed by the attention and guidance the monk had shown him. He wondered what he meant by his being reborn. He was intrigued by his insistence that his future had many potential pathways but that there was only one true one for him to follow and that it may relate to the allegories he had selected. What was most daunting was Biko's assertion that the most difficult task for any human being is finding and following their true pathway.

Nevertheless, his conversation with Biko convinced him that he was right to leave the retreat at this time, for it was clear his destiny lay elsewhere. In any case, he thought that now was a good time to leave for he was not a practicing Buddhist and neither did have any desire to become one, although he deeply respected those that chose to follow such an enlightened calling. In addition, he felt he would be taking advantage of their warmth and kindness if he were to stay there any longer.

After saying his warm farewells, Peter left on the morning of Thursday, December 15 2011, in readiness for his meeting with the Dean the following day.

Just as he was about to drive away, Biko came rushing over to him, his powerful robust figure making him look like a Welsh rugby pack forward in full flight. Peter feared he would knock over some of the other monks in his way, but he luckily steered clear of them. Biko then wished him all the best and placed his hands over Peter`s in a mutual prayer-like gesture. Peter dreaded such physical contact would send him into one of his draining visions, but nothing happened; he guessed this was because Biko had a pure heart and was free from any unresolved issues. Biko then reached into his back pocket and handed him an envelope, before saying.

"I have just written a new story for the prayer path; it came to me last night after our walk. I had you in mind when I was writing it down. It was like a vision; although it pales into insignificance compared to your own…Will you please do me the honour of accepting it? Don't worry, I have made a photocopy for myself which I can use to transcribe other copies from." Peter gracefully accepted Biko's warm gift.

As he drove out of the main gates, he began to cry; he could not help himself. He cried like a young child taken away from its mother for the first time. It pained him to leave such a peaceful retreat, whose gentle inhabitants had shown him so much love and support, at a time when he needed it most.

When the tears had faded and he managed to calm his emotions, Peter wondered what new story Biko had so kindly written for him. Their talk the previous day then came to mind again, especially his thoughts regarding Peter's true destiny. The words that resounded with him most of all were "*Only you can save yourself.*" He then remembered this was the same message he felt the ocean Gods were saying to him when was engulfed and `spat out` by the giant wave in Porthcurno.

Chapter 4

His despair in leaving the retreat was somewhat allayed by the inner strength he felt from Biko's parting advice, for he recognised that they held the secret to his mental and spiritual freedom. They may also hold the key to unlocking the mystery that lay at the heart of his theory. The only problem was that he did not know how to discover his true destiny and save himself. He feared that unless he could comprehend the true nature of his purpose in life, he would forever remain a lost soul. A feeling of nausea gripped him. He felt very much alone in the universe.

However, as he drove through the beautiful Welsh countryside on a bright crisp winter's day, his despairing thoughts slowly disappeared. The scattered towns and villages with their inhabitants going about their business in an unhurried way, contrasted with the frenetic pace of life in London, whose blind inhabitants were powerless to break free from their daily flight from themselves.

But as he journeyed along the largely deserted roads, something kept trying to connect with his consciousness from the deep recesses of his psyche, but he could not figure out what it was. Eventually, after several hours of travelling, a collective energy, like a hidden entity, emerged from the shadows and transformed itself into the following words, `The only way to save yourself is by healing the wounds of your past.`

He knew exactly what these words meant. He had to resolve the trauma of the sexual abuse he had suffered as a child at the hands of a man called Max Cameron in Cardiff. The emotional damage from this experience accompanied him throughout his life. The all-powerful, self-destructive, negative feelings it engendered, had made his life a living hell. The following decades were an accumulation of unresolved grief as he was unable to heal and forgive his disintegrated and disempowered soul. He had desperately tried to free himself from this torment but he could never find a way through. He was painfully self-aware that he was trapped in a mental prison from which he was powerless to escape. Nevertheless, he obstinately neither would not, nor could not give in, even though he was so emotionally unwell.

Peter now saw that his destiny lay in resolving these heart-wrenching events from his childhood; he also sensed that the deeper meaning of his theory would finally be revealed to him once he came to terms with them.

What could he do, he wondered, that would finally set him free from this terrible burden? Surely, (his negative mindset told him), anything he tried would be doomed to failure. Then, all of a sudden, the nebulous energy that had just emerged from his subconscious suddenly revealed the way forward for him-*he had to go back to the origins of the abuse and face his abuser.* Crippling fear had preventing him from taking this step before. He now knew that the game was up and that he would finally have to confront Max. As these experiences had occurred in Cardiff, he decided to journey towards his home city to seek him out, on route to London. However, he had no idea what he would do if he found him. `Do I make him confess to his crimes; do I forgive him; do I punish him?` Nevertheless, making this decision helped to lift the confusion from his mind.

His journey to the retreat had been at night and he had not been able to get a real feel for the land of his birth, but he was now beginning to reconnect with it once more. The Welsh hills, now held in the grip of winter, possessed a haunting, magic-like quality, that had its roots in the distant Celtic past. Its beauty took his breath away. The azure sky was like a protective cloak thrown over the Earth from the heavens above. A light veil of mist covered the mountain moorlands, which were painted in thick brush stroke shades of emerald bracken, amethyst heather and golden gorse. Swathes of burnt charcoal swept across several hillsides, the result of autumnal burning. The rolling hills seemed to take the form of sleeping giants waiting in vain for their next call to defend their land. A guard of scattered leafless trees stood like frozen skeletons along the lower valley sides, as if in readiness for battle, their only purpose to stand as sentinels against any threat to the mountain Gods above.

It was this impression of sleeping Gods and sleeping warriors that finally clarified what he had to do if, and when, he met Max. `*Revenge! Revenge! That's it!* My fate lies in taking vengeance on the man who abused me and destroyed my life! Only then will my torment end; only then, will I save myself. After all, didn't Biko say that he thought the allegories might have some special significance regarding my true purpose in life? Perhaps the *Revenge* parable holds some relevance to my own life after all. However, unlike the jealous man who took terrible retribution upon his innocent brother, mine would just and might finally set me free. `

However, he was aware that it was highly probable that Max had long since passed away. Even if he was still alive, he would be a very old man by now, and then what would he do if he found him? `Do I *force* him to admit to his crimes and understand the evil he did to me? Do I then *kill him*? Surely not! ` Also, he deliberated, if Max were still alive, the likelihood is that he would have moved house by now and how would he then find him?

Yet, Peter felt that he was now travelling along the pathway of his true destiny. He took great comfort from this. It was decided! He would go to Cardiff that day and track Max down, before continuing his journey to London.

It was experiencing the beautiful majesty of the Welsh countryside again that helped him to achieve this clearness of vision. He now understood that he had to bring some closure to the traumatic events of his childhood. Not once, since that time, had he thoroughly examined the nature of the sexual abuse that he had been the victim of; his life had been one long escape from facing up to these demons of the past. He still dreaded confronting these terrors head on, but what he could do, as a first step, would be to revisit the geographical location of these events and find out if the perpetrator was still living there.

Peter continued his journey for several more hours, his mind focusing on his new-found mission, until he eventually found himself looking up at the sign for the link road that led to Ely, the huge council estate in the west of Cardiff, where he grew up. His was full of trepidation at the thought that he would soon be driving down the street and passing the house where the abuse had taken place. He had not been back there for forty years.

He finally turned into Sevenoaks Road, where Max had lived. The street had changed dramatically since he last saw it. Stark block brick walls replaced the green privet hedges that once fronted the front gardens of every home. The Council had painted over the red brick front of each house with cream paint, which had since faded and now looked smudged. Several houses had torn dirty curtains, rotten window frames and piles of rubbish in their gardens. Some homes were boarded up. The overall effect of these changes was to make the street seem impoverished, bleak, and inhospitable.

The large concrete bastions that stretched across the road half way up the street to put off joy riders, only added to this feeling of deprivation and menace.

"There it is! Number sixty-two," he said to himself, noticing an innocuous looking end of terrace house where Max Cameron lived. He pulled his car over to the curb a few doors down the road from the house. It was once the nicest looking property in the street and was one of the first on the estate to be purchased from the Council. Now, however, its appearance had markedly changed. It looked tired and neglected. The garden was overgrown with weeds. The house martin nests that had nestled under its eves had long since gone. The magnolia tree, whose beautiful yellow blossom would fill his damaged heart with hope in the springtime, was also absent.

`What if Max is still there? ` he reflected to himself in panic. His whole body became gripped with a disempowering fear, which made him incapable of thinking or acting clearly. He took a few slow deep breathes to calm himself down and tried to reason with himself. He soon acknowledged that he was not in the right frame of mind to challenge him. Hopefully, he would be ready one day soon, but now was not the time…that was assuming he is still alive and living there. Nevertheless, finding this out was something he could establish before he left.

Therefore, rather than knock on the door of Max's house, he chose to enquire about its present occupants from the neighbour next door, who he could see standing by his front gate.

He got out of his car and walked up to the fellow, a well-built man in his thirties, who was smoking a cigarette. He had a pale complexion and tough looking features. He wore a string vest even though it was the middle of winter.

"Excuse me? Would you mind telling me who lives in the house next door, number sixty-two?" he said pointing to his former abode. "I just called there, but got no reply," he fibbed.

"Sure, but would you first tell me why you want to know?" he replied suspiciously.

"I was wondering if an old chap called Max Cameron still lives there; I used to be a friend of his?"

This seemed to put the man at ease, which allowed him to open up a little to this stranger.

"Oh no, a young couple live there now…they've only been there for a couple of years and before them an older couple lived there for a while."

"Did you know Max?"

"No, I never saw him myself and I've been living here for over ten years. Mind you, I sometimes come across people on the estate who talk of him-quite a character I hear. He was obviously well liked and respected in the neighbourhood."

"You wouldn't happen to know where he moved to?"

"No, sorry mate, I haven't a clue."

"Never mind… many thanks."

"Sorry I haven't been of much help," he replied, this time with less mistrust in his voice. "Why don't you call on number sixty-four on the other side, the chap living there might know more than me?"

He then called on this house. A middle-aged man answered the door. Regrettably, he didn't know Max, because he had moved house by the time he arrived, but he did have a faint recollection that someone had once told him that he had gone to live in an old people's home.

Peter felt reinvigorated by having taken this, albeit somewhat obtuse, first step in returning to his past. However, he was unsure what he would have done if he had come across Max. He wondered, because of his confused state of mind, whether any actions he may have taken would have been the right ones. He therefore got back into his MG and drove away, his unusual car catching the eye of some of the locals.

He pondered over his next move, whilst drinking a pint of Welsh ale in the Farmers Inn in the beautiful nearby village of St Fagans on the western outskirts of the city. It became apparent to him, that in spite of the days dead end, he would eventually have to track Max down and make him face up to the sins of his past. Although, now was not the time to pursue this goal, because he wasn't in the right frame of mind to face him, he knew that he would be back soon…when he was ready. But first, he had to address his family and work dilemmas.

Peter then remembered the unopened envelope containing the allegory Biko had handed to him that morning. As he retrieved it from his rucksack, he noticed the words `be open to love, ` written on the gummed flap. Opening it, revealed a beautifully handwritten story entitled *Love.* It was written in blue ink on three single sheets of handmade parchment paper. Its border was decorated with various word inscriptions written in different languages. He wondered if these were various spellings of the word love. The whole manuscript must have taken him all night to write and adorn, he thought. This is that story.

Love

Simon had been living rough on the streets of London for over two years, ever since he came down from Liverpool, when he was sixteen years old. It was after his father had kicked him out of the family home. His parting words to Simon were. "Now we no longer have to legally look after you, it's time you went out into the real world and made a living for yourself. I *won't* have you scrounging off us any longer."

He had not expected this to happen, even though he knew his father could be cruel and callous at times, like the night he drowned six kittens in the Mersey. He had put the poor little things in a sack laden with bricks and chucked it over a jetty near the Albert Docks. There were also the times when he would beat Simon on his back with a leather belt for daring to speak up to him. Sometimes the belt would draw blood, after which his father would keep Simon home from school for a few days, fearing his son's wounds might be discovered. For some unknown reason, his father had always hated him; Simon could not remember a single time when he was loving or affectionate towards him. When he asked his mother why this was, she said that he really did care for him. When Simon pressed her further, she revealed that he was treated very cruelly by his own father in Manchester when he was a boy. However, this information didn't make Simon feel any better.

Over time, the outdoor existence on the streets near Holborn, where he had his cardboard box home, had taken its toll. His face had lost its healthy complexion. The regular diet of super strength cider and lager hadn't helped either. He was lonely and cold. He lived off food handouts from soup kitchens vans. He twice slept in a hostel but was asked to leave both times; the first time for drinking alcohol on the premises and the second for stealing another vagrant's packet of cigarettes.

He had no real qualifications, poor social skills, (which included a short temper), and no belief in himself whatsoever. He felt hopeless; many a time he seriously considered putting an end to his suffering by jumping off the nearby Waterloo Bridge into the River Thames. The only time during the day he felt better was when he saw the lovely face of Layla serving food from the back of the soup kitchen van in Victoria. She was nice to all of the down and outs, many of whom had grown to `love` her. However, Peter felt that he was the only one who *truly* loved her.

Layla was petite in stature, gentle by nature, quiet and reserved. She dressed in dark, drab clothing and never attempted to pretty herself up. But Simon could see a beautiful person hiding beyond this camouflage. However, she had been coming around less often lately. Every time she failed to turn up, he would feel a physical pain in his chest. One nice old vagrant, Stan from Essex, who had noticed his crush on her, suggested that he ask her out for a date, to which Simon jokingly replied.

"Fuck off, Stan! There is absolutely no way in a million fucking years that she would say yes!"

"I know Simon-you are probably right. But if you got yourself together then perhaps it might be a different story." This suggestion got Simon thinking; what if he was right, what if he cleaned myself up, found a place to stay and got a job-perhaps then...who knows?

But nothing changed for a while until the time when Layla stopped coming completely. Simon was devastated. He found out that she had found a job as a teacher, but he wasn't sure where. From that moment onwards, Simon made a concerted effort to end the vicious cycle of homelessness. He asked Stefan, one of the soup kitchen helpers, for some advice on how to break free. Stefan, seeing Simon's genuine desire to escape, managed to pull a few strings and find him a place in decent sheltered accommodation.

Simon gradually pulled himself together over the next few months. He even let go of the `crutch` of the demon alcohol. One day, he asked Stefan if he could help him serve the food. Stefan said that he had a better suggestion "Why don't you see if there is a job going in the First Help charity headquarters near Leicester Square where they make the soup that is distributed by the vans. As a permanent employee, they will even pay you a decent wage Simon. Come back this time tomorrow and I'll have written a letter of recommendation for you to pass on to them."

He returned the next day to pick up the letter and after an interview a few days later, was offered a job, to which he devoted his energies for six months before getting a grant to study for a one-year full time crammer course to retake his GCSE's. During the evenings, he worked in the ticket office of the Odeon cinema in Leicester Square in the West End.

Five months later, he asked Stefan if he would give him Layla's telephone number so that he could ask her out for a date. Stefan was naturally wary of giving him this information, but over the preceding months, he had grown to trust and respect Simon. He therefore took the risk of giving him her number, on the proviso that he would never tell her, or anyone else, that he had given it to him.

Simon called Layla that evening from a payphone in Piccadilly. He was so nervous his hands trembled, making him, bizarrely, wonder if Layla would pick up the vibrations on the other end of the phone. Layla was shocked to hear his voice once more and bluntly asked who gave him her private number. "I'm afraid I can't tell you that because it might get that person in trouble." He replied.

"Do you remember me, Layla?"

"Yes, I do."

"Well, I've been off the streets for over a year now." He then explained what he been doing to improve himself.

Layla, once her initial suspicions had subsided, seemed very interested in what he had to say and was very pleased for him.

He then braced himself before saying these fateful words.

"Layla, I would like to tell you the real reason why I contacted you." Then, mustering all of his courage, he continued, "I would like it very much if you would come out on a date with me?"

He carried on, awkwardly. "That is presuming you don't already have a boyfriend. And, even if you don't, I'd understand if you turn me down."

There was a long pause before Layla replied "No."

However, Peter, presuming that she was rejecting his request, quickly interjected, "It's OK, I understand. I'll just hang up now. Don't worry Layla, I won't bother you again."

Layla continued, "I mean no, I don't have a boyfriend."

An infinitely long interlude then followed before she finally replied to his request, "Yes, I would like that very much Simon."

Simon's world turned upside down when she said those lovely words. His whole body was captivated by a mysterious energy. His thoughts turned to mush. His legs felt like rubber. Eventually he managed to collect himself a little, before grappling together the following words.

"My God! I was convinced you would turn me down Layla!"

"Why, just because you used to be a down and out doesn't mean that I wouldn't be interested in you. Look Simon, I don't know whether you knew this, but I always had a bit of a thing for you when I used to serve you from the van. I used to pray that you would one day free yourself from the streets and make something of yourself."

They arranged to meet the following night for a meal in China Town.

That was ten years ago. They had a sweet courtship before marrying and having three lovely children. Simon managed to pass his GCSEs and later his A levels. He then studied for a law degree in University College London and ended up becoming a successful barrister specialising in defending the rights of the underprivileged in legal aid funded cases.

....

Peter pondered over the possible meaning behind this story. Was Biko trying to tell him that finding romantic love was the ultimate key to his life but that he had to sort himself out first? If this were true, then how could he reconcile such a story of redemptive love with his newfound quest for vengeance? He felt undeserving of receiving Biko's gift, especially now that he was harbouring such dark thoughts.

He then headed for the M4 motorway to continue his journey to London; it was getting late and he would not arrive there until the middle of the night.

Chapter 5

As Peter drove into London along the elevated Westway section of the M4 motorway, bisecting the illuminated modern headquarter offices and the distant views of suburban residential expansion beyond, the enormity of the metropolis overwhelmed him. All those people milling about down there he thought. With the exception of his family and a few close friends, he had no wish to meet any of them. However, he knew that if was ever to move forward in his life, he had to return to London and face up to his home and work problems.

His line manager's instruction that he meet up with the Dean, had come after he had told his children that he would be coming back to visit them on Christmas Eve, which would be a week later. They were unaware of his earlier return because he had not called to inform them, as he wanted this to be a surprise. But as it was nearing one o'clock in the morning when he finally reached central London, he decided that it was too late to go back home to Hackney that evening and drove instead to the main car park of Imperial College where he was to have his meeting the following day. He parked his car in an out of the way space, went to the back seat, pulled his warm overcoat over himself and promptly fell fast asleep.

He was disturbed from a deep slumber early the following morning by one of the College security staff frantically knocking his fist on the side window of his car. The guard admonished him for sleeping overnight in the car park, emphasising that it was against the College rules.

He mellowed somewhat when Peter explained that he was one of the College Professors and had one too many drinks at a Departmental Christmas party the night before. Peter then had a wash and shave in the College toilets. He also changed into a pair of jeans, casual shirt and jacket-he had no wish to impress the Dean by dressing smartly in a suit and tie, for such pretension was contrary to his nature.

Peter then walked the short distance to the shopping centre in South Kensington to get some breakfast. He wanted to avoid hanging around the University too much in case he accidently bumped into any of his colleagues, for he feared that they might ask him about his absence. But doubtless, the Cambridge debacle and his subsequent disappearance had long become common knowledge via the express delivery of the campus grapevine.

For the rest of the morning he sat in a quiet backwater of the nearby Natural History Museum, out of the way of the mass hordes of visitors. As he looked up at the glass display case in front of him, he noticed that it contained the stuffed specimen of an extinct Tasmanian Tiger. Its powerful jaws were wide open, as if it had just taken its final breath before being transfixed in a moment of frozen time. For all Peter knew, it could well have been the last breath from the last Tasmanian tiger to have lived on the Earth-this thought made him feel melancholy.

He was dismayed that such a significant reminder of the harm that human beings can do to the living creatures on our beautiful planet was `hidden ` in a remote part of the museum. He saw a parallel with another momentous exhibit, Crick and Watson's original metal construction of the DNA molecule in the neighbouring Science Museum, which is submerged amongst giant steam powered engines.

In the afternoon, he walked to the nearby Kensington Gardens from where he could see his garret window in the apartment block across the street. However, he had no intention of visiting his room, for fear of meeting one of his students or work mates. Instead, he took in the sights and sounds of the Park once more. The squabbling of water birds on the Serpentine, the incessant barking of dogs and the joyful noises of children at play, mingled in the air with the soothing sound of the Park's majestic wind-blown trees. Absorbing these familiar sensations once more, helped to raise his spirits in readiness for his forthcoming meeting with Professor Richard Eastbury, the Dean.

"Come in…come in," he called out, quickly responding to Peter's sheepish knock on the door.

The Professor was once a distinguished cosmologist at Imperial, before taking on the mainly administrative and political role of Dean of the Science Faculty. He was about sixty years of age with a shiny red bald forehead leading to swathe of long white hair which ended in a braid tied ponytail; he looked for all the world like an old hippy, except for the smartly tailored formal suit and tie he wore and the antiseptic office room in which he was based. He seemed like a man out of place with his time and environment.

Peter and he hardly knew each other. They had only met on rare occasions, usually at formal College functions, but had never engaged in serious conversation.

"It is so nice to see you again Peter, after such a long time. Please sit down whilst I make a cup of tea for us both-is that alright with you?"

The Dean's friendly greeting took him by surprise. He then directed him to two armchairs situated towards the side of the room, away from the more official surroundings of the main desk area. Peter sank deeply into one of the cozy seats.

"It's nice to see you too, Richard," Peter replied warily.

There was an awkward silence whilst the Dean made the refreshments, before placing a tray with the cups of tea, milk, sugar and biscuits on a coffee table between the two chairs. He then sat in the other armchair; the Dean's expression seemed to noticeably relax as he `disappeared` into it.

"I could have asked my secretary to make the tea but she never makes it strong enough," the Dean whispered, as if fearful of her overhearing him, even though she was in the next room.

"Comfy chairs aren't they! I bought them for a fiver each in a local junkshop in Fulham Road over twenty years ago. A fiver! Can you believe it, imagine what you would have to pay for them *now?* They are the only thing I really like in this office. I find this place so stuffy and officious, which… to be frank with you, is not really me."

The Dean's words helped to put Peter at ease and make him naturally warm towards him.

"Look Peter, I don't know what James told you about this meeting, but it will not be as heavy as you might think-I just need to hear your side of the story. But first of all, I think it best if I tell you how I view your situation. To be honest with you, your scene in Cambridge brought the Faculty and the College much embarrassment-my God, the headlines in the press the next day! In addition, you just left your post without letting anyone know what happened to you or where you went. A short phone call of explanation would have been enough and I would have been more than happy to give you some compassionate leave. Who do you think gave your lectures, took your tutorials and managed your section? What's more, you even failed to see a doctor and send in a sick note! If you had only done that you, would have been covered legally with the University authorities, who have been breathing down my neck wondering what on Earth is going on."

"I'm so sorry for all of the trouble I have caused and for not having contacted you sooner," Peter interjected.

The Dean continued, "Please stop that! I don't need you to give me a groveling apology. What I want is your account of what took place in Cambridge and what you have been doing these last two months, for only then can I give you my opinion. I just need the *truth* from one respected scientist to another."

"Certainly…I will tell you everything."

Peter proceeded to convey to the Dean his side of the story, starting with the moment he made his breakthrough discovery of the Mystery Field and how this had deeply disturbed him. He explained how revealing his revolutionary new theory in Cambridge had finally pushed him over the edge and that he then fled to the Buddhist retreat in Wales to recover. He said he had been in such a dark place that he was incapable of contacting the outside world. "I guess I had a nervous breakdown," were his concluding words.

The Dean paused for a moment before giving his reply.

"Do you know, James told me the words that you had asked him to pass on to me, "Please consider for a moment that I may be right?"

After a long pause, the Dean continued, "Can I speak to you off the record, as the journalists say? Can I have your word that what I am about to say will only ever remain between us?"

Peter gave his word.

"Several years ago, when I was researching binary stars in the Keck Observatory in Hawaii, I had a very strange experience. It followed a drunken whisky argument I had with a famous Professor from Princeton. It concerned the benefits, or otherwise, of scientific specialisation. I argued that this was a good thing and that it would lead to even greater discoveries in the future. He reasoned that the cost of over-specialisation is the danger of losing sight of the bigger picture of the universe and our place in it. Well, I stormed out of the common room to resume my observations of the night sky. Whilst examining the beautiful image of a dense region of local galaxies, an overpowering sensation took hold of me. It felt as if I was somehow *known* to the universe and that there was no distance between the stars and myself; in fact, that we were one and the same. When I snapped out of this wonderful experience, I realised that the Professor was right; scientists are failing to see the grander picture as a whole, one that may even include... *God*."

"I can't believe I have just revealed this secret to you Peter. I have never told another soul about this before, not even my wife! I feared being branded a crackpot, like yourself; no disrespect intended."

"None taken," Peter replied, laughing.

Peter felt great relief in hearing him say these words for it established a common connection between them.

"Well Peter, to put it more bluntly, I am open to the possibility that you might be onto something, *that you may in fact be right*. I know what a superb, open minded, scientist you are, and if you found something that points to some kind of divine aspect to the universe, well I, for one, will not rush to call you a madman."

"I suspect that you didn't expected me to say those words to you...did you?"

"No, Richard, I had absolutely no idea. To be honest with you, I was expecting the sack!"

"I had no intention of firing you and losing someone as special as yourself from the Faculty. *No way.* You can have some more time off if you still need it, just as long as you go through the proper channels this time and get a sick note from your doctor. Then, when you are ready to come back to Imperial, you can even work on your theory, but it would have to be done in absolute secret, for if anyone else gets wind that you are investigating the `God stuff` again, there would be one almighty uproar. If, and when, you get definitive proof of your hypothesis, then you have my blessing to go public with the news."

"Richard, you don't understand-I *have* the proof already."

"What do you mean? How can that be possible? How can you have found what no one else in the history of humankind has been able to discover before-*the Philosophers Stone*?"

"Didn't James Renshaw tell you how I found a new kind of energy using the new quantum detector in Manchester?"

"Yes, of course, I am fully aware of that, but I was informed that it relates to some kind of peripheral `waste` radiation associated with all matter?"

"No! What I did not tell James, or anyone else, was that the results provided the definitive evidence that my theory was true-that there is an intelligent energy field actively creating the universe."

"Please explain yourself some more Peter; my classically trained mind is finding it hard to take it all in."

"The energy we discovered exactly matched that predicted by my God Field equation. It is released when the physical world is seeded from what I call the God Field. The two worlds interact along a multidimensional boundary, across which the Field seeds the real world whenever there is the potential for greater order. This even includes catastrophic events, such as a supernova explosion, which lead to more complex orderly systems afterwards."

Peter added, "I even listened to what I can only describe as the `voice` of God, when I converted the detector results into sound form. I cannot truly convey in words what this was like, other than it felt as if my whole being was bathed in a loving harmony."

The Dean then sharply interrupted and said, "I don't mean to put you down Peter, but this is starting to sound like some new age mumbo jumbo."

"*Nothing* can be further from the truth," Peter responded assertively.

He continued, "Dean, I am moved that you shared your spiritual experience with me. I am also touched by your

74

offer to give me more time and space to recover and work on my theory. Nevertheless, I have decided to hand in my resignation, (Peter had only come to this decision at that precise moment), for I don't know how long it will be before I sort myself out and I do not want to keep the College waiting in limbo any longer. Also, it is imperative that I take more time out to face up to some issues that relate back to my childhood."

God, or `Sonny, ` as he preferred to call himself, was listening attentively to their conversation. He was sat on the sharp corner of the office desk, longing to sit in the comfort of one of the occupied arm chairs. Having just witnessed his conversation with the Dean, `He` was very worried about Peter's future, for even `He` didn't know exactly what would unfold for him because the God Field only followed broad lines of unfurling potential energy.

They carried on talking amicably for a while; in that short space of time, they had become friends. However, neither of them again broached the spiritual nature of the God Field, or Peter's proof of its existence. Peter promised to contact Richard soon to let him know how he was coping and, in particular, how he was progressing with his theory. He wished Peter all the best and said that he would find him a position in the Department if he ever changed his mind in the future.

Peter left the Dean's office with a sense of satisfaction in having taken such decisive action in simplifying his life. He was well aware of the risks, especially financially, he was taking in resigning from his distinguished position at Imperial, for his savings, which he had been living off for the last two months, would eventually run out. Also, The College administrators had stopped paying his salary after two months, as they had not heard from him or received a doctor's certificate. Furthermore, in rejecting the Dean's offer for him to continue working at the College, he was probably jettisoning any chance of gaining an academic post in another university, for it was highly unlikely that another establishment would take him on after the Cambridge `farce. ` Yet, notwithstanding these concerns, Peter was satisfied with his decision to quit his job. However, there now remained the problem of his pending divorce to deal with.

Unlike the work problem, the one concerning his home life had been largely taken out of his hands by his wife's insistence on getting a divorce; he could have contested it but he knew it would be a mistake to pursue this avenue, because his marriage had come to an end a long time ago. They hadn't slept in the same bed or had sexual relations for over five years and they only talked to each other when it was absolutely necessary to do so, for instance when it related to the children's welfare or paying the bills. They had mainly stayed together for the sake of the children, but now that they were grown up this wasn't such a priority any more. But there was another reason for their not having parted sooner-their own natural fears of being left alone. Eventually, though, their marriage had to end, as the tension in their relationship had become intolerable. Even temporarily living apart from one another for a while was now out of the question, for they both knew their differences were irreconcilable. Sian had lost patience with his emotional insecurities and neediness and he could no longer excuse her cold and uncaring nature.

As his MG drew nearer to his Hackney home, Peter became increasingly fearful of facing his wife again, mainly because of the guilt he carried for his part in their marriage breakup. He knew that she had justifiable cause for wanting the divorce, for he had not been the husband and father that she wanted and needed. Most of the time he withdrew into himself and was incapable of opening up to others and participating fully in family life. He may have had good reason for being so insular, but this was not much help to the people that needed him most, his wife and children, for they required him to be an `awake` and proactive participant in family life. Peter was well aware of his frailties and deficiencies, but he had been unable to free himself from them, no matter how hard he tried.

Peter especially bore a lot of regret for the early years of their marriage when he was an addictive gambler, spending much of his income and time betting on the horses, dogs and fruit machines. When he invariably lost, he would proceed to drink himself into oblivion in various public houses, in an attempt to forget his losses and his hide his shame. The real reason he gambled and drank was to numb the overwhelmingly powerful black emotions which engulfed him, ever since the abuse at the hands of Max when he was a boy. These `fixes` helped him to anaesthetise the pain somewhat, but they had a destructive fallout, especially on his family, who had to put with his long absences, mood swings and financial hardship, as they were caught up in the throes of his addictive behaviour. Eventually, he discovered Gamblers Anonymous and had not gambled since.

He parked the car in the only parking space left in his street, some way from his home. He sat there for a while, trying to gather himself. As he was about to get out, he saw his wife walking along the opposite pavement. She was so wrapped in her own thoughts that she failed to notice his distinctive car, or her husband inside it. Seeing his wife so unexpectedly, instilled Peter with an overwhelming feeling of self-doubt, which convinced him to postpone meeting her. Therefore, when she had disappeared into their house, he quietly drove away and parked the car in a parallel road three blocks away. He then left his vehicle to walk to his favourite Hackney pub, The Anglesey Arms, in Dalston, where he had a meal and a pint before heading back to his car to sleep for the night. It was cold and it had started to rain, the continuous, mist-like drizzle, which seems to penetrate right through one's clothes.

Peter was woken up early the following morning by the strange piercingly guttural sounds of two cats in a standoff on top of his car. An almighty scrap then ensued, until they both fell off the roof onto the pavement next to him, followed by slowly descending tufts of torn off multi-coloured cat fur. Peter quickly opened the car door and screamed at them; both cats then looked towards him, perplexed by this unexpected interruption, before scarpering off. Peter, fearing a similar nasty confrontation with his wife, took the cowardly way out and drove off. He made up his mind not to return home until the following Saturday, Christmas Eve, when, in any case, they were expecting him. However, he was unsure what he would do and where he would sleep in the meantime.

Chapter 6

Biko's advice to find an insight into his true destiny, kept on resurfacing in Peter's mind as he drove towards central London. Although he now believed that this first involved taking justifiable revenge against Max, he still needed to find some deeper purpose to his life.

He parked his car near the British Museum. Once he had placed enough money in the meter to cover the maximum stay of four hours, he had breakfast in the Bar Centrale café, a favourite eating place of his next to Russell Square Tube Station. He then purchased a Travelcard, boarded a train on the Piccadilly Line, changed for the Circle Line at Kings Cross and travelled for several hours watching the passengers going about their daily business

Peter found that he could observe his fellow travellers with a dispassionate eye, without being self-conscious. He was amazed to find he could look at them without their being aware that he was doing so. He had never before looked at other people in this way, due to his acute shyness, but now he was aware that he could look at others with virtual impunity. Also, because the passengers rarely returned his stare, he didn't have to worry about being drawn into their souls and suffering the incapacitating consequences he experienced since his discovery of the God Field. He took this opportunity to try to learn something about the people travelling on board the tube-perhaps this might give him an understanding into his own predicament.

He was fascinated by what he saw; the way people's faces seemed to reveal their natures and how almost everyone seemed to be in their own tiny bubble of personal space. `This is *very interesting*, ` he thought, `the tube is a ready-made human laboratory from which I can learn something. `

Each time the train made one full circumference of the Circle Line, he would have to change platforms at Edgware Road Station to resume his journey. He noticed that it took about fifty-five minutes to make one full loop around central London. He travelled around the entire perimeter three times before rushing to catch the Piccadilly line train from Kings Cross to Russell Square to collect his car before the meter ran out. He arrived at his vehicle five minutes late and had to use all of his powers of persuasion to convince the impassive Parking Officer not to give him a ticket.

His tube travels fascinated him; he was intrigued and wanted more of this experience. He was hooked. He therefore decided to spend as much time as possible on each of the forthcoming days leading up to Christmas Eve, observing passengers travelling on the London underground. His next task was to plan how to do this effectively.

He drove his car a little further away and parked in Lincolns Inn Fields. He put enough money in the parking meter to cover him until 6.30 in the evening, after which time it was free until 7.00am the following morning. He then had a bite to eat in the cafe there and went for a walk; he eventually ended up near Holborn Library where he decided to stay for a while and complete his tube study plans.

It occurred to him that he could park his car for free in the evenings in Lincolns Inn Fields and sleep in it until the following morning. He would have to make sure that he slept unnoticed, for there were sure to be policemen patrolling the area, who would take a dim view of him using his vehicle as a mobile hotel. But where could he park his car in the daytime he wondered? Most parking spaces were very expensive and had a maximum time limit of between two to four hours, after which time he would have to move on. There was no way he could keep breaking his journey in order to move to another parking space. He googled 'cheap all-day parking in central London' into the web browser of his mobile phone and found a reasonably priced car park beneath the Brunswick Centre close to Russell Square. He could leave his car there all day and into the evening before picking it up sometime before the midnight deadline, (after which he would have to pay an exorbitant premium). He considered paying this extra fee and sleeping there through the night but he thought the duty attendants would surely see him. He still had enough funds to stay in a cheap hotel but he wanted the anonymity of sleeping by himself away from any place where people congregated. He therefore decided to sleep all night in his car in Lincoln's Inn Fields before dropping it off in the car park early the following morning. After breakfast, he would then catch a Piccadilly Line train from Russell Square tube station to Kings Cross Station where he would board a Circle Line train and begin his observations. But how long would he travel along the line? Where and when would he eat, drink and go to the toilet?

He finalised his plan in the Library and wrote down a daily timetable into his notebook.

Timetable

6.30 am. Wash, shave and change clothes in Lincolns Inn Fields public toilets.

6.55 am. Park the car in the all-day car park beneath the Brunswick Centre.

7 am. Have breakfast at Bar Centrale next to Russell Square Tube station.

7.30 am. Buy a peak time zone 1 Travelcard, take the Piccadilly Line to Kings Cross Station and change for the Circle Line.

7.45am-1pm. Travel on Circle Line train in a clockwise direction, making observations.

1-2pm. Disembark at Edgware Road Station and have lunch/toilet break.

2-7pm. Travel on Circle Line in a clockwise direction, making observations.

7-8pm. Disembark at Edgware Road Station and have dinner/go to toilet.

8-11pm. Travel on Circle Line in a clockwise direction, making observations.

11pm. Change at Kings Cross for Piccadilly Line to Russell Square Tube Station.

11.05pm Collect car from car park and drive to Lincoln's Inn Fields.

11.15pm-6.30 am. Park car in an out of the way part of Lincolns inn Fields and sleep in the back seat for the night.

(N.B. Extra items I will need to buy beforehand-warm blanket to keep me warm/ small notebook to record observations /small rucksack/bottles of water for tube ride/dry snack foods/pocket torch).

He decided to make observations for the five days of the forthcoming working week. He would approach his study in a controlled manner like a behavioural anthropologist might do. He was well aware of the limitations of his mini experiment. The duration of his study would be very short and would not include a weekend. He would also be the only observer without the confirmation, or otherwise, of the corresponding observations made by others. Furthermore, he would be limited by his own bias. He therefore made it a sacrosanct pre-condition that he would observe others with an impartial and non-judgmental mind. Furthermore, he would only make conclusions from repeated patterns of observed behaviour. Nevertheless, the study had its advantages as a controlled experiment, because it was confined to a specific spatial location and its changing temporality between dawn and night time might reveal how people may differ between these times.

Peter stood back for a moment to question why he was really about to undertake such a random experiment. Was it a sign of an unbalanced mind, he wondered? This may well be the case, he thought, but he knew there was no going back down from his little project now. But he convinced himself that it might help him to find a way forward in his life.

Although he was approaching his study in a scientific manner, he realised that what he was really seeking was a vision of some kind, not unlike that sought by individual members of tribal aboriginal cultures who went on a vision quest. But whereas they had to go through a period of a few days of enforced deprivation, in which they neither eat nor drank, whilst exposing themselves to the elements in some sacred wild place, Peter had no intention of going without food, water, shelter or sleep. He wanted any vision that he may have, to come from a clear mind, not one hallucinating through lack of sustenance. Unconsciously, he felt that he had already experienced enough suffering in his life as a consequence of the sexual abuse experienced and that he had `earned` the right to receive such a vision from the Creator. He was of often prone to such childlike naivety. However, he was unsure how he could gain such a vision from a series of detached observations.

Peter therefore decided to undertake a journey into unknown spiritual waters-he chose for the first time to `give God a chance. ` He would take the plunge and let God, if `He` was out there, reveal himself in some way to him. It was an innocent wish, but one that he was compelled to seek. It was `hearing` the `sound` of God from the ghost detector experiment results that spurred him into to undertaking this quest to receive a vision of his true path. He was also hoping to be blessed with an insight into the mysterious underlying nature of the God Field.

A strange similarity occurred to him between his experiment around the Central Line and that of the Large Hadron Collider (LHC) in CERN in Switzerland. Both structures are seventeen miles in circumference, both underground. Both use an induced force to propel objects, the LHC uses electromagnets to speed up subatomic particles whilst the tube trains are also driven by an electromotive force along the trackway. The LHC fires particles, (at great speed), in opposite directions to collide with one another at enormous energies and the Circle Line sends passenger trains also in opposite directions, (although they travel at much slower speeds and their pathways do not collide!).

Peter couldn't think of anything on the Circle Line which was equivalent to the LHC's detectors, (if one excludes its thousands of security cameras). However, it then occurred to him that it does have a detector-*himself*. The LHC detectors look out for the derivatives of, mainly proton, collisions, whereas, he, on the other hand, has the potentially more complex task of trying to understand human behavior, albeit based on a brief snap shot of travellers on board the London underground.

There was one further fascinating link between the two experiments. The primary experiment being carried out at the LHC at that time, was the search for the elusive so-called Higgs Boson or `God` particle. One of Peter's aims was to gain some understanding of the true purpose of the God Field he had discovered. He could act as a counterpoint to help bridge the gap between the Godless scientific worldview and those who blindly believe in a deity. Understanding the underlying meaning behind his theory may prove, for the very first time, that both parties are really singing from the same hymn sheet, namely that of a divine Creator who is as real as the sun and the moon.

However, this kind of thinking was beginning to trouble him, for *who was he* to dare to know the mind of God? `I must be out of my *stupid fucking mind*. What a fucking self-important *twerp* I must be, ` he reflected, chuckling to himself as he did so. `After all, I am nothing more than a burnt out, disillusioned, mocked, scientist. ` Peter reproached himself for such conceit and made up his mind to stay humble and grounded. After all, his was a puny little study of some passengers travelling on board trains. He made a point of just getting on with his mini project with the minimum of fuss and seeing what may transpire.

As it was getting late on Saturday night, he headed back to Lincolns Inn Fields to get some sleep. He decided to use the following day to make the final preparations for his experiment.

The next day he went to Oxford Street to purchase the things he needed for his five-day study. As well as the items on his list, he also bought some new clothes from Primark, so that he could change into something clean during the period of his study.

It was late in the evening by the time he finished his preparations. He then headed for Lincolns Inn Fields and curled up in the backseat of his car with the blanket wrapped warmly around him, trying to look as inconspicuous as possible from the outside. He was excited about his investigation, which would begin early the next morning. Finally, he set the alarm on his phone for six o' clock before soon falling asleep.

The alarm interrupted a vivid dream he was having about a lost herd of caribou on the London underground. As it felt like an important dream, he switched on his torch and immediately wrote it down, in case he forgot its details later.

Dream...I find myself in a large passenger tunnel in London's underground. Suddenly, a large herd of Arctic caribou come charging towards me, almost filling the tunnel. By some miracle, they didn't trample me underfoot as they pass by. I could feel their warm breath and smell their musky fur as they rushed past. Two other men, and myself, excitedly chase after the herd but we soon lose sight of them. The strangers then run on further ahead and go down onto a platform; I follow but go onto one opposite theirs. A tube train then pulls up at their platform. Its automatic doors open on both sides of the train, including the side that faces the open train track. They board it in the belief that it will follow the path the caribou had taken. Trusting their judgment, I quickly go down onto the track and rush across to board their train before it leaves. About half way across, I realise the danger of what I was doing and rush back to the platform I had just left. As I do so, I see another fast approaching train heading towards me. On reaching the platform edge, I ask a friend, Alan, to lift me up. He pulls hard on my arms but is unable to help me. The train is moving so fast that there isn't enough time for me to escape, but luckily there is a narrow gap between myself and the train as it passes by. When it comes to a stop, its doors open to reveal an old Inuit Eskimo in full native dress standing in the carriage in front of me. I climb on board the train and join him on his journey. I am aware that he knows the correct path the caribou had followed; it was opposite to the one the two strangers had taken.

. . . .

Peter sensed there was a message for him in the dream and wondered if it was that he should follow his own path, not one chosen by someone else.

It was the first morning of his project. At 6.30, true to his plan, he headed for the public toilets in Lincolns Inn Fields where he washed himself, cleaned his teeth, shaved and put on some clean clothes. The duty attendant didn't seem bothered by his actions. Peter was joined by a middle-aged gentleman, who followed a similar routine to his own, except for the change of clothes. He looked quite well to do, with his smartly tailored pin stripped suit, quality white shirt and yellow silk tie. It was odd to see such a seemingly rich man scrubbing himself up in a public lavatory. His guilt-ridden face, however, may provide a clue as to why he was there. Peter speculated that he had carried out some lascivious misdeed the previous night. The empty packet of condoms, which then fell out of his pocket, seemed to confirm this. He wondered whether his wife had just kicked him out of his home as a consequence.

As Peter headed for his car, he saw the man get into his top of the range black Mercedes and quickly speed away. Peter then drove to the car park beneath the Brunswick Centre where he paid thirty pounds to park his car until midnight. He put a bottle of water, notebook and a pen into his rucksack and headed for the nearby Bar Centrale. He dived into a hearty fry up breakfast and sipped from a cup of a delicious strong tea-the kind you can stand a spoon in. Whilst there, he found a spare electrical socket on the wall to recharge his mobile phone. He also browsed through a well-thumbed copy of the Observer Magazine; his blood raced at the sight of some `artistic` pictures of half-naked woman. This made him conscious of the lack of intimate feminine companionship in his life, which made his heart ache. When he had finished eating it was 7.30 am-he was bang on schedule. He then walked to the tube Station next door and made for its deep spiral staircase, rather than take the lift. As he walked down it felt as if were descending to the underworld. He then gloomily contemplated to himself: `Are the tube travellers the living dead? Am I also one of these, for it feels as if it my soul abandoned me a long time ago? `

He then took the short journey to Kings Cross Station where he caught a Circle Line train and began his experiment.

What follows are selected extracts from the extensive first and last days of Peter's notes. The detailed records for the intervening days were of a similar nature. He scribbled outlines of his observations on the train and then wrote them down in more detail when he later went back to Lincolns Inn Fields.

Observations of people travelling on the Circle Line in London.
DAY 1-Monday 19th December 2011.
Morning peak time (7.45 to 9.30 am)
Board the Circle Line train at Kings Cross Station at 7.46am. Unable to get a seat at first because it is so busy... so *hectic*. I finally find one, but it is difficult to observe others as there are so many people standing in the way.

Everyone is wearing dark clothing-mostly grey or black trousers, skirts, jackets and raincoats. Thank God for the lighter coloured shirts and blouses brightening up their otherwise funeral procession-like appearance!

No one is speaking; there is a strange silence, a silence of knowing, a silence of social fear. The only noise is from the train as it journeys through the tunnel. It sounds like the constant `rushing` sound of a strong wind, except when the train crosses some points which produce a deafening, disjointed, ratter-tatter sound, or a piercing screeching noise when the brakes are applied.

These people are in their own little worlds, their own insulated bubbles.

The vast majority of passengers are engaged in some kind of solitary activity, usually involving their smartphones, (but not for making phone calls as there is no reception on the underground). What are they using their phones for? After watching many different passengers, it appears that they are using them for the following main reasons: -

1. Playing computer games.
2. Listening to uploaded music.
3. Watching uploaded movies or TV programmes.
4. Checking saved social media messages and making draft messages.

Some of the remaining passengers are reading a book on their Kindle or tablet computer or listening to portable music players. A few are reading a newspaper, mainly the free Metro and fewer still an old-fashioned hardback or paperback book. *My God,* will paper newspapers and books soon become a thing of the past?

Everyone is isolated. NO ONE TALKS TO EACH OTHER.

After morning peak time until lunch (9.30 to 1pm)

Fewer travellers, less hustle and bustle. There is a more relaxed atmosphere than during the peak time.

The make-up of the passengers has changed, with more non-workers, several travelling with friends or family members. There are a few small groups of overseas and British tourists judging by the intermingling of foreign accents with UK regional dialects. They are quite chatty and animated and seem largely unaware of the silence of the other passengers. They must be in London to celebrate Christmas. They are much less self-conscious and their conversation is often interspersed with laughter.

If any of the non-working groups have young children with them, it is noticeable just how uninhibited and excitable they are-they put us self-aware adults to shame.

N.B. Is it this innocence that we lose when we grow up; is this God's innocence? The above is a naïve statement, but perhaps there is a powerful truth in its simplicity. What if the purity of children is related to the God Field?

Lunch above ground near Edgware Road Station (1 to 2pm)

After lunch until evening peak time (2 to 5pm)

There are fewer passengers than in the late morning but the carriages are still quite full of people, although the numbers vary greatly at different points along the Circle Line. For instance, they are more crowded at the tube stations linking the main railway terminals such as Paddington, Euston, Kings Cross, Liverpool Street, Charing Cross and Victoria.

Just as in the later morning, there is more chatter, mainly from small groups of visitors. Likewise, those who are alone, are engaged in one of the private pursuits already mentioned.

At Temple Station, I caught sight of a young, rake-like, white man in long dreadlocks, boarding the next carriage with his dog. Not long after the train has pulled out of the station, the interconnecting door to my carriage opens and he walks in. His clothes are dirty and disheveled; loose threads from his jumper hang down over his dirty hands. He has a Labrador-collie cross-like dog held on a string lead behind him. One of its eyes has an opaque/milky colour to it; is it blind in that eye? The passengers catch sneaky nervous glances towards them. He walks quickly, whilst talking to himself, occasionally stopping to ask for money; whenever he does so he would say, "please don't worry-I only need a few shillings to help feed my dog. It's *not* for drugs or drink, I promise you." Nevertheless, he seemed a druggy to most of the passengers; the strong smell of skunk didn't help to dissuade them from this impression. One shy looking chap gave him a fifty pence piece, it seemed more out of fear than a genuine act of charity, but then I may be mistaken. "Come on Lady, that's a good girl," he calls out in an affectionate tone to his dog who is trying to stick its head down a horrified passenger's

MacDonald's food bag. Eventually, he gently pulls the dog away, before heading for the next carriage.

Evening peak time (5 to 7 pm)

Train packed. Everyone seems stressed out and tired. There is mostly silence, as there was in the morning rush `hour, ` except for the sound of the train hurtling down the tunnel and the screeching of brakes.

There is a little more talking than during the morning rush hour, possibly because there are more tourists and shoppers in the crowd, but a few of the other workers seem to be occasionally chatting to each other.

A heavily pregnant woman boards the train at Liverpool Street Station. Initially, no one offers their seat to her until a gentleman in a smart suit sitting some distance away, beckons her to take his seat. The other passengers squirm in embarrassed silence for not having offered theirs.

Many have their heads buried in their mobile phones, but fewer than in the morning rush hour. I guess they are too tired, after a stressful day's work, to concentrate on this task.

Dinner above ground near Edgware Road Station (7 to 8pm)

Night time (7 to 11pm)

Early evening. Not too busy. Generally, a different crowd than before; mainly people heading for the West End nightspots, I guess. Most passengers are dressed in smarter, more colourful clothes. There is more animated talk going on.

Late evening. Quite a few drunken revellers board the train; several young men and women are absolutely smashed; they are very merry and often shout to their friends who are sometimes just standing or sitting right next to them.

When the train approached Paddington Station, one chap, obviously so drunk that he didn't know or care about what he was doing, proceeded to urinate next to one of the carriage doors. The other passengers, with the exception of his mates, (who didn't seem bothered), look on in shock and disgust.

One of their friends, a drunken woman of about twenty-five, sat next to me and started chatting.

"What's your name then? … What's your name? Come on, please tell us! Don't be shy!"

"Peter," I shyly replied.

"What do you do for a living?"

I hesitated, before responding, "I'm a scientist."

On hearing this, she shrieked with hysterical laughter, before calling out to her friends.

"Sal, get this, this chaps a fucking scientist-can you Adam and Eve it!"

She then leaned over and whispered into my ear: "Do you know what Peter, I've got a soft spot for brain boxes like you; how's about you coming back to my place tonight and teaching me a *fucking* lesson," after which she rolled off her seat laughing. One of her friends then picked her up and apologised for her behavior.

"I'm so sorry sir-she's never like this normally," she, explained.

DAY 5-Friday 23rd December 2011. Observations Morning peak time (7.45 to 9.30 am).

Early. Waiting on Circle Line platform at Kings Cross. Very crowded; people seem less self-conscious than when on the train. They move their body and heads more because they have a little more room to manoeuvre, although they are very careful not to encroach on the personal space of anyone standing next to them. Most of them seem to be looking at the other passengers a bit more and generally taking in more information from their surroundings. They are carrying out fewer solitary tasks than when on board the train, no doubt due to the short time before the trains arrival and the difficulty of carrying out these activities whilst standing up. Nonetheless, many are still absorbed with their smart phones, doing something or other.

Once the passengers cross the yellow line on the platform edge and step onto the train their behaviour changes dramatically; as they sit down, they become rigid and shut off from the outside world, before engaging in one of the isolated activities referred to before. They rarely look around and investigate their surroundings and even less do they look at the other passengers. Why is this I wonder?

At 9.00 am, an old woman boarded the packed train at Notting Hill Station. She seemed overwhelmed by the overcrowded carriage. Her bright red painted lips and pink blushed cheeks, rather than making her look younger, only emphasised the shadowy crow's nest wrinkles radiating from her lips and eyes. Her desperation was there for all to see. When she leant her head to one side to rest it on the palm of hand, it was as if she was trying to elicit some compassion from the other passengers. Was she asking them to remember the beautiful young woman she once was?

N.B. Note the inevitability of aging. The inexorable continuity of time. But universal time is independent of our daily reality, as it intrinsically intertwined with the bizarre predictions of the unreal quantum world and relativity. Even our cells biologically age at different rates according to the speed at which we are travelling, albeit impeccability so.

After morning peak time until lunch (9.30-to 1pm)

As for the previous days, there are more small groups of passengers-tourists, students, leisure break seekers and some workers. The general atmosphere lifts somewhat and there is more movement and sound emanating from their direction. The overall feeling is less isolating and impersonal than during the rush` hour` death run.

Three portly African ladies in colourful dress are talking loudly in their native tongue, (Nigerian I think). Everyone in the carriage can hear them, yet they seem oblivious to this and carry on talking, laughing and gesticulating in energetic movements of their face, hands and body. They seem uninhibited, unlike the other lone passengers.

Lunch above ground near Edgware Road Station (1 to 2pm)

After lunch until evening peak time (2 to 5pm)

Several school groups come onto the train at different times. The younger children seem so free and happy, the older ones perhaps about aged 15-16, seem to have taken on the pattern of restless, hormonal adolescents.

N.B. Perhaps the God Field. and therefore, our innocence is diminished when we enter the world of biological sexual maturity.

I overheard two women teachers talking to one another. They are accompanying a group of young secondary school children returning from a trip to the British Museum. One of them, perhaps in her forties, was talking in a loud American accent. She had a burnt-out appearance, typical of so many teachers these days.

"Teaching in UK schools is *so different* now compared to when I first came over from New York, nearly twenty years ago. Teachers these days rarely make a positive emotional connection with their pupils and rarer still do they inspire them."

Her teaching friend concurred with her colleague, giving an example from her own upbringing.

"I remember `Scratcher` Harris, my English teacher in school. We called him this because he was always, unknowingly, scratching his head and private parts. The class found it hilarious. Nevertheless, we learnt a great deal in his lessons, especially through stories and the use of humour. We didn't realise that we were learning at the time because we were so absorbed in his performance. His lessons were often riotous fun. However, when it came to the exams, we usually all excelled. But he would not last a second in today's teaching climate before being shown the door by some unimaginative headteacher."

"You're absolutely right," came an unexpected reply from an old gentleman sitting opposite them, who had overheard their conversation.

The two women, taken off guard by his interjection, only gave a short reply of acknowledgment, the kind aimed at deterring any further comment.

At one point, the school children became so noisy and restless, that their teachers had to get up from their seats to calm them down, which was a difficult task and took some time.

Undeterred, the old man again intervened and, looking at the teachers, said.

"I understand now what my granddaughter has to go through in school-she is also a teacher," to which the American woman replied.

"You're absolutely right; most people have no idea just how demanding it is to teach kids these days," a comment that stirred up the pupils even more, as they responded with boos and hisses directed towards their teachers. Everyone found this situation funny and a heartfelt laughter simultaneously erupted from passengers and pupils alike.

Evening peak time (5 to 7 pm)

Quiet chaos, passengers jam-packed in the train carriage. Everyone seems either exhausted, pissed off, or defeated, or all of these things, after a hard day's work. The vast majority are mainly office and shop workers, as in the morning rush hour.

N.B. Why are they so mentally beaten, is it because they have been undertaking work which is contrary to their soul's nature. There is no way they can be doing the kind of labour the Lebanese poet Khalil Gibran says human beings should be doing, namely work that is `love made visible. ` But, who am I to judge, someone who has only ever worked in the cozy world of academia?

Dinner above ground near Edgware Road Station (7 to 8pm)

Night time (7 to 11pm)

Early. Generally, a very lively bunch tonight-it must be the Friday night crowd on their way to a pre-Christmas booze up.

Late. Most passengers are in different stages of inebriation-one man puked up nearby-a disgusting sight, which was soon followed by the smell of sick permeating throughout the confined space of the carriage. When the train pulled up at the next station, Westminster, I quickly changed carriages, only to find myself standing next to a couple embroiled in a nasty argument. I was unable to move out of their way because the train was packed with so many partygoers returning home. A chap, about twenty years old, with a bloated and pale completion was being extremely rude and intimidating towards his girlfriend. However, rather than backing down, she kept on riling him up by pressing all the wrong buttons. I was worried that he was going to strike her, but rather than asking them both to take it easy and calm down, I did nothing, fearing he might attack me if I intervened. Luckily, for my sense of dented pride, they got off at the next station.

This was the last daily entry of Peter's London underground observations.

The following morning, Peter woke up a little later than normal, before cleaning himself up in the public toilets. He intended to use the day ahead to clarify his findings from his mini experiment. He also decided to record a strange series of meetings he had with an Eskimo-like vagrant outside Edgware Road Tube Station during his lunchtime breaks.

Key findings from my observations of the weekday Circle Line tube passengers

The lone passengers, (no matter what time of day), are stuck in a silent, isolated, protective cocoon of their own unconscious choosing. The enclosed space with its lack of natural light and fresh air, along with the proximity of so many strangers, upsets their equilibrium and they become disconcerted and withdrawn. They shut themselves off as a means of minimising their feeling of exposure to the eyes and perceived examination of their fellow passengers, especially those seated opposite them. As a result, they bury their heads in some form of lone pursuit, usually involving their smart phones, and to a lesser extent, tablet computers and Kindles; fewer still read a newspaper, or an old-fashioned book.

Are they afraid of being exposed for who they feel they really are-fearful and flawed individuals? Are they afraid that others might see their fragile ego, character defects and poor image of themselves?

The morning and evening rush hours are almost totally made up of such lost souls. They sit in a state of quiet separation. They are like fundamental particles attracted by some hidden force to their devices and repelled by their fellow travellers. Collectively they make up a lost tribe. Although this level of estrangement diminishes around these peak times, as more native non-workers and tourists on route to some leisurely foray, join the train, it is still always there in the background.

Sometimes, these quiet scenes were interrupted by some incident that reveals the humanity, either good, bad and sometimes ridiculous, that lays just beneath the surface, such as the dread-locked chap with the dog and the importuning drunken lady I observed on Monday. Such incidents had the effect of temporarily shaking the other `hidden` passengers out of their shells.

Alienation is a word that most appropriately describes the way many of the passengers feel; they are alienated from themselves, each other, and the society around them.

They are divorced from any meaningful connection with the natural world; this is why they fear disclosure on the tube; it is because they are scared, unfulfilled individuals, without any real spiritual meaning in their lives. Like most of the rest of human kind, they are lost little naked souls, unable to make any sense of their lives on this little blue dot in space.

As human beings, we are so easily conditioned, so predictable in our behaviour. Conditioning from the media and other tentacles of the consumer society, has made us nothing more than consumption entities. I had watched a small sample of such beings in my mini study. When they enter the train carriage, there is no place for them to hide and so they are momentarily laid bare. So, what did they virtually all do? They buried themselves in their portable high-tech devices. This way, they could mask themselves from possible public exposure.

We have become blind technological junkies. What is worse, these little machines are used as a means of influencing and controlling us. The `pop up, ` and other forms of advertising they flood us with, directly fuel the production market. They also act as a distraction from free thought, which might make us aware that we are trapped monkeys in a human zoo of material gluttony. Technology neutralises and helps to quell any potential dissent that could bring about positive change. It nullifies the only thing that could change society for the better, a mind that is free to question. Each one of us is a mass produced empty little grey box, save for an accumulated bank of received subliminal messages on how to be a, (soulless), participant in mass consumerism. We are incapable of seeing and thinking outside of this box to see that we are helpless pawns in the `game` of exploiting our beautiful planet to satiate the inherent greed of our species. The worst crime of all is that nature suffers as a consequence of our rampant plunder. We even call the wonderful animal life, plant life, oceans, land and air, *natural resources,* as if they are only there for us to use and have no intrinsic value in themselves. Even people are now described at *human resources*, which implies that they are only there to be used as a means of production, whether in the manufacturing, agricultural or service industries.

The big joke, of course is that we are tricked into believing that we have free will in our lives. This is the ultimate malignant weapon in preventing any dissention, for why would one want to rebel if they already believe themselves to be free?

There are a few, rare, independent souls, who know that they are imprisoned in this way and the reasons for this. Sadly, authority, friends or neighbours, often object to their non-conformity and seek to crush their spirit.

We are caught up in unstoppable tide that is the force of our consumerist culture imprinting its indelible mark upon our freedom. Each of us is stuck, to a greater or lesser degree, in a cycle of unbridled over-indulgence that is destroying the natural world, extinguishing the very thing that could save us and give meaning to our lives.

The greatest tragedy of all is that there seems to be nothing that we can do to stop this `fall,` because as a species we seem INCAPABLE OF REAL SPIRITUAL CHANGE. For this reason, I see no hope for our future.

This message is nothing new to the world, but it is new to me, for I had not been fully aware of it before.

But where is God in all this, where is the God Field? It must surely be that a God, working through the God Field, has no effect on our daily lives. If `He` did have some influence, then he would wake us up to `His` truth and empower us to end the destruction of our planet and, therefore, our inevitable demise as a species. He would also use `His` influence to prevent our terrible cruelty to each other. Although, I have proven in my ghost detector experiments in Manchester that the God Field is intricately involved in the unfolding development of living beings in the embryo, (and probably childhood), it appears to have no influence when we become adults.

....

Nevertheless, however strongly the feelings Peter expressed about the plight of the human race above, he remained uncertain as to how the findings from his little study related to his own destiny.

Chapter 7

During the five days of his study, Peter had a series of unusual lunchtime encounters with a vagrant outside Edgware Road Tube Station. Although these were outside the remit of his study, because they took place above ground, he felt compelled to write them down as they were of such significance. He was also hoping that they might provide him with the guidance he was seeking.

Encounters with an `Eskimo` Vagrant
Monday 18th December

As I left Edgware Road Station at 1pm to get some lunch, an elderly, dirty and unkempt vagrant caught my eye. He was begging for money, but I sadly feigned ignorance to his pleading and walked on past to a nearby café. I sensed that he had been staring at me intently however and felt guilty for having taking such sneakily evasive action to avoid giving him any change. However, in my defence, I was surprised to have suddenly come across him and anyway I had other things on my mind.

The vagrant was not there when I later excited the station again at about 7pm to have my evening meal break.

Tuesday 19th December

On leaving Edgware Road Station to take my lunchtime break, I once more saw the vagrant sitting down on a blanket placed on the cold stone floor. He had an empty polystyrene cup in front of him into which I placed a measly ten pence piece. As I bent over to drop the coin into the cup, I was shocked when I got a clear view of his face.

He looked exactly like the old Inuit Eskimo I saw on board a tube train in the dream I had on Sunday night about a lost herd of caribou on the London underground. The resemblance was uncanny-the same wavy black hair, large roundish face, dark reddish-skinned completion and piecing, slanting eyes; even the thick moustache and beard, were an exact match. His clothes too, a thick Parker jacket with a `fur` rimed hood, were very similar.

The vagrant, on seeing my paltry donation, looked up and gazed purposely into my eyes. This made me feel even more ill at ease, for my meanness had been found out. I then quickly headed for the café across the road for lunch, where I sat on a seat by the window with a clear view of him.

From a distance, I began to doubt his likeness to the Eskimo in my dream and convinced myself that his looks were typical of down and outs who had been living rough for many years. The ravaging effects of the weather, strong alcohol and malnutrition, sculpts their faces over time to reveal ruddy, bloated, pock-marked, puffed-up, darkened features with stretched skin around their eyes; all which make for an Eskimo-like appearance. But in spite of such reasoning, I was still unsettled, so much so that when I later headed back to the tube station to resume my observations, I pointedly avoided looking in his direction, fearing I might again be shocked by his resemblance to the Eskimo in my dream.

The vagrant was also absent when I later came out of the station, at about seven, for my evening break.

Wednesday 20th December

The sight of the homeless man had been on my mind for much of the previous night. I was apprehensive at the thought of seeing him again at lunchtime. Could he be the same man as in dream? I even considered taking my break at another station but was loathe to change the conditions of my experiment, albeit it an arbitrary sociological one. I therefore knew that I had no choice but to leave from the same station again. However, when I was exiting it later, I noticed a young police officer trying to move him along. I stopped to put a pound coin into his polystyrene cup, as much to show to the policeman my support for the vagrant as it was a gesture of financial aid. In doing so, I caught sight of his face again and would still swear that it was the same person as in my dream. This repeated shock threw me off my stride and I found myself saying to the police officer.

"Can't you leave him alone -he's not harming anyone is he?" I could tell that the vagrant was aware of my attempt to defend him.

The officer then replied, "Look, I don't like having to do this either, but it's my job."

On hearing this, I said nothing more and left for the café for lunch and resumed watching the vagrant again from afar, who by now had moved away from the station to the corner of a nearby street to avoid any more of the policeman's harassment. I once again, convinced myself that he wasn't the same person as in my dream and that it was just a freak accident of nature that he happened to look exactly like him. This settled my mind a little.

When I later emerged from the station for my evening break, there was no sign of the vagrant, (or the policeman for that matter).

Thursday 21st December

This time I gave the vagrant a two-pound coin as I left Edgware Road Station. He looked up and gazed intently into my eyes once more, but said nothing, which unnerved me. I quickly headed for the café across the road for lunch. As I was finishing my meal, I looked towards the station and saw the same police officer talking to him. On seeing this, I grabbed my rucksack, walked angrily towards them, stood nearby and listened to the policeman as he spoke to the vagrant in an intimidating tone.

"Look, I told you that I didn't want to see you back here again-is that *clear*. If I see you here next time, I'll lock you up. But that's probably what you want isn't it. That way you'll get a warm night's sleep and a meal, wouldn't you?" The officer said mockingly.

On hearing this, I couldn't stop himself and had to intervene to defend my `Eskimo` doppelgänger.

"Haven't you got anything better to do than to pick on this elderly gentleman?"

The vagrant was closely watching the situation from below.

The officer's head turned sharply towards mine, his eyebrows furrowed, his face contorted in an antagonistic expression. He then replied, "Aren't you the same guy that spoke to me yesterday? Look, I suggest you keep your nose out of this; as I told you before I'm just doing my job!"

He then leaned forward and whispered into my ear.

"Now piss off son, unless you want me to take down your details and lock you up instead of him! If I see you back here as again, *I'll fucking nick you mate*, make no mistake."

I then sheepishly, tail between my legs, headed down the stairs to resume my observations, shaken by the officer's unexpected aggression and threats.

I was understandably anxious about my planned evening break at the Station. When I arrived there later, I tentatively climbed the stairs leading up to the exit before scanning around carefully for any signs of the officer but could see none. I concluded that his shift must end in the afternoon. There was no sign of the vagrant either, who must head off to somewhere else in the evenings.

Friday 22nd December

When I exited Edgware Road Station at lunchtime I stealthily looked around for any signs of the police officer-but luckily, there were none. I therefore went over to the vagrant, who was sitting on the floor with his head bent down and placed a two-pound coin into his cup. He looked up at me and then straight away picked himself off the floor and moved towards me with his arms out stretched.

When he got closer, I noticed he had tattoos on his forearms. On looking more closely at them, I could see they were of a hunting scene. The vagrant then proceeded to wrap his arms around me in a great big bear hug.

"Thank you so much for trying to help me with that copper yesterday," he said.

"No problem at all, I didn't like the way he was pestering you."

After a short pause, I continued. "Do you mind if I take a closer look at the tattoos on your forearms, they look amazing?"

The vagrant rolled up his sleeves some more to reveal a beautifully designed image of Eskimos hunting a herd of caribou.

I was flabbergasted at the connection with my dream. Here was a man that looked exactly like the Eskimo in my dream and had tattoos on his forearms depicting a scene of Eskimo huntsmen pursuing a herd of caribou, again linking it with my dream.

I immediately realised that this synchronous event might have some portent for me. I therefore asked the vagrant.

"Do you mind if I ask you a question about the tattoos?"

"What would you like to know?"

"This may sound a bit odd, but can you tell me where the herd of caribou were heading for?" I could tell from his face that he didn't think this question too strange.

"They are going to the place where their heart is."

"What do you mean by that?"

"Their heart lies in the next place of fresh pasture. It is their destiny to keep on travelling, otherwise they will perish."

"Can you tell me where you think my destiny lies?" I boldly asked.

The vagrant paused for a while and then looked intensely into my eyes. It was as if he was trying to peer into my soul.

"Your future lies in your healing the wounds of your past; only then will you find yourself. Only then can you unblock the way to your heart."

"How can I heal these wounds?"

"The only way is by confronting them and forgiving yourself...Only you can do this…only you can save yourself."

His unexpected answer, in which he seemed to know something of my own history, disturbed my equilibrium. This advice was the last thing I expected. It unnerved me. My reaction was to get away as soon as possible. I therefore hurriedly hugged and thanked him, before bidding him farewell.

Peter then examined the meaning of this encounter with the vagrant. His conclusions are written down below.

Thoughts

There must be a link between my dream of the lost herd of caribou on the London underground and the `Eskimo` vagrant; it has to be more than a coincidence; surely it has some spiritual significance? Was the Great Spirit, (the God Field?), speaking to me through the `Eskimo` vagrant?

Perhaps the link is in the lost herd of travellers I observed: are they like the lost herd of caribou? Are they lost souls whose salvation lay, like the caribou, in finding their heart? Does the path the caribou had taken represent the direction to our true heart and soul, one that is in tune with the God Field I discovered? The passengers on the Circle Line can board one of two trains going in opposite directions, one in tune and one out of tune with the `Great

Mystery; ` every moment, we are faced with a decision to select one of these two pathways. Because of our negative upbringings, we invariably make choices which take us on the wrong path, away from our true heart and soul. The only way to turn this around is by understanding our past failures, traumas and conditioning. For myself, this means facing up to and healing the wounds from my childhood.

The `Eskimo's` advice to me, to heal the wounds of my past, is the only way I can open the closed doors to my heart. It confirms that I must find Max and exact my revenge. But revenge? Surely, a merciful GOD would not countenance taking reprisal in an attempt to right the wrongs of the past. He would want forgiveness and reconciliation. But perhaps revenge is too harsh a word, for would I not be making a man accountable for the evil has done? Therefore, from now on, I will see my intention as one of natural justice, rather than of revenge.

....

Once he had finished writing down these last words, Peter put his notebook and pen into his rucksack and switched his torch light off.

He felt empowered from the gift of insight the `Eskimo` vagrant had given him into his future destiny. This emboldened him to return home the following day to face his wife and discuss their impending divorce.

Peter slowly drifted into sleep in the back seat of his car in Lincolns Inn Fields. He dreamt that he met a lovely, but troubled, woman and they eventually fell in love. However, on waking, he could not recall any specific details of the dream, only its bare outline.

Chapter 8

The next day, Peter went shopping for Christmas presents before heading to his family home. When he arrived, he tentatively knocked on the front door of the late Victorian house in Hackney; it was over two and a half months since he was last there. It was two o'clock on Christmas Eve afternoon.

His wife and children were waiting for him expectantly inside, completely oblivious of his tube wanderings over the past week.

Sian answered the door and stood looking blankly at him for a moment. Her mind was unable to process the information it received from the sight of his visible presence; it was log jammed with several conflicting emotions: -resentment and forgiveness, bitterness and compassion, judgement and empathy.

"Please come in," she finally said.

His children were in the living room watching TV; they jumped up in delight upon seeing him, throwing away any hurt they carried for his lack of communication since he had been away. They hugged him dearly and made him feel at home.

Whilst Sian was making him some tea for him in the kitchen, he sat with the children in the living room and once more explained to them why his mental disintegration was the reason for his lack of contact over the last few months. He again mentioned the distress that his breakthrough had caused him and how he needed to get away. He also told them of his having just resigned from his position at

Imperial. They could both tell that he was in now in a much better place, both mentally and spiritually. Julia explained that she had abandoned travelling with her New Age friends for a while so that she could stay at home and help mum.

Having now composed herself, Sian entered the room and politely asked Peter if he would like some dinner, to which he agreed. He later joined her in the kitchen and they made some small talk for a while, before deciding to leave any discussion of the divorce until after the Christmas celebrations. Both were mentally tired and in no fit state to think rationally about such an important matter.

In the evening, Peter went for a drink with his children in his local; although he invited Sian to come along, she declined.

Once everyone had retired for bed, Peter slept on the couch in the living room, rather than in the spare bedroom.

The next morning, after breakfast, Peter helped his wife and children tidy the house and prepare the Christmas meal. Later on, at about midday, they exchanged presents. He gave Julia a copy of the *The Mabinogion* and George Borrows *Travels in Wales* to Stephen, as he wanted them to learn a little more about their Welsh roots. He also gave each of them a cherished turquoise chert flint arrowhead which he had he found in a ploughed field when he was a teenager. Julia gave him a signed copy of the Dalai Lama's book on *The Art of Happiness* and Stephen gave him an elegant antique brass pocket compass. Peter gave Sian a book on yoga; she, however, did not reciprocate with a present of her own; she was too upset by the collapse of their marriage.

They all had a happy Christmas day together, especially as Peter and his wife had agreed to bury their differences for a while. They played several games including Charades and Articulate; Peter was rubbish at both, which added to the hilarity.

Sian's relations came over on Boxing Day and everyone had a pleasant day.

Early the following morning, Peter decided that it was time to face up to the matter of the divorce and asked his wife if she was ready to talk about it. She agreed, but he could tell that she had been dreading this moment just as much as he had. They both sat down in the kitchen in readiness to discuss the inevitable.

Peter asked Sian if she could agree to talk amicably and without any bitterness about their marital situation, to which she, (reluctantly), concurred. He explained that he had every intention of signing the papers and not disputing them.

He apologised to his wife for the embarrassment he had caused her in his `thankyou` speech at Cambridge and for having `disappeared` afterwards without contacting her.

Sian replied that she appreciated his saying these things. She conveyed her regrets for the cruel things she said to him in Cambridge.

Peter then expressed his remorse for his part in the failure of their marriage. He was especially regretful for the early years when he had been an addictive gambler and excessive drinker and for the consequences of such behavior on the family. He explained to Sian that he could not help himself because of the emotional illness brought on by Max's abuse, which he had told her about many years previously.

"I was trapped in a prison from which I could not escape. Sadly, I didn't have the right key to unlock the jailhouse door."

"But why did you gamble and drink so much-surely they only made things worse for you?" Sian asked, wanting to fully understand the real reasons for his actions.

"They helped to deaden the pain I was suffering. The buzz from the gambling and the anesthetic from the drink helped me to dampen the hurt. I just can't describe in words to you what this was like, other than to say it was like being in a *living hell*."

"Why didn't you tell me about this before?" She replied.

"I did so, several times, but neither of us was in position to really listen to one another."

"I'm sorry for not having listened to you Peter…I'm so sorry." His honesty had lifted her antipathy towards him and tapped into her natural integrity.

He continued, trying to hold back the tears.

"Please forgive me for all the pain I have caused you Sian."

This was too much for her to bear and she burst into tears. A deep hurt came from some dark place within her. Julia, having overheard her mother's heart-felt distress from the living room, came in to console her, but Sian politely asked her to leave, saying that she was alright and not to worry. As she exited the room, Peter stood up from his chair, went over to Sian and put his arms around her. They were entwined in a place of mutual empathy; this shared instant would, from then on, help them both to discuss their divorce without too much acrimony.

When Sian had calmed down, they chatted convivially and heartily for a while. It was as if the touching moment they had just shared had blessed them with the grace of forgiveness and this had temporarily lifted the shroud of hurt they both felt.

Sian then explained her side of the story. She said how his irresponsible behaviour had made it very hard for her to cope. She told him how his gambling, drinking and black moods, had affected her and the children.

These words from his wife hurt him badly for they were true; but he let these feelings stay with him rather that run away from them as he had done in the past. He deeply regretted not having been able to free himself from his tormented soul.

Sian continued with a list of his failings. She wanted to express to Peter what it had been like for her and how she felt. Peter listened in silence, although it was hard for him to hear these facts.

When she had finally poured out all of her accumulated misgivings and released all of the pain that lay within her heart, she stopped talking. She then looked at Peter to see if he had taken in all that she had said. It was clear from his broken countenance that he had listened. Sian was not, by nature, a cruel woman and knew that it was time to back off; she had no desire to crush her husband.

Peter then calmly said that he would sign the divorce papers. Sian fetched them from upstairs. He quickly read and signed them, drawing a bold line underneath his signature, which symbolically represented drawing a line in his marriage; he knew he had to do this for both of their sakes, if they were ever to have their lives back again.

He then told Sian that he had resigned from his position in the University. She was very surprised by this and worried for his future.

Feeling compassion and concern for him, she enquired, "What do you intend to do Peter?"

"I'm not exactly sure. I do know that I will have to leave London for a while. I also have some old stuff in Cardiff which I have to face up to in the near future."

Sian knew instinctively what he was referring to.

"You're *right* to sort that matter out," she said with feeling.

Her understanding of his situation made Peter warm to her.

"What will you do yourself, Sian?"

"To be honest with you Peter, I'm not really sure-I think I'll work on things that will make me feel better about myself."

"That is good to hear-you are a very special person. I hope you know that?"

Sian remained silent to this question due to her feelings of regret and self-loathing. She partly felt responsible for the break-up of their marriage, particularly for her cold and bitter stance towards her husband's struggles. She was starkly aware of her emotional distance from him, which she saw as 'tough love,' but was also a means of punishing him for his perceived failings. This lack of intimacy and love had been like a dagger to her husband's heart.

Peter stayed for another week. They all joyfully celebrated New Year's Eve on Primrose Hill from where they watched the spectacular midnight display of fireworks from the River Thames in the distance.

Stephen was due back to work in a couple of days and Julia was soon to meet up with her New Age friends to resume her travels.

Julia and Stephen, when they found out about their parents having signed the divorce papers, felt a kind of release, for they knew that there was no longer, as they had once hoped, any chance of turning the clock back.

Peter had a great time with his children that last week. They had fun taking walks and cycle trips together in London and the surrounding countryside, as well as wading through the West End post-Christmas sale crowds.

He would never forget two comically surreal cycling trips they had together. The first was organised by his daughter, who had signed up her dad, (without his knowledge), to participate in one of London's *Secret Cyclists Club* mystery rides. They are an eccentric group whose members receive a text on the day of the outing informing them of a rendezvous to meet up, from where they would be told of a secret destination to cycle to, where a special event would take place.

Peter, therefore unexpectedly, received a text one morning instructing him to meet at Speakers Corner in Hyde Park at 8 pm that evening. Sensing his daughter

113

might be behind this `mischief,` he showed her the text and she had to come clean on her subterfuge. When she explained the tenets of the cycling club to him, he was up for a laugh and looked forward to their bike ride that evening. Stephen was already aware of the trip.

They set off at six o'clock, travelling along the busy London streets, their bicycles seemingly oblivious to the traffic. Peter, worrying about the safety of his children, tried to get them to cycle on the pavements wherever possible, but this was usually in vain. He asked if they could take the slightly longer central London route via Euston Road towards Edgware Road Tube Station and then to Hyde Park. He did this in the vain hope that he might see the `Eskimo` vagrant once more, although he knew that he was never at the Station in the evenings.

As expected, the `Eskimo` vagrant wasn't there when they later passed by the Station, leaving Peter with a saddened feeling as one would feel if a long-lost friend had failed to show up for a meeting. As they cycled along Edgware Road itself, he caught sight of a small gathering of rough sleepers on the corner of a side street, outside the Lebanese restaurant, *Maroush*. They appeared to be receiving food handouts from a side door of this famous eatery. Most of the crowd were young people down on their luck. Many were of East European descent, judging by the faint accents he could hear in the distance; their homeless numbers had dramatically increased in recent years. As he turned his head to look more closely at this scene, he caught sight of the unmistakable outline of the `Eskimo` vagrant once more. His spirit lifted. As if sensing his presence, the vagrant then turned around, looked towards him and waved; Peter waved back. He then rolled up his sleeves to proudly show off his tattoos to Peter once more. Peter responded by shouting, "it's wonderful to see you again," realising for the first time that they didn't know each other's name. But that brief re-connection with the

`Eskimo, ` filled his soul once more as they continued the short distance up the road to their meeting place in Speakers Corner. Julia and Stephen, who had been cycling behind their father, were bemused by the exchange they had just witnessed.

When they approached the Park, many other cyclists joined them. Inexplicably, several of the riders were stark naked, except for a rucksack on their backs, which presumably carried their clothes. They must have been freezing in the bitter cold. Peter wondered what was going on. As they pulled up at Speakers Corner, they joined a large assembly of other cyclists, a least a quarter of whom were stark butt naked! A swift enquiry to one of the other clothed cyclists revealed that the *Buff Cyclists Club*, a renegade offshoot from the *Secret Cyclists Club,* had decided to hijack the event. None of the clothed group, however, dared to show their objections, seemingly not wanting to appear to be `uncool. ` At about 8.15, the groups were told their secret destination was Arch number 23 near Waterloo station, where an event would start at 9.30. Everyone then set off in that direction. Seeing so many naked cyclists in the middle of winter, must have seemed a strange sight for the late-night shoppers along Oxford Street!

On their arrival, Peter and his children locked their bikes alongside many others on the railings running beside the Arches and headed towards a pink neon sign entitled `NUMBER 23`. The Arches are cavernous dome shaped spaces beneath the dense network of railway tracks and sidings leading to Waterloo Station and its approaches. Once they had paid a ten pounds entrance fee, they tucked into a hot food buffet, soft drinks and wine. Having eaten a hearty snack, they entered a huge, dimly lit, adjoining room and sat down on the floor. In the kerfuffle, Peter and his children were separated from each other as the nude and clothed cyclists rushed to grab a `seat` near the front. By chance, they each found themselves sandwiched between naked cyclists on either side of them.

A young woman with long auburn hair, wearing a thick red Afghan jumper and jeans embroidered with `crystal` beads forming patterns of stars and tigers, announced that they were to watch a screening of the film *Casablanca.* They all waited in excited anticipation. Before the film started, someone accidently turned up the lights to full brightness, causing the clothed cyclists much embarrassment as they tried their hardest to avoid looking at the naked cyclists and their dangly bits. The `in the buff ` lot didn't seem to give a fig either way.

Eventually, the lights were dimmed, (to the obvious relief of the clothed lot), and the film began. There was much fidgeting when they reached the famous scene when Ingrid Bergman says to the pianist "Play it once, Sam. For old times' sake." Several of the clothed group had unforced mental images of the naked cyclist next to them playing with their naughty bits.

When they later cycled back to Hackney in the early hours of the morning, along largely deserted streets, Peter and his children had great fun recalling the events of that evening. Peter told them how he had accidently dropped a hot dog sausage into the lap of a naked cyclist beside him and wondering, "Do I pick it up, or not?" and "if I do, I hope I grab the right sausage!"

The other bizarre journey they had together concerned a cycling trip to Epping Forest. They were having a great time weaving their way along its muddied tracks, until they got lost and didn't have a clue where they were. Peter's Bear Grylls-like attempt to ascertain their position using the position of the setting sun just visible above the trees, came to no avail as they ended up in exactly the same place they had started from. As they did not have any headlamps, they had to dismount and walk their bikes when night time came. The only light they had to guide them was the torchlight from their smartphones. The fun of their situation soon vanished as darkness drew in and they felt the cold bite of the air. It was then that they started to panic a little.

Having scrambled through dense undergrowth for over an hour, they heard the sounds and saw the lights of motor bikes in the distance. Feeling relieved, they headed in that direction, ploughing their way through dense thicket. Soon they could make out voices through the trees. Eventually, the terrain opened up to reveal the surreal sight of about a hundred or so motor cyclists gathered around a tea hut in the middle of the forest. As they nervously approached, they could see that they were members of the Essex Chapter of Hells Angels, judging by the emblazoned emblems on the back of their leather jackets. The bikes had big engines, several of which were of the laid-back chopper variety; many adorned with images of angels, eagles and wolves.

Peter, wishing to protect his children, emboldened himself to go up to the most fearsome looking chap, who appeared to be their leader and ask in the most gentlemanly voice.

"Excuse me, but we are lost, can you kindly show us the right way back to London?"

The leader, having remaining silent for a moment, as he took in the sight of the strange threesome emerging from the darkness, then replied.

"You're lost! You must have been *scared shitless* in the forest. Then coming across us lot in the middle of bloody nowhere!"

"Look, before I tell you the way back, would you do me the honour of joining myself and my crew for a cup of tea and a piece of cake-you guys look as if you need it-you must be fucking freezing!"

Peter was temporarily thrown off guard by this unexpected warm response. He then called to his children to come over and get some refreshments.

"Red," as he called himself, called over to the chap in the tea hut to prepare some tea and cakes for his newfound friends.

He made them feel welcome and introduced them to some of his crew, telling them that they were not as frightening as they appeared. Therefore, Peter and his children ended up spending several hours chatting over tea and cupcakes with a bunch of Hells Angels on a cold winters night in the middle of Epping Forest! But they all absolutely loved the experience.

Peter had lost all track of time when he suddenly realised that it must be getting very late and he still didn't know where they were. Red informed them that they were about four miles from the nearest railway station in north Chingford and if they took a nearby main road, they still had time to catch the last train. Peter knew this particular line stopped at Hackney Downs Station, near their home. As they left, the bikers gave them a resounding farewell from their `revved` up engines, beeping horns and flashing headlights. They easily found the right route back and managed to catch the last train home.

Before his departure, Peter had several meaningful talks with his children. He listened caringly to their worries and dreams for the future and only gave advice when it was solicited, or if he thought it might of some real help.

He needed more time to get his mind right before returning to Cardiff to confront Max. After some careful thought, he decided to go to a place that held happy memories for him-a quiet, secluded cottage in Dorset, where he had stayed with his family a few years previously. It was one of several holiday cottages managed by the Nettlecombe Estate in Symondsbury, near Bridport. On

New Year's Day, he called the Estate Letting Office who revealed the cottage he requested had no vacancies, but a smaller one nearby had no forward reservations for quite some time. He therefore booked and paid for a two month stay there, until Saturday March 3, just in case anyone else was interested in renting it in the meantime.

He left London the next day, Monday 2 January 2012.

Chapter 9

Peter was in a daze for most of the journey to Dorset. His mind was clouded by the dawning realisation that his marriage and work predicaments had come to a formal end. He arrived at the Nettlecombe Estate Office in the dark. It was situated to the side of a large house although he couldn't see it clearly from the Office. He then picked up the keys for the Owl Cottage where he was to stay. On his arrival there, he dumped his bags on the hallway floor and went straight to bed.

At nine o'clock the following morning there was a "tap, tap…tap, tap," on a downstairs windowpane, followed, after a longish pause, by a slightly louder "tap, tap...tap, tap...tap, tap."

The sound finally woke Peter from his deep slumber. He quickly sat up and rubbed his eyes. `Who could be calling at such an early hour, he wondered? ` Still half asleep, he went downstairs to see a woman's face peering through the porch window. He opened the front door to see a shy looking woman, with her head slightly bowed, standing in front of him. He guessed that she was in her thirties. He couldn't make out her features clearly, because her long brunette hair fell partly over her face. But he could see a nervous face hiding behind this mask.

"Can I help you?" he asked politely.

"I'm so sorry to disturb you. My name is Alice, I clean the cottage. I only found out late last night that you were moving in today, so I didn't have time to fully prepare it for you. The place is virtually ready; it just needs bed linen, bin liners and a few other bits and pieces." She murmured these words in a barely audible voice, whilst making every effort to avoid making direct eye contact with Peter.

"Certainly, by all means…do come in…that's no problem," he replied.

"By the way, my name is Peter. It's a pleasure to meet you."

Alice didn't respond with a similar friendly gesture of her own, probably out of bashfulness. She quietly came in and set about her duties, not wishing to intrude upon his privacy for any length of time. She still hasn't caught my eye, he noticed. Making eye contact with another person was something he long had a problem with himself. He never really fully understood why this was. However, it would not be long before he would discover the reason for this.

It took Alice half an hour to finish her preparations. She said that she would be back every Saturday morning at nine to do the cleaning. She pointed out that she had left a few welcome gifts of food in the kitchen, courtesy of the Estate.

"Goodbye," she said softly.

"Goodbye, and many thanks, especially for the gifts," he replied… `Strange woman, ` he thought.

The gifts included locally produced milk, bread, butter, jam and cereal, which he hungrily sampled as soon as she had left. He then set off for the local village of Symondsbury. Although the food refueled his depleted energy reserves, he nevertheless left the cottage feeling a little wretched, as he was unwashed and unshaven.

"How are you?" came a confident voice from an elderly gentleman walking his dog along the road. "A bit on the chilly side today isn't it, cold enough to freeze the brass balls off a wooden monkey."

Peter, surprised by the old man's friendliness, replied.

"Good morning. I'm fine thank you. Beautiful day isn't it?" … 'I've got a feeling I might like this place, ` he thought.

Peter continued his walk along the deep-set country lane. A small flock of fledgling long tail tits accompanied him for a while as they skipped along the ancient hedgerows which lined the top of the steep banks. He wondered how such a late brood could survive the cold winter months. `They will need a big heart to do so; I must somehow reconnect with my own, ` he reflected soulfully to himself.

On entering the village, he was struck by how few people were out in the streets; in fact, the only person he saw was a postman hurrying back to his van, having emptied an old red VR post box.

He made his way to the village shop, which he had used regularly on his previous stay. The shopkeeper gave him a cordial greeting; he was the same man, now on his late forties, who had served him on his earlier holiday some ten years earlier, but he clearly hadn't remembered Peter. His full-faced ruddy features matched his happy nature. Peter stocked up with enough provisions to last him for a few days. The shopkeeper asked him where he was staying.

"The Owl Cottage, about a mile outside the village."

"Lovely place. It's a Nettlecombe Estate cottage isn't it? They have many holiday lets around here. Don't mind Alice the housekeeper, she seems a bit odd, but means no harm."

"Yes, she seems very shy-I wonder why that is?" Peter said, being a little nosy.

"No reason-it's just the way she is."

Peter knew instinctively that this wasn't true and that there is always a reason for the peculiarities of human character and the bigger the inflection the more profound the cause. To push a static juggernaut lorry requires an immense external force to move it, but once moving it possesses a great inherent momentum of its own. Disturbed people-those with neurotic, psychotic or darkly depressive tendencies-always have something in their past which made them that way. It could almost form an eleventh commandment read out by Moses on Mount Sinai: -`Show me the hurt child and I will show you the hurt adult. `He understood that his introspective nature had its origins in his own childhood trauma.

He could recognise something of himself in Alice, not least, the way he also used to arch his head forward and avoid eye contact.

Peter was unaware of how much she was on his mind, even though they had only met once.

He explored the village for a while. It was built around a crossroads with a village green at its centre. This was surrounded by several quaint thatched cottages, a village hall and a picturesque pub, the Foundry. There was also a beautiful old church, St Edmunds, hidden out of sight from the village green. Peter walked around the circular graveyard of this beautiful eleventh century church, which retained much of its ancient stonework. He noticed a rusted, corrugated roofed, lean-to building at the back. It was dappled with various shades of moss and algae. It sheltered several ancient Celtic crosses in various degrees of preservation; some with runic symbols inscribed along their edge. In the centre of the tallest cross, he could just make out the roughly carved alien-like figure of a saint with a halo above his head.

The church grounds were full of old tombstones. There were also a few recent headstones; one with a large ornately decorated headstone of red marble caught his eye-it was inscribed:

In loving memory of Lord James Traherne.
Born April 7th 1937. Died March 17th 2006
"He was a good man, who cared for others."

However, what was most striking about it was that someone had sprayed blue graffiti paint over this lament. Not a nice gesture to have occurred in such a seemingly friendly place he thought. A finely sculptured portrayal of Lord Traherne's head and shoulders, chiselled in light relief, occupied much of the remaining space beneath the inscription. It gave its subject the appearance of gravitas and nobility.

There were several other gravestones nearby bearing the same surname. He remembered it as the same name on the headed paper of the receipt he collected from the Estate Office the previous night. The Traherne family must be the historical owners of the Nettlecombe Estate, he concluded.

Peter struggled to carry the bags of shopping back to the cottage. The now heavily overcast sky changed the mood of the landscape to one of foreboding and gloom. He walked as fast as he could to avoid the rainstorm that threatened. On his return to the cottage, he sunk into a comfy armchair. After a short while, he ignited the wood burner; its light and warmth soon lifted his spirits.

The following morning, Peter explored the old cottage and its grounds. The inside of the seventeenth century cottage had many exposed oak beams and white washed stonewalls. These complemented the, generally sparse, interior, which had been updated in a tasteful way with various items of Victorian and Edwardian furniture. He chose the smallest of the three upstairs bedrooms to sleep in because it had a beautiful view overlooking nearby fields and woodland. The opulent kitchen, with its Aga stove, American style fridge and tastefully designed country kitchen units, also seemed a welcome place to unwind.

The living room had a worn leather upholstered sofa and armchairs and a large wood burner, set in an old inglenook fireplace. The large collection of books on classical literature and local interest was impressive. There was also a specially published guide on the history of the Estate, as well as a visitor's book with glowing entries from previous holidaymakers who had stayed there. Peter felt very much at home; `I will get better here, ` he mused to himself.

He then went outside into the garden to be greeted by the bright blue sky of a refreshing winter's day. The surrounding countryside consisted of green fields of pasture, thick hedgerows, woodland copses, interspersed here and there with an occasional farmstead, cottage, hamlet and village. This beautiful vista lifted his spirits. Fewer people and more of nature was what he needed.

The cottage looked impressive from the outside with its cream coloured plastered walls set within a framework of black ancient oak beams. The curved edges of the thickly thatched roof gave it a simple symmetry. It seemed `content` with its place in the landscape. In the large back garden, there was a summerhouse in one corner, and a large lawn swept in a wide curve towards another corner, besides which stood a tar painted timber garage and an adjoining playroom. Several battered old stone outbuildings backed onto these. They were probably former cattle and sheep sheds but were now in a severe state of decay and dilapidation. The buildings had an enchanted feel about them with their lichen covered stone, twisted old rusty roofs, overrun with climbing thorn and ivy. He felt the urge to investigate them further but was put off by prominent signs reading, `DANGER! KEEP OUT! ` In any case, they were so choked with dense vegetation, it seemed impossible access to them.

He did very little for the rest of the day, except sit in the living room reflecting upon his situation. The events of the last few months began to weigh heavily upon his mind: the `eureka` moment of his discovery, the visions, hearing `God's` voice, the Cambridge `revelation, ` his breakdown, quitting his job, the `Eskimo` vagrant experience and his divorce, had all left him emotionally drained.

His inner self was like a shattered vase, its countless pieces piercing his conscious mind. He was aware that it could never be restored to its beautiful original form. He had been this fragmented vessel ever since he was a fifteen-year-old boy on the council estate. The subsequent decades had been a time of terrible emotional disturbance for him. Disempowered, he had lost his force as a human being. He felt like a young child stranded in the black mire of a forgotten island. The mud clung to him and sapped him of his life energy, making it impossible for him to escape. He was a bog child, seemingly forever preserved in that putrid place.

The only way of escaping from this metaphoric island, upon which had been a prisoner for so long, was to resolve his childhood wounds. He hoped that this would then free him to uncover the secret of the God Field. Although his God Field equation possessed an awe-inspiring beauty, its deeper meaning remained elusive.

Mentally weary, Peter fell asleep in the armchair when it was still daylight. Several hours later, he awoke with a start to find himself in complete darkness. He panicked, as he was not used to the pitch-blackness of the countryside, for there were no lights on in the cottage, the only illumination coming from a faint lamp light in the outside driveway. He fumbled for the light switch, eventually found it and filled the room with a welcoming light. The clock on the wall read nine o'clock.

He was then blessed with an insight, which could bring light to his own darkness, as he said the following words to himself without knowing from whence they came:

`Alice will help you find the secret. `

The words came from none other than God himself, who was sitting unseen in the armchair opposite him. He let the words drift through the God Field.

Peter felt very much alone. There was no one else who could help him in his mission to find Max. He was concerned that, even if he found him and made him accountable for what he did, he might still feel the same afterwards and be forever doomed to remain in his emotional prison. He made a vow to himself, that if this proved to be the case, he would take his own life, rather than carry on as before.

He then headed for a pint in the Foundry, using the light from the pocket torch he had purchased in London to guide him. On entering the Tudor beamed building, he made for a quiet alcove and proceeded to drink himself into oblivion. The taste of the first pint of real ale was like a balm to his troubled spirit. He knew that this was only a temporary lift and too much of this stuff would be his downfall, but this fear was not enough to override his desire to forget.

Once he had downed several pints in quick succession, he walked deliriously back from the pub, along the deserted road. After a while, feeling too tipsy to carry on, he lay down on the tarmac in the middle of the road and looked up to the cloudless and moonless night sky. The starlit heavens shone with a majestic light. It was as if God had haphazardly sprinkled stardust on a blank canvas of nothingness. The magnificence of the Milky Way overwhelmed him as its great arch swept across the sky, like a fine veil of jewelled silk.

A rage then arose from some hurt part of him and made him call out with child-like innocence.

"So, there you are God, oh elusive one. Please tell this humble human being, what exactly is your *fucking* game? Please tell this wretched creature, what are you *fucking* playing at?" Peter then became aware of the comical aspect of his pathetic pleadings to the Almighty and proceeded to roll about with laughter on the hard, cold ground.

He then continued to scramble his way back to the cottage where he passed out on the kitchen floor.

Peter did very little for the next few days except sit on the couch staring into empty space. He was in a deep depression, defeated by thoughts of a failed marriage, an abruptly curtailed academic career and grappling with the bizarre fall-out of his God Field theory. At that moment, nothing could motivate him. He did not wash or shave himself and neither did he put on a change of clean clothes.

"Tap, tap…tap, tap." Peter was woken up by a tapping sound from downstairs. He quickly checked his phone for the time; it was nine o'clock. `Is it Alice, the cleaner? ` Right now, I'm in no fit state to see anybody. ` The truth was that had completely forgotten about her visit… he didn't even know what day it was.

Peter picked himself up from the kitchen floor, wondering how he got there and rushed to open the front door of the cottage.

"Good morning, Mr. Fellows." Alice looked directly at him for the first time, albeit for a fraction of a second. She was surprised by his rough appearance. She felt a natural human sense of concern for him…`Why would he let himself go like this, he must be going through a difficult time, ` she conjectured. Although feeling embarrassed, he was pleased to see her again. He warmed to her troubled innocence and felt drawn to know why she was so introverted.

"Please come in, Alice."

He was careful to avoid touching or engaging in prolonged eye contact with her, as he had no wish to connect with the source of her hurt.

Nevertheless, he really wanted to look into her eyes because she intrigued him so much. He felt compelled to know more about her. Alice, on the other hand, expended all of her emotional energy trying to avoid his stare.

However, when she suddenly glanced back at him and their eyes met, it happened; Peter was transported back in time to witness Alice cowering in the corner of a bedroom. She was a young girl of thirteen, paralysed with fear.

"Are you in there Alice?" Came a chilling enquiry from a male voice outside the door.

It felt as if her soul had been pierced with a black bladed dagger.

"Can I come in?"

The man's mobile phone then rang and he reluctantly went outside, where the reception was clearer, to answer it, cursing under his breath as he did so. This gave Alice a brief moment of respite before his inevitable return.

Peter suddenly snapped out of his vision when Alice asked him in an anxious tone, "Mr. Fellows! Mr. Fellows! Are you alright?"

"Yes, I'm OK, thank you," he replied unconvincingly.

"Your eyes suddenly closed and your body froze; I thought you were having a stroke!"

"No…no Alice, please don't worry, I sometimes have these momentary blackouts."

"Shouldn't you see a doctor, it could be something serious?"

"Oh no, there is nothing wrong with me, I've had them ever since I was a child," he feigned, albeit with the good intention of alleviating Alice's worries.

The glimpse of a past moment of her distress had shaken him; he wondered what was about to happen to her. Feeling for her suffering, he let down his normally reserved guard and said.

"It's nice to see you again. Would you like to join me for a quick cup of tea before you start?" He was uncomfortably self-aware of his apparent directness.

Alice, caught off guard by his kind words, said a quick, "No thank you, Mr. Fellows, I have to leave shortly as I have several other cottages to attend to." She let him know of her other duties so as not to offend him by her refusal to join him for tea.

"Would you mind, then, if I ask a favour of you?"

"Certainly", she responded, without yet knowing the nature of his request.

"Would you please call me by my first name, Peter?" Even though he introduced himself by his Christian name when they first met on Tuesday morning, Alice had since only addressed him by his surname.

"Yes, certainly sir," she responded, somewhat reluctantly, Peter sensed.

The return of his uninvited capacity to connect with the inner pain of others, made him distraught. "Why God have you cursed me so…why can't you just heal me instead…why have you abandoned me?" He found himself, once again, somewhat pitiably, pleading with God he still refused to let in. Even the confirmation of his theory and hearing `God's voice` in the computer room, could not remove the wall around his heart.

When she had finished her chores, Alice said, as she was leaving.

"Good bye. I'll see you next Saturday. Don't forget to use the summerhouse, it's a nice place to unwind, even now in winter time. It has a paraffin heater to keep you warm. I occasionally use it myself, when the cottage is empty."

As she was leaving he said, "Do you have a key for the cottage, Alice?"

"Yes, I do." She replied.

"Please let yourself in next Saturday and at any time you need to get into the cottage… There's no need to knock."

Alice said that she would do so in future.

The following morning, he took Alice's advice and visited the summerhouse. It was a hybrid structure made of old vernacular stone and with a small veranda of modern pine. Both parts, however, somehow complemented each other.

The interior was simply decorated in whitewash paint. A battered old armchair and small round coffee table occupied its central space.

A reclaimed wooden Georgian panel covered the whole of the back wall, the upper part of which had been converted into several bookshelves, the lower part retaining its original unmodified features. Several tins of paint and open cardboard boxes, full of DIY equipment, were stored in front of the panel, along with a weathered looking paraffin heater with a box of matches on top.

Peter then examined the books on the bookshelf. One in particular, "The Last Huntsman," caught his eye. It was about the plight of the Bushman hunter-gatherers of the Kalahari Desert. There were several books on a similar theme of primitive peoples in peril, including `Wipe-out` about the past decimation and present-day struggles of the Australian aborigines.

As it was getting cold, Peter retrieved the paraffin heater from the back, but was unable to light it because it had run out of fuel.

Judging by the scattering of dry brown leaves and a thin layer of dust on the floor, the summerhouse had probably not been used since the autumn.

Peter liked its quirky appearance and isolated position in the grounds. It seemed content with being so marginalised and alone. Peter wondered if this was the reason why Alice also liked the little building so much. `I'll be back here a lot, ` he ruminated to himself.

Later that day, Peter took a leisurely walk to the village to stock up on food and drink. He felt a little better in himself; his mood was less down. He was more optimistic about his situation now, especially as he was convinced that he was staying in the right place at the right time. The key thing was to continue his recovery before his journey to Cardiff to track down Max.

He made his way again to the summerhouse the following morning. As he was about to open the door, he noticed a wooden sign lying on the grass next to the veranda. He picked it up to see the name Haseya amateurishly burnished onto it, presumably from a hot piece of metal. He placed it back onto a hook on the door, probably from whence it had fallen.

Rummaging around the back of the summerhouse, he found a nearly empty plastic canister of paraffin, along with an empty paraffin lamp, hidden under a dust sheet. He topped up the heater and the lamp with the meager supply of fuel. He then ignited the heater before placing the canister at the back of the summerhouse next to the panelled wall. As the space warmed up, he examined the contents of the bookshelf once more. Most of the books were romantic historical fiction novels except for those concerning primitive tribal cultures but these, strangely, were distributed `randomly` amongst the other books, as if they had been deliberately placed in such a manner. He started to read the book about the Bushman he found the previous day. He soon became engrossed in reading its contents in his peaceful `hide-out. `

Peter read for several hours, until the heater ran out of fuel. He then drove to the petrol station between Symondsbury and Bridport to refill the canister. The thirty litre container was now very heavy and he struggled to carry it from the car to the summerhouse where he refilled the paraffin heater and lamp. However, as he went to store the canister at the back, he accidently knocked the lower part of a Georgian panel, causing a `secret` cupboard door to spring open. He could see that it had been kept closed by a small spring lock. Looking inside, he noticed a small recess where a few small stones had been carefully removed. Curious, he pulled the `door` fully open, switched on his pocket torch and shone its light into the space to reveal a circular tin box and three books hidden inside. He cautiously removed them, making sure to remember how they had been originally arranged, for he felt that he was somehow intruding upon someone's private space.

He placed the items onto the coffee table and, guiltily, opened the lid of the Heroes chocolates tin. It contained about thirty small animal and bird figures carved in soft stone; they included wolves, bears, bison, deer, owls and eagles, amongst several others. Each figure had been carefully hand crafted to show the finer detail of each wild creature. There were also several non-precious, but beautifully shaped coloured crystals such as rose quartz, amethyst and blue agate, as well as a small leather medicine pouch which contained about a dozen tiny round pebbles of many striking colours. At the bottom of the tin, there was a small American Indian dream catcher, a bunch of dried wild sage, (with parched tips), and a silver lighter with the profile of an Indian brave engraved on its side.

One of the books was entitled *Healing the Shame that Binds You*, by John Bradshaw. It seemed to be an academic self-help book of some kind. Flicking through its pages, he couldn't help but notice the mass of tiny annotations written in blue ink in the margins. Another book, entitled *Alive*, by Piers Paul Read, concerned the Andean mountain aircraft disaster in 1972 which chronicled the survivors fight for survival which eventually led to them eating the flesh of the frozen corpses. There was also a notebook, about 6 by 8 inches, the first half of which contained hand written poems, mainly of a spiritual and mystical nature. Running from the back of the book were dated notes of further, more detailed analysis, of the Bradshaw book. The first entry was dated 12 June 2006 and the last, January 10 2007.

Feeling uneasy in having looked at someone else's personal possessions, Peter carefully replaced the items in the recess, leaving them exactly as he had found them, except for the Bradshaw book, which he kept as it had struck a chord with him. It crossed his mind that the owner of these effects would realise straight away that the book was missing, but he was intrigued to take a closer look at it. He then pushed the panel `door` back in place –it fitted seamlessly-it was impossible to tell from the outside that it was a concealed door.

Through the glass windows of the summerhouse patio doors he could see a great red sun just sinking below the horizon, sending its crimson light in a futile endeavour to fend off the inevitable march of darkness. The land was still, the trees silent; a shroud of translucent mist caressed the valley beneath like a child lovingly placing a cloak around their sleeping grandmother. The screeching calls of fighting owls in a nearby woodland, heralded the close of the day and onset of the night.

Peter then went back to the cottage to grab a quick bite to eat before returning to the summerhouse where he lit the paraffin lamp and heater. He started to read the Bradshaw book and was soon consumed in its contents. He couldn't put it down and read to the early hours of the morning. He read the book in the summerhouse during every spare minute over the next five days, only stopping to sleep and carry out the daily essentials in the cottage.

The book examined the intense feelings of shame the victims of sexual abuse feel; Bradshaw called this, toxic shame. Peter learnt about the tragic irony that it is the victims, rather than the perpetrators, who feel this most shame. "Toxic shame is unbearable and always necessitates a cover-up, a false self. Since one feels his true self is defective and flawed, one needs a false self that is not defective and flawed."

The book was a revelation. It moved him like no other. The author of the annotations clearly felt the same as he did. The primary ideas it expressed of the way victims of sexual abuse respond to this trauma, equated with his own.

It allowed him to explore a hidden corner of his mind where past secrets lay buried, a place he had avoided visiting all of his adult life, for he was terrified others would see his shameful self. He was convinced that he was fundamentally a bad person because he felt that he was the one who had done something wrong, not the abuser. He became frozen in time, ensnared by toxic shame. These feelings had placed him in an emotional prison, where he retreated from the world and practised a form of social self-apartheid. This hindered his social growth and maturation.

Reading further on, he came across the following passage, which moved him deeply. "Only when the dark events that caused the trauma are resolved can the individual begin to live a life on his/her own terms and begin to play a proper part in society/community."

He cried when he finished reading the book. Tears fell onto the open pages of the book sending outward splashes of water like miniature exploding hand grenades on the muddied ground of a battlefield. They came flooding from his broken soul, which, for the first time since his childhood, was allowed to grieve for the death of itself. It was unable to mourn before because it was so fragmented, but now the parts came back together in a temporary whole. He was like an insane man who, given day release from a secure mental asylum to attend the funeral of his mother, attains a moment of clarity when he remembers the woman who bore and raised him.

The book helped him to revisit and understand his own childhood anguish, just as it must have done for its owner. Peter had tried, for decades, through reflective self-analysis, to find a way through this psychic impasse, but he was unable to let his feelings connect with the origins of his suffering because the emotional pain was too great for him to bear.

He had also embarked on an obsessive search for a personal God as a way of saving himself. This was the reason why he first became fascinated with physics. However, he gave up this quest when it proved to be a fruitless struggle. This happened just after he had finished his PhD at Imperial. He initially chose a doctorate in quantum mechanics in the hope that it would somehow reveal a path to the divine creator behind all existence. He dedicated several years to theorising and testing events at this minuscule dimension of `reality. ` However, to his dismay, he always received statistically flawless results substantiating their random nature, without even a hint of a `supernatural` deity. He therefore saw no other option than to abandon his search for God through science. He was twenty-four years old at the time.

From this time onwards, the only solace he found from theoretical physics was in producing mathematical majestic descriptions of the fundamental laws governing the universe. Regrettably, no God ever revealed `Himself` in such formulations. However, over the last few years, he found the inherent hollowness of these equations increasingly hard to accept. He likened them to a lifeless desert forever scorched by the sun, where nothing could survive, not even a simple blade of grass, not even a flower. He was reminded of a quote from the Nobel Prize Winning physicist Steven Weinberg.

"The more the universe seems comprehensible, the more it seems pointless."

Weinberg was implying that there was no need for divine explanations of existence. However, Peter found the alternative scientific explanations of reality to be vacuous, although he never found any direct evidence for the hand of God in creating the universe.

Having finished reading the book, he carefully placed it back in its hiding place. He then removed the A5 sized notebook, which he intended to read next.

"Tap.tap…tap.tap." The tapping on a downstairs window suddenly woke him up. It's Alice! It must be Saturday morning, he thought, although he was unsure of the exact day, because he had been so absorbed in reading the Bradshaw book. However, the expectation of seeing Alice again, stirred his heart a little, although he was unaware of this. He quickly got out of bed and rushed downstairs to see her walking towards the kitchen.

"Good morning, Alice."

"Good morning Peter. I hope you don't mind my letting myself in, I didn't want to wake you up," Alice responded demurely. He was pleased that she had let herself in and addressed him by his Christian name for the first time.

"No, not all. I'm delighted that you're finally using the key. Would you like a quick cuppa before you start?" He was aware of his uncharacteristic forwardness again, but he just couldn't help himself.

Alice hesitated a little before accepting his offer.

He remained mindful of avoiding any direct contact with her, for fear of regressing again into her past.

They sat down at the kitchen table and proceeded to make awkward chatter, each as pathetically bashful as the other. They came over as a distinctly odd pair as they talked about inconsequential matters such as the weather and the cost of fruit and veg. However, both took comfort in communicating with another individual who they found to be non-threatening. Each warmed to the other`s bashfulness. By the time their conversation was over, they sensed for the first time that they might like each other. When Alice was aware of this, she became unbearably self-conscious and quickly terminated their conversation.

"Thank you very much for the tea Peter, but I really need to get a move on with the cleaning."

"Sorry to hold you up. It was interesting talking to you." He wanted to let Alice know that he enjoyed her company.

With these unexpectedly kind words milling in her mind, Alice made her way upstairs to start her cleaning tasks.

When she had finished and was about to leave, she asked Peter if he would help her carry a heavy old chair from the hallway to the Estate van outside; Lady Traherne wanted it transferred back to the `Great House` from whence it originally came. As they placed their arms around the opposite sides of the chair, their hands momentarily touched, straight away sending Peter back to the same time and place of his previous visitation of Alice, when she was a thirteen-year-old girl in her bedroom.

There was a gentle knock on the door from the same man as in the earlier vision. He continued,

"Please hold on a moment," Alice replied, terrified as she braced herself for was about to take place.

"Can I come in?" He repeated, this time with more assertion.

The young girl failed to respond to his requests, so he opened the door by himself.

`Someone had carelessly left the downstairs front door open, anyone could let themselves in, ` he said, trying to deflect the conversation away from his intended purpose.

Alice then sat on the desk chair with her back to him. He then stood behind her. She froze with terror, for she knew what was going to happen next. She unconsciously placed a protective mental cloak around herself into which she withdrew. Alice then let her mind drift to a fantasy world in which she was playing happily with her friends in a beautiful meadow.

The man then proceeded to slowly to move his hand down to touch her breast. Alice was powerless to speak out and powerless to stop him, just as she had been in the past, for the abuse had been going for over sixth months.

He then laid his hand between her legs, making her tense up with abject fear. This continued until he told her in a menacing voice to lie on the bed where he proceeded to have sexual intercourse with her. Sadly, during this most violating of experiences, she was unable retreat to her imaginary world, for the trauma was so horrific and immediate. All that she could then think about were thoughts of suicide, for ending her life seemed the only way out.

Peter then abruptly came out of this regression. He felt utterly beaten and empty just as he had felt from all of his other flashbacks. Every time a vision happened, it was as if someone had dipped a ladle into the pool of his soul and removed a part of it. He also felt despair in his inability to intervene and change these events. He could not take many more such episodes.

His heart went out to Alice. Because her situation mirrored that of his own, he felt her pain even more poignantly. But his connection with her would never be the same now that he had been a witness to her anguish.

Once they had managed to manoeuvre the chair into the back of the Estate van, she thanked him and bid him farewell. Peter only gave a muted goodbye, prompting Alice to wonder if she had offended him in some way.

That evening he made his way along the dark country lane to the Foundry pub using his pocket torch. He needed a drink to help him forget the upsetting events of that day. Once again, he hid away in an alcove. The landlord, Phil, who was a friendly old man, tried to engage in chit chat with him, although he was aloof at first. Peter eventually relented because he had earlier observed him place some very heavy logs onto the large open fire in the public bar, rather than ask the barmaid to do it. He sensed that he was a decent and uncomplicated individual, someone unburdened by unresolved issues, unlike Alice and himself. They had `stuff' happen to them in their childhoods which had thrown them off their natural life-course, like two swallows steered away from their traditional migratory flight path by a mysterious, invisible, force.

When they had chatted for a while, Peter asked him about the Estate and its history. The landlord replied with animated, usually complementary detail, except when he described the late Lord Traherne.

"It sounds as if you didn't care for him much?" Peter enquired curiously.

"Most of the locals liked the old man, but I didn't have much time for him myself."

"Why was that?" Peter cheekily probed.

The landlord paused for a while, as if unsure whether he should open up to someone he had only recently met. However, having assessed Peter as being a good sort, he continued, for he clearly had something he wanted to get of his chest.

"Many years ago, I had a lovely collie dog called Lefty. We called him that on account of how he would chase his tail by running towards the left, never to the right. I really liked that dog. Sometimes he would disappear and run around the local Estate fields where he would harass the sheep. The tenant farmers would be understandably upset, although Lefty would never harm them. When Lord Traherne got wind of this, he asked me, (kindly at first), if I would put a stop to this. I then kept Lefty in the back garden, only taking him out for walks attached to his lead. But Lefty, being an intelligent, hyperactive sort, sometimes managed to escape and terrorise the sheep again. Well, after scaring them during the lambing period, Traherne, for if you don't mind I'd rather address him by leaving the Lord out, warned me to stop this from happening once and for all, or he would have to take the matter into his own hands."

"I then made renewed efforts to stop Lefty from running off; I even put up a secure new fence around the garden. One day, though, my daughter accidently left the back gate open and he was off at once on one his farmland escapades. When I later discovered he was missing, I immediately went looking for him around the Estate. After several hours, I had to abandon my search when it got dark. When I got home I received a phone call from one of the Estate workers, a friend of mine, informing me that Lefty had been found with his leg caught in a fox trap. I rushed over to where he said I could find him. I cannot tell you how shocked I was when I saw him lying ensnared on the grass, his front leg bloodied and shattered; I will never forget his piercing cries of agony. Sadly, I had to have his leg amputated; that put a stop to his wanderings."

"However, to finally answer your question. I received a phone call from a friend on the Estate a few months later. He said he had overheard Traherne's Land Manager telling a fellow worker how his boss had told him to deliberately lay fox traps on the likely route that Lefty would take from the pub to the Estate lands. Well, you can imagine the horror I felt on hearing this-I was close to going over and throttling the bastard; fuck his old age, he was *evil*. But I held back."

"What stopped you?"

"Well, I thought about my family. If I had hit him I'd have lost the pub tenancy, which I lease from the Estate and was due for renewal at that time. I would have then lost my livelihood and my home. I feared that my family might become paupers again-for we were once very poor. But I never forgot what he did."

"I don't think the old fucker had any regrets for what he did afterwards. When we next bumped into each other, I could see in his eyes he knew that I knew that he had trapped Lefty, but I could tell he just didn't care…he may even have gotten off on it. All the locals thought he was some kind of saint-if they only knew the truth! However, as the years went by, I realised that it would be best if I forgave him, for what he did to Lefty reflected a disturbed soul. After all, what type of person could have done such a thing to such a lovely dog? In the end I just pitied him."

It crossed Peter's mind that Phil was probably the person who sprayed the blue graffiti paint over Lord Traherne's gravestone.

By the time, he had finished a few, `on the house, ` drinks from the landlord, Peter was smashed. He staggered home. The stars were once again out in all their full glory. They seemed to be his travelling companions through the darkness; he sensed a strange connection with his night time friends. His body tingled. For one brief moment, he felt at one with the God Field. But this sensation was soon extinguished by the shining headlights and loud noise of a fast approaching tractor, which forced him to back up against the side of the road as it rushed past. The driver must be drunk, he thought; why else would he be driving so recklessly. He made a point of remembering the `nutters` face, having caught a glimpse of him in his cabin.

The horrific vision of Alice's childhood sent him into a deep depression. He stayed holed up in the cottage for the next few days, doing very little. He worked his way through two large bottles of cheap Russian vodka he found in the back of a kitchen store cupboard. He looked and felt rough. Letting himself go like this was not his style. However, revisiting Alice's childhood fears had let down the draw bridge to his own.

Eventually, on Thursday evening, he returned to the summerhouse and began reading the notebook he recovered from the hiding place. He lit the paraffin heater and lamp, drank some black coffee from a flask to help sober him up and relaxed in the armchair. He liked being there perhaps for the same reasons as the secret note taker. It was like a childhood den. It had a comforting mother's `womb-like` secure feeling about it. He proceeded to devour the pages of notes anayalsing the Bradshaw book. The final entry appears to be a crystallisation of the note takers interpretation of how its contents pertained to their own life: -

Trauma.
Toxic shame.
Powerlessness.
Frozen in time.
Forgiveness of self.
Liking oneself, (how?).
Loving oneself, (how?).
Forgiveness of abuser, (can't).
Letting go and surrendering to God, (how?).

It was uncanny, but Peter could have written the same words himself, with the exception of the statement relating to handing over to God, (which he could never see himself being able to do). He felt a deep empathy and a strong common bond with the author.

On Friday afternoon, having finished reading the notebook, he returned to the recess, but not before intriguingly flicking through the poems, which took up the first half of the notebook: he was keen to read those next. He then returned to the cottage.

The insights he gained from reading the Bradshaw book, the notebook and witnessing Alice's childhood tragedy, meant that he was now ready to re-live the events of his own trauma for the first time.

Having thought of several possible ways of reconnecting with his past, he came up with an idea. Whilst unpacking his things on his arrival at the Owl Cottage, he accidently came across some old correspondence from Max hidden in a zipped-up pocket in the lining of an old travel bag he had taken to Cambridge for the award ceremony. The letters were dated from October to December 1979. It occurred to him that he could use them to regress back to his time at Max's. Peter rushed back to the cottage to retrieve them and then quickly returned to the summerhouse. He composed himself before slowly taking one of the letters out of its envelop. He was very anxious but had to carry on. On pulling the pages out and opening them, even before he could start to read their contents, he found himself transported back in time to an April evening in Max's house when he was a fifteen-year-old boy. A vivid flashback to his childhood then fleetingly crossed his mind.

"Please don't go, I really need you to stay at home with me," Max pleaded with him. Max was hiding behind the front door next to him, He was the `father-like` figure who had `befriended` Peter some months earlier.

"Come on Peter, Wendy Thomas is going to be there," Ryan, his best friend, called out to him from outside the front gate to the house. "She is only coming because I told her you were going to be there." He was trying to convince Peter to attend a party he had organised that evening at his house. Peter was about to say that he would go, especially as he had long had a crush on Wendy, who was the prettiest girl in the School, when Max quickly intervened and said in a pathetic and persuasive voice.

"*Please* don't go…*please* don't go Peter." He was once more using subtle psychological power to manipulate Peter to his own ends.

He did not go to the party that evening. He would not see his best friend again for forty years.

Peter then suddenly snapped out of this regression. He felt shattered but he knew he had to carry on. He therefore proceeded to remove the letter completely from the envelop and start to read it. However, after reading the first few words he was sent back again to his childhood.

"Do you know Peter, the ancient Greeks believed that the highest form of love was between two men and this was seen as a much greater love than that between a man and a woman?" This was the latest instance of Max's grooming, in readiness for what was about to happen next. Max then placed his hand on his inner thigh. Peter, although shocked, felt some sexual pleasure from this. It was only many years later, he found out that this was a common response and was simply due to teenage hormones and not any latent homosexual tendencies the victim may have. Max then moved his hand further up his leg and rubbed his crouch before unzipping his own fly and removing his penis. Max then took his penis out, masturbated and ejaculated over a stunned Peter. He was powerless.

Peter then came around from this trance feeling violated and confused, just as his younger self had felt. He was breathless and sweated profusely, his heart palpitating as if it was about to burst from his chest. He lay back in his seat as if he had just witnessed the death of a loved one... his younger self.

When he had recovered a little, Peter felt proud of himself for having the courage to finally go back to the source of his hurt. He then made himself remember, for the first time, the regular sexual abuse that followed this first invasion of his soul; it carried on for two years afterwards. The worst times were when, upstairs in the bedroom, the decrepit, gnarled, old man would put his penis in Peter's mouth, masturbate and then cum. On other occasions, he would attempt sexual intercourse with the defenseless boy. These events destroyed him. They were his kryptonite. The scars of these wounds were still with him.

He first visited Max's home to receive help from him in his studies, for he had fallen behind. Max was a former teacher and writer who had somehow ended up living in the huge council estate of Ely, on the western outskirts of Cardiff. Ely was sometimes referred to as the `Cardiff Bronx, ` as it was seen as a tough place to live. The community were fooled by Max's cunning and charm into believing that he was a loveable, wise old man; little did they know that he was paedophile who prayed on young boys.

What made the situation even more perplexing for Peter during this time, was that Max had become a surrogate father to him, giving him the care and attention he craved, for his real father had not been able to provide it for him. Being abused by a person he loved as a father figure made the scars run all the deeper-so deep that they caused the obliteration of his soul.

His older brother Michael was also living in the same house. Max was teaching him the craft of writing plays for the TV and radio. Michael had no idea about the abuse because it only ever took place when he was out of the house and Peter was too traumatised to tell him.

Peter looked forward to the regular `expeditions` he had with his brother to the nearby Vale of Glamorgan. They would often explore its ancient landscapes, searching for buried treasure with a metal detector, or digging up an old farmhouse rubbish dump looking for Victorian bottles and ceramic wear, or simply scouring its ploughed fields picking up interesting finds.

He had a great camaraderie with his brother who was a great source of support for him. This, along with his thirst for knowledge, agile mind and sense of humour, helped a little to alleviate the emotional devastation the abuse had brought upon him.

Peter tried to make sense of the momentous events of the last few days. For the first time, through reading the material he found in the summerhouse and his regressions back to Alice's childhood trauma, he was able to revisit his past ordeal at the hands of Max by opening his letter. This enabled him to recall the history of his own abusive childhood for the first time. This was a pivotal moment in his life, for he knew that unless he did this, he would never be able to break free.

God, who always seemed to be nearby, was deeply upset when he witnessed Peter's flashbacks. Nevertheless, `He` knew that they would steer him towards the pathway of closure and recovery. He was accompanied by `His` beautiful, graceful, helper Petra, who collected the psychic energies from Peter's regressions.

`Surely, Alice is the author of the Bradshaw book annotations and the notebook? ` Peter surmised. After all, my visions revealed she was the victim of sexual abuse. She also said that she liked spending time in the summerhouse. She must have used the Bradshaw book to help her understand what had happened to her. If this is the case, he conjectured, then what if she discovers that he had found and `spied` on her most private belongings. She would never be able to forgive him. This possibility pained his heart.

It was late on Friday afternoon. Alice was due to return the next day, completely oblivious of Peter's preoccupations in the summerhouse over the previous week.

That evening he retired to bed feeling satisfied that he had taken the first step in unraveling his past. He had his first peaceful sleep since arriving in Dorset.

The following morning, at 9 am, there was a "Tap…tap" on the window. Alice was back to using this form of entry, rather than using her key. Taking a deep nervous intake of breath, he opened the door; their eyes met for a split second, but with insufficient time for Peter to fall into one of his relapses, but enough for each to experience a satisfying glow from their momentary intimate connection.

Alice again accepted his offer of a "quick cuppa." They then sat down and a chatted at the kitchen table for a while. Their conversation this time was of a less awkward nature, although to an impartial outsider they must have appeared a peculiar pair. Neither looked directly at the other, as they relayed barely audible threads of trivial information to one another.

However, they could not help but notice the other's odd behavioural traits. Alice observed the comical way he would sometimes lick his finger with his tongue and use it to clean some blemish on his jumper, rubbing it in with some persistence until it had disappeared. She also noticed, when she occasionally glanced at him, how his eyes looked everywhere except towards hers. And as for his strong Cardiff accent, she could barely contain a smile.

Peter was aware of how Alice would sometimes nervously shake her feet from underneath the table, no doubt as a release from the anxiety she must be feeling. She was oblivious of this habit, until she sometimes inadvertently touched a table leg, causing the cups and saucers to vibrate loudly, as they resonated in harmony with her shaking feet. Peter was also struck by the way she arched her head forward and chewed on some strands of hair. He also noticed how she would occasionally purse and bit her lips with her teeth, breaking the symmetry of her face. Nevertheless, he could see through all these odd mannerisms, lay a woman of innate beauty and grace. Alice, however, saw herself as odd, ugly and unlovable.

Their friendship was slowly developing, something they both needed. But what they desired most of all, however, was a loving friendship based on mutual trust, which would allow them the freedom to be themselves.

Alice said that Lady Traherne had asked her to pass on an invitation to a party she was hosting next Saturday evening for the workers of the Estate. All of the holidaymakers renting the cottages were also welcome to attend. Peter said that he probably wouldn't go as he didn't like such big social functions.

"I would like you to come." Alice said. She had to collect her emotions after saying these words, for it was contrary to her nature to be so daring, but they just came

148

out of her mouth before her self-conscious mind could stop them.

Peter, touched by her rare outward show of feeling, replied.

"In that case Alice, I would like to go."

"That's good," she responded.

Their conversation ended there for they were both feeling uncomfortable for having let their guard down.

Alice then carried out her cleaning tasks. When she had finished, she left quietly without saying goodbye. Peter guessed that this was due to her coyness, especially as she had been so open earlier on.

The next day he went to Bridport to stock up on food, drink and paraffin. He was gradually settling into his temporary home. On his return, he eagerly returned to the summerhouse to look over the poems in the first half of the notebook. Each of the sixty or so poems were written in meticulous handwriting, with few corrections, just like the notes on the Bradshaw book in the back half of the notebook. They were mainly of a mystical theme, often using beautiful natural imagery. It seemed that the author was on a mission to free themselves from their own mental incarceration. Some poems also revealed a romantic need to break free and find love; like the following.

Surrender
I cast aside my defiant will,
And childhood's bitter pill.
Relinquish my need to be free,
My longing for God's mercy,
And surrender to another realm,
One of strangeness and charm,
Where fear hides its false face,
And I, her love, shall embrace.

Some poems, however, seemed to touch upon a darker side. However, these often possessed a mysterious quality, as if their author was trying to purify some shadow aspect of themselves. The following poem is one such example.

Frozen

The falling light of a setting sun,
Scatters through crystalline snow.
The white carpet cloaks the meadow,
Where tender plants stand rigid,
 Forever enslaved in a frozen grasp,
 Making them resistant to the wind.

A groomer fox's deep imprints,
Outlined a malevolent pathway
Of red steps back to bloodied snow,
Where, sadly, lay a devoured rabbit,
Its lovely innocence destroyed.

In the nearby forest all was still
As the nuclear light began to fade.
A wonderful silence was present,
Permeating everything around
In an infinite loving continuum,
Filling my soul with its mystery,
       ...healing me.

Peter woke up very early the following morning to finish reading the poems. He then read the book entitled *Alive* in one continuous session lasting twelve hours. It transfixed him, but he couldn't figure out why. It told the true story of a plane crash in 1976 in a cold and isolated part of the Andean mountains along the Chilean and Uruguayan border. Its passengers were mainly Uruguayan rugby players. Once their food supplies ran out, they were driven by hunger to eat from the cold preserved corpses of those who had perished during the initial crash. It was a harrowing decision to eat the flesh of their dead comrades, but one that ensured their survival.

Alive was not annotated like the other books but it clearly held some special significance to its owner because it was hidden with the other items; Peter, though, was at a loss to identify what the link might be.

However, early the following morning, he suddenly grasped why the book was of such importance to the person who hid it in the summerhouse-it was because it was concerned with the shameful feelings the survivors experienced because of their cannibalism. This equated with the shame the survivors of sexual abuse feel. The book made the reader understand the devastating power of shame.

He then removed the last item from its secret hiding place, the Heroes tin box, containing the small animal carvings, crystals, stones, sage sticks, silver lighter and dream catcher. He wasn't sure why they were significant to their owner, other than wondering if they were used in some kind of purification ceremony, for he knew that crystals and sage were often used in sacred healing rituals.

Peter had now carefully examined all of the objects he found secreted in the summerhouse recess. The books, notebook contents and the objects in the tin, must have been Alice's way of trying to heal the wounds of her past. He felt guilty for having looked at them in such detail but he couldn't stop himself, especially when they connected him with his own disturbed childhood.

Chapter 10

The following Tuesday evening, Peter was disturbed by a loud knocking on the front door. It couldn't be Alice, he thought, as she taps the window or lets herself in with a key. In any case, she isn't due back until Saturday. He then went to investigate the persistent banging.

"Hello! I'm Lady Traherne, but please call me by my first name, Sylvia. I am the owner of the Estate. Since my husband James passed away five years ago, I've been running it by myself. You must be Peter. I hope you're having a pleasant stay. " She delivered these words with the assured confidence, bordering on arrogance, of a person with an inflated sense of their own importance. She was a healthy, vigorous and wiry lady, probably in her mid-seventies. With her grey hair blowing wildly in the breeze and an unruly set of twisted white hairs on her chin, she made for quite an unnerving presence. Her angular facial features, sallow complexion, shadow lines and deeply sunken eyes, reinforced this feeling.

"I am sorry to hear that…Please do come in."

"Thank you…he had a good innings... Do you know, this is our favourite cottage on the whole of the Estate, and we let out fifteen of them in all, most much grander than this one? I like its simplicity. My husband and I used to stay here sometimes when it was vacant, as a break from the demands of our main home, Llanmaes, although most locals call it the `Great House. `"

"That's nice to hear-I've taken quite a liking to it myself."

"I've come along, not just to wish you a pleasant stay, but also to invite you to Llanmaes on Saturday for an open buffet and wine evening, starting at 7 o clock. It is my annual thank you to the Estate workers, but you and the other cottage holiday guests are more than welcome to attend. Alice mentioned to me that you might like to go."

"Thank you very much for the invitation. I'll try to make it," knowing this response gave him the option to opt out quite easily, although he had already promised Alice that he would attend.

"Excellent, I look forward to seeing you."

Sylvia intrigued him, for he sensed that she wasn't the person she portrayed from this less than flattering first impression. Every nuance of strained facial sinew and taught muscle contour, hinted that she was carrying a deep hurt inside.

Peter was wary of making closer contact with her for fear of connecting with this pain. He had so far managed to avoid making full eye contact with her, which was quite some feat, given that she was the kind of person who stared intently at others. But he could not refuse her outstretched hand when she said goodbye. When their skin touched, he was immediately taken back to when she was a nine-year-old girl sitting at the family dining table having their evening meal. Suddenly, there came forth a scolding rebuke from her stern father.

"How dare you rush saying Grace. That's the second time you have done that this week. Now go to your room and dwell on the sin you have committed. *You have dishonoured our Lord!*"

She apologised and left the room, head lowered to the ground. Her father's admonishment had crushed her young spirit and she felt totally rejected by him. She cried on her bed until emotional exhaustion made her fall asleep.

Sylvia quickly pulled her hand away from Peter's, for he had held it tightly whilst in the throes of his vision.

Sylvia, disturbed by his strange behavior, instinctively sensed that he had somehow been divining her soul. She felt vulnerable, fearing her innermost hurt may have been exposed. Peter knew this was the reason why she put on such an austere public persona. Inside, she was that scared abandoned little girl who had been brought up by a brutal and unloving father.

She quickly said a shaky "Goodbye" to Peter, who, overcome with emotion, mumbled "Goodbye, and thank you for the invite," in return.

This flashback shook him up badly and left him feeling disconsolate. Every new regression had taken away a little bit more of his life force. From now on, he would make a more concerted effort to avoid being drawn into them.

Peter reflected on the unpleasant pairing of the late, but cruel, Lord Traherne and his surviving wife, Sylvia, with her tough exterior. Woe betides any children they may have; having them as parents must have severely emotionally blighted them. Wealth and status are no prerequisites for love and security, he concluded.

Peter returned to the summerhouse the following morning to double check that he had replaced all of the hidden items exactly as he had found them. He was worried that Alice might check her hidden possessions, and finding them out of position, suspect him of having looked at them, for she knew that he was now using the summerhouse regularly, as she had suggested. Satisfied that everything was in its right place, he was about to close the back-panel door, when he noticed a small piece of masking tape dangling down from the inner side of the panel above the recess. As he gently pulled on it, a small leather pouch came falling down. He eagerly picked up the small bag and pulled out a small notebook. It was full of minute ink writings, along with several full-page sketches of different cottages. As he flicked through its contents, tiny flecks, of what looked like gold dust, fell to the ground.

He sat down on the armchair to inspect his latest discovery. It appeared to be a record of someone's thoughts and experiences. The first date of entry was September 1 2003 and the last January 1 2004, although the entries were not kept on a daily basis, but on odd days here and there. Written several years before the larger notebook and the poems, the writing, although much smaller, was clearly from the same hand-Alice's? Judging by the thick layer of dust covering the notebook, it had been there for some time, possibly since the last date of entry. It must have held a special significance, above all of the other effects, as it was hidden in the most inaccessible place, its owner clearly never wanting its contents to be revealed. If it wasn't for the deterioration of the masking tape gum, causing it to hang down, it might never have been found. Convinced that this new find also belonged to Alice, Peter was wary of discovering any new secrets it may reveal. He therefore decided not to rush into reading it and carefully returned the notebook to where he found it, this time firmly pressing down the masking tape.

Peter needed time to think. He slumped back in his chair. It might well be, he thought, that its contents were of a relatively innocuous nature, but this seemed highly unlikely. What if it revealed something so disturbing that it would get in the way of him being able to take his growing friendship with Alice any further?

He was in a dilemma-should he read the notebook or not?

Peter pondered for several hours about the right course of action to take. He finally came to the conclusion that he would read it, for he thought that if their relationship is to develop, it was important to know more of her past sufferings, no matter how distressing they were. However, he promised to himself that he would, one day, tell Alice he had discovered her secret lair and all of its contents; he would also tell her of his own traumatic childhood.

In the evening, he returned to the summerhouse and removed the small notebook once again and, with much trepidation, started to read its pages. The writing was so small that he interrupted his reading to go back to the cottage to search for a magnifying glass to help him read the minute script. After a long search, he finally found one in a sideboard draw in the living room.

As soon as he began reading its contents, his heart sank, for it described in harrowing detail a catalogue of relentless sexual abuse to a young girl, perpetrated by an unnamed individual. It started when she was thirteen and finished when she was sixteen years of age. No names, places, or dates were given by the author who was clearly too afraid to give full disclosure.

The writings were a testimony to the tragic events that had befallen the victim. It was as if the author wanted someone to read it one day in the distant future, perhaps after her death, so that they would bare retrospective witness to this great injustice. The notebook's obscure hiding place, clearly showed that she didn't want anyone to discover it for a long time.

The entries ended with a short poem.

Soul stealer
If I succumb to illness overnight,
Before my virtue could ever flower,
Or, if I extinguish my own light,
Before Nature's designated hour.

Or, if you find me lying prostrate,
Catatonic in a sanitorium room,
Or, one day, to strangely evaporate,
And never return to Nettlecombe.

Then please examine this space
For the stealer who stole my soul,

He who came and took my grace,
Shattering a vessel, once whole.

Peter felt nauseous and physically sick in the pit of his stomach. The distressing content of the small notebook had shaken him to the core. He quickly put it back in its hiding place, rushed out of the summerhouse and climbed over a fence into a neighbouring field, where he cried. Silent tears fell from his eyes.

He felt like one of the undead, fated to walk the Earth in a subsumed state of reality, unable to make contact with the realm of the real world and its people.

In an effort to get in touch with his real physical self, he took off all of his clothes and ran into the pitch-blackness, scaring the life out of a flock of sheep, which scattered in all directions. He then collapsed naked on the cold damp grass and looked up at the heavens.

Overcome with rage, he proceeded to scream obscenities once more to an invisible God, "You poor excuse for a compassionate, loving omnipotent being. You are nothing more than *sick sadistic fuck* who just loves to watch us poor pathetic souls suffer."

He eventually managed to find his way back to the cottage and lay naked in front of the burning log fire where he quickly downed a bottle of wine before falling asleep.

Early the next morning he was disturbed by the sound of hailstones battering the living room windowpane with great force; for a moment, he thought Alice was tapping the window. His thoughts immediately returned to the contents of her little notebook. He felt for her. He internalised her pain. He was determined, if it was at all possible, to help relieve her suffering. But who is the perpetrator, he wondered? What if he is still alive today and living nearby; he could come back to threaten or harm her to prevent her from revealing his identity? Peter would have to examine the notebook again to try to discover the name of the abuser, which the *Soul stealer* poem implied lay hidden inside. Peter had no wish to read the unsettling account again, but he felt that knowing the identity of the person would help him protect her.

He got dressed and left the cottage in the pouring rain to retrieve his sodden clothes from the nearby field. The sheep, remembering his wild antics from the previous night, looked at him with an incredulous stare.

Peter did not return to the summerhouse for the rest of the week leading up to Alice's next visit. As regular as clockwork on the Saturday morning there was a "tap…tap," on the window to signal her return. She clearly preferred this method of entry to using her key. He felt edgy in her presence having just discovered and read her secret little notebook. She seemed to sense that something was wrong. During their morning cup of tea together, she once again asked Peter if he was going to Lady Traherne's party that evening. He reluctantly replied in the affirmative but really had no wish to interact with a crowd of strangers, especially as the upsetting details of Alice's suffering remained foremost in his mind. However, as he had promised to her that he would attend, there was now no way that he could back down now.

Later, having cleaned himself up and putting on a fresh set of smart casual clothes, he set off for the `Great House. ` He decided to walk there, rather than drive, as he anticipated having a few drinks that evening. There was a short cut to the house across some fields but he decided against taking this, as it was now dark and feared that he might get lost. He therefore headed along the road to the village, before taking the country lane that led to the house.

Some half an hour later, he came to some wrought iron gates with the name Llanmaes engraved on a brass plaque above them. He then followed a poorly lit winding track of tall, dark, cedar trees to the house. Guard dogs barked menacingly in the distance, perhaps sensing his presence. After a long walk he came across the Estate Letting Office where he had collected the cottage keys a few weeks before. A little further on, he caught the full sight of a grand Georgian country house. Its beautifully proportioned splendour wasn't what he expected, for his imagination had anticipated a `Hammer House of Horror` edifice. The forecourt was full of cars, land rovers and vans. A din of excited chatter and laughter emanated from inside. He knocked the large antler shaped doorknocker and was soon greeted by a middle-aged lady dressed in an elegant evening gown, making him feel as if he was under dressed. She led him to the cavernous rectangular `Great Hall. ` A huge marble fireplace occupied the centre of one interior wall, opposite which were several magnificent windows looking over the gardens at the back of the house. The walls were mainly adorned with vast tapestries depicting rural hunting scenes. There were also two smaller fireplaces at either end of the room. Roaring log fires were raging from all three fireplaces.

The space was packed; the Estate must employ a good hundred plus people judging by the dense throng, Peter imagined. He was relieved to find the guests attired in a variety of clothing, from casual to very formally dressed, which meant he could easily blend in. A long dining table occupied the heart of the room; it was full of buffet finger foods which included Italian cold meats, cheeses, olives, salads, various fresh breads and dips. Most of the guests gathered around this delicious banquet or a large long side table full with alcoholic drinks; mainly bottles of wine, high strength local beers and ciders. Everyone seemed engaged in hearty conversation.

As soon as he had a snack and poured himself a glass of wine, Peter made for a far corner of the room, where he hoped to `hideaway, ` undisturbed. From this vantage point, he could view the other guests as a neutral onlooker, as he been on his recent London tube study. However, he knew that there was no such detachment in the quantum world, where the observer is inevitably embroiled in some kind of `conspiracy` with the phenomena that is being observed.

He was surprised by the almost complete absence of any family paintings or photographs on any of the walls or mantelpieces, with the exception of one large portrait of the late Lord Traherne above the nearby fireplace. His pasty-faced completion complimented an impassive countenance with no distinguishing facial features.

The lack of family pictures made him wonder if Lord and Lady Traherne didn't have any children of their own.

Although the room was grand and the spread of food and fine wines impressive, Peter noticed that the tapestries, curtains and carpets were faded, worn and dusty; they gave the impression of a place that had not been properly maintained. The Estate might not be as affluent as it once was, he conjectured.

Peter braced himself for the time when he would have to engage in conversation with some of the guests; his aim was to keep this to a minimum, however. He reminded himself to avoid making any prolonged eye contact or physical connection with them, especially Alice and Lady Traherne, who must be in the room somewhere.

"*Hello* Peter. I'm glad that you made it." The unmistakable, but gentle sound of Alice's voice snapped him out of his detached bubble. The fire light had illuminated Peter's face making him visible to Alice from across the room, who immediately made a bee-line for him, intent on making him feel welcome. It took all of her courage to overcome her social anxiety and go over to him. Her heart felt a gentle pang on first seeing him; she was not used to feeling this way and was both confused and excited at the prospect of exploring this unknown land of attraction.

"I'm fine, thanks Alice-it's nice to see you again."

"Ah Peter! I hope my daughter is doing a good job looking after the cottage for you?" Lady Traherne then appeared suddenly out of nowhere, (having also seen his radiant face from afar).

He was flummoxed by her words, for he had no idea that Alice was her daughter, for neither of them had ever mentioned it before. He never imagined the daughter of the Lady owner of the Nettlecombe Estate to be one of its cleaners and that she would be Alice.

"She's doing a grand job, Lady Traherne." He replied trying not to let on that he had been unaware that she was her mother.

"Please call me Sylvia," she said confidently. "Alice wasn't always a cleaner you know. She studied English Literature at University and taught in a local school for a while, but eventually she had her fill of that." She said these words as if she was trying to justify her daughter's existence.

"Why was that Alice, if you don't mind me asking?" Peter dared to enquire, keen to learn more about her.

Alice, clearly embarrassed by her mother's disclosure of personal details of her life to a comparative stranger, responded truthfully, for it was against her nature to lie.

"I found it very draining having to manage and control the kids. It got in the way of my passion for my subject and just left me feeling stressed out all the time."

Her mother then quickly interjected, "I never knew that Alice...you never told me that was the way you felt. I thought it was because you didn't get on with the other staff." She was clearly hurt by Alice's omission.

In an attempt to relieve the tense atmosphere that had suddenly developed, Peter said how difficult he found it when he first started lecturing undergraduates, who were not much younger than himself. He recalled how one precocious student kept interrupting his lectures with challenging questions and how he often struggled to find a satisfactory answer to them. This caused him great anxiety and humiliation at the time.

It was during this uncomfortable moment that Peter's and Alice's eyes met properly for the first time. He took the risk of yielding to one of his visions by holding eye contact with her. But this time he did not succumb to one of his regressions.

They both took a massive risk by letting their guard down in this way, for they were highly sensitive and wounded individuals.

Each knew their relationship had now taken a new course, but both were willing to take the risk of embarking on the unknown journey that may follow.

"Do you know that Alice is a brilliant writer; her poems, in particular are very beautiful?"

"Please mum, you are embarrassing me! I only wish that were true-I just like to dabble a bit. There is no way that a publisher would take my work seriously."

Alice's natural modesty made Peter warm to her even more.

Lady Traherne encouraged Peter to mingle in the gathering and to make himself feel at home, before taking her daughter's arm to meet another guest. It was clear that Alice did not want to be there and was only doing so to please her mother.

Peter was now left alone to observe the social interactions in the room once more. He soon focused on Lady Traherne's loud voice as she was talking to a small audience nearby. She was berating someone who had failed to attend the party as they had promised. "It is so typical of him not to come. Do you find that you can't trust him either?" she continued, placing the guests she was addressing in a difficult position. Soon, each of them concurred with her judgment by proffering denigrating remarks about the targeted non-attender. As Estate workers, they were clearly very careful not to upset their `boss. ` Peter wondered if they came to the function more out of fear rather than respect for her.

He also heard one of the other guests talking in a muted tone about some impending cutbacks that were about to take place on the Estate. It was clear that many were worried about their future job security, now that the Estate was clearly experiencing financial difficulties. This explained the poor upkeep of the `Great House`.

The whole situation had something of a mediaeval air about it; so much for progress and democracy, he thought; Sylvia was the feudal `lord` who `ruled` the Estate and its workers with an iron hand.

After a few glasses of wine, Peter summoned up the confidence to mix with the other guests.

Peter got very drunk and left very late. Luckily, someone called a cab and helped him into it. He had a faint recollection that it was Alice.

He woke up the following morning, remembering little of the previous night's celebrations. He hoped that hadn't made too much of a fool of himself.

However, he did remember meeting Alice's eyes and not succumbing to one of his soul-sapping visions. This made him feel gratified.

That morning, for the first time since leaving Cambridge, he felt a glimmer of hope for the future. The numbness that gripped his mind like a vice had receded a little. He was beginning to feel more responsive to the outside world, judging by his albeit faint memory of merrily mixing with the other guests in the function the night before. However, it was his recollection of connecting with Alice's eyes that lifted his spirit most of all.

Chapter 11

When he had finished breakfast, Peter headed straight for the summerhouse where he intended to spend every spare minute leading up to Alice's next visit, analysing the text of the little notebook in a search for the identity of the unnamed offender. The author must have laid down some clues for someone else to decipher.

He carefully read the text, looking for all kinds of links: the first and last letter of each chapter, every twentieth, thirtieth or fortieth letter, bracketed word codes, codes that may follow colons or semicolons and so on. But all this was to no avail, for even he, with his brilliant capacity for fathoming out the mathematics that describe the workings of the universe, was at a loss to find any constructive leads.

A further five more days of intensive scrutiny also proved fruitless.

Alice's unmistakable, but welcome, "Tap,tap…tap,tap," sounded as usual on the Saturday morning. She was more reliable than the best alarm clock. They had their usual cup of tea and chat together, but this time she opened up a bit more about herself, talking a little about her teaching experiences and her mother. Peter reciprocated by mentioning his pending divorce and resigning from his position at Imperial. A bond of trust was growing between them which was gradually cementing their friendship.

That weekend Peter gave himself a mental break from his code breaking efforts. He often found such `times outs` led to a breakthrough for a particularly vexing theoretical problem. He also made a point of taking better care of himself in order to keep his mind fresh. This included a commitment to eating well and drinking less alcohol, as well as taking regular walks.

He resumed his study of the notebook on Monday, February 6. He had been in the cottage for over a month and for most of that time he had been absorbed in Alice's personal world. When he became aware of this, he felt uncomfortable, for he was not by nature a nosy person; but here he was delving even deeper into her secret past. He therefore put the notebook away and didn't look at it again again until the Friday.

When Alice came as usual on the Saturday, his mind was full of the unsuccessful permutations he had used to unlock her enigmatic code. She had made solving the puzzle a very challenging task, even for someone with his brilliant mind. Nevertheless, he was delighted to see her again and they had their usual beverage and talk together. He loved her shy mannerisms and the gentle way in which she spoke to him. She opened up a bit more to Peter and told him a few more details about her life, in particular, that she had a brother, Jeremy, who lived in Southampton.

In the evening it occurred to him to examine the eight sketches of the picturesque cottage scenes for clues, for the writing had given him none. It was a desperate attempt, for he could not see how they could hide a missing code. After several hours of close examination, he drew a blank and retired to bed.

The following morning, he resumed his study of the sketches. He noticed that each cottage had a very distinctive porch area, which seemed to be the primary point of focus of the artist, as if they intended to draw the viewer's eye towards them. No two porches were alike; each design was unique and based around some of the following features: arches, columns, architraves, paneling, and inlaid windows, (some with stained glass). Some had a letterbox, (if the porch front was level with the front door), a few had a house name plaque and two had hanging baskets.

Peter sketched each porch design onto separate sheets of plain paper. It was difficult to clearly make out the first porch as the ink used to draw it had faded a great deal. He could see the name Merlin Cottage and some of the main features but struggled to pick out all of the finer detail from the original drawing. The second sketch was also quite faded and the third less so; he therefore had less difficulty reproducing their original compositions. The final five drawings of cottages were all in perfect condition and he could consequently copy them accurately.

He looked at each of his drawings individually and then compared them with each other, looking for some kind of common link, such as concealed symbols, letters and words. He had a gift for uncovering patterns that lay hidden in sets of data, but after eight solid hours of intensive but unproductive research, he returned to the cottage to cook his evening meal.

Peter was at a complete loss as to what step to take next, for he felt that he had exhausted all possible lines of enquiry. His talent for resolving complex puzzles had for once deserted him; he hated being defeated by a challenge in this way. He had to overcome numerous, seemingly insurmountable, stumbling blocks during the development of his God Field theory, but each time he succeeded in finding a way through. However, this time he had to admit that he was outfoxed by a little notebook written by a mysterious, but troubled, woman.

He was woken up in the early hours of Thursday morning by a strange dream. At dusk, he saw a great flock of cackling black crows take flight from a ploughed field. As they headed towards a woodland on the top of a nearby hill, they seemed to slowly fade into the trees and become immersed in them. He then saw himself walking across the field in the direction of the same trees and also gradually dissolving into them, like a silhouette that fades into the night. He contemplated on the meaning of the dream. Could it perhaps be a clue to untangling Alice's missing code? After all, his dream about the caribou on the London underground had some real-life connection when he met the `Eskimo `vagrant.

This insight did not come to him unaided, however, for God had been up to his old tricks, again through one of Peter's dreams.

Peter looked for a connection between his dream and the text in the notebook, but to no avail. He then examined his copies of the porch sketches again. Other than their distinctive designs, how were they different from one another? Then it came to him-the first few original sketches had shown decreasing signs of fading, just like he and the crows had slowly disappeared into the woodland. Putting his own copies of the sketches aside, he scanned the original notebook sketches for clues. Did Alice deliberately intend the sketches to diminish over time and, if so, why? Was her purpose to gradually reveal the identity of the perpetrator?

When he looked intently at the remaining details on the first faded sketch he noticed that a few fragments from the area around the porch seemed to show no sign of fading at all. They appeared to be small random jottings of no apparent significance but he still copied them down onto a piece of plain paper. It was more difficult to identify such fragments from the second sketch and even harder from the third. When he compared theses `pieces` extracted from the three sketches, he could find no pattern other than that they looked symbol-like. However, having rearranging them many times he found that they fitted together to form three sets of individual letters, one for each cottage. In sketch date order they were:

SE   AMJ   RAT

By themselves, each set of letters were meaningless, so Peter typed SEAMJRAT into an online anagram solver website, but none of the results produced were like a person's name.

Peter, therefore, turned his attention to examining the five remaining drawings, but none showed any contrasting details around the porch area. He wondered what he could do to reveal any symbols that may lay hidden there.

He surmised that Alice had sketched each drawing in a different dilution of water-based ink. This ink would naturally fade over time due to the effects of heat causing it to evaporate and therefore diminish in intensity, so revealing the fragments. When she finished each sketch, she must have added the extra symbols to the porch area in permanent blue ink, that would not fade with time. Therefore, when the main details of the sketches eventually faded these symbols would remain.

But how could he reveal the missing symbols on the last five drawings? After much deliberation, he wondered whether he could artificially accelerate the fading process by increasing the temperature the ink was exposed to. It would have to be heated very carefully to prevent other, non-symbol, details of the sketches from disappearing, for Alice would then know that someone had interfered with the sketches and may have unearthed the secret name. Peter therefore decided to focus only on heating the porch area, leaving the rest of the drawing alone.

He had intended to use the paraffin heater as his source of warmth but rejected this idea for its heating effect would be too widespread. He decided instead to purchase a micro warm air torch, the kind that artists use, because he could more easily control its heat output as well as the focus of the flame.

Peter headed straight away for Bridport, to obtain the items he needed. He purchased a range of blue water-based inks in an artists supply shop and made colour photocopies of the sketches in a print shop. However, he had difficulty in finding somewhere that sold the micro warm air torch. He eventually purchased one in an Artists Emporium on the outskirts of the town.

When he returned to the cottage, he headed for the summerhouse and started to, very carefully, heat the fourth sketch in the notebook. Having placed the torch on its lowest setting, he held it at a sufficient distance to blow a very gentle heat over the porch area of the drawing. Nothing happened for ten minutes but then the water-based ink slowly began to evaporate to expose the hidden symbols. After half an hour he was satisfied they had been fully uncovered. He then heated the rest of the drawings, one by one, until their secret markings were also revealed. He then copied the symbols, in date order, for all five drawings onto plain paper, placing them alongside those from the first three cottages.

Using the same tone of water-based ink he then very carefully touched up the details lost from each of the original drawings due to the heating process, using the photocopies of the sketches as a guide. The finished product was virtually indistinguishable from the original. All being well, Alice would never know that he had modified the sketches.

He then rearranged the fragments for each cottage into letters and wrote them down next to those from the first three cottages,

SE AMJ RAT REH EN MY TAF HER

He then typed in all of the letters and then various combinations of the sets of letters into an online anagram solver on his mobile phone. But little came out that made any sense and nothing that resembled a name.

Peter therefore reverted to relying on his own mental processes to crack the code. He was now in the zone of mental processing for which he exceled-looking for a pattern in seemingly random information.

He stared at the letters for a while, rearranging the order of all of the letters, groups of letters and the order of the letters within each small group, looking to see if they spelt a name or a meaningful word. He tried various combinations for several hours before resigning himself to the realisation that he would not be able to solve the riddle before Alice's return the following morning at nine. He was disappointed with himself for failing to solve the problem in time, but it wasn't through want of trying. Eventually he had to give up his search for it was past two o'clock in the morning and he was very tired.

Peter fell asleep in the summerhouse mulling over different variations of the groups of letters in his mind. He woke up very early the next morning and looked over the original sketches once more to see whether his focus on them and the hidden symbols had been a false trail. He concluded that he was on the right path and was close to working out the mystery name. He again scribbled down many possible combinations of the reordered letter groups but without success. It was seven thirty and the time for Alice's visit was drawing near-he would have to leave the summerhouse soon or there was a chance she might discover him and what he had been up to over the last few weeks. In one last-ditch effort, he put down his pen and just stared at the clusters of letters for half an hour before it suddenly came to him-*there it was*, the identity of the missing person he had been searching for so obsessively:

MY FATHER JAMES TRAHERNE

`It was her *father* the *evil bastard*. I should have suspected it was him after my talk with the pub landlord. It was Alice, and not the landlord, who must have sprayed graffiti over his gravestone lament. ` Peter frantically looked through the large cardboard boxes containing various DIY accessories stored in the back of the summerhouse and soon found a can of spray paint which matched the light blue colour sprayed on the gravestone. But before he could fully digest the shocking discovery of her father's guilt, he could hear the faint sound of someone calling his name from the direction of the cottage.

"Peter! Are you there…Hello Peter are you home?" It was the unmistakable voice of Alice. She was calling from the back door of the cottage, having let herself in. It was eight o'clock. Alice could not see into the summerhouse as its entrance faced away from the cottage towards the countryside beyond. For some reason she had arrived earlier than usual. `On now of all days…on now of all moments. Many thanks…*you malicious fucking God*! ` Peter once again cursed the Creator.

He panicked like never before. In a fraction of a second, he placed the notebook in its leather pouch, tied the cord around it, leapt up from the armchair, rushed over to the panel and stuck it behind using the original masking tape. In his state of over excitement, he hadn't pressed the tape firmly enough on the inside of the back panel and as he closed the door he could hear the notebook fall down. He frantically put it back again, this time making sure that the tape firmly held the notebook in position. He then gathered his sketches and photocopies together, folded them in half and stuffed them in his back pocket. He then quickly grabbed a book from the shelf and sat down in the armchair pretending to read it. He was breathing so heavily he was close to hyperventilating. He inhaled several deep breaths of air to calm himself down and not assuage Alice's suspicions. Her face then suddenly appeared from the side of the doorway and she said in an animated tone.

"Good morning Peter! I'm sorry to disturb you. I hope you don't mind, I've come along a bit earlier as my mum wants me to go with her to visit my brother Jeremy in

Southampton. Didn't you hear me calling from the back door?"

He paused before replying, "No, sorry. I was so absorbed in reading this fascinating book… That's no problem Alice-by all means do your chores a bit earlier-that's fine."

But she knew immediately that something wasn't quite right with him; her acutely sensitive intelligence had sensed his anxiety. This, along with the red complexion on his face and small beads of perspiration on his forehead, convinced her that something was wrong.

Recognising her suspicions, he quickly interjected, "Sorry I didn't hear you calling Alice," before standing up to greet her.

He continued, "I like this place a lot and I've been spending quite a bit of time in this place recently. As you suggested, it's a great place to chill out." He suddenly realised that he had repeated the word "place" three times; a fact that was not lost on Alice.

"I love it too…. Do you know, it's about time I gave it a good clean, don't you think? It hasn't been touched since the autumn. It's best that I give it the once over, especially now that you are using it. Shall I do that now?"

"That would be great," Peter lied, for the last place he wanted her to look around was the summerhouse. `What if she finds out I have discovered her secret possessions? ` But he was confident that he had placed everything back exactly as he had found it. He then left for the main house to give her space to clean it.

When Alice had cleaned the summerhouse and then the main cottage, Peter caught sight of her quickly heading for the front door and called out, "Goodbye Alice. Many thanks," but she failed to respond with a reply. `She must have surely heard me, ` he thought. All of a sudden, he was overcome with a terrible feeling of foreboding that she had found out he had discovered her concealed possessions and uncovered her deepest secrets. Why else would she leave in silence, especially as they had grown closer together? He was mortified with grief; it felt as if the opportunity for developing a loving friendship with someone he had come to care for and respect, had ended in an instant. There would be no chance of any possible recourse, for how could she ever forgive him for his intrusive breach of trust. She must feel violated, the very thing she wrote about in her little notebook. The pain of this realisation hurt him like a vice around his heart. He felt ashamed for what he had done, even though he did it for the noble reason of protecting her. But he thought he understood her well enough to know that there was now no going back from this catastrophe.

Once he heard her drive away, he rushed over to the summerhouse. She had cleaned it thoroughly, just as she does in the main cottage. When he checked the recess, nothing at first glance seemed out of place. However, as he closed the concealed panel door it dawned on him that the tiny specks of gold dust on the carpet had gone; she must have cleared them with her mini hand-held Hoover. They had fallen out of the little notebook when he had first opened it. He berated himself for not having registered them laying on the carpet and removed them. She must have deliberately placed some gold dust in the pages of the notebook as a way of checking if someone had looked at it.

He was gripped with feelings of remorse. He tried to blank them out by thinking about the revelation he had unearthed that morning. He had discovered that the "soul stealer" Alice had alluded to in her poem, was none other than her father. He now also understood why she hadn't revealed his name in the mini notebook-it was because he was still alive when she wrote down the entries and made the sketches. His nearby presence must have had some kind of disempowering constriction upon her, like a strait jacket of the mind and soul. It was only after his death that she was able to begin the process of self-healing, for it was soon afterwards that she began writing the poems and analysing the Bradshaw book. This must have provided some degree of relief from her emotional suffering. However, she would sadly never see her father brought to account for his crimes.

Peter further concluded that the abuse must have taken place in the various cottages depicted in the sketches in the little notebook. Her parents must have regularly stayed in them, (when there were no bookings), as a break from the pressures of the `Great House. ` Her mother had said that she and her late husband used to sometimes stay in the Owl Cottage. Sylvia was no doubt frequently away on Estate business. Her father must have taken the opportunity of her absence to prey upon his daughter.

Alice didn't return the following Saturday to do her cleaning chores. A young Polish lady came instead. Her absence hurt him badly, as did his sense of guilt. He tried to catch sight of her in the village and the surrounding Estate, but without success. He walked for many miles along county lanes and across fields in the vain hope of seeing her.

When Alice failed to return on the second Saturday, he was convinced that she knew he had found her belongings in the summerhouse recess. He asked the new cleaner if she knew why she had stopped coming. She said that Lady Traherne had reassigned her to new duties in the main house. Peter thought that she must have asked her mother to do this for her.

Once the new cleaner left, he considered whether he should leave the Estate for good but the thought of doing so pained him, for Alice had taken a hold on his heart. However, his booking was due to end shortly, on March 3, when he intended to go to Cardiff. He had been uncertain whether he would return to Dorset afterwards. However, now he was drawn towards Alice and her tragic story, he felt a strong yearning to return. But he was in danger of losing out on extending his stay at the `Owl, ` for it may have already been booked after his two months stay comes to its end. But how could he stay if she was never going to speak to him again? How could he remain if their relationship would now never develop as he, and no doubt she, had once hoped? Living there would then be insufferable.

After much deliberation, he decided to return to the Estate after his trip to Cardiff; he cared for Alice so much that he could not bear to be apart from her, even if they were not speaking with one another. He would commit himself to staying for another six months in the `Owl, ` or some other cottage, on the Estate, if any were still available. He had grown very fond of the cottage in his time there and did not want to lose it to someone else. He kicked himself for not having booked it earlier and was convinced that it must already be let. He therefore wasted no time and decided to head for the Estate Office at once to see if there was still time to secure the `Owl, ` or some other cottage. In addition, there would be a chance he might `bump` into Alice, for the Estate Office was in an annex building not far from the Great House; his heart raced at the thought of this opportunity.

He quickly jumped into his car and speeded out of the driveway, sending a shower of gravel behind him, some of which spattered against the downstairs cottage windowpanes, luckily without breaking them. As he exited into the country lane, he almost collided with a tractor, whose driver he identified as the same person who almost ran him over in the middle of the night some weeks previously. Now Peter was the `nutter` driver. All that he could think about was the chance of seeing Alice again.

When he approached Llanmaes, he slowed the car down, for he did not want to draw attention to himself. He knocked on the main door of the house, rather than go to the Estate Office. He was hoping that Alice might answer it.

Sylvia answered the door and invited him into the lounge where he asked her about booking the cottage. Whilst inside, his eyes frantically scanned around looking for any sign of Alice, but she was nowhere to be seen. After a quick cup of tea and a chat, Sylvia took him to the Estate Office to check the bookings register. After close examination, his heart sank when she said there were already three bookings over the next six months to the beginning of September. She said that she had kept the `Owl` free from bookings until recently in the hope that Peter might extend his stay there, but as he hadn't heard from him, she had penciled in these other bookings recently. His heart lifted again when she said that she would transfer them to one of the other cottages-she was obviously pleased to have a guaranteed source of income for the six months, especially now that the Estate was under financial pressure.

She was very friendly towards him and even said what a pleasure it was to have him living on the Estate. Unknown to Peter, she was aware of Alice's attachment towards him. She had guessed the reason her daughter had asked to end her cottage cleaning duties was because they had fallen out with each other.

As he left the Office, he looked to the many upper windows of the `Great House` hoping to see Alice, but sadly, he caught no sight of her. However, as he pulled the car door open, he was aware of some figure hiding behind one of the upstairs bedroom curtains and wondered whether it might be her.

His only hope was that, when he returned, Alice would slowly mellow and perhaps forgive him in some way. He knew that he would have to one day explain his actions to her; perhaps she would then forgive him? But right now, he was heartbroken. Alice, who had been watching him from behind the curtains, felt the same.

Chapter 12

A week later, Peter left for Cardiff. As he quietly pulled his car out of the cottage driveway and slowly drove towards Symondsbury Village he absorbed the beautiful countryside he would not see again for a while. A light dusting of snow covered the higher ground. Mist lay on the river valley below. The low angled rays of the morning sun pierced through the tree branches like a blessing. A cock pheasant scrambled ahead of him along the country lane, unable to cope with its steep banks; its intricate tail feathers seemed like an inscription.

As he approached the village, he saw someone park their car outside one of the rental cottages belonging to the Estate. He was shocked to see Alice climb out of it; their eyes met, but neither acknowledged the other. However, a great deal passed between them in that brief moment: Alice experienced feelings of love and betrayal; Peter felt love and shame.

He surmised that she must have resumed her cottage cleaning duties and was preparing this particular cottage for the arrival of the next group of holidaymakers. It was also Saturday, the day when most changeovers took place. He wondered whether she would also be cleaning the `Owl` again; if so, he would meet her once again on his return from Cardiff.

When his car exited the village, and turned onto the fast road to Bridport, he put his foot down hard on the gas pedal and accelerated in a bid to blank out the painful memory of his brief encounter with Alice. He soon exceeded the speed limit but was soon snapped out of his `trance` by the sight of young woman with a pram crossing the road ahead of him, forcing him to come to an emergency stop. The woman looked understandably furious but said nothing. He recognised her as the Polish cleaning lady. It crossed his mind that Alice might have taken her job and that she might well now be out of work.

Seeing Alice again had unsettled him deeply. Although he tried not to think about her, she occupied a subliminal part of his mind for the rest of the journey to Cardiff. He was largely oblivious to the countryside as he it passed by.

It was midday when he parked his MG outside his mother's house in Ely, in Cardiff.

He had phoned ahead to say that he was coming home for a break. When he entered the house, his mother, Katherine and his brother, Bruce, gave him a very warm welcome, followed by a hearty meal. Katherine was now ninety-one years old but was still in reasonable health for someone of such a great age. Bruce, who was now in his mid-50's, looked after her. He had also taken care of his father for a while until he passed away a few years previously. His three other brothers lived in different parts of the city, as did two of his three sisters, the other living in the South of France.

Peter mainly stayed indoors that weekend. He only ventured out for a walk to the nearby River Ely along a stretch of flood plain called The Lauries and for an evening pint with Bruce in the local Glamorgan Wanderers Rugby Club.

Katherine had brought up her eight children well, each of them growing to be decent and authentic individuals. Ironically, both she and her late husband William, were only children and yet they made up for this later by having a large family of their own. She was small in stature but possessed a strong constitution, no doubt bolstered by good genes and her love of the outdoors, for she was always active, whether gardening, walking, cycling and enjoying all manner of other pursuits. Her sharp intelligence and creative gifts expressed itself in her love for painting and playing the piano, probably inheriting these gifts from her mother, who was also a fine artist and musician. Katherine was a striking woman in her younger days. Even now, she retained the kind of beauty that old people who have lived a rich and full life possess, where the wrinkles and creases of their countenance, radiate an endearing quality of wisdom and maturity. The elderly, on the other hand, who had led false and bitter lives, betray this in the twists, contortions, and dark shadows on their faces.

Nevertheless, his mother had a hard life bringing up so many children and often struggled with mental illness. She had several nervous breakdowns and on occasion had to be admitted to Whitchurch Mental Hospital in the north of the City. In fact, she was there during the first year of Peter's life. Katherine, then in her forties, could not deal with the stress of having one more child after a gap of several years to the last, his sister Lilly.

Her husband William, had come from a very different background to his wife's. He was brought up in a poor area of Nottingham called Sneinton. His parents were Irish immigrants. His father worked as a labourer on various building sites, but sadly died when he was only six years old. He was a very strong man, for William once recalled seeing him carrying two heavy flagstones, one under each arm. His mother later remarried a man who had been a champion bare knuckle boxer. William's education was meager and this left him with a feeling of inadequacy throughout his life. But he had several hidden talents which included writing, he even wrote a 400,000-word novel based on his working-class roots in Nottingham. He later tragically burnt the book after he received scathing criticism of its grammatical and literary credentials from Max.

Perhaps these contrasts attracted his parents to one another when they first met towards the end of the Second World War in Saundersfoot in Pembrokeshire, where William was on recuperation leave from the Royal Marines. Katherine was also, no doubt, impressed by his dashing good looks and smart dress sense. His father was always a snappy dresser. They met in a local dance hall and soon fell in love. They got married just after the War when William moved to live with Katherine in Cardiff where they lived in her grandparent's house.

His brother was a strongly built and darkly handsome man with movie star features. He was also very intelligent and was by far the most outstanding pupil in his primary and secondary schools. He regrettably failed his 11+ exam in curious circumstances, when it was suspected that a place at one of the City's grammar school had gone to a boy from a more affluent part of the City. This lost opportunity was to affect him all of his life, for he could never find an outlet for his brilliant mind, other that in computer software programming and even then, he wasn't using his abilities to their full potential. Given a normal education in a normal area, he would have been a guaranteed Oxbridge student.

Although he finished top in his secondary modern school, he left with few recognisable qualifications and drifted between mundane jobs, working in Wiggins Teape Paper Mill and Brains Brewery, amongst other places. He later got a job as croupier in Les Croupiers casino in St Mary's Street in Cardiff. His sharp mind and natural charisma perfectly suited such a role. This led to him to working for several years as a croupier on board luxury cruise liners which travelled the world. He had a wonderful time and met many a beautiful woman. It was whilst on such cruise that he met his future wife Sofia, a stunning Puerto Rican lady.

Before they married, Bruce in an endeavour to improve his prospects, studied for a six months Government initiated `TOPS` course in computing. He discovered that he had a natural talent for computer programming and came first in his class. This propelled him into his career as a highly paid computer programmer repairing software faults on large mainframe computers for such companies as BP and Rank Xerox.

But sadly, after several years of marriage and two lovely children, his relationship with Sofia broke down. She eventually went back to Puerto Rico with the kids. Bruce was devastated and never recovered from this blow. He bore deep mental wounds from the loss of his family and the guilt he felt for causing this.

Bruce carried on working for major computer companies for a while but these opportunities eventually dried up because his specialism became outsourced to India where the labour costs were a lot less. So, when his money ran out, he returned to Cardiff to look after his elderly parents to whom he showed selfless love and support.

One Sunday evening, the day after his arrival, Peter opened up to Bruce about his problems. He told him how marital and work stresses had resulted in him having a breakdown. He failed to mention the specific cause-how his theory had infiltrated and disturbed his psyche. He said that he needed to stay for a short while in Cardiff to help him recover from this difficult period of his life. He also omitted to tell Bruce about the real purpose of his stay, which was solely to track down his abuser Max and exact `justifiable` revenge.

However, his brother never once opened up to Peter about his own problems.

On the Monday morning, after breakfast, Peter began his search for Max. He knew from his brief stopover in Cardiff after his stay in the Buddhist retreat that he no longer lived in his old address in Sevenoaks Road. Other than the comment from the next-door neighbour that Max may have gone to stay in an old people's home, he had no other leads as to his present whereabouts.

Peter first googled Max Cameron into his mobile phone but none of the several individuals which came up with that name seemed to match the Max he knew. His next step was to search the online records of the General Register Office for evidence of a Death Certificate for him, as he thought it quite likely that he had passed away, because he would be 86 years old by now. But Max wasn't listed there. As this only recorded deaths after the sixth month of passing, he needed to check his local Register Office for deaths which happened during this time. He therefore headed for the Cardiff Council Registration Service in the City Hall, to search through the Death Registers there. But he again drew a blank. Peter thought it highly unlikely that Max would have moved away from the Cardiff area and his death recorded there.

He left the Office with a feeling of optimism for it looked as if Max might still be alive. But where could he now be, he wondered? On the Tuesday, Peter headed for Cardiff Central Library to continue his search. He tracked down the names, addresses and telephone numbers of all of the Retirement and Nursing Homes in the city and then phoned each of them to see if they had a Max Cameron staying with them. Regrettably, Max wasn't resident in any of them and neither had he been in the past.

Over the next three days he continued his search for evidence of Max's whereabouts. He particularly focused on the possibility that he was in an old people's home near Cardiff, but again he could find no leads. He then decided to leave his pursuit for few days in the hope that he might then come up with some new idea that might help track him down.

He chose, instead, to use this time to look for his best friend from his childhood, Ryan Stephens, whom he last saw when he was a boy of fifteen. Hopefully, he might still be living in Cardiff somewhere. Unfortunately, he had also lost contact with all of his other school friends so he could not get in touch with them to ask if they knew his address.

Googling his name produced no positive leads. Peter then searched through a hard copy of the local telephone directory, which revealed seven people with the same name. It occurred to him that Ryan may not even be one of them if he is X directory, didn't have a landline or had moved out of the region. Nevertheless, he had no other option than to call each of the numbers in turn. Luckily, his mobile phone contract was for unlimited calls and data. However, once again, his enquiries came to nothing. Nevertheless, his smartphone was proving to be of invaluable help in his search, even by swiftly ruling out potential leads.

He then recalled a glimmer of information buried deep within his memory banks of having read an article about Ryan's band, The Lighthouse Boys or The Light Boys, in the local *Echo* newspaper; but that must have been over twenty years ago. The following day, he re-visited Cardiff Central Library to look for evidence of the band in past copies of local music magazines and newspapers but was told that they were stored in the Glamorgan Archives building in nearby Leckwith in the Cardiff district of Grangetown. However, his subsequent search there produced no positive results. One of the archivists suggested he ask in some of the local music shops whether they knew of Ryan and his band.

Peter quickly drove back to the City Centre and headed for Wales's oldest record shop, Spillers, now in Morgan Arcade. Luckily, the elderly owner, said that he had heard of the Lighthouse Boys, but they had long since disbanded with some members forming a new band called The

Greenstreet Boys. He recommended Peter visit a local music haunt called The Rock Den and ask some of the old timers there if they knew anything about Ryan. The venue is in the infamous Tiger Bay area of Cardiff's docklands. But the area is no longer recognisable as the seedy, rough district where sailors used to enjoy their shore leave; over the last twenty years it has been gentrified into a trendy place to live and hang out.

That evening, Peter visited The Rock Den, along with his brother. Bruce had once been in a `Hippie` band himself, with the comical, folksy, name of Ninety Nine Percent Mom and Apple Pie Rock and Roll Band. Peter held a faint memory of one night, (when he was about nine), entering the front room of his parents' house to be met with a wall of marijuana smoke. He could just about make out the faces of about a dozen young guys, all cramped together, listening to Credence Clearwater Revival's, `Bad Moon Rising, ` being played on the old-fashioned record deck. Later, some of the band members played a few of their own tunes on their guitars especially for him-the sound was intoxicating to his innocent ears, a feeling no doubt enhanced by having passively inhaled the heady fumes which filled the air.

Bruce and Peter enjoyed listening to the music from the several blues bands that played that night in the `Den, ` as the venue was usually called. Peter thought that it did Bruce the world of good being there and was a nice change from drinking in the Wanderers. However, he was concerned to see his brother down so many pints of strong lager in quick succession; although Peter drank his fair share as well. During the course of the evening, he asked some of the older musicians and members of the audience whether they had heard of Ryan or his band, but regrettably no one had.

The following night Peter returned by himself to the ` Den.` Again, his enquiries about Ryan came to a dead end. When the last band, Rebus, had finished playing and retired for a joint in an alleyway by the side of the Club, Peter bravely approached them. They were a bunch of seasoned old rockers and he had a hunch that they might know something. Sure enough, the band leader Leonard said he sometimes used to play with Ryan and that he was now in a band called The Blue Jeans and that they were booked to play a gig in the Plough and Harrow pub in Monknash in the Vale of Glamorgan this coming Friday night. He described them as a fusion band mixing several different styles in their set.

Peter explained that they had been best friends in School but had completely lost touch since then.

Leonard then described how Ryan was an accomplished, self-taught musician who wrote and sang his own songs as well as proficiently playing several instruments. He had been in several different bands over the years which mainly played in the South Wales area. He had never married but had child from a relationship a long time ago.

"What is he like now?"

"He's an OK guy, I always had a lot of time and respect for him. He is straight with people, which could sometimes rub them up the wrong way. But he is cast iron honest guy and true to his mates. Friends he never lets down." It sounded as if he was talking from personal experience.

"Has he led a happy life?"

"Well, his life has been his music. But he's had a tough life and got into drugs, skunk mainly-not too much of the heavy stuff though. He never had much dosh either and was often on the bread line.

"Do you know where he lives now?"

"Yes," then after a short pause he continued- "I see no harm in giving you his address; I'm sure Ryan won't mind-he'll be glad to see his old mate again."

He then pulled off the outer covering of a beer mat and wrote down Ryan's address and telephone number on its plain surface. It read, `top floor Flat, 4A Seymour Place, tel no' 0222 376882. *Don't forget to knock hard on the downstairs door.* ` Witnessing Leonard use the beer mat in this way, reminded Peter how he often used to write `mystical` poems on them after a day's heavy losses during his old gambling days. He could easily clear a nest of pub tables of their beer mats.

Once they had exchanged mobile phone numbers, Peter warmly thanked Leonard for his help.

"It's been a pleasure meeting you Peter. I hope you get in contact with him," Leonard said in a genuine manner. "Don't forget to come and check out my band again soon- we play regularly on the Cardiff circuit."

"It's been nice meeting you as well. I'll definitely do that sometime soon."

Rather than visit or call Ryan straight away, he chose to wait until his gig in Monknash. He was excited at the thought of meeting up again with his old mate. But he wondered if he might carry some resentment towards him for disappearing from his life for so long.

He spent much of the daytime hours of the days leading up to the gig, sat at home thinking of a way of finding Max. On a few occasions, he walked around the estate looking for any of the old faces that knew of him in the past. Unfortunately, he did not recognise anyone, not even those who used to hang around the betting office Max often frequented. He also called at several more houses in Max's old street, aside from the neighbours with whom he had already spoken, to make enquiries of his whereabouts, but to no avail.

Peter was shocked to see just how much the Estate had changed since he was last there. A huge underclass now lived in Ely, many living on benefits. Drugs taking and dealing was everywhere. A sinister air now pervaded ever street. Few cars lined the roads; most were parked in driveways to avoid either being stolen or vandalised.

Luckily, Susan who lived next door to his mum's, had kindly let him park his distinctive sports car in her unused driveway for safety. The car had already drawn the attention of the local gangs. Bruce told him how his own car had been recently stolen twice in one day. It was first taken from outside the house and abandoned in a street about half a mile away, where the police placed a black and yellow checked, `do not touch…stolen vehicle` tape all around it. But, this proved to be an ineffective deterrent as it was stolen again that day and burnt out in local playing field.

He sensed an undercurrent of fear as he walked around his old neighbourhood; he never felt this as a kid playing in the streets. A genuine working-class community existed in those days when most people had jobs, were friendlier and cared more for one another. But now, groups of menacing, pasty-faced youths, wandered the streets. If they `eyeballed` him, Peter would take great care not to return their stares. He could handle himself, but this was somehow different: there was a definite threat of impending, possibly armed, physical assault. Although he grew up on the same streets, he now gave off the look of an educated, well to do, ` out of towner, ` which had the effect of stirring up their resentment towards him.

The youths were often brought up by a single mother, who was burdened by the daily struggle to feed, clothe and provide for the material needs of her family. Drugs, (skunk, solvents, heroin and crystal meth), debilitated many of the youngsters, with the consequent damage caused to their neural pathways. They were hooked on sensation- seeking highs to dampen the hopelessness of their existence. Many became vacant, uncaring, insensitive sociopaths.

Many Ely teenagers, lacking a stable home life and good role models to look up to, sought identification in their local gang, the `Fam, ` as they called it, for this gave them a feeling of belonging they never had before. With no stability at home, poor qualifications and little prospect of a job when they left School, they felt despondent, scared and desperate.

He knew there was no way that he could deal with such a group of lost souls, even though he was one himself, albeit for different reasons. He therefore decided, for reasons of personal safety, despite his wish to explore his old stamping ground, to keep his street wanderings to a minimum.

Peter's childhood recollections, before he went to Max's, were happy ones. Unlike the situation now, the streets then were a wonderful place to explore and have fun. He recalled how he and his friends had a great time mucking about playing such games as `rat a tat ginger, ` `British bulldogs. ` and `kick the can. ` He had many such fun memories playing with his mates, some of whom had comical sounding name, such as Paul Crapper, Simon Whitty and Arthur Herring.

He recalled some of the pranks they used to get up to. One involved tying a rope between the door handles of two houses on opposite sides of the street. Their inhabitants would get a shock when a passing car drove into it pulling both door handles completely off. When his dad later found out about his part in this escapade, he gave him a severe beating and kept him grounded at home at night for several weeks afterwards.

Above all, he loved playing football in his street, usually using the old privet hedges as goals, especially Mr Hagg's next door. He was an elderly, Welsh-speaker, who would sometimes speak `in tongues` during the Sunday morning service in the local Baptist Chapel. His hedge was the best kind of goal because it was tall, thick and wide. Unfortunately, he hated it being used for this purpose because youths would often have to go into his garden to retrieve the football, damaging his lovingly kept flowerbeds. He used to gain his revenge by letting out his vicious Welsh corgi, `Suzie,` from his house to attack the kids, who would scarper and scramble over some hedge or fence to evade her sharp teeth.

Having made some enquiries, Peter regrettably found out that none of his pals now lived in the street. He heard that several had experienced tragic deaths: one had died of a glue sniffing overdose, whilst another was crushed under a lorry after riding his racing bike along the busy nearby Cowbridge Road. Strangely, it was along the same stretch of road that another friend `committed suicide` by running in front of speeding traffic not long after he discovered he had AIDS.

However, Peter now had the opportunity of renewing his friendship with his best mate from his schooldays. They first became friends in bizarre circumstances. Ryan had newly arrived at Windsor Clive School, in Ely, from the South Wales valleys. He was ten years old. As he entered the playground for the first time, he saw a chaotic scene of kids screaming and shouting, whilst engaged in all kinds of rough play. "It was like going into the liar of the `backstreet kids,` '" Ryan used the say. Martin Lamb, (the best sportsman in the School), Stephen Flynn, (who had the blond goods looks of the late Steve McQueen) and Lee Pauling, (who had fists like mallets), came forward and told him that they were in charge around here and he had to first prove himself before he could be accepted. They then pointed to another member of the gang, Peter, who stood across the other side of the playground; at that time, he apparently presented a large, tough and imposing presence. "You have to fight Fellows over there," pointing to Peter. Ryan, terrified, then went over to Peter and told him what the other gang members had said. Peter arranged for them to meet for a fight at eleven o'clock the following day, (a Saturday), by the gate in the Half Mile Field, which was just outside the nearby village of St Fagans on the outskirts of Cardiff. They dully met and began circling each another, arms outstretched and fists clenched, in readiness to fight. After throwing several `sparring` punches they inexplicably called a truce and decided, instead of engaging in a full-blown fight, to go `catching` great crested newts in a nearby pond.

From that day onwards, they were the best of friends. They had a great time together playing `footie` and mucking about in the streets. They also had a passion for nature and often explored the nearby Vale of Glamorgan with its winding rivers, luscious meadows, mysterious woods and sultry marshland. They went fishing, searching for bird eggs, catching snakes, lizards, toads, frogs, newts, or collecting insects, which they gassed with chloroform and preserved in formaldehyde, before mounting them onto cork boards with sharp pins. (The chemicals were given to them courtesy of a local thief who had broken into a local laboratory).

He recalled one comical memory, which took place during the long summer holidays, when they were thirteen years of age. They had set out to re-visit a copse in an area of farmland near the village of Michaelston. The previous day, they had set a trap there in the hope of catching a weasel. Peter went into the tiny woodland ahead of Ryan. Upon approaching the trap, he was startled to see a weasel run out of it and then head in his direction, before sidestepping him and running between Ryan's legs. As they sat down to reflect upon having just missed out on catching the weasel, it quietly returned, seemingly oblivious of their presence. It then proceeded to grab one of her babies, who had been hiding in the grass, by the back of its neck and take it to the relative safety of a larger woodland nearby. She returned a further five times to pick up the rest of her litter.

One of his greatest regrets was having lost touch with his best pal. He remembered Ryan as an intelligent and energetic individual who was always open to new experiences. His outgoing nature, however, masked an insecurity born out of an unsettled upbringing. He often had to move with his family to a new home, as they followed their father who worked for the RAF. His dad was an old-fashioned disciplinarian who, at that time, was unable to show his son much love and affection. Moreover, his parents were often in conflict, which was exasperated by their peripatetic existence. Ryan's sensitive nature was affected by these influences and his response was to carry an inner hurt and anger.

In the evenings leading up to Ryan's performance on Friday, Peter went for a drink with his brother to the `Wanderers` on the outskirts of Ely. He would also sometimes meet his brother Martin there. He noticed that Bruce drank a lot, every night he would quietly get drunk. Peter was worried for him. He got to know Bruce a little better during those evenings but his brother still remained a very private person and would never proffer personal information about himself. He bottled up all of his worries and was unable or unwilling to revisit hurtful events from his past.

However, one evening, he accidently touched upon his brother's inner wound when he saw the pleasure and deep sadness in Bruce's face as he looked upon Martin's children, who had popped into the pub to pass on a message to their father. Peter could see in Bruce's eyes how much he missed seeing his own children growing up. When he caught Peter looking at him, he instantly knew that his brother was aware of his contrary emotions on seeing Martin's children. Peter's direct eye contact with his brother then sent him into one of his flashbacks. It was his first vision for a while, but now he had been taken off guard and had connected with his brother's pain.

Peter found himself upstairs in a snooker hall, above some take-away kebab and fish shops in Caroline Street, in Cardiff City centre. Bruce was on one of his weekend breaks from computer contract work in Marlow, in Buckinghamshire. He would spend his evenings having a good time in the City centre pubs and clubs. It was three o' clock in the morning. The place was a real dive and was frequented by some of the City's toughest characters. Peter was observing, (although he was invisible to everyone else), his brother easily beat a guy from the valleys in a game of snooker. They were playing each other for quite a large sum of money. His opponent took great offence to losing and accused Bruce of hustling him, for his brother had lost heavily to him in the earlier games they had played. However, the real reason for Bruce's improved form was due the increased levels of alcohol in his system which calmed his nerves and greatly improving his snooker skills.

Bruce, fearing serious trouble, took his £100 winnings and left straight away. Whilst waiting in a deserted taxi Rank in nearby St Mary's Street, he felt a sudden thud on the back of his head as the lad from the Valleys pummelled him from behind with his fist. Bruce fell to the ground, but as he was trying to get up to defend himself, he was met with a relentless torrent of nasty kicks and punches from the gang. Only when an approaching mini cab driver pressed his car horn continually and draw the attention of everyone nearby to the incident, did they stop and run off. Bruce lay still. He was covered in blood. Two young men, who had been watching the incident from a distance, but were too afraid to intervene, then came rushing over to help him.

It was over half an hour before Bruce was able to sit up. Meanwhile, the taxi driver who had beeped his horn had called for an ambulance and the police, who soon turned up. Bruce declined their assistance and asked the cabby to take him home. Luckily, the thugs in their excitement had forgotten to take his wallet with his winnings inside, so he could afford to pay for the taxi fare. As soon as he got back to his mother's house, he went straight up to the bathroom to clean his wounds. He placed his torn and bloodstained cashmere jumper and Saville Row shirt into a black bin liner and chucked then into the wheelie bin outside. He then washed his trousers in the sink and hung them from a hanger in his bedroom, where he crashed out to sleep.

He woke up the following day feeling aches and pains all over his body. When he caught sight of himself in the bathroom mirror, he was shocked at the number of cuts and bruises on his face and worried how he would explain them to his parents. He decided to say that he had accidently fallen heavily on a city centre pavement, having had one too many drinks. He hated lying but could not divulge the whole story as it would worry them too much.

When Peter came around from this flashback, he was shocked to have witnessed such an upsetting scene from Bruce's life. But it was reading his brothers subconscious thoughts as he lay in bed reeling from the pain of his wounds, which really distressed him. His brother felt as if he had deserved the beating as punishment for being, as he saw it, mainly responsible for the breakup of his marriage.

Peter was left utterly exhausted. He made up an excuse and quickly left the pub, leaving his brother feeling somewhat confused. Peter walked towards the blackness of the rugby pitch feeling listless and empty; it was as if a part of his soul had again been sacrificed for the `gift` of a vision. Some twisted gift he thought.

The following evening, Bruce and Peter were having a great time chilling out together until Peter changed the direction of their conversation. His vision of Bruce made him take the risk of further opening up about his own troubles in the hope that it would prompt him into talking about his own. Peter told Bruce about the sexual abuse that he had suffered as a boy at the hands of Max. Bruce was the first member of his family in Cardiff he had ever talked to about these events. Peter was extremely upset by his brother's response when he said, "it is important to get over these things you know." Peter was disappointed that his brother's intelligence did not extend to empathising with his own suffering.

Peter then broached the most sensitive subject in Bruce's life-the breakdown of his marriage. "It must have been tough getting over your spilt from Sofia?" To which Bruce sharply retorted, for Peter had touched a raw nerve to his heart, "Peter, take no offense, but I have no wish to ever *go there* thank you," whereupon he stormed out of the pub.

Chapter 13

Peter had been to the Plough and Harrow a few of times in the past; it was a lovely stone-built pub near the beautiful Glamorgan Heritage Coast, not far from Bridgend. It dated back to medieval times and lay in the grounds of a ruined ancient priory, which further enhanced its charm.

As Peter entered the main door, he was greeted by the welcoming glow from a blazing log fire, set in a huge stone fireplace. Its light lit up walls covered with rural artifacts, such as old horse harnesses, stuffed animals and split cane fly fishing rods. The public bar was crowded with what appeared to be locals and visitors from further afield who had come for the gig.

There were also a few surfing youths present who are attracted by the big winter breaks which unfold onto nearby sandy bays.

"I was absolutely *stoked*," one of them exclaimed, which meant that he had a great ride on one of the big storm waves that hit the coast that day.

Peter could see some of the members of the band setting up the equipment in the far corner of the bar - but there was no sign of Ryan. He ordered a pint of local ale and sat down in a quiet corner towards the back of the pub. A few minutes later, Ryan and another band member entered the room from a side entrance and helped the rest of the band get everything ready. Peter baulked at the sight of his old friend whom he had not seen in forty years. He looked very different from when he remembered him, although he could still make out some of his distinctive features, which gave him a mischievous `Jack Nicholson` like appearance.

He positioned himself so that several members of the audience shielded him from the band. He was anxious at the prospect of seeing his old friend again and was in two minds whether he should make a quiet exit. But before he could make his mind up, Ryan introduced the band, whilst cracking a few hilarious bawdy jokes about them. "And on the saxophone, we have Stan, who makes love to his instrument like only a man can." The audience laughed out loud.

The band consisted of a keyboard player and vocalist, (Ryan), Stevie on double bass, Digger on trumpet, Mic the percussionist, Rockabilly on electric guitar and Stan who played tenor sax.

The tracks they played were a mix of jazz, blues and ska. They sounded great to Peter and the rest of the audience. Several people got up to dance, even though there was very little space to move; they just couldn't help themselves for the music had the power of overcoming their natural restraint. One chap even climbed onto a heavy oak table to dance, only to be severely reprimanded by the harsh landlady. The pleasure he got from listening to the music and watching his mate perform, convinced Peter to stay.

Once they had played several numbers, Peter became aware of a pair of eyes staring intently in his direction-they were Ryan's!

Ryan then asked the other band members to stop playing for a moment. Then, addressing the crowd, he said "I'm sorry to interrupt the performance, but I've just caught sight of a friend I haven't seen in a very, very long time…My God! Is that *you* Peter?"

Peter stood up to acknowledge his old friend. They then tentatively walked towards each other. When they met, they formally shook hands before warmly embracing one another. Then Ryan said, "I can't believe it's *you*." Peter responded by saying, "It's great to see you again mate."

Witnessing this touching moment prompted the audience to give a resounding round of applause. Ryan then returned to the microphone to explain to the crowd that he had just seen his best mate from School for the first time in forty years. Being the professional he is, he completed the set before going back over to Peter and asking him to go the beer garden for a chat and a smoke.

They sat outside on a picnic table. It was a crisp and clear night; an Atlantic front had recently passed over, washing the land and purifying the air.

"I don't believe it! I don't believe it!" Ryan said.

"Peter, where the heck have you been?"

"It's a long story-I'll tell you all about it later. It's wonderful to see you again Ryan."

"It's great to see too mate."

"The last time we saw each other was when I came around to invite you to a party; we must have been fifteen at the time…*Jesus,* that was a long time ago."

"Let's not worry about that right now." Peter said.

Ryan then called over to the other band members to come and meet his old friend.

"Look Peter, come back to my place for a proper talk and a drink after the gig. Whatever, you do *don't disappear again.*"

Peter gave him his assurance that he would stay.

Several other band members also came around to Ryan's flat afterwards. In the noisy melee, the two old mates had little time to properly talk to each other. Once they had all left, Ryan's first question to Peter was, "where the *fuck* did you go?"

Peter replied that after their last meeting, he continued to live at Max's for a while but was too traumatised to seek out his old mate.

"What do you mean by *traumatised* Pete?"

"It was due to Max-the old guy in the house. Remember him? He fucked me up."

"Of course, I remember him. I could well believe he did something bad to you. I could tell that he had some kind of unsavoury hold on you."

"It was he that persuaded me not to go your party that night, or to seek you out later."

"Do you know, I called around a few times in the months afterwards, but you weren't in? Every time, Max tried to dissuade me from coming back again in the future. He said that it was best if I didn't come around for a while, so that you could concentrate on your studies. He made me feel guilty. So, I eventually stayed away completely."

"The *bastard*-I didn't know that," Peter replied angrily and with uncharacteristic uncouthness.

"Please accept my apologies for disappearing from your life; I just couldn't help myself-I was so disempowered."

"What happened there, Pete?"

Peter then told Ryan about the abuse and the destructive effect it had upon him later.

"I'm absolutely shocked-what an evil fucker!".

Ryan continued, "I'm extremely sorry for what happened to you but hearing this helps me to make sense of your `vanishing` from my life afterwards. I blamed myself for your not wanting to see me. I lost my way not long afterwards. After leaving school, I trained to be a quantity surveyor for a while, before leaving that job to focus on my music. Unfortunately, I also got heavily into drugs. These and the aftermath of several disastrous relationships, messed up my head."

"There's something I need to tell you," Ryan continued. "It concerns an event, which I can now see, explains what happened to you."

"What do you mean?"

"About five years after the party, I bumped into Max and Michael, who were walking near the Village of St

Georges. I was on my way to collect magic mushrooms in some nearby fields. They said you were away in Uni at the time. However, Max invited me back to his place, where we shared a few whiskies and got a little tipsy. Max and I were then alone together in the room. I then became aware of him staring intently at me. Then, all of a sudden, he dropped his trousers and underpants to reveal his erect penis and blurted out, `Please Ryan, touch me *there*, ` pointing to the underside of his."

"Although shocked, I nevertheless felt compelled by his insistent pleading to do as he asked." Peter was aware of how powerfully persuasive Max could be.

"He came straight away."

"I hope you understand Peter -I'm not gay, it was just the way he begged me. But, even to this day, I don't really know why I went through with it."

He continued: "So what happened to you now makes sense to me. The dirty old pervert."

"I can well believe Max doing that." Peter responded, before adding, "I'm sorry that we lost touch... He had so much control over me. Please accept my apologies Ryan-I need you to do that for me?"

"Look, Peter now that I know the truth, I can forgive you. But for a long time, I hated your guts for rejecting your best friend. I kept thinking, how could someone dump their best mate like that!"

Having cleared the air, they carried on chatting, laughing and joking for a few more hours. They reminisced a lot about some of the antics they got up to as kids. Resentment slowly left Ryan. The sense of lost time that had so pained Peter, lifted for a moment. They eventually fell asleep on the armchairs.

Peter stayed at Ryan's place for the rest of that weekend. They talked a lot about their lives after they lost touch with one another. Before Peter left, they exchanged telephone numbers and agreed to meet at Ryan's next gig in a few days. More importantly, they vowed never again to lose touch with each other again.

As they parted, each felt a great sense of release from having met again. This helped to lift the feeling of unresolved hurt from their shoulders. They both, however, needed the space of the next few days to help them come to terms with their sudden reunion.

Peter had another, as yet unaccomplished, aim to fulfill-tracking down Max's whereabouts. Meeting Ryan again had made him more determined than ever to find him. The sense of loss he felt from being deprived of Ryan's friendship, due to Max's manipulation and control, fired his purpose even more.

He had come up with a few new possible new areas of enquiry. One was to try and make contact with an old social services friend of Max's, George Crewkerne. However, Peter soon found out he had regrettably passed away. He remembered him as being a lovely, warm-hearted individual, a true gentleman.

Another potential lead was an artist called Lewis, who used to be a great friend of his. But he discovered that he had also sadly died a few years previously. Peter met him many times when he used to visit Max. He was an intense character, a seriousness that stemmed from feelings of inadequacy due to a poor education. He channelled this anger into his art, creating outstandingly original paintings.

The only remaining possible new line enquiry he thought of was to find Max's younger brother, Sam. But if he were alive, he would be an old man now. They had met occasionally in Canton, an inner-city district of Cardiff. He was a dustman then but must have retired a long time ago. Unfortunately, a check through a hard copy of Yellow pages and Thompsons local directory, proved to be unsuccessful, as did his online searches. Clutching at the last straw that seemed available to him, he decided to walk around the Canton shopping area in the slim hope of catching sight of him. This he did for most of the daytime hours over the next few days, but without success. Finally, late on the afternoon on Friday he decided to abandon his search there. Sam was probably dead now anyway, he thought. But as he boarded the number 13 bus, opposite Canton police station, to make his way back to Ely, he caught sight of a face on the opposite pavement which seemed familiar to him- Sam's!

Allowing for the effects of aging over the intervening years, his features still bore the unmistakable resemblance of the Sam he remembered, with its distinctive angular chin and high cheekbones. However, age had left its indelible mark in the wrinkles and dark sunken canyons on his face. But Peter was certain that it was him.

When the bus stopped at some traffic lights, Peter politely asked the driver if he would open the doors. The driver replied with a rude response, "Who do you think I am, a bleeding taxi driver!" He was no doubt used to having to deal firmly with the troublesome youths who board the bus on this notorious route to the Ely council estate. Peter, in desperation, pulled the emergency exit cord for the doors and left the bus. There was no way that he would let this of opportunity of finding Max slip by. He ran across the busy high road, almost getting run over by the passing cars as he did so. "I'm going to report you! I've got your face recorded on video," the irate bus driver shouted at him. "This is a *fucking* emergency!" Peter shouted back at the top of his voice.

"Excuse me…excuse me!" Peter called out towards the figure walking away from him. The person turned around, he could see at once that it was Max's brother.

"Are you Max's brother?"

The man stopped and looked Peter up and down, as if vetting him.

"Yes, I am. Who are you, may I ask? And why did you mention my brother's name?"

"Well, I have been trying to find him. I don't know if you remember me, but I am Michael's brother-we used to live together in Max's house in Sevenoaks Road?"

Sam took a closer look at Peter's face before replying: "Yes, you do look familiar; I remember seeing you with Max and Michael many years ago."

"I have been living in London for a long time and have come back to stay at my mother's house in Ely and try to reacquaint myself with my old friends, Max being one of them, although I haven't seen him for many years. Do you know where he is living now?"

"Couldn't you find that out from Michael?"

"He has disappeared from Cardiff. No one knows where he now lives. We think he is living somewhere in Italy, but we have no idea where exactly."

"It's a shame that you can't find him-he was a lovely guy. Max taught him how to write didn't he? He became a gifted playwright if I'm not mistaken." Sam clearly had fond memories of meeting Michael.

Sam continued, "Yes, I do know where he is. He is living in an old people's home near Pontypridd, called Bethlam Retirement Home. I'm sure he'll be glad to see you, he doesn't get many visitors now. He is very old you know-you might be surprised by his appearance when you see him. I have to be honest with you, I rarely see him much myself these days."

"How is he?"

"Well, for a very old man, he's doing quite well physically, although he can only walk unaided for a short distance. Mentally, he fluctuates-sometimes he seems lost in another world, where no one can get through to him, and at other times he's as sharp as a button!"

Sam then gave him a card with the address and telephone number of the retirement home on it.

"Promise me that you will see him soon and tell him that Sam says hello."

"I promise… I can't thank you enough for your help."

"It's a pleasure helping someone as nice as yourself. I remember you now-you were a pleasant young man… I can see that you have grown up to be a decent fellow as well." Peter was touched by his sentiment.

They bid their farewells and went they separate ways, probably never to see each other again. The thought of this likely eventuality, having only just met Sam again for the first time in forty years, pained his heart. Life's fleeting connections with simple honest people, such as Sam, is a tragic lost opportunity we all share. Sam, although he was the rejected bastard child of one of his father's many dalliances, nevertheless had developed into a special human being.

As he departed, Peter could barely contain his excitement in having finally discovered Max's whereabouts.

When he returned to his mother's home, he retreated to his bedroom to collect his thoughts. He did not want to make a rash decision and do something he would regret. He stayed there for so long that his brother and mother knocked on his door several times to ask him how he was.

Peter eventually fell asleep, with the correct course of action to take regarding Max, unresolved in his mind. However, when he woke up the following morning, he knew with certainty what he had to do. He would seek out Max, gain his trust and when the right opportunity came, kidnap and murder him.

Chapter 14

It only took a few seconds for Peter to track down the location of the retirement home using Google Earth. He found out from Wikipedia that it was built on the site of an old mental asylum called Bedlam and was later re-named Bethlam Retirement Home in remembrance of its former name and because of the Christian link with Bethlehem. However, Peter could not understand why someone would want to retain the memory of an old lunatic asylum in its name.

He stayed indoors all day on Sunday, chatting with his mother and brother. He also helped with the cooking and cleaning. His intention was to allay any worries they had about him before his visit to Max.

The following morning, he headed for Pontypridd.

He had a little difficulty in finding Bethlam, which was situated on its own at the base of a bleak hillside just outside the eastern part of Pontypridd, a town famous for being the birth place of Tom Jones.

"Hello," Peter said politely to the young receptionist, Sarah, judging by her lapel name badge. "I was wondering whether you had a Max Cameron staying with you. I am an old friend of his and I'd like to pay him a visit, if that's OK?"

"Yes, we do," she replied straight away, without even checking the books. "Would you like to see him now?"

Peter had not counted on the immediacy of seeing Max and had to brace himself before replying that he would like that very much.

"Who shall I say is visiting?"

"Peter Fellows," he replied nervously. "Would you please remind him that I used to live with him in his house in Ely, along with my brother Michael."

"Would you mind taking a seat whilst I ask one of the staff to go and tell him he has a new visitor?"

Peter waited for what seemed like an unduly long time; he wondered if Max was in a state of shock on hearing his name and was pondering on whether or not he should see him. Or perhaps he was in one of the absent states of mind Sam referred to and could not remember his name at all.

Whilst waiting, he looked around the Home. It was a large building probably built in the nineteen sixties judging by its drab modernist yellow brick design, aluminum framed windows and the antiseptic nature of its interior design. He thought the place had a depressing feel about it and wondered if the elderly people living there felt the same. The dark concrete inner courtyard with its large potted plants struggling to grasp the meagre light, only added to this gloom.

The staff member, Lucy, who Sarah had sent to inform Max of his new caller, returned some ten minutes later. The receptionist then beckoned Peter over to the counter.

"I'm sorry to say that he says he can't remember your name. Isn't that right, Lucy?"

"Becky, the duty assistant, said he seemed to be in one of his blank moods today, but that it would still be alright for you to see him," Lucy replied.

"Excellent," Sarah responded. "Lucy would you be so kind and take Mr Fellows to see Max?"

As Lucy walked him along the corridor, the powerful odour of stale urine and the unpleasant waft of floors having been cleaned with a dirty mop, filled his nostrils.

There was also the residual smell of hospital food in the air. She led him to a small lounge where several elderly people were seated quietly. He caught sight of Max sitting in a Derbyshire armchair, similar to his favourite seat in his old Ely home. He was looking at a copy of the "Racing Post."

Peter was so apprehensive he could barely breathe and think properly; he feared his nervousness might betray his true intentions.

"Hello Max. I'm Peter. Do you remember me? I lived with you and my brother Michael in Ely for a while, when I was a boy."

Max looked straight at him. The demeanor of his face changed in that moment of first contact, as the blood left his cheeks and his face dropped. Peter knew he recognised him.

"Of course, I do…how could I forget. I helped you with your studies, as I recall." Max replied coherently, having clearly come out of his mental torpor.

"It's so nice to see you again Max. You helped me to catch up a lot…I'm a scientist now."

"Isn't that wonderful," Max replied with pride, his face regaining some of its lost colour. "I knew you would do well one day-I could see that bright spark in you-well done son."

Peter remembered that he used to address Michael and himself as his sons, no doubt because he had abandoned his own after a disastrous relationship with a famous, alcoholic, actress.

They talked for an hour or so, until Lucy kindly brought them some tea and cakes. Little of his old wit and sharpness had deserted him-this was remarkable for a man of his age. Peter realised he must still remember everything he did to him; he wondered if he felt any remorse for what he had done but doubted whether he did. Max's retention of his mental agility and memory reassured him, for he needed him to recall what he had done…when the right time came for him to exact his revenge.

After their tea break, they resumed talking and didn't stop until the duty assistant interrupted them when it was time for Max's lunch. Peter then left, after agreeing to Max's earnest request that he come back to see him very soon, "Please…in a couple of days." Peter could see he was very lonely old man, who cherished any visitors, even those he had done harm to in the distant past.

Peter, kept his promise and came back two days later. This time, he was taken directly to Max's room on the ground floor. It had French window-like fire escape doors overlooking a large expanse of garden, now barren of colour, except for several evergreen trees and shrubs.

He visited Bethlam once more that week. It was a clear, warm winters day. Max did most of the talking, as he had done in the past, often reminiscing about his childhood and his days as a young man in Cardiff. He reminded Peter of his school teaching days in Wood Street School in the City Centre. It was based in an old Victorian building, which later became the headquarters of the Cardiff Bus Company, before it was demolished. He loved his time as a teacher there. As he spoke, Peter carefully planned how he would carry out his act of `justifiable` homicide.

When Peter suggested they go for a walk in the gardens, Max eagerly agreed. "I'll just check to see if it's alright with the Becky," Peter said…to which she duly agreed after giving him an overcoat to keep Max warm. She opened up his foldable lightweight wheel chair, (upon which she placed a blanket), suggesting that Peter take this in case Max got tired along the way and needed some rest.

That evening, he finalised the details of his plan to kidnap Max. He made a list of items he would need: camcorder, tripod, spare batteries, torch, binding cord, disposable gloves, cardboard, some old shoes, an overcoat and a pair of baggy trousers. He would also need to use Max's lightweight foldable wheelchair and blanket.

Peter intended to abduct Max and drive him about ten miles to a car park on the top of a beauty spot called Caerphilly Mountain. It wasn't really a mountain as such, but a rounded hilltop about fifteen hundred feet in height, covered in bracken and gorse. He guessed that lovers in their cars would sometimes visit it in the warmer summer months but hoped that it would now be deserted in wintertime. However, love was the furthest emotion from his mind. His aim was to make Max confess to his crimes onto a camcorder and leave him naked to die of exposure on the hill top; he surely wouldn't last for more than a few hours there he thought. This way his death would, all being well, not arouse too many suspicions. However, once his body was discovered and the cause of death established, hopefully, by natural causes, the police would still need to know how Max ended up on the top of Caerphilly Mountain. Luckily, Peter had heard from one of the staff at Bethlam that Max would sometimes leave the building by himself, often at night, to catch a bus to some random place miles away before being rescued and taken back. Peter knew that there was a regular bus service that stopped outside the Home that went over the high pass near the top of the `Mountain. ` With this information in mind, and as long as he did not leave any physical evidence behind, he believed that he would not be caught. There was, though, the real possibility that he would be interviewed by the police because he had been a frequent recent visitor to Max. He would have to prepare himself for this eventuality.

That weekend he gathered all of the items he would need to carry out his plot.

Early on Tuesday morning, he woke up to the sound of the local Dragon Radio Station reporting that a bitterly cold Arctic front was due to hit South Wales the next day. The night time temperatures would fall to well below freezing and the cold spell would last for four or five days. He knew that this was the right time to carry out his plan, for he might never have such an opportunity again, especially with spring not too far away.

He visited Max again the following morning and took him for a short walk in the gardens. He could just about manage to walk unaided without the use of his wheelchair. Peter could feel the sudden drop in air temperature, which signaled the onset of the approaching cold front. On their return, he carefully placed a piece of cardboard between the lock of the French doors as he closed them behind him. As he drove back to Cardiff, he felt a nervous euphoria now that his plan was beginning to unfold.

At midnight, he put the items he would need into a rucksack, silently left his mother's home and drove to Pontypridd. He parked in a quiet lay-by, around the corner from Bethlam. It was bitterly cold. He got out of the car and speedily put on some old baggy trousers over his inner pair, a pair of old boots, an overcoat and some disposable gloves. He returned to his car seat to calm himself down in readiness for the abduction.

Peter remained there for two hours, wracked with indecision. Eventually, it dawned on him that there was no way that he could go through with his plan. He was no murderer, even if Max's death was justified. Despite his burning need to fulfill his `destiny` to confront and bring closure on his past, first intimated to him by the Biko and `confirmed` by the `Eskimo` vagrant, he was unable to follow through with his perceived means of bringing this about. Peter was devastated, for he could see no way, other than by ending Max's life, that would release him from emotional slavery.

A feeling of doom slowly and inexorably descended upon him, like a black fog that moves inland along the creeks and inlets of an estuarine shore, bathing the landscape of his being with despair and strangling his soul.

The events of the last few weeks and months hit home hard. They had disturbed a part of him that he had kept hidden for a long time, for he had been unable to resolve the terrible feelings that stemmed from his sexual abuse at the hands of Max. He had avoided `going there, ` to face the feelings, for over forty years. He was still really a frightened little boy who had his innocence stolen from him.

The drinking, the gambling, the isolation, were all ways of blocking out the pain these feelings aroused. But now, they re-surfaced in his conscious mind and shook him to the core. The visitations of Max's abuse and those of Alice's past had opened up the wound and made it raw. It hurt so badly, it felt as if it had been released from its ethereal domicile and made physical. It was like a beating heart that was having its blood squeezed from it by some dark mysterious force.

He reflected deeply for the first time in his life on all the things he had lost: the friendship of his best friend, the loss of close contact with his parents, brothers and sisters in Cardiff, lost romantic relationships. There was no way he could reinvent the past and make up for this lost time.

The grief he now felt was devastating. It was as if it had imperceptibly accumulated behind the walls of a great dam and was all of a sudden released.

Peter retreated to his room for the next two days, emerging only briefly, when there was no one else around, to grab some food and water. Bruce and his mother were concerned for his mental state. But when they ventured to knock on his door to enquire upon his welfare, he somehow managed to placate their anxieties about him.

He just wanted to remain alone with his `stuff. `

When he finally cleared his mind, he knew exactly what he had to do. The only way he could be released from his suffering would be to end his life. He had made a promise himself to do this if he was unable to go through with taking

Max's life. He was now convinced of this action. But how? He was too much of a coward to cut his wrists with a sharp instrument and was unsure if an overdose of tablets would succeed- he had no wish to survive with his insides permanently damaged.

He thought about leaping off the nearby Wenvoe Transmissions Station mast which overlooked Cardiff from the west. But when he finally left his room to drive there, he ruled this out because of the formidable barbed wire fences surrounding its base.

After careful thought, he made a decision to drive to the nearby coastal town of Penarth later that night and jump off its pier to be taken away by its receding waters. The force of the Severn estuary tide, the second most powerful in the world, would quickly take him out to sea where the effects of the freezing water would soon close down his bodily systems, leading to a swift death.

He would inform his mother and Bruce that he planned to go fishing off the pier that evening. They knew he was a keen sea fisherman and would hopefully believe his death to be an accident.

A quick check in the South Wales sea fisherman's `Bible, ` the *Gary Evans Tide Timetable*, showed the high tide would turn just after midnight, which would be perfect for his plans.

Over dinner that evening, Peter engaged in friendly conversation with his mother and brother. He wanted them to have no suspicions that he might do something so drastic as to take his own life. When he told them of his intention to go sea fishing later that night, they were surprised and a little concerned because of his recent reclusive behavior. But their fears were somewhat placated when he explained that he needed the fresh air to clear his head. When they had both retired to bed, he collected his sea fishing gear, some frozen mackerel from the freezer to use as bait and headed for Penarth.

Peter started fishing from the end of the pier at just after midnight. Several anglers were already there watching their rods with the light from the old lamplights which also illuminated the wooden entertainment buildings that straddled this classic fossilised Victorian edifice. He would have to wait until they had all left before jumping to his death, for he wanted to die alone, without any chance being rescued.

It was not until two in the morning that the last fisherman had left. There was silence all around. The air was still. The waters of the sea beneath were calm. Even the usually frenetic and chatty seagulls were now perched quietly on the electrical cables that bridged the ornate cast iron lampposts.

It felt like a good time to die he thought, alone in the universe, with no answer as to why he was here. No meaning to the universe, just existence, then no existence. He had paradoxically discovered the falsehood of these assertions through his God Field theory, but he just wouldn't let himself accept its divine implications. He also still refused to accept that the sound he heard in the computer room in Imperial was God's voice. `For why would God communicate with someone like me? Because I discovered the God Field? I cannot accept that. How dare I have the temerity and arrogance to think I had revealed the ultimate divine meaning of the universe and would be blessed with hearing `His` voice? ...*fool.* `

He inhaled a deep breath of the bracing sea air, then climbed onto the metal railing at the end of the pier and held onto to its outer most lamppost. Its light shone like a beacon, a calling card to an absent God. "Dear Lord, please show yourself to me," he cried out pathetically.

But God, who was watching, did not answer. He was saddened to see that the first person on Earth to have discovered `His` God Field was about to end his life. It pained him to have to witness this, for he knew that Peter's redemption was near, if he would only stay alive.

However, although God could have directly intervened in Peter's case to save him, because his discovery of the God Field had entwined him in its creative process, he held back. This was because he knew that a synchronous event was unfolding from the God Field, which he hoped would result in him not going through with his intention of killing himself.

Peter could see the exposed seaweed, algae, sea urchin and limpet encrusted iron pier supports below. Life's tentacles endeavor to holdfast everywhere, he thought. He then said a short silent prayer, wishing all of his family and friends long, happy and healthy lives. He said one final prayer to Alice wishing her love and happiness-his last words were "Alice, I think I love you." Peter was fully aware of the irony in praying to a personal God he still could not believe in. He then steadied himself in readiness to jump.

"Don't...don't do that!" came a loud, aggressive call from a male voice from some unseen place behind him.

This was followed by a polite, "I would very much appreciate it if you would refrain from jumping."

Peter peered closely towards a dimly lit area of sheltered seating nearby. An old man emerged, his face now revealed by the pier lights. He then said in an almost scolding voice, "You *must not* do that! If you come down now, I will tell you why."

The contrasting rebukes and polite request had the desired effect of momentarily taking Peter's attention away from leaping off the edge of the pier.

Neither person said a word to each other for a few minutes. The old man then sat down on a nearby classic, curved backed, Victorian bench.

After a short while, Peter began to climb down from the fence. As he did so, the old man immediately got up from his seat, rushed over, firmly grabbed a hold of his arm and led him to the bench.

They both sat in absolute silence for ten minutes. The old man was wondering if he shouldn't have interfered in Peter`s imminent suicide attempt. Peter sat beside him in a state of abject confusion. The old man then brought out a flask from his ruck sack and proceeded to pour a hot cup of coffee from a flask and offer it to him, along with a chocolate digestive biscuit. Peter hesitantly accepted his offerings.

When Peter had finished his drink, the old man said assertively, "let's go for a walk." They then made their way along the pier and onto the deserted promenade of Penarth sea front.

The old man then said, "Do you see that church on the hill up there?" He said, pointing to a large, floodlit, Victorian church overlooking the small town beneath.

"If you look closely enough, you can just about make out a graveyard-that is where my son, Stefan and my daughter, Hayley are buried. They were nine and ten years old when they died. That was thirty-five years ago."

Peter then spoke his first words to the old man. "I'm sorry to hear that."

"One night, before I left the house to go to the pub, I accidently dropped the burning stub of my joint down the side of the settee. I was a heavy cannabis smoker at the time. The settee and house then caught fire and my children died from inhaling the poisonous fumes."

"I'm very sorry," Peter soulfully repeated.

"What is your name by the way?"

"Peter Fellows."

"I'm Sterling Reed. It's a pleasure to meet you Peter."

"Likewise, Sterling."

"Look Peter, as you can well understand, I rightly blamed myself for what happened and went on a downward spiral of drink and drugs for many years afterwards. My wife could not take any more of my self-pity and finally kicked me out of the house. I eventually saw that the only way to end my pain was to kill myself, for I could not deal with the guilt and shame anymore. Like yourself, I choose Penarth Pier as the place to end my life. I waited for one late winter's night with an outgoing tide that would take me out to sea."

"Yes, you're right, that was my thinking too…Do you mind telling me what stopped you from killing yourself?"

"Love! Love for my wife, Grace. As I stood in the same place as yourself, looking out to the sea, I knew I couldn't go ahead with it. I suddenly saw how selfish I had become. I realised that I had to help her, especially as she had recently been diagnosed with bowel cancer. I could not leave her alone. Therefore, I left the pier that night with a mission to support her and try to reawaken the love that we had once felt for one another. Every year since, I return to this same place and thank God that I did not go ahead with killing myself. Tonight, is the thirtieth anniversary of my thwarted suicide attempt; any other night and there would have been nobody here to save you-you would be dead by now. But that is what you wanted isn't it, to die alone?"

Peter didn't reply to his question but instead asked Sterling what happened after he put off his suicide bid.

"I went back to my wife and persuaded her to accompany me to the graveyard, for neither of us had been there for many years because we found the experience too painful to bear. After paying our respects to our diseased children, we proceeded to argue and shout at each other. All the pent up hurt and regret we had kept inside us came flooding out. Afterwards, we sat down on a battered old wooden bench in the churchyard, exhausted. I then asked her if she would give me one more chance. I promised I would not let her down and if things did turn bad again, we would separate for good. Well, she did take me back and we have lived together happily ever since. And, against all the odds, after two years of chemo and radio therapy, she defeated the cancer for good, (fingers crossed). We went on to have two lovely daughters afterwards."

"Do you know, the most special thing of all was that we rekindled our romantic love for one another. It was amazing, the feelings we began to feel for each other were wonderful. We are still madly in love to this day."

"I feel I now owe it to you Sterling to tell you my own story."

"Please don't be offended, but I would rather you didn't."

"All that I ask is that you give life one more chance, understand what is destroying you and let your heart be open to love."

"I'm very sorry Peter, I have to go; my wife will be worrying herself sick about me. Thank you for not jumping and listening to my story. It is now up to you whether or not you go back to the pier. But may I say that it was a real pleasure meeting you…goodbye and good luck."

"Goodbye Sterling…thank you so much."

Peter watched him disappear into the distance. He then headed straight back to the pier. His purpose this time, however, was not to end his life but to collect his fishing tackle.

He knew exactly what he had to do to end his suffering- to follow through with his intention of ending Max's life.

Peter picked up his fishing tackle and drove back to Ely.

The following day was still in the grip of the cold spell. He eagerly awaited the nighttime when he could finally fulfill his plan.

Chapter 15

Peter double checked that he had all the items he would need for Max's abduction in his rucksack. Then, precisely at midnight, when his mother and Bruce were asleep, he silently left the house and drove quickly back to Bethlam, where he again parked the car out of sight. He got out and once more put on a change of clothes and a pair of disposable gloves. It was bitterly cold. This time, without hesitation, he stealthily walked through the gap in the hedge into the grounds until he came to the back of Max's room. He carefully pulled the French doors open. The piece of cardboard fell to the ground. He turned on the torch, walked over to Max and placed a piece of duct tape over his mouth. Max stirred violently on the bed as Peter wrapped his hands and legs together with some cord. He then lifted him into his wheelchair and exited the French doors, placing the piece of cardboard between them as he did so. He calmly wheeled him across the gardens, placed him in the back seat of his car, folded up the wheelchair and placed it in the boot.

The journey to Caerphilly Mountain was uneventful except for the flashing lights and noisy siren of a passing police car, which he thought for one moment, was pursuing him, but luckily carried on speeding past. He noticed the two officers laughing in the front seat as they went by.

He pulled up in the deserted car park whereupon he set up the wheelchair and lifted Max into it. It was very dark, the moon a thin crescent. The stars were there to greet him again, shining in all their blazing glory, like diamonds in the sky. The lights of Caerphilly town glistened in the distance.

Peter then untied the cord from Max's hands and feet and bound them to the arms and legs of the wheelchair. "Max, do not scream or shout when I remove the tape from your mouth, otherwise I will push you off the hill. *Make no mistake-I will do it.* No one will hear your cries up here anyway." Peter carefully removed the tape; Max gasped for breath, but said nothing, terrified for his life.

He pushed him to a nearby bench and sat down.

They were alone, just two lost souls on a desolate hillside, bracing themselves from the icy wind.

After a prolonged silence, Peter said, "You know why I have taken you here Max, don't you?"

"No, I haven't fucking clue. What the hell are you doing kidnapping an old man and bringing him out here in the middle of this freezing night…you must be crazy! What's wrong with you?" Peter saw at once that this was Max's belligerent way of trying to reclaim the power of the situation; he was an expert at that.

"One more loud noise from you and I swear to God you will go down the hill." As he said this, he pushed the wheelchair to the top of a steep ledge with a dark chasm looming below.

"Down there!" exclaimed, pointing to the sheer drop.

Max remained silent, visibly traumatised by the ordeal. He showed his great age and looked pitiful. Peter had to fight off any sentiment, however, for he had taken him there with a purpose to fulfill.

"What do you want? I knew you were up to something, why else would you visit me?"

"Have you forgotten what you did to me?Your sick actions ruined my life…you evil fucking man!"

Max remained silent, petrified that Peter's seething anger would make him push him over the precipice to his death.

"This is the deal Max-either you confess the full truth of your abuse to me, or I will leave you out here all night long to freeze to death. Don't worry, I'll be OK; your death will be determined to be from natural causes and although the police might suspect foul play, they will have no evidence to prove it. They will just put it down to one of your occasional `escapes` from Bethlam. I'll give you three hours maximum before you perish in this cold. Do you know, it is minus ten tonight? Either way, I will have my revenge, but for you, the only way you can survive is by talking into the video camera and telling the whole truth."

"I'll take my chances; if I can survive being shot down and living with painful shrapnel in my spine, I can get through this night." Max responded in a typically defiant tone, for he possessed, like so many people who have done bad deeds, a powerful personality. He remembered that Max had lied about to his age to join the RAF when he was sixteen. He became a rear gunner on a Lancaster Bomber before it was hit by a German fighter plane whilst flying over the English Channel and crash landed in a field in Kent. He tragically saw his best friends face ripped apart next to him. Max miraculously survived but was left with shrapnel in his back.

Peter was determined, however, not to let himself feel sorry for him, no matter what he said.

"But you won't stay alive for long when I remove all of your clothes." Peter said in a calm voice.

Max knew he was defeated but decided to play for more time in the hope that someone might pull up into the car park and discover them. However, unknown to them, this might have been a real possibility a few weeks previously because it had become a regular `dogging` hangout until the police `busted` it and made several arrests. Hardly anyone now came to the car park at night, except the occasional police patrol car looking for `doggers. `

Peter put his rucksack on his shoulder and a blanket on the back of the wheelchair. He then pushed Max along a narrow tarmac path which led to a more remote area of higher ground about two hundred yards away. He unbound the cord from Max's arms and legs and removed his clothes, leaving him wearing only a vest, underpants and socks. He was too frail to put up much resistance. He then carried him to a nearby park bench.

A stalemate then ensued. Neither spoke. An hour slowly passed by. Max was visibly shaking. Another hour went by. Max then curled up naked in a fetus-like position on the bench, sobbing quietly at first, then uncontrollably.

A further hour elapsed. Max was now motionless on the bench. Peter thought that he might be close to death for it was so bitterly cold, but he was determined to wait.

Eventually, a muffled exclamation came from Max. "All right, all right…*stop*. I will tell you everything." Max knew that Peter was for real and would have let him die out there unless he admitted the truth.

"Everything?" Peter enquired.

"All of it."

Peter untied the constraints, put his clothes back on and lifted him back to the wheelchair. He then wrapped the blanket around him and pushed him close to a nearby lamppost which overlooked the car park below. He set up the camcorder on its tripod and carefully positioned it to get a clear view of Max in its viewfinder.

He told Max to state his full name, age, place of birth and that he is about to give a full and honest confession, made without duress, to the camcorder He positioned it so that the lamplight lit up his face and the background was completely dark so that no one would recognise where it was filmed. He then switched on the camcorder.

Max began, "My name is Max Cameron. I am eighty-six years old. I was born in Canton in Cardiff. What follows is a full and honest confession made of my own free will and without duress." He then added, "This is the complete truth."

Peter noted that Max had added `made of my own free will` and `this is the complete truth, ` without being prompted; this could only add to the validity of his statement.

Max then gave a full account of his sexual abuse of Peter; it lasted an hour until Peter was content. He had covered every main detail.

Peter turned the recorder off and placed it carefully, along with the folded down tripod, into his rucksack.

"Well Max, you finally did it. How do you feel-are you by any chance sorry for what you did, sorry for ruining my life! Well speak up!" he said threateningly.

"I'm so sorry Peter-I couldn't help myself-I had this demon inside me; I had this overwhelming need to pursue young boys for my sexual pleasure. *I beg you* to please forgive me."

"Well Max, your suffering isn't over yet. I'm afraid I lied to you before." He took away his blanket and proceeded to remove all of his clothes, leaving him completely naked. This time, Max resisted with all of his might but to no avail for he was old and weak.

"What are you doing? What are you doing Peter…you promised?"

"As I said, I lied to you. I had no intention of taking you back to Bethlam; I always meant to leave you out here to die. Even this is nothing compared to the suffering you caused me."

Peter placed his clothes and blanket on the wheelchair. He then carried Max back to the wooden bench. He expected him to plead for his life but instead there was an air of acceptance in his face. Neither did he call out to Peter as he pushed the empty wheel chair down the path with Max's clothes, his rucksack and the blanket on it. Along the way, he carefully scattered his clothes onto some bushes, making it look as if they came off Max when he got lost. When he reached his car, he folded up the wheelchair and placed in the boot along with the rucksack. He chucked the blanket onto the back seat. It was three o'clock in the morning. He looked up the hill to where he had left Max and could just about make out his still form on the bench near the lamppost.

Peter calmly drove away. Max would not have long to go now-perhaps an hour or two at most. Peter felt nothing, not even the glimmer of a sense of release, not even any guilt.

He drove his MG back in the direction of Cardiff before taking the turning for Ely. But as he approached the council estate he inexplicably took a road leading in the opposite direction and headed for the Vale of Glamorgan. After a few miles, he pulled up in a lay-by between a river and a railway line just outside of the ancient village of St Georges.

He sat back and reflected upon his actions. He had just left an evil old man to die. `But why do I feel nothing? ` He said to himself. The closure he had expected had not happened. `Why do I not feel any sense of release …Why? …Why do I just feel an emptiness inside? `

Peter questioned whether he had make a mistake in `killing` Max.

His mind wandered to remembering Jacob Bronowski in the famous BBC series *The Ascent of Man*, when he was filming in Auschwitz, where many members of his family had perished. He visualised the heart-rending scene when Bronowski knelt down and placed his hand into the rain sodden ground to pick up a handful of the burnt ash remains of those incinerated in the nearby crematorium. He then said the most moving words, as he addressed all those who have power over other human beings.

"I beseech you in the bowels of Christ to think that you may be mistaken."

`What does this mean for me? ` Peter wondered.

For some reason he then leant over to the back of the seat to pick up the blanket he used to cover Max. As he did so, a silver locket fell to the floor. Peter turned on the dashboard light to look at it more closely. He opened the locket to see a picture of Max's estranged son Benjamin; he must have been about fifteen. Peter recognised the resemblance for they were uncannily alike. Max must have held it in his hand as he waited for his fate on the hillside.

As he closed the locket he was suddenly taken over by the `process` again and could see Max when he was a young man, perhaps in his early twenties. He was driving an open topped sports car. (Peter was looking down from above the moving vehicle, as if he were in a `flying` dream). His wife was sitting next to him with a young baby in her arms. They had been married for two years. They were fiercely arguing with one another, as they had been doing more and more often recently. They always argued over the same subject matter-Max's addictive gambling. He had just been to the Cheltenham Festival and had lost a substantial amount of the money he had recently inherited from a rich relation in South Africa. Their squabbling became so intense that Max lost concentration, veered the car to the other side of the road and crashed head on into a fast approaching car. His wife and child were killed instantly. Max and the passengers in the other vehicle, walked away relatively unharmed. Although he escaped physical harm, Max was to suffer mental and emotional scars from this accident for the rest of his life.

Peter came around from this regressive vision feeling beaten and exhausted.

He knew straightaway what this meant-he had to go back and save Max. Dr. Bronowski's profound message was a carrion call for human beings to show humanity and refrain from carrying out an act of cruelty, even though they may feel justified in what they were about to do. The vision of Max's past gave him an insight into the anguish he had experienced as a young man and although this did not absolve him of his paedophile crimes later on, it stirred in Peter feelings of empathy and forgiveness. Peter had to show compassion and save him, just like the mystery person in the Buddhist retreat allegory, who gave lifesaving gifts of food and water to the outcast pregnant young Turkish girl.

It might not be too late for Peter to do something... he hoped. But time was now of the essence, for Max may have already died of hyperthermia.

He drove frantically along the M4 and then along the connecting road to Caerphilly Mountain. The same policemen as before, saw him speeding past, but for some reason did nothing. His car came to a screeching halt in the car park. He was sweating profusely with anxiety. He then ran up the hill. But there was no sign of Max. Grabbing the torch from his pocket, he walked around the hilltop looking for him, but without success. He then ventured through the dense bracken in the lee of the hill until he caught sight of a white figure lying on the ground ahead of him-it was Max. His naked and lifeless form resembled that of a concentration camp victim. Max had walked quite a distance, strangely in the direction away from the car park and his possible rescue there. `Did he want to die? `Peter wondered.

Peter crouched down, fearing the worst; he held Max's pulse. He could only detect a faint murmur. But he was still alive. He ran back down the hill to the car to get the wheelchair and blanket. As he ran back up, he retrieved Max's clothes from the bushes. He then quickly, but with great difficulty, for Max was lifeless, put his clothes back on and wrapped the blanket around him. He then vigorously rubbed his hands and feet in an effort to revive his circulation. He opened the wheelchair, placed Max's fragile body into it and covered him with the blanket. He then pushed it at a frenetic pace down the hill to his car. He then felt his pulse again-it had not improved.

He then drove like a maniac to a nearby all-night McDonalds and parked the car in a remote part of the car park. He purchased a cup of tea, hamburger and fries. He put the hot cup to Max's mouth but he did not respond. However, after several minutes, he partially opened his lips and drank a few sips. After a while, he ate some of the chips. Max gradually replenished his energies and slowly but surely came around, murmuring the words "I'm sorry…please forgive me Peter."

Peter then drove back to the care home where he carefully lifted Max into the wheelchair and pushed him back to the outside of his room where he pulled open the French doors, releasing the piece of cardboard. He laid Max on the bed, changed him into his pajamas and pulled the sheets and blanket over him. He was fast asleep, but he now felt warmer and his pulse was beating much more strongly than before. On his way out, Peter picked up the piece of cardboard and placed it in his back pocket before closing the doors behind him. He then went back to his car and changed back into normal clothes.

It was as if nothing had happened that night-the only people who knew what had befallen were Max and himself. He very much doubted that Max would ever tell anyone what had taken place because of the risk of his evil past being exposed. He would then be left hoping that Peter would not make his film confession public.

God and Petra had been observing this all along. Petra collected the precious psychic energy of Peter's compassion and forgiveness of Max.

Peter headed back to Ely but again took the detour to the lay-by in St Georges village. The events of that evening had taken its toll on his fragile spirit. Furthermore, the vision he had of Max' s past had tapped into his last vestiges of energy. Every vision, whether of himself, Alice, Alice's mother, Ryan, Bruce, and Max had depleted him further.

However, he still felt nothing now he had spared Max; the closure that he had hoped for, still eluded him. He now had no choice- this time he would go through with his previous intention of killing himself. Sterling's reasons for living were not for him.

His mind was made up-he would end his life that night. However, rather than drive to Penarth and jump off its pier into the cold sea, he decided to leap to his death from the top of the nearby Wenvoe Telecommunications Station mast. He could see its very tall frame lit up on the top of the hill less than a mile away. It was now six o' clock in the morning; there would still be time for him to go through with his intention before daybreak.

He then drove to the mast and parked in a dark corner of the car park, out of sight of the security cameras, which overlooked the main gate. A strange blackness surrounded the car. Even though it lacked any physical form; it was like an unearthly being. God, who was next to him in the car, knew that it was the negative effect on the God Field of Peter's aim of killing himself. Petra, God's beloved assistant, who sat in the back seat of the car, could also feel this shadowy interaction.

The communications tower was nearly nine hundred feet in height and its position on top of a hill gave it a prominent position overlooking Cardiff. It transmitted radio and television signals. It was unmanned and relied on tall fences, security cameras and regular patrols to prevent unwanted intruders. Peter did recall, though, how one local farmer, a well-known local character, nicknamed Blackbeard, had somehow managed to circumvent its defences and jump to his death from the top of the mast. Apparently, he had just lost his farm to debt collectors. A strange note was found in his pocket afterwards, which read, "The true countryside is now dead, like me. I love you Zina. Please forgive me."

Peter would have to scale a razor sharp topped outer fence and an inner one surrounding the spiral staircase leading to the top of the mast. He also had the problem of a security camera by the outside gate to deal with; he didn't want to be seen on camera and his suicide attempt subsequently thwarted by security guards. He wondered how he could circumvent these obstacles? His solution involved using a small old carpet he found dumped on the edge of the car park and the blanket from the car

Without a moment's hesitation he walked over to the main gate, climbed it from the blindside of the security camera and covered it with the blanket. He then went back to the car and pulled it up alongside the gate before retrieving the carpet. He climbed onto the top of the car roof and covered the top of the fence with the carpet. He then managed to straddle the fence using the carpet and scrambling down the other side, pulling the carpet down after him, He then scaled the shorter interior fence and covered the top with the carpet before climbing down the other side. He was amazed his plan had worked.

Peter then began ascending the tightly twisting staircase. It was an exhausting ordeal; he had to take several breaks along the way until he finally made it to the top. Once he had recovered for a few minutes from his exertions, he looked out towards the lights of Cardiff in the distance; they shimmered like a pulsating life force. He then looked up at the heavens, which were cloudless and full of stars. "Hello again, my fellow travellers," he said in a gentle tone. He walked to the edge of the fence that overlooked the ground beneath-he would have an uninterrupted fall. He then climbed on top of it and sat down with his legs dangling over the edge. He did not look down again for fear of being too scared to jump.

He then prayed to a God he did not believe in.

"Oh Lord, please forgive for what I am about to do. I do not wish to cause my wife and children any more distress but I cannot carry on living like this. He stood up and held onto one of the supporting posts before outstretching his arms in a last gesture of homage to the heavens.

He leapt over the edge like a descending angel. As he fell, the updraft of air brushed passed his ears, battering them with a reverberating sound.

Chapter 16

As the ground rushed towards him, he was suddenly aware that he was changing direction, as he moved from a vertical descent into a curve. In a split second he found himself travelling parallel to the ground, some three hundred feet below. He was flying, or rather gliding, effortlessly through the air with his arms and legs trailing behind him. He could this be, his stunned mind wondered? `Am I dead? Am I spirit? ` ...He wasn't sure.

He flew over several fields until he was `flying` above a new retail park on the edge of the city where, before it was built, he once found two beautiful turquoise chert flint arrowheads in a ploughed field. He then glided over Ely and his mother's home, before heading towards Canton where he had met Max's brother Sam two weeks previously.

He then moved his arms out to his side like the wings of an eagle riding on a thermal of rising air.With his mind focused on the city centre lights ahead of him, he felt something touching the tips of the fingers of his outstretched right hand. He turned his head to see a beautiful woman in a white flowing dress clasping his fingers. She then guided him upwards towards the night sky. Their speed gradually increased until they were travelling at an unimaginable velocity. She then smiled at him and said.

"Don't worry Peter, don't be afraid, you will be alright. By the way, my name is Petra."

"Am I dead?" He asked incredulously.

"No, far from it-you are very much alive."

"I am taking you on a journey to a very special place."

As they travelled, Peter saw flashes of his life history quickly pass by, from adulthood right back to his childhood They began with the most recent events, starting with his descent from the communications mast, then Max crouching naked on Caerphilly Mountain, Sterling talking to him on Penarth Pier, discovering Alice's secret little notebook, meeting the Eskimo vagrant outside Edgware Road Station, his wife crying in the kitchen, the translucent twisting creature in Cambridge...and ended with his birth in St David's Hospital in Cardiff.

Then in an eternal moment, in a measureless distance, he found himself in darkness, except for the sight of small white circular platform below, surrounded by a dark sea. There was a man at its centre.

Petra carefully steered him to gently land feet-first in front of the man who was seated on an armchair.

"I have to leave you now; it was nice to meet you. Remember there is no need to be afraid." Petra had been so reassuring to him, he thought.

"Howdy!" said the man in a friendly and uplifting voice. He was middle aged, tall, with longish straight black hair and a high forehead. He looked very much like Carl Sagan, the charismatic scientist who made the wonderful *Cosmos* TV series in the 80's. But the naturally impressive good looks of the odd man in front of him, were dimmed somewhat by the black mole on the side of his nose, a few days old stubble, and a noticeable paunch. It also looked as if he had not washed or changed his clothes in a few days. Nevertheless, Peter's first impression was of someone comfortable in their own skin.

"Don't be afraid Peter. Please sit down...I am so happy to meet you at last...please sit down, then I will explain everything to you."

"Where in the hell am I? What the fuck has happened to me? My mind feels as if it is about to *explode*."

Peter, rather than sit down on the empty chair opposite the stranger, walked to the edge of the floating stage and peered over the side into the wide expanse of what he presumed was water, covered by mist. In the distance, he could see a large dark spherical `cloud, ` about a mile across, `floating` on the `sea`. The surface of the huge ball was continuously twisting and turning. It sent forth streams of luminescence, like burning dust.

He leant his feet over the edge, through the mist, to test the `water` beneath. He was surprised to find that his feet touched what felt like a fluid but were unable to sink into it. He stood, falteringly, on this dynamic `liquid` with its great surface tension and then ran as fast as he could over its wobbly surface. It was like running over a giant waterbed. He found it impossible to remain steady and fell over several times. He ran into the black void beyond, determined to fulfill his intention of ending his life. But it only led into emptiness where there was no means to kill himself, no objects to grab, no edges to fall off.

Peter then headed for the giant orb in the distance, but no matter how far he ran, it seemed to maintain its distance from him, as if it didn't want him to come any nearer.

After a while, he turned around and looked back towards the platform; he could barely make it out in the distance. He felt painfully alone.

He stopped to reflect upon what had just happened to him, but his mind could not take it all in. `Am I dead? I can't be, because I feel alive, ` he thought and bit his hand to feel the pain to make sure. `I must be alive, ` he concluded. After pausing for a while, he began walking back towards the point of light with the silhouette of the strange man on it. He was exhausted when he finally reached it, before clambering on board and sitting on an armchair opposite the man.

Peter looked around to see a dining table set for a meal for two, with a small TV on it. There were also two London public `Boris` bikes parked in stands nearby.

"Please don't run away again Peter, I mean you no harm. All will be well, you'll soon find out." The stranger said reassuringly. He wore a shabby, cream coloured `war correspondents` suit over a faded khaki shirt and loafers that had seen better days.

"I hope you like the armchairs? You might recognise them. They are the same as the ones in the Dean's room. Remember- you saw him a couple of months ago. I was also there, but invisible to you of course, listening to your conversation with him. I sat on one of the armchairs when the Dean got up. Wow! It was so comfortable, so relaxing, I just had to get some for myself. It took me *ages* to track another pair down."

He continued, changing the direction of the conversation, "You had me worried just now Peter...when you tried to kill yourself again by jumping off the mast."

"How could you possibly know that?" he asked, disbelievingly.

"Because I saw it happen... because I saved you. Well, more accurately, I asked Petra to save you."

"Who are you? What the hell are you talking about- being in the Dean's office listening to our conversation? Saving me?... *What the fuck is going on? Who are you? Where am I?*" Peter asked, his mind in a state of hopeless confusion.

"Who do you think I am?"

"Well, if you saw me jump off the mast and saved me to bring me here in the middle of, I don't know fucking where, then I guess you must be...GOD!" he said flippantly.

"*Right* on the button there, mate," God replied humorously.

"My God!" Peter exclaimed.

"No pun intended I hope." God responded in jest. Peter laughed unintentionally at the absurdity of the joke and his situation sitting opposite *God himself.*

"Whilst you're at it, please tell me how you got the chairs delivered here-by DHL I guess?" Peter asked in sarcastic vain.

"Now Peter, please don't be facetious. Let me be clear to you…*I really am*…God."

"Please forgive me, I just can't take this all in. I'm recovering from another failed attempt at ending my life and being taken by a flying woman called Petra across the universe to meet someone who calls himself God!"

"Yes, all of that is true…and I really am… the ONE."

After a long silence, Peter said. "If you really are `Him`…then what do you want from me? Why did you bring me here?"

"I do not want anything from you Peter, other than the pleasure of your company for a short while. After all, you did discover my magic elixir…the God Field."

"Shall we have a chat over dinner…you must be ravenous after the cold night on top of Caerphilly Mountain?"

`He knows that I tried to kill Max, ` Peter thought.

Peter looked towards the dining table to see Petra, (who had just landed nearby), standing beside it, seemingly ready to serve them.

They both went over and sat down at the table. God encouraged Peter to "get stuck in".

"It's my favourite," he said. Welsh lamb with mint, Jersey royal photos and Savoy cabbage. With onion gravy-mm mm. It's one of your favourites too, isn't it Peter?"

"Would you like some red wine?" Peter nodded his head in agreement. Petra, would you be so kind and pour us a glass of wine each. It's Malbec-I know you are partial to it. The grapes for this wine were grown in the rich volcanic soils beneath Mount Sagrado in Argentina. Nice isn't it?"

Peter nodded in the affirmative, unable to formulate and articulate speech, as the enormity of what was happening to him had still not sunk in.

He began to eat the food, which tasted delicious.

God, in particular, could not hide his pleasure and made strange eating noises, which conveyed his delight in tasting its wonderful flavours.

"Please forgive my noisy eating habits Peter-it is so rare that I get to experience eating human food."

When they had finished eating they sat back on the armchairs

"Shall we watch a bit of TV before we have our chat?"

Peter again nodded his head in silent approval.

God got up from his seat, walked over, and switched on the old-fashioned analogue TV. The film *Carry On Camping* was showing.

"I love the *Carry On* films, don't you? They are comedy classics. The characters are so funny and the humour so bawdy. And, as for the lovely acting `assets ` of Barbara Windsor, if you know what I mean, please don't get me *started*."

There was then some interference in the TV transmission. God got up from his chair, walked over and hit the side of the TV with his hand, which seemed to correct it. He then jokingly exclaimed.

"It's probably a fault with the Wenvoe Transmission Station. You know that place pretty well, don't you Peter."

Peter finally broke his silence and said in a bitter tone, "Yes, well done, you do know everything about me. Yes, I do like the *Carry On* films and yes, I do like Malbec wine. *Congratulations*." He was seething with anger from being saved against his will from certain death, by someone who believes themselves to be God. But what also rankled with him, was that his `Saviour, ` seemed to be a, slovenly, louche, know it all… albeit with a good sense of humour."

"I'm sorry Peter, I didn't mean to offend you. I was only trying to crack a joke."

They quietly resumed watching *Carry On Camping* until God said, "Kenneth Williams and Charles Autrey are also great in this film. Max knew them both from the days when he used to write plays for BBC radio."

"Yes, I *know* that," Peter said in an attempt to regain the independence he felt he had lost.

"Do I call you God, or something else?" Peter asked, as he finally came around to accepting the incredible identity of the being sitting opposite him.

"Actually, I would prefer it if you would call me Sonny, the name of the character in the first *Godfather* film. He's my alter ego-he had such charisma and just got things done without making a fuss. The ladies loved him as well… As you can see, when I take on human form, I get taken over by your world with its likes and dislikes."

"I can see that. I never thought God would be a fan of the *Carry On* films!"

"Do you know about the Max stuff?" Peter asked.

"I'm afraid, I know all about it. I understand it was at the root cause of your suffering in life and your attempted suicide just now."

"I feel better knowing that you know, God." Peter was beginning to warm towards him.

"Please call me Sonny."

"Sorry, Sonny."

"Do you mind if we go on a short cycle ride?" God asked.

"To where?"

"If I tried to explain the destination, you wouldn't believe me Peter."

"Try me! I've just taken on board the craziest shit imaginable."

"Well this might be a bit too weird, even for your undoubted powers of acceptance?"

They each pulled out a `Boris` bike from the racks.

"I'd better not ask you how you got these?" Peter said in jest.

"No, its best you dont," God guiltily replied.

"Be very careful riding on the surface; try to roll with the wobbles. You take the lead Peter-just head for the sphere."

Peter led and God followed. He had great difficulty staying on the bike and fell off several times.

Eventually, Sonny called out. "Peter, for Christ's sake! You're riding like a lumbering Bernard Bresslaw, (of *Carry On* fame). You should just ride with the carefree abandon of the late, but great, Sidney James." Whereupon God took the lead and rode like a maniac towards the approaching orb, waving His legs back and forth. It was not long before He disappeared into its flux. Peter, followed, terrified, but believing that if it was all right for God to enter, then it should be safe for him to do so.

As he entered the sphere he was greeted by thin sheets of curving and twisting energy passed in front of his amazed eyes. Upon these membranes he could see many images of people and strange alien-like creatures engaged in moving and animated conversation. Some were laughing, some crying, some seemed sad, some wise. Occasionally, he would catch a word or a phrase of what the human beings were saying. "Please forgive me." … "I will support you no matter what." … "I am so sorry." … "I love you."

When they finally left the giant ball of energy, they emerged onto a sandy shoreline, surrounding a large round lake about a mile across. God was just ahead of him. He struggled to cycle through the sand and soon had to dismount `His` bike and push it to the lakeshore. Peter followed suit. He became aware of beings on either side of him and scattered at intervals along the perimeter of the lake. God then mounted `His` bike and glided over its strange surface. Peter got onto his bike and warily followed `Him. ` The lake wasn't liquid at all but a sea of intertwining harmonic sine waves which somehow offered a smooth surface for the bikes to ride upon.

Sonny stopped and dismounted his bike half way between the shore and the centre of the lake. He asked Peter to do the same. They laid their bikes on the energy field. God then kneeled down and crossed his legs, Peter following his example.

Peter noticed that everything was slowly turning in a spiral towards the centre of the lake. God, Peter and the bikes were moving, almost imperceptibly, along with it. Barely discernible, circular pulsating waves, emerged from the centre and radiated outwards.

"We can now have our chat, if that's OK with you, Peter?"

"Where are we Sonny?"

"Believe it or not, we are in the singularity from which a new universe will arise, once it `explodes` that is. Don't worry; it won't happen for a while yet. Anyway, it isn't really an explosion that happens but a rapid expansion of space and time from a single point - the centre of the lake."

"But what is this lake?"

"You already know the answer to that question, don't you? It is the God Field you discovered!"

"*The God Field*?" After a pause, Peter continued, "This is all too much. I just can't believe that I am getting confirmation of the Field from none other than God himself!"

"There is no surer proof is there Peter? The lake is a nascent singularity, a God Field that we are developing. When it is ready, it will rapidly expand and seed the new universe across a matrix of multidimensional membranes.

But *come on* Peter, you know all about this from your theory."

"Why did you bring me here? Why did you stop me from killing myself?"

"I had to intervene, because it was not your time to die. I am unable to normally interfere in human life, but I can in your case because you had become entangled in the creative process of the God Field. I held back directly from saving you on Penarth Pier, hoping the synchronicity of Sterling Reed being there would save you. But it was too close a call, so I had Petra save you the next time you tried to kill yourself when you jumped off the mast. The only other way I can intervene, is in selecting certain individuals to help me. I call them my Beautiful Collectors. Petra is one of them."

"I saved you because you have unfinished business in your life. You have to find the real meaning behind the God Field."

Peter interrupted Sonny to ask, "Why don't you just tell me the answer now, straight from the horse's mouth as it were; and I don't mean the horses head in the movie producers bed in the first *Godfather* film either! You would save me a lot of trouble. After all, I might never even find the answer by myself."

God was pleased that Peter was now feeling relaxed enough to crack jokes. He loved a good pun.

"*Very* funny Peter. I wish I could tell you the answer, but I would be disturbing the fabric of the Field with potentially disastrous consequences, just as I would if I were to directly intervene to relieve the suffering of people on Earth."

"All I can say, is that you will you feel the answer when you discover it. It is your destiny to find it, for the human race is now ready to learn about the God Field and its deeper meaning."

"A great help you are Sonny. A God with limitations, that's a new one," Peter replied with ironic humour. God laughed.

"You have another equally important piece of unfinished business to attend to Peter and it is also related to your search for the meaning of the God Field. You have to go back to Dorset, seek Alice's forgiveness and get to know her better. She is also a major part of your destiny, because you can help each other heal the wounds of your pasts, since you are damaged souls with similar tragic childhood histories. Meeting Alice was no coincidence, for your discovery of the God Field enabled me to create the conditions for your paths to cross, via the very Field itself. This is why you experienced strange visions and regressed to witness the suffering of others. Normally I cannot intervene this way, unless, as I have already said, it is to select a Beautiful Collector."

Sonny continued. "I so wanted to meet the first person to discover my Field. Can I say it has been a privilege to make your acquaintance? I can see that you are a special human being."

"Thank you, God. Sorry, I mean Sonny."

"Do you have any further questions?"

"Why didn't you prevent me from attempting to kill Max?"

"I could have done so, but on this occasion, I had to leave it to yourself to eventually show him mercy, although this wasn't preordained."

"Who are those beings on the lake shoreline? What are they doing?" Peter then asked.

At the `water's` edge, he could see many people and alien-like creatures. The aliens were of a variety of different forms; some had weirdly shaped heads and many limbs, a few hovered, others were android-like and appeared to be made from a semi-organic/synthetic material. It was a bizarre sight. They would suddenly appear from empty space, make their way to the edge of the shore and kneel down, (if they were able to so). They would then open a glowing golden orb and release a stream of 'light' energy into the 'lake'. The ripples it produced would move outwards and interact with the sea of harmonic waves in the lake. They would then hold the orb to their heart, bow their heads and say some kind of prayer in a myriad of strange languages and sound inflections. Peter could make out the words the human beings said: "to all the souls who have given me this gift, I thank you." They would then 'walk' into the 'lake' and swim joyfully in its 'waters' for several minutes before 'walking' out and 'melting' into space.

"They are my Beautiful Collectors. I had specially chosen each of them to, invisibly, observe the interactions of intelligent life forms on other planets. Their task is to look for a moment when some individual reaches within to reveal such feelings as joy, compassion, love, sorrow and pain. They then collect this psychic energy and store it in a golden orb. Once they have collected enough energy, they make an instant journey, by means of quantum entanglement, to release the energy into this, or some other, embryonic singularity pool. This happens across many different universes."

"Why?"

The psychic energies such as vulnerability, compassion and love, will seed the Field so that there is greater propensity for the living beings in the planets of the future to develop into more loving, feeling beings. All of this will unfold when the singularity expands. Only then can a species grow spiritually, only then can meaning in the universe evolve."

"Aren't the interacting ripples in the lake like those formed when your children threw some pebbles into the Round Pond, which gave you your first inkling of a special field at the heart of everything?"

"Yes, that image came to my mind when I was watching the Beautiful Collectors releasing the energy from their orbs into the lake."

"But why do the Beautiful Collectors also collect negative energies such as pain and suffering?"

"This is so that the God Field will help future species develop in ways that will lessen such hurt."

"As I have told you before, I am unable to get involved directly and stop human anguish or make people love each other more. I can't stop human misery, no matter how much I want to. I'm not omnipotent you know. Well that is a bad choice of phrase-I guess I *am almost omnipotent*, because, although I can do most things, I can't do *everything* -even I have my limits." Sonny laughed out loud from his portly belly.

"The only way I can express myself is through the unfolding of the God Field."

"Why do the Beautiful Collectors swim in the `lake` before they leave?" Peter asked.

"The psychic energies they release move in a spiral towards the centre of the pool from where a special kind of energy is released outwards in all directions. It is like a form of light and yet it is not, it feels like a gentle breeze and yet it is not the wind. It is a kind of grace, which fills their soul. This gives them the strength to leave and continue with their task."

"What exactly is this grace?"

"It is my *voice*…it is my *grace*…You felt it when the perfect harmonic sine waves you observed in the `ghost` detector were transformed into sound form."

Peter's body tingled as he absorbed the words that God had just told him.

They watched the Beautiful Collectors on the shoreline for a while. They seemed to be in a state of utter bliss as they bathed in the energy of God's grace.

"I love watching them." God said.

"What is the sphere that we just passed through?"

"It is a collection of stored psychic energies, collected by the Beautiful Collectors, which can to be drawn upon when needed. They are being transformed in readiness to be transferred to merge with the God Field in the lake. The sea around the platform where we just had dinner is also a store of psychic energies but they are in their raw, unprocessed state. These energies will be moved to the sphere when needed."

"As you are no doubt now aware, I am everywhere and in everything. This is why I can be anywhere, at any time. This is why I have been observing you during your recent turbulent times. But I can't intervene directly. It is only through the unfolding of the God Field that I can manifest myself."

"Wow! I find it impossible to comprehend all of what you have been telling me." Peter was overwhelmed by all that he had heard, but he knew that to make the most of this special `moment` and keep asking God questions.

"How do you choose your Beautiful Collectors?"

"Sometimes, very rarely, I see an individual on some planetary system where there is intelligent life, who shows a special capacity to empathise and give of themselves selflessly to others. Petra was one such person. She was a maid in a royal household in ancient Mesopotamia. She took the risk of saving a baby rejected by a lady of nobility and brought it up lovingly as her own. After that, she befriended many other rejected children and set up what was probably the world's first children's orphanage. She treated every child as if she were its mother and lavished heaps of love on all in her fold."

"Peter, I would like you, one day, to be one of my Beautiful Collectors, but not just yet."

"Thank you for the privilege. I would love to help you out, plus I get to live forever and travel a bit!" Peter replied with joyful humour.

"Just a bit… across a universe or two. Not much really, an all zone London Transport Travel Card should just about cover it." Sonny replied, before giggling irrepressibly.

"Sadly, it is time for you to go back to Earth, if you don't mind Peter. The real reason I saved you and brought you back here was to give you some belief in yourself by confirming your God Field theory and reminding you of your unfulfilled destiny. I also very much wanted to meet you."

"Sonny, I have *so many* more questions to ask you."

"I'm sorry Peter, but you have to leave now because the conditions for instant travel are perfect at this moment."

"I just can't tell you how much you have helped me. You have not only saved my life, you have saved my soul. That is in spite of your noisy eating habits, dirty sense of humour and eclectic taste in films." On hearing this, God chuckled again.

"Any more insults? What about you! You cheeky Welsh git with your unintelligible Cardiff accent. A Scouser's dialect is like perfect BBC English compared to yours!"

Sonny continued, "Petra will take you back to planet Earth. You will then find yourself continuing your descent from the communications mast until you hit the ground. But don't worry, you will not be hurt. After that you are on your own-I can't help you then. Well, I guess in your case I could, as I explained to you before, but it would not be right for me to interfere too much. Although I have told you of your true path, it does not mean that you will find it; only you can make it a reality. Remember, though, you can always make conscious contact with me through prayer."

"I've never been much good at that."

"Well take a tip from none other than God himself-it works, if you try it. It's like falling, safely. Just learn to hand yourself over to me without thought or question."

God stood up, walked over and lifted Peter up from the pulsating `floor` and gave him a warm hug, which Peter reciprocated. He told him what a great joy it was to have met the first individual to discover the God Field.

Petra then appeared from out of nowhere, took a hold of his hand and lifted him upwards. In a moment, they were gone. This time, Peter experienced flashbacks of his life in reverse, from birth to adulthood, ending with his plunge from the mast.

He continued his fall and hit the ground hard, but unharmed. Petra was no longer with him; he was alone. The cold morning dew on the grass washed his face like a baptism. He stood up, and looked up to the sky, aware that he could remember everything that had just transpired. He knew it was all real and not an illusion. He had met and talked with God himself.

As he walked towards his car, he could hear the sound of a police car siren approaching from the direction of Cardiff. He wondered if someone was coming to investigate the loss of communication from the security cameras, or perhaps he had been seen climbing, falling or `flying, ` from the tower. He ran as fast as he could to his car and speeded out of the car park, for he had no wish to be apprehended by the police, for he now had some very important things to do.

When he turned the car onto the A48 on the brow of the hill, he caught sight of the first rays of the sun rising over the horizon from the east, its golden light almost blinding him. The light lit up the Earth and touched a part of Peter that had lain dormant for a long time.

He drove back to Ely and quietly parked his car in Susan's driveway before going to his mum`s house next door. As far as he was aware, no one had noticed his exit or his return.

Peter then retired to bed, feeling an inner glow from having just met the Creator.

Chapter 17

Peter followed his usual routines for the next few days: helping out with the chores around the house, going for walks in the nearby countryside and having an evening pint with his brother in the `Wanderers.` He intently watched the local TV news and carefully scanned the local daily newspaper, *The Echo*, for any report on Max's kidnapping and attempted murder but found nothing. As expected, Max had kept quiet, fearing Peter would expose him if he were arrested.

He also read with interest a report from a local farmer who witnessed a man falling from the Wenvoe mast and then `flying` over his land. But because he was a relative of the late, but mad, `Black Beard,` who committed suicide by jumping off the same structure, no one took him seriously.

Over the next few weeks, Peter began turning his life around. He was more confident in himself. He felt empowered for the first time in his life. The events that night on top of Caerphilly mountain, had cauterised a canker that had besmirched his soul. Having thought his destiny was to take `justifiable` revenge on Max, he instead found that it lay in forgiving him; this helped Peter to finally bring closure to his childhood trauma. His later meeting with God that same night, after `He` had intervened in his suicide attempt, finally gave him the absolute proof he so much needed in `His` existence. This affirmation came from none other than God himself, as did the confirmation of his God Field theory. But it was the faith and love God showed him which finally touched his heart.

Something had changed within him; he could not define or articulate its architecture, but a shift had taken place, a subtle schematic movement of the inner compass in the core of his being. The shroud that had covered his spirit, and hindered its natural expression, had lifted. For the first time in his adult life, the dark shadow of the abuse had quietly drifted away without a smidgen of resistance. The great power that it had on his life, made manifest through the malevolent `self-saboteur, ` had been rendered harmless; the horned devil had been neutered. In reality, it was a sniveling little coward, like his abuser.

Peter was now more relaxed and less self-conscious when communicating with people, for he now held the key to unlocking the secret door to the outside world where they lived. The door was his shadow self and its key, self-love. He could now hold eye contact with others without fear for the first time since he was a boy of fifteen, some forty years previously. His greater openness made meant that others could now recognise him for who he really was. His former closed off demeanour had acted as a barrier to people fully acknowledging him. This feeling was very liberating for him.

God, as usual was watching, although Peter was still unaware of his presence. He knew that Peter had finally let go of the toxic shame that had ruled over him. He was now free to live the life he was meant to lead and in so doing be in a position to uncover the true meaning of the God Field.

Peter had long, enjoyable and meaningful talks with his mother and Bruce. Katherine talked a great deal about her love of nature. She reminisced about the beautiful cliff-top walks along the Pembrokeshire coastal path she had with her late husband William. She described the flowers and the birds they came across, her eyes lighting up as she did so. She remembered her happy childhood with her mother and how they used to go for long walks with their cocker spaniel along the River Taff, through Sophia Gardens, Llandaff Fields and onto Taffs Well at the foot of the Rhondda Valley.

Connecting with Bruce though was much more of a challenge. His brother had withdrawn behind a high wall to protect his feelings, just as Peter had done. Getting him to talk about his past was a touchy subject, as Peter found out a few weeks earlier, when Bruce had snapped back at him. But his brother slowly opened up to him, no doubt because he could see that Peter himself had let go of something which held him back. He talked about his time as a croupier on board luxury liners and recalled his many experiences undertaking computer contract work throughout Britain, Europe and beyond.

One evening, Bruce even mentioned his regret in losing his wife Sofia and their children, due to `my stupid fucking immaturity-I just hadn't grown up Pete. ` He said how he struggled to accept the responsibility of family life and was often out playing sports, drinking and gambling. Although some others wondered if he had gallivanted with other women, he denied this ever happened and said that Sofia was the love of his life. Bruce would be the first to admit his character defects, but nevertheless, he was an outstanding individual who possessed a great many gifts and qualities, not the least of which were a giving and caring nature. His real problem was his inability to open up to his feelings for he was `old school, ` like his father, who also found it difficult to express them because he saw it as `unmanly `to do so.

Peter also spent a lot of time with Ryan. They chatted much more comfortably this time without any signs of the concealed bitterness or regret that accompanied their first meeting. They became like two old Ely boys again. Ryan took him sea fishing a few times. They even fished off

Penarth Pier where Sterling had rescued him from his first suicide bid a few weeks earlier. Unfortunately, Peter never caught a fish, resulting in Ryan giving him the nickname *no fish Fellows*. `What a cheek, ` Peter thought, but he took it all in good humour.

He saw Ryan's band a second time and enjoyed it just as much as the first. Ryan loved performing and the audience greatly enjoyed the music and his interaction with them. Both mates saw several other bands playing in different music venues throughout the Cardiff and the Vale, including *Rebus*, who's band leader, Leonard had first told Peter of Ryan's whereabouts. Peter also met several of Ryan's mates who seemed to have his best interest at heart. The two became great friends again. Peter noticed Ryan was smoking less `draw` than before. He seemed happier and more animated. He felt these changes had something to do to his re-acquaintance with his best friend of old. Peter himself reduced his drinking to sensible proportions for the first time in a long while.

One of the most tragic consequences of Peter's entombment inside his own enclosed world was the loss of contact with his parents and family in Cardiff. Max had deliberately placed a wedge between them. He now understood that this was a common deliberate action of sexual abusers, who sought to create a physical and emotional bridge between the target victim and their family. Max nurtured a resentment in Peter towards his parents by poisoning his mind with negative comments about them. Although Peter did not believe these words, they still infiltrated his mind and created a further barrier between himself and his parents. Max executed his plan expertly, for it was not long before Peter rarely visited or slept at his parents' house.

His mother, understandably, felt deeply hurt by the loss of her son, no two sons, for his older Michael was also living there. She must have felt neglected and unloved by their preferring to live at Max's, believing they cared more for him than they did for her. Sadly, for Peter, he felt the fallout from her pain and had to listen to her recriminations for his staying at Max's. Peter was caught in an emotional tug of war between his mother and Max. This tortured him with guilt and messed up his mind even more.

The sad reality was that Peter needed the care, love and attention Max showed him, for he had not received them from his father. Max became the father figure he needed. The great tragedy was the person he came to love as a father figure then sexually abused him. This confused him and left deep emotional scars.

In later years, he found staying at his mums would reopen these painful memories, especially the guilt he felt for not having gone back to stay there when he was a boy.

However, now he could let go of these negative memories and feelings because they no longer had any power over him.

During this time, Peter met up with his other brothers and sisters he had lost contact with. They enjoyed each other's company and no one seemed to harbour any bitterness towards him for his former isolation. He had lost touch with them over the preceding decades because he had withdrawn into himself. He was incapable, due the results of acute trauma, to meet and communicate with them. On the few occasions when they had met, he was paralysed with shyness and fear. This loss of contact with his siblings had regrettably meant that had not been around to witness their lovely children growing up.

Although it was impossible to get this time back, one thing that he could now do was to forgive himself for this `distance` from his family in Cardiff. He now knew he was innocent and this avoidance of their company was not his fault, but Max's, who was the cause of this collateral damage. This realisation meant he could let go of the guilt he felt for losing contact with them.

In the weeks following his meeting with Sonny, he noticed his visions had completely stopped. He tested this out by looking directly into the eyes or `accidently` touching the hand of several stranger's he sensed carried inner wounds from their past. He now felt or experienced nothing. Although he was relieved they had ceased because they had become increasingly draining, he was also, in some ways, saddened to have lost this special gift to peer into the souls of others.

However, as time went by, Peter felt a growing restlessness. Something was troubling him. One afternoon whilst shopping in Canton, he saw a copy of the book *Alive*, (the same book that Alice had hidden away), in a charity shop window. Seeing this again, unlocked the source of his unease- it was time to see Alice again and as God himself had suggested, make amends with her. He was nervous at this prospect, however, for he feared that she would never forgive him. Nevertheless, he had to go back; he had no choice because the compulsion he felt was too powerful to withhold, for it was a force driven by emergent love…He would have to leave for Dorset soon.

He decided to leave in three days' time after spending a little more time with his family and Ryan in Cardiff. It was now over four weeks since, in the time and space of one long Friday night, he had kidnapped and released Max, was saved from attempted suicide and taken to the cradle of a new universe to meet God and `His` Beautiful Collectors.

Peter gently broke the news of his departure to his family and Ryan, explaining to them that he would come back to visit them very soon. He made sure that he clearly relayed this message to Ryan to eradicate any doubts he may have that he would not return again for a long time.

Over the next few days, he hung around with his mother and Bruce, as well as his other brothers and sisters. When he was not with them, he chilled out with Ryan.

However, his mind was so full of expectation at the prospect of seeing Alice again that he could hardly sleep at night.

He left for Dorset on the early morning of Tuesday May 1 2012.

Chapter 18

As Peter approached the Owl Cottage along the ancient country lane, he felt a deep longing, for he was going back to the cottage he loved, where he met the enigmatic woman whose story had turned his life upside down.

By returning with the intention of seeking reconciliation with Alice, he was following the guidance of none other than God himself. Receiving `His` blessing, now moved his spirit with a relentless momentum. It was as if a seed had been placed in the palm of his hand, ready to be planted into life's fertile soil.

On entering the cottage, everything seemed the same except for a thin layer of dust over the furniture and a faint musty smell in the air. `Alice hasn't been her at all since I left, ` he thought. He lit the wood burning stove to dry the air and sank into his favourite armchair. He then made a baked bean pasta dish, using the only edible ingredients he could find in the kitchen. For most of the rest of the day, he relaxed watching TV. Afterwards, he fell asleep on the sofa.

Early the following morning, he heard the inimitable sound of "Tap, tap… tap, tap" on the windowpane next to the front door. "Tap, tap…tap, tap," the sound repeated itself. Shocked, he stood up with a jolt, not knowing what to do. `It must be Alice! But its Wednesday; she never cleans on a Wednesday! Anyway, she had stopped cleaning the cottage. `

Peter rushed to the front door. He felt a million contrasting emotions-the fear of rejection, the `ache` of love, the desire to escape, the need to see Alice again. Just as he was about to, gingerly, open the door, Alice opened it with her key and almost fell into his arms. She was visibly shaken to see him again, so unexpectedly.

"Hello Alice, long time, no see… I've been away for a while, visiting my family in Cardiff."

"I know, but I wasn't expecting you back yet," she said, barely able to conceal her anger towards him. She had known from the last time they met in the summerhouse and seen the gold dust on the carpet beneath the back panel, that he had found her hideaway with its secrets. This intrusion had made her livid with rage and bitterness towards him, for she felt somehow violated by the very person she had grown to care for. However, her wrath had gradually diminished over the following months, especially when she found out that he had left the cottage. She missed him badly. Seeing him again melted her heart. She mellowed. Love was trying to take its place but it was held back by a deep hurt.

"Sorry, I didn't mean to disturb you. I was just going to freshen up the place. The `Owl` has just been put on my new cleaning rota again. I am due to come every Wednesday morning, although I could change it back to Saturday if you would like?" Alice looked at him, waiting for an answer, with eyes wide open, in spite of her acute bashfulness... She had to devour him…she had to take in his essence again.

"Would you mind coming on a Saturday? Could you return again this coming Saturday-I can see the place needs a lot of cleaning." He only asked her to come back then so that he would see her again sooner.

"That's no problem Peter…it's almost as dusty as the summerhouse before I last cleaned it in February…you remember, when I found you reading a book there?" He noticed that she had, no doubt intentionally, brought up the time and location of their falling out, the place where he had discovered her secrets. `It is still fresh in her mind, she is still furious with me, ` he thought. `But she did address me by my first name- perhaps she doesn't despise me so much after all? ` He wondered.

He looked at her and felt his heart skip a beat. Her natural awkwardness, pale skin, bowed head and dowdy clothes…all stirred his attraction for her again. He knew they disguised a woman of great beauty.

Most of all, Peter wanted to apologise to her for his previous intrusion upon her privacy in the hope that she would forgive him; but now was not the right time.

When Alice had finished her errands, she left abruptly, having politely declined his offer of cup of tea.

Over the next few days, Peter was hardly ever in the cottage. He had no wish to hide away anymore. He met many of the locals, both old acquaintances and new faces. One lunchtime, he even volunteered to do the cooking in the Foundry, when the chef was unable to make it in due to personal problems. "Probably hung-over," he overheard the landlord, Phil, murmur to his wife. Phil, with whom he developed a casual friendship before he left for Cardiff, surprisingly took him up on his offer. He did a good job as well, judging by the positive feedback from the diners.

Peter's biggest challenge, though, was when and how to broach the subject of the bleak obstacle that had come between Alice and himself. He decided, in the end, to approach it head-on, for he preferred to be straight with people. He intended to speak to her on the coming Saturday.

"Tap, tap…tap, tap," that lovely staccato sound, which he had grown so found of hearing, resonated throughout the cottage like the call of a mythical lover. It was nine o`clock on Saturday morning.

He rushed to let Alice in. They were both secretly glad to see each other.

"Lady Traherne, (as usual, she addressed her mother in an impersonal manner), sends her best wishes. She asked me to tell you that she is delighted that you are back." Alice then proceeded to perform her duties as professionally as ever. As she was about to leave, Peter asked her if she would, "do me the honour," of joining him for cup of tea. She seemed in two minds as to whether or not to accept his offer before agreeing, but his natural charm had won her over.

After several minutes of polite chitchat, Peter said, "Do you mind if I speak to you honestly about something that concerns us both?"

Alice became very agitated for she seemed to know what he was going to discuss.

"No, not at all, that is the way I prefer to be treated," she replied bracing herself for the worst.

"Well, not long after I arrived at the `Owl, ` I accidentally knocked a lower back panel in the summerhouse which turned out be a secret cupboard door. I found several things hidden inside: two handwritten notebooks, two published books and a Heroes chocolates tin with several objects inside."

Alice stood up to leave, overcome with emotions she could not articulate. Peter gently took her hand and politely asked her to remain. She relented but could say nothing. Her feet vibrated uncontrollably under the table, vibrating the cups with her nervous energy.

As soon as he said `notebooks, ` she knew that had not only discovered the main collection of her personal items, but also the little notebook hidden above these.

"Over the next few weeks, I read the notebooks and the other books. I just could not stop once I had started. But it was the contents of the small notebook, which I found taped behind the panel, that shook me the most, for it made for harrowing reading. It concerned the suffering of a young girl who had been the victim of sexual abuse by a man whose name isn't mentioned. At first, I wasn't sure who the items belonged to, or who the girl was, but after a while I wondered whether they were…. Yours Alice… and whether the young girl was… you?"

Alice looked directly at him. Her complexion had paled even more than normal; her features were blank and expressionless. Peter braced himself for the bitter recrimination that he was sure would follow. But she remained silent for what seemed like an inordinate amount of time, as if she was uncertain about how to respond to what he had just told her.

Finally, she replied, "I *knew* that you had found my private belongings. You should be ashamed of yourself for prying into someone else's innermost secrets. *How could you*." She hesitated before continuing. "You were right to infer that the person referred to in the little notebook is me." It suddenly dawned on her that it was the first time she had ever admitted her childhood tragedy to anyone else. She felt a sense of release. Something had lifted from her body, like a ghostly ectoplasm leaving a possessed person after an exorcism.

She continued, "Just when I was beginning to like you as well. I knew, as soon as I saw the gold dust I placed in the little notebook had fallen onto the summerhouse carpet."

"That's why you never came back to do the cleaning again?"

"Of course! I hated you after that. *Don't you see*-you betrayed my trust. It felt like an intrusion. I thought I could never forgive you. I couldn't function properly for weeks afterwards. Instead, I holed myself up in my room in the Great House and wondered if you would tell someone else about my shame…perhaps my mother. She was very supportive of me at the time; she knew I was upset about something, but she never asked me the reason why. I think she presumed that we had argued with one another."

"Alice, I am deeply sorry for what I did… I guessed that you knew I had found out about your secret possessions. I was mortified with guilt. It really hurt… you're not coming around again. I really missed your company because …if I can still be honest with you…I had grown very fond of you. Eventually, I couldn't stand the pain of your absence any longer and left for Cardiff. My only hope was that you might one day forgive me."

"*Why* did you read the notebooks?" She asked directly.

"Because I had a similar torment to the author… yourself. I too was sexually abused as a child, in Cardiff, by a friend of my family's, called Max. Until I read the your notes I had never dared to think about these past experiences, but the pain I could feel from the victim in the pages brought it all back to me. I was shaken to the core. Your notebooks helped me to face up to my own demons and the terrible emotional suffering I experienced. Up until then, I had spent all of my life, `not going there. ` The Bradshaw book also helped me, along with your annotations, to understand that toxic shame was at the heart of the self-torture I put myself through since the abuse-I had no idea about it until then."

"Terrible emotional suffering?"

"Yes, I have lived in an emotional hell all of my adult life."

"Just like myself," she replied, before continuing. "Now you know my full story Peter; I think you owe to me to tell me more about yours."

Peter then told her all about his abuse at the hands of Max and the price he had paid ever since. He talked about his self-loathing, chronic introversion and living a life in a state of perpetual fear. He also mentioned how his lack of self-confidence had hindered his making relationships.

"Just like myself," Alice repeated.

When he had finished, Peter bowed his head in defeat. Tears of surrender trickled down his face. As he lay there, he could hear Alice's tearful sniffles as she buried her head into her bosom. Feeling a deep sense of compassion, he arose from his chair, walked over and put his arms around her. He held this embrace until her sobbing stopped. He then gently lifted up her chin and said.

"I'm so sorry Alice…I never meant to hurt you. Can you ever forgive me? I want you to know something…I care for you *very much*?"

Alice looked into his eyes. Momentarily losing all sense of self-consciousness, she said.

"I had no idea you had a similar story to mine. I could sense something was troubling you but I didn't expect it to be the same thing as myself. I now understand why you read my secrets…knowing this means that I can forgive you Peter… In some strange way, although I was angry, I felt a sense of relief that someone else finally knew about my past."

She paused for a moment before continuing, "I like you also. Do you know, I was so saddened when you left? I thought I would never see you again?"

"I have another confession to make to you Alice. I know who abused you-it was your father wasn't it? Your poem in the notebook hinted that the name of the abuser lay hidden inside. I eventually deciphered the code concealed in your sketches of the Estate cottages."

"But why did you do that Peter?" She replied, barely containing her ire.

"Once I had guessed the victim in the notebook was yourself, I felt protective of you and I just had to figure out the perpetrators name in case he was still alive and could potentially cause you harm. Although I was shocked to discover that it was your father, I was relieved that he had passed away and could no longer be any danger to you."

"You're the only person, other than myself, who knows the truth. I am now glad you are the first one to find out. I so much wanted the truth to come out, but my father was such a dominant force, I was too petrified to tell anyone. But his death was a turning point, for it was only then that I could begin the process of healing myself... Thank you for being so protective of me Peter."

This tumultuous interaction would change their lives forever. They both knew that this was a positive turning point in their relationship. Peter therefore handed out an olive branch which he hoped might bring them closer together again.

"Alice, can we become friends again and get to know each other better?"

"I would like that very much."

Peter, ecstatic that she had seemingly forgiven and warmed towards him, then asked. "Would you like to continue our chat over a snack and glass of wine here tomorrow evening?"

Alice hesitated before replying in the affirmative.

"About seven-is that OK?"

"That would be fine."

When Alice left to continue her cleaning duties elsewhere, she was still reeling from the emotional upheaval of their encounter.

God, who had been anxiously observing them, was deeply moved by what he witnessed. Tears welled up in his eyes. He was pleased that Alice had forgiven Peter. Petra was also there, collecting the psychic energies from their confrontation and resolution, before transferring them into her golden orb.

Peter barely slept that night. The turbulent events of the day rebounded in a confusing medley of thoughts and feelings in his mind. He was also concerned that Alice might change her mind and hate him again.

When he opened the door to let Alice in the following evening, his heart lifted. It didn't matter to him that she had seemingly done her best to hide her natural beauty. This was masked by the thick brown   nalyz jumper, black jogging bottoms and worn shoes she wore; he even noticed a small hole in one of them, through which he could see her a part of her big toe. Her brunette hair was all over the place, in part, because it was windy outside. Although he had made an effort to look smart, he was no better dressed with his shabby jeans and dated black polo necked shirt. The trainers he wore were only suitable for the bin. In spite of his attempt at combing his hair, it was still unkempt and he did not even have the wind outside as an excuse.

"Please come in...I've missed you." ... He felt a fool for being so brazen.

"I've missed you too," ...The words infiltrated his heart.

"I've got some nibbles, but I was wondering if I could cook you a meal-it won't take long? Have you eaten?"

"No, but my mum has dinner waiting for me at home."

Alice reflected for moment before committing herself. "Yes, if that's alright with you. I can always eat mum's dinner tomorrow."

"It's no problem-I love cooking; I even helped out in the pub the other day when the chef couldn't make it in."

Alice then called her, somewhat surprised, mother, to say that she was having dinner with Peter and would be home later.

Peter cooked steak, chips and peas served with his much-loved Malbec wine. He had bought the food and wine from Bridport earlier that day in the hope that she might stay for dinner.

Alice greatly enjoyed the meal and thanked him for his efforts.

"Shall we continue our talk in the living room?... Please bring along your glass of wine with you."

Alice sat on the sofa and Peter on the armchair next to her.

"I am so glad that we have cleared our differences, Alice."

"Me, too."

"Are you still Ok about yesterday? You're not still angry with me, are you?"

"No! No! Not now, as I told you…now that I know *your* story."

Alice felt self-conscious sitting alone with a man in the more intimate surroundings of the living room. She had rarely dated before and her deep insecurities with the opposite sex re-surfaced. Sensing her discomfort, Peter cracked a few jokes and did everything he could to make her feel at ease. She eventually relaxed and they went on to have an enjoyable evening together.

They did not talk about their tragic histories other that Alice asking whether Max was still alive. Peter said that he was now living in a retirement home, not far from Cardiff. He refrained from mentioning the recent dramatic events of Max's kidnapping, attempted `homicide` and subsequent release and his own recent suicide attempts. He intended to tell her about them soon. And as for when he would relay his meeting with God in the emergent singularity, he was unsure, for he feared that she might think him of unsound mind.

Just as she was about to leave, an idea came to him on how they could help each other's recovery.

"I hope you don't think that what I am about to say is inappropriate. Please stop me if I overstep the mark. I was wondering if we could meet more regularly, perhaps once a week, to work on our `stuff` together? We could be like psychotherapists, albeit amateur ones and help each other by talking about our histories?"

"I'm not sure about that Peter. As you know, I've not spoken to anyone about my past, other than our brief talk with you yesterday. Do you think it might be of help?"

"I'm not sure, to be truthful with you. But look, what else has helped you… *nothing*."

"Well, writing down my story in my little notebook and nalyzing Bradshaw's book were of great assistance to me." She responded, somewhat indignantly.

"Yes, I'm sorry. Of course, they helped you and also myself for that matter, as they gave me an insight into my own plight." Peter replied, having felt a fool for having said such a comment without thinking.

"I also, sometimes, perform a kind of purification ceremony on my own using the dried sage, crystals and figures you found in the Heroes tin."

"That sounds very interesting-would you mind telling what you do exactly?"

"I have found a quiet hidden place in the old stone farm outbuildings at the back of the cottage. I know a secret way to get inside. I place the crystals in a wide circle and then position some of my totem animals, usually the owl and the eagle, in the centre, which I surround with the small pebbles. I then take off all of my clothes, step into this sacred space, and say a few words to the Great Spirit. After this, I light the sage sticks and brush my body up and down with the smoke. This is a form of healing the North American Indians used to perform. Finally, I wash myself with pure water from a bottle I filled from a nearby spring… I hope you do not think this sounds a bit weird and hippy-like? You're the first person I have ever told about this?" Alice couldn't believe that she had revealed something so personal to Peter.

"Thank you for sharing that with me Alice. I don't think it strange at all. Your ceremony sounds very special and healing. I wondered why you collected those items in the Heroes tin. I hope you don't mind me asking, but what exactly did you ask the Great Spirit?"

"I asked him to take away the pain from my wounded soul. But I have to admit that I doubt he ever listened to my

pathetic words, because I still felt sick inside afterwards…
Has he ever been there for you?"

"That's a *big one*…Let's say, I recently had an experience of God, or shall I say *with* God. One day soon, I will tell you about it. It will blow your mind! It happened to me during my recent visit to Cardiff. I'm worried, though, that you might think me delusional if I told you about it?"

`Sonny` was observing all this with amusement. He was seated uncomfortably on a tiny wooden stool, beside the warm fire. `She's in for a shock when he tells her, ` he thought.

"Even crazier than my little ceremony in the old barn?" Alice asked.

"Yes…a whole lot madder than that."

"Try me-then I'll let you know."

"Not yet Alice, if you don't mind."

She then finally responded to Peter's suggestion about their meeting up for mutual support sessions.

"Perhaps we could give your idea about supporting each other, a go."

"That's brilliant! When is a good time to meet?"

"What about every Saturday evening?"

"At seven?

"Yes, that's fine."

"Do you mind if I cook dinner as well-I'd like that?"

"That would be nice... I must be heading back home now; mum will be getting worried."

As she was leaving, Peter said what a pleasure it been sharing her company again. Alice reciprocated. Their eyes met directly for the first time that evening. Something magical passed between them.

God smiled. He was pleased that their friendship was growing. He then quickly scan-read a copy of Shakespeare's love sonnets he saw on a nearby bookshelf. He didn't need to retrieve the book from the shelf, he just absorbed its contents from a distance. Its hypnotic words of love sent a strange sensation running down his spine. His heart burned, for he was an incurable romantic at heart; his favourite film, after *The Godfather* and the *Carry On* films, was *Notting Hill*. He fell in love with the Julia Roberts character in the film. Mind you, he often fell in love with the heroine in the films he saw.

Chapter 19

When Alice arrived on Saturday evening, it was clear to Peter that she had made more of an effort to dress up this time. However, the long beige dress and mustard coloured woollen cardigan she wore, fell over, rather than fitted, her body shape. Her hair was also still shaggy and looked a bit like a mop. Nonetheless, he was no dashing Valentino himself. He had put on a pair of too-tight black trousers that once fitted him in his leaner days, but now clung to his body like a cyclist's spandex. His formal blue shirt, with its open top buttons, also ill fitted the occasion and made him feel uncomfortable. He looked a bit like an overweight disco dancer from the seventies. All that was missing was a heavy gold medallion chain hanging from his neck. The only consolation was that his new, smart, haircut suited him.

That evening, he cooked seared scallops and king prawns served in large scallop shells covered with a grilled mixture of gruyere cheese, breadcrumbs and oregano. The accompaniments were fresh asparagus in melted Dorset butter, a chicory and fennel salad and freshly baked granary bread. He served this with a glass of Malbec wine, (God, of course, had been right about his favourite choice in wines). He did not prepare a starter or desert, for fear of making the occasion seem too much like a romantic date and scare her off; he needn't have worried about this, for his dress sense was enough to do that.

They ate on the kitchen table. She loved the meal. They made incidental chatter.

He asked her what wine she preferred; she tried in her usual awkward way to politely say that she didn't like reds but preferred dry whites, preferably a Chardonnay. Peter got the message and loved her for her innocent clumsiness; he was no better. He made a point to himself to buy white wine for their meals in future.

It was only when they later sat down in the comfort of the living room that they conversed on more serious matters.

The details of the talks regarding their tragic childhood histories and how this affected their lives afterwards, are outlined below.

The sessions

They duly met every Saturday evening for the next eight weeks. They gradually opened up to one another, every week daring to reveal more sensitive details about their lives. The sessions followed a similar pattern-dinner with white wine followed by their retreating to the living room, where one of them would talk for a while, whilst the other listened. They hardly ever interrupted each other and made very few comments when each had finished. They just needed to talk about their `stuff` to a safe listener, someone whom they could trust, someone who was non-judgmental. They needed a silent witness rather any deep psychoanalysis. Occasionally, Alice would break down in tears. Peter would then put his arms around her and say comforting words. He cried a few times as well. They eventually revealed everything to each other.

Peter told Alice how Max had groomed him to be his victim, although he had no idea at the time that he was doing so. Max would shower Peter with the praise for the study work he did. He also gave him the attention he craved. Peter liked being there. After a short while, he would occasional sleep overnight. In a few months, he was living there all the time. It was then that the abuse began.

He talked to her about the disgusting and degrading things Max used to do to him when his brother was out of the house and the immense shame he felt from this. He mentioned how he couldn't reconcile how a person he saw as a loving father figure could abuse him.

Peter said how he then retreated into a kind of bubble. He recalled one occasion in his youth that pertained to this. It was whilst he was walking one morning with Julia Shawcross along `Birdies Lane` to Cantonian High School in the neighbouring district of Fairwater. An image suddenly appeared in his mind in which he is inside a large oval egg shell. He understood that he would spend most of his life chipping away at it from its dark inside, until many years later, cracks would appear, allowing chinks of light to enter. Gradually, small pieces of shell would break off until there was enough space for him to escape. That time has finally arrived, he said.

He described how he became mortally withdrawn and would often engineer ways of avoiding people, especially if it meant closer association with them, such as in a job interview or having his haircut. He explained how he was never fully aware of what was going in his mind and emotions; it was all a mixture of unfathomable fears. His subconsciously understood that the Max `stuff` was at the core of his troubles, but this only occupied a dim place in his consciousness behind a mass of troubled feelings which inhabited his mind like spiders. They dominated almost every waking moment, especially when he visited the real world outside. These black emotions made his life a living nightmare. Tragically, he could find no escape from them, even when the abuse came to an end. They would rule his life with unrelenting mercilessness for the next four decades.

Alice listened searchingly and compassionately. She could feel the rawness of his wound. His suffering was a mirror image of her own.

Peter continued. "I would walk with my head and shoulders bowed forward and chew my hair, which I let grow long. I remember one boy calling me `Hottentot` because of the way I stooped forward with my rear end sticking out prominently. I could hear the other boys laughing at this. This hurt me deeply at the time."

Whilst in the sixth form, Peter continued to avoid people. One of his favourite hiding places was his class form room where he would sit alone every lunchtime. He avoided the common room because it made him self-conscious and triggered powerful negative emotions of self-loathing and inadequacy.

During lunchtimes, he would retreat to this room to quietly catch up on his reading, as he tried to make up for his poor education in Glan Ely High School. He recollected how he once went through a stage of only reading books on Alexander the Great, consuming ten in a short space of time.

He told Alice of one incident, which helped him to get along better with some of the pupils and relieve his isolation in Cantonian High School. It was when members of the sixth form Chess Club began to also use his form room at lunchtime as a base. Once, one of the boys, also from Ely, was rude to Peter, who responded by half-jokingly telling him to "*shut up*". The boy took great offence to this, came over and punched Peter full in the face before proceeding to beat him up. Peter retaliated and gave him as good as he got. Afterwards, Peter became something of a hero to the group, who invited him to join their Club. From that point onwards, he was treated like a cool `Ely boy, ` who could handle himself. This incident helped him to mix a little better with the other students but he was still burdened by crippling shyness.

He also described his time as a physics undergraduate at Imperial. As in the sixth form, he was paralysed with fear, unable to engage in normal communication with others, except when he had no other option, for example during tutorial discussions. He was really fucked up emotionally. His self-awareness of this, as a pathetically shy anti-social introvert, made him feel all the worse about himself. Surely, no one could like me he thought. Much of his free time was taken up wandering the streets and parks of central London or staring out of his digs or College library window. Except for a brief friendship with a girl in the first year, he never had any girlfriends; nor did he have any male friends either. He was ill and no one either knew, or cared, about this. How he got through his degree was something of a miracle for his negative feelings about himself were all consuming.

Peter then went on to study for his PhD at Imperial. Although the main reason for this was a love for the subject, it was also because it meant that he could continue to shelter from the real world and avoid seeking employment. His PhD, on the morphogenesis of the Big Bang, was a brilliant piece of work and was published in the journal *Nature*. He told Alice how he held high hopes, at the time, that he would somehow find the fingerprint of God somewhere submerged in the mysterious world of quantum physics but found nothing. He had to wait another thirty years before he gained his first divine insight, when he discovered the God Field. When Alice asked him what this was, he said he would explain it to her later.

He revealed how the following three years as a research fellow at Imperial, were also a way of avoiding the outside world. By this time, he had lost some of his passion for his subject because he had not found any sign of Gods `hand` in creating the universe. This hurt him deeply because it meant that he finally had to forsake the spiritual meaning he so much craved. This left him having to accept a

Godless universe but he found to be a hollow, sterile and soulless place.

His career after this time, as a member of the tenured staff at Imperial, meant that he could continue to hide away in the cloistered confines of the College. His subsequent rise up the academic ladder from a lectureship position to a Professorship was due to his original research record and inspirational skills as a teacher. But his inner demons never left him.

Peter told Alice how he first met his wife when she was organising a conference aimed at forging links between schools and universities. She was working as a consultant for the Department of Education at the time. He was attracted by her inner confidence, sharp intellect and striking beauty. Peter thought Sian was drawn to him by his shy disposition and quirky mannerisms. They later met up to develop the Faculty's outreach programme for London schools. It was a great success. She slowly broke through his defences and they eventually dated; their love blossomed and they soon got married.

However, Peter eventually got sucked into drinking and gambling as a way of escaping from his black feelings. He remained in this mental prison for the following decades. He tried so hard to break free of its confines, but to no avail, until recently. His inventive mind was more of an encumbrance than an aid in solving this particular dilemma. For how does one reassemble the thousand pieces of a shattered vase into its original form? It was like solving an equation with a thousand variables. His failure to break free, made him feel more and more hopeless.

Alice's testimony made for equally disturbing listening. She told Peter how the abuse only ever took place in the holiday cottages. It was when her parents were having a few days stay in one of them, as a break from the pressures of living in the main house. It never happened in the

Llanmaes, probably because there were too many people around and therefore the greater risk of discovery. Her father would wait until Sylvia had left the cottage, usually on some Estate business, before seeking her out.

She said she was unable to stop the abuse, which started when she was thirteen, because of her father's powerful personality. If I objected, he would insist that it was her duty to give him pleasure. If she protested more vocally, he would threaten to tell her mother and say that she had led him on.

"I wanted to die. I knew that my life was over. There was no way of undoing what had been done to me. I desperately prayed for God's help but it never came, just as `He` didn't come for you. I lost faith in God then and have never really believed in `Him` since. I felt sub-human. I now realise I was mortified with toxic shame. The only thing that stopped me from killing myself was the upset it would bring to my mother."

After saying these particular words, Alice sat listless, staring vacantly into space. Then, as if decades of internal anguish had suddenly been released, she broke down like a rag doll and fell into Peter's arms, tears pouring from her tormented soul. When she stopped crying, they remained in a motionless embrace, like two petrified corpses from Pompeii.

She later went onto to explain how the abuse had continued for several years, "until I reached sixteen when it all of a sudden stopped." She didn't know why. "But afterwards, I still lived every day in fear that it might start again and only felt safe when I left for University."

Alice explained how she had withdrawn into herself at school, was unable to make friends and had a morbid mistrust of the opposite sex. Like Peter, she could never look into another person's eyes and had a terrible inferiority complex, believing herself to be unattractive and worthless. She was also the target of verbal bullying from the other girls because of her odd persona and extreme introversion.

After the sixth form, she left home to start a degree in English Literature in Exeter University, some forty miles away. However, she felt the same painful dark feelings as before. She suffered from acute social anxiety, like Peter, and was unable to make friends. She often thought of taking her own life, like so many other victims of sexual abuse do; it seemed like the only way of ending her suffering. Above all, she loathed herself and felt contaminated by feelings of self-disgust. Her only escape was to withdraw into herself.

Nevertheless, she excelled in her studies because she could lose herself in her passion for literature. She also developed a real gift for writing, especially poetry. It served as a way of relieving her mental suffering. She took great solace in creating an imaginary world of tiny animals that could speak. She passed her degree with distinction, gaining a double First-class honours, the first there for many years in her subject. Her teachers thought she had a great future ahead of her as a poet and novelist. After University, she returned with dread to the Llanmaes. Her father, though, now posed no obvious threat to her for he had become morbidly insular. It was as if something was deeply troubling him. She knew what it was - his guilt for what he had done to her as a child. This was clearly apparent from the way he could no longer bear to look at her.

However, she lacked the confidence to find a job. After a year at home, she returned to Exeter to study for a one-year teacher training P.G.C.E. She then returned to the Estate and taught for a while in a nearby comprehensive school. She hoped that facing children in the classroom would force her out of her crippling shyness. It never did; if anything, it made her feel even worse because she felt more exposed. She would take any criticism to heart, no matter how slight and use it to convince herself that she was a bad teacher. She took everything personally. God knew that, in reality, Alice had the potential to be a gifted teacher, but she never had the faith in herself to make this a reality.

As a consequence, Alice soon left her teaching position because the negative feelings it stirred in her were so painful. She then undertook private tuition for several years but ultimately gave that up as well. She eventually ended up cleaning the cottages, which she did with the fastidiousness of someone with OCD. Alice told Peter that she now realised that the reason for this was a subconscious need to wash away the dirtiness of the places where she had been abused, as if it would somehow make her clean again. This explained the thoroughness with which she carried out her cleaning duties in the `Owl, ` Peter thought. Her mother encouraged her to find a job that suited her gifts, but Alice was too afraid. What she loved most of all was to write but even that stopped after a while, for years of self-torment had incapacitated her mind.

"I thought there was no way out for me. But when my father died, I slowly began to think differently about myself and life in general. It was as if a shadow over me had partially lifted. After I sprayed his tombstone with graffiti, I came by chance upon the Bradshaw's book which I used to help me carry out my own form of self-psychoanalysis." (Peter then interrupted her to say he knew that she had sprayed the gravestone because he had found the can of spray paint in the summerhouse). "This helped me to begin to understand what I had been through at the hands of my father and the damaged it caused me. I saw how this affected me as an adult. Gradually, the shackles on my creativity lifted and I began to write again. In due course, I felt brave enough to write down in detail in my notebook, (the one that you discovered taped behind the panel), everything that he did to me. It was my testament of truth.

But I wasn't ready to reveal his name in case my mother found out; I knew it would break her heart and that, selfishly, I would be left with no one to care for me."

She told Peter how the three relationships she had with men had all ended disastrously when it came to their consummating their association. Up until that point, they had developed in an amicable, but awkward, way. On two occasions, she was unable to go through with full sexual intercourse and had burst into floods of tears. In her last relationship, she finally lost her virginity but woke up next to her partner feeling great self-revulsion, which led to her being physically sick on the side of the bed. Understandably, she told Peter, all three courtships only lasted for a short time.

Alice told Peter that it was the emotional damage caused by the trauma of the abuse which stopped her from developing a proper loving relationship and having children. Because of this, she felt like a failure as a woman. She interrupted herself at this point to exclaim.

"That *bastard* robbed me of my womanhood." Her anger seethed, contorting her features with its pain of loss.

She deeply regretted not having the confidence to leave the Estate once she had completed her studies. "I had this dream of travelling and writing novels based on the people and places I observed. But, like yourself, I retreated from the world. I was a coward. Well, I now know that this wasn't really the case; in reality I was a mentally sick person."

"I was unable to confront my father with the truth and therefore bring some closure on my past. Although this can never happen now, there is something I could do that may help." However, she did not explain to Peter what this was.

At the start of their eighth and final session, Peter asked Alice if she wouldn't mind telling him about the secret imaginary world she created whilst at Exeter University.

"I created a fairy-tale land of tiny birds who lived like ordinary people. They had hospitals, prisons and played football. Many a ball was pierced with their sharp beaks and talons. They argued, they loved, they could be cruel and kind to one another. They lived in a miniature world, barely the size of basketball, but because they were so small, the `planet` had many hundreds of such independent communities living between vast areas of wilderness where dangerous, giant `human-like` beasts roamed."

"Some troubled individuals had psychotherapy in order to help them get by. Lucy Watson was one such girl. Lucy was based on myself. She was a Little owl. She survived by eating tiny mice. Her therapist was a Harris hawk, Jacob, who was famed for his ability to empathise with others. Lucy sought out his aid to help her overcome the death of her twin sister Mary, who was found dead with a picture of her deceased lover in her hand. Jacob suggested that she take a `pilgrimage` to visit the great Snowy owl in a cave on the top of Mount Sinera, in a great mountain range in the wilderness called the Spirit Lands. Its peak was so high that it was permanently obscured by clouds. It was several days flight away."

"The following morning, Lucy set off on her journey to the find the great Snowy owl. She flew at night over the treacherous wild region in between. Only the moonlight from the planet's seven little moons illuminated the land beneath.   Several times, giant `human-like` creatures would suddenly jump up from the ground and try to grab and eat her. Exhausted, after flying for seven nights and hiding in the trees during the day, she finally caught sight of the Mount Sinera. She flew upwards through the dense white clouds near its peak, which soaked her feathers, making it difficult for her to ascend further. Eventually she reached a dark cave and called out to the great Snowy owl but received no reply. She then, warily, entered the cave only to find the burnt ashes of the owl lying in a blackened pile on the ground. There was a giant white egg on a downy nest next to it. She thought she could hear something stirring inside it, but she wasn't sure. Feeling utterly shattered and spiritually broken after her failure to see the Snowy owl, she returned home."

"On her return, Lucy stopped having therapy sessions. She became a daylight addict, wishing only to stay awake in the daytime, never at night. The other owls rejected her for this, but she could not give up her addiction for she needed to see the world as it really was, not hidden in darkness. What she saw was often painful, but at least it was the truth. However, the light hurt her eyes and damaged her internal organs. One day, close to death, she heard a voice calling out to her. It was her `dead` twin sister, who had come to save her. She took her to a shaded woodland in a part of the wilderness, where no human-like creatures roamed, where they could live safely under the shadow of the trees."

`This is where the *in-betweeners* live, ` her sister said.

`Who are they? ` Lucy asked.

`They are the innocent who had been harmed by others and have not yet been saved. `

`Who can save them? ` Lucy asked.

`God, ` she replied.

`How do you know, Mary? `

`Because `He` brought me back to life. `

`But where is God? `

`He is inside you, in the centre of your being. `

`How can I find him? `

`By letting go of your hurt Lucy. `

Sadly, Lucy couldn't let go of her hurt for it clung to her like a limpet."

. . . .

"This is the stage I am still at now Peter; like Lucy, I cannot fully let go of my past. Because of this, I am unable to find the God I secretly hope lies within me."

Peter had been captivated by Alice's tale. He then paused for a moment as he thought carefully of an appropriate response.

"Perhaps there was a Snowy owl in the egg, waiting to hatch?" He said, but this resulted in no response from Alice.

He then continued. "I was the same as yourself, I refused to let God into my life. But this all changed after my recent visit to Cardiff."

It was then that he told Alice the real reason he went back to his home city- to bring an end to his suffering by kidnapping Max, making him confess to his crimes and then killing him. He said how his remembrance of Jacob Bronowski's pleading at Auschwitz concentration camp, made him return to save him and take him back to the care home. He told her how he then tried to kill himself by jumping off the communications mast but found himself `gliding ` and being taken by Petra to meet God at the source of a new universe. He recalled his conversations with God, including his love for the *Carry On* films and his penchant for Barbara Windsor. He told Alice about the giant sphere, the mystical lake of harmonic waves and the strange Beautiful Collectors who seeded it. (He loved talking of his time with the Creator and the Beautiful Collectors). He said how meeting God and freeing Max had finally allowed him to let go his past.

When Alice tried to assimilate this bizarre account, she thought he was playing a trick on her, as a kind of clever joke. Then she wondered if he had made up an imaginary story of his own, just as she had. But it soon dawned upon her, that Peter was for real. She was stunned when she realised this. Then, without warning, she got up from her seat, walked out of the front door, got into her car and drove away at high speed. Peter did not know what to make of this unforeseen response. He feared she would, once again, keep her distance from him. `It was too early to tell her…It was too early to tell her. `He kept repeating to himself.

Alice returned, two hours later.

"Tap,tap…tap,tap…tap,tap," came the familiar sweet sound from the window. He opened the door to see her looking very flustered. "I'm sorry for storming off like that, without saying a word. I just couldn't accept the incredible things you said to me. They disturbed me greatly. You were right-it is a lot crazier than my little ceremony in the old farm buildings. You met *God!* How can *anyone* accept that! But it has now sunk in a little and I would like you to know that I hope to, one day, accept what you said. My mind isn't closed; I am open to learning new things, however outlandish they may be. But the truth is, nothing can ever be stranger than what you have just told me!"

Having calmed herself down, Alice continued. "I would like to thank you for listening to my personal history over the last few weeks-it has really helped me to accept what happened to me… Thank you so much Peter."

He praised her for her great honesty and courage.

Peter warmly thanked Alice in return. He then stood up, walked over and hugged her. She felt loved; this was a new experience for her, one that she cherished.

Their final session had come to an end. They neither questioned nor analysed their sessions. They just needed someone else to listen, in a sympathetic way, to their story.

They both agreed the meetings had helped them enormously. They confessed they had dreaded the thought of digging up the past but that a great weight had lifted from their shoulders.

"Before you go, I would like it very much if you would continue to come for dinner on Saturday evening? We don't have to talk anymore about the heavy stuff from our pasts- it will just be a social thing. We could just meet as friends."

"I would like that very much Peter…just as friends. Shall I see you the same time next Saturday then?"

As she left, Alice made an almost skip-like jig, like a little girl, to her car.

Petra placed the psychic energy that she had collected into her orb.

Sonny had been eavesdropping, as usual. He was a real nosy parker. Alice's and Peter's testimonies over the previous weeks had pained his heart but their reconciliation and growing closeness had filled it with joy.

Chapter 20

Alice looked noticeably different when she arrived the following Saturday evening for their first post session meal, although Peter could not figure out how at first. As she entered the hallway, he looked more closely at her. He could now see that her clothes lacked their usual woolly-dowdiness, although they were still plain in colour. They also appeared to hug her figure more closely, revealing the hint of a sensual figure, but it was still too difficult to tell for sure. Her hair was less disheveled than usual and had clearly been brushed more carefully. Peter wondered whether she had made more of an effort to look nice for him.

Peter had also smartened himself up. He wore black chino jeans, a new green polo shirt and a brown casual jacket. Although he did not need to wear the jacket indoors, he wore it anyway because he wanted to look decent for Alice.

As usual, they ate in the kitchen where they had a main course meal with a bottle of white wine, usually a chardonnay. Afterwards, they moved to the living room to relax and watch a film on TV. This pattern carried on for several weeks. Never once did they bring up the subject of their confessional sessions together. They had no wish to return to the pain of remembering their pasts. They just enjoyed each other's company. Alice cherished not feeling uncomfortable in the company of an adult member of the opposite sex. They both liked talking to each other as friends, without the complication that a romance would bring.

When Alice occasionally used her hand to move her fringe away from her face, he would catch a glimpse of her features, which were very pale, accept for some areas of redder skin. She had a very unhealthy complexion he thought-all she needs is some outdoor exercise and fresh air to bring colour back to her face. But what could not be hidden were the beautiful sinuous curves of her brow and her mysterious green eyes, which shone like Tahitian pearls in their shells.

He really liked Alice. He loved her company. He loved to talk to her. He loved to look at her. But he steered clear of thinking about any closer involvement.

Alice warmed to his good manners and sensitivity. She also liked his handsome features and quiet disposition. But she could also see hurt in his eyes, although she felt that would disappear once he found love. It crossed her mind whether she might be the one to give him the love he so desperately needed, but she was nervous about contemplating a passionate relationship with Peter; she didn't want the risk of destroying the lovely friendship they were developing.

As they were getting on so well together, Peter suggested that they go for walk one weekend, (he thought a trek around the local fields would be good for her health and well-being). Alice seemed happy to comply. They agreed to go the following Saturday morning, once she had finished her cleaning duties.

Their first walk was across some undulating fields to Bridport, some five miles away. The pure air and warm sunshine revitalised their spirits. They were pleased to discover a mutual passion for nature. They each had a particular feeling for the inherent majesty in a landscape. Alice also had a keen eye for seeing the beauty in smaller things. She brought Peter's attention to a beautiful damp grotto of fern, moss and fungi at the base of fallen tree and the frozen `giant` dew drops on the wings of a tiny winter moth. She was adept at observing the wildlife in the surrounding countryside and took great pleasure in informing Peter of something interesting she saw. One such instance occurred at dusk when she noticed a group of badgers emerging from their set on the edge of a secluded woodland.

He loved to listen to her voice, which was smooth and innocent. If a beautiful orchid flower could talk, it would have the same tone as Alice's speech, he thought.

This first walk was the springboard for many more afterwards, usually to different parts of the Estate's extensive lands, or to other nearby fields and villages.

It was noticeable how the locals in Symondsbury, thought her odd. They judged her and yet they did not really know her, or her story. Also, seeing her and Peter together in the village raised a few eyebrows, because many thought Alice incapable of attracting a partner. In reality though, she and Peter, were still nothing more than close friends.

Usually the villagers felt sorry for her, but some mocked her, especially the local `lads`. He observed how she would visibly close up whenever they came across them. She would then lower her head and chew the end of her long fringe with the corner of her mouth. Once, when they were having a drink in the Foundry together, Peter overheard one of the `lads, ` who was as drunk as a skunk, making fun of her to his mates: "look at old miss frumpy over there. You'd need to put a bag over head first before you shagged her." When he turned around to look at the rude idiot, he was shocked to see that he was same person who had almost run him over in his tractor a few weeks previously, when he was returning from the pub. This made Peter's blood boil all the more. It was touch and go whether he would go over and give him a piece of his mind, but he held back on this occasion, for he did not wish to upset Alice

However, what Peter hated most of all was the patronising way some of the locals would talk to her, as if she was some kind of lesser human being to be pitied. Peter, by now, knew she had a wonderful spiritual grace and hidden behind all of her messy hair, drab clothing and bowed head, there lay a beautiful jewel waiting to shine.

After several walks together, Peter could clearly see that Alice had a much healthier complexion, was fitter and had clearly lost a few excess pounds. She was also noticeably more confident and less withdrawn.

If their developing relationship could now be considered a courtship, it had so far circumvented the normal direct channels, for there was no outward show of love and affection. This allowed them the freedom to express their independent selves without the attachment a romantic association would bring. However, both were now ready to take the next step towards closer involvement.

Over dinner one Saturday evening, Peter asked Alice out for the very first time. "Would you do me the honour of going out on a date with me to Bridport next Saturday evening? Perhaps we could have dinner first and catch a film later?"

Alice knew that this invite meant their relationship had taken a different course. She felt nervous. Until recently, she would not have been able to cope with a new romance, especially as she had such a disastrous track record in that area. But she was now ready to take the risk of embarking on a new journey with Peter, for she had felt a growing passion for him. Peter's heart was also hurting, it pained him so much that he had no other option than to take this leap into the unknown and ask Alice out for their first true date.

"I would love to come Peter. Thank you for asking." Peter was surprised and pleased by her sudden acquiescence.

Both agreed to meet outside Bridport Library at seven; they had decided, after the meal, to watch the new James Bond film, *Dying of the Light*. They would both come separately in their own cars; both still needed that little bit of independence.

They were like two naïve teenagers entering their first serious relationship, excited by the prospect of discovering more about the opposite sex. They now had some say and control over their future destinies; this excited them both. They were a couple in the first throws of love; the feelings aroused were like nothing they had ever experienced before; and they wanted more, no matter what might befall them. This hunger that stems from the loss of time is like no other, its power is merciless and unrelenting in its quest for justice, which can only be realised by reclaiming one's life.

Peter waited with excited apprehension outside the Library for Alice to arrive. It was Saturday, August 11 2012. He was to remember this date very well for it marked a watershed in their relationship. He wore a smart pair of his favourite Levi 501 jeans, a green hemp shirt, a new loosely fitting beige linen jacket and a new pair of brown brogues.

Alice arrived exactly on time. She wore a long dark grey dress that went well below the knees, a dark blue blouse and a long tweed patterned cardigan. Although her wild hair was now tide back, it left her looking a bit like a frumpy, off duty nurse. Her poor self-image had once again done its best to suppress her natural beauty; a beauty she was still totally oblivious of.

They ate in a small Italian Restaurant that had caught his eye when he visited the town during the week to buy the jacket and shoes. He booked a table for the coming

Saturday evening as he wanted to guarantee a place, for it was full even then, on a mid-week afternoon. The restaurant, from the outside, seemed to meet with Alice's approval. As they were led to their table, Peter asked if could take her coat which he passed onto the waiter to hang up. Peter then pulled her seat back for her to sit down. She was surprised by his gentlemanly conduct but she also liked it. He could not comprehend why he was behaving in such an old-fashioned way but wondered if it was because he wanted to treat Alice with the respect he felt she deserved.

Alice was clearly anxious about dining out, especially in such an intimate place. She was worried that she might come across someone she knew and her old feelings of inferiority well up to the surface. For who was she to be dated by such a nice, handsome man? One of the reasons she dressed so plainly was so that she could remain unnoticed in the background. However, Peter's courteous behaviour, wit and charm helped to ease her worries to some extent. But it was knowing that he liked and cared for her, which really boosted her belief in herself and helped her to relax in the crowded little restaurant.

They had the same starter of local lobster bisque soup, which was delicious, as was the main course, a shared platter of locally caught seafood, fresh salad and Italian breads. The fresh taste of the monkfish, langoustines and shell fish, were intoxicating to their palates. Because they had being having such a fun time together, they had to skip the desert, as they were running late for the start of the film. When they had finished their meal, Peter once more pulled her chair back and helped her to put her coat on. He got some quizzical looks from the other diners for his chivalrous ways.

Once the film was over, which they enjoyed, they headed back to their separate homes. They had a lovely evening together. Peter knew it would be the wrong approach, at this stage, to be too forward with Alice and it would be a while before they could become more intimate. Now, even holding her hand or giving her kiss on the cheek would be inappropriate.

After this first date, their Saturday nights out together became a regular event, following an earlier afternoon walk. After several weeks, they also met at other times as well, about two or three times a week, usually over a cup of tea and a chat at the cottage. They enjoyed each other's company so much they hated being apart from each other for too long, but this was counterbalanced by neither wanting to be seen to cramp the other's space.

All this time, Peter never once visited the `Great House` to pick her up. On the odd occasion when he came across Alice's mother in the village, she would say a polite "hello" and perhaps exchange a few words. She had been wary of him ever since their first encounter when he connected with her inner pain. But he could tell she knew of his developing relationship with her daughter and did not resent it.

On their third date, Peter gave Alice a single red rose he had carefully selected from a larger bunch in the florists, as he was so keen to pick out the perfect one for her. When he handed it to her, she blushed. He continued with such romantic and gentlemanly gestures-he became an expert at holding doors and being polite in general.

During their fourth date, he was bold enough to kiss her on the cheek when they first met outside the Library. Alice trembled with pleasure when he did this. It was obvious to Peter that her assurance in herself was growing. Her dresses, although still long and plain, were now made of a sleeker material and showed a little of her luscious curves. She had also abandoned her dowdy cardigans, replacing them with a lighter coloured ones made of cashmere, which caressed her figure like fine lace. Her innate beauty was beginning to emerge.

By the time of their seventh date, she looked stunning. Her clothes, for the first time, closely followed the contours of her feminine form. Her newly cut and carefully brushed hair had lost its messiness and now fell elegantly over her shoulders. The fringe had gone and he could see right into her eyes, which were the colour of absinthe. She now held her head up high, abandoning her characteristically forward gait. When he first saw her like this walking towards him, he rushed towards her, embraced and kissed her on the cheek, almost touching the edge of her lips.

"You look absolutely amazing Alice! No one will recognise you!"

"Thank you very much, Peter, but I`m sure no one will notice." She replied modestly.

His compliment was soon proven true, for on their way to the restaurant the crazy tractor driving `lad, ` who had recently been uncouth about her in the pub in Symondsbury, looked at her lustfully, but without remembering her. Peter asked Alice to excuse him for a moment, whilst he rushed back to inform him that the beautiful person he had just walked past was the girl he had mocked in the village pub some weeks before. The `lad` then stared in the direction of Alice, who was closely observing what was going on, although she was unaware of what they were discussing. Peter could see the shock on his face when he realised it was her. He then apologised to Peter for his stupidity saying, "Once I've had a few jars, I can become a real asshole- I'm very sorry for being so rude about her mate." After this meeting, they sometimes crossed each other's path in the Foundry and became occasional drinking buddies. Peter later found out that his father, who worked on the Estate, had physically brutalised him as boy, which might partly explain the way he turned out as a man.

Later that evening in the restaurant, Peter handed Alice a small gift box. She opened it to reveal a mother of pearl pendant engraved with a scene of Bushmen hunting a herd of antelope. He had purchased it from a local charity shop for just three pounds, the shopkeeper not realising its true value. As soon as he saw it, he recognised its synchronicity with his dream of the Eskimo hunting caribou and his meetings with the `Eskimo` vagrant with his similarly tattooed arms. He could not believe his luck in finding it; to him it was priceless. She gazed at its beauty, but at first refused to accept it, until Peter eventually persuaded her to keep it.

Peter's feelings for Alice continued to grow. He loved her innocent purity. He likened her to a beautiful crystalline formation, drip-fed from the mineral rich waters of a subterranean cavern, suddenly illuminated by the penetrating beams of a blazing sun. He couldn't help thinking in such imagery, for he was, like Sonny, a hopeless, old fashioned romantic at heart.

There was something magical in two damaged souls emerging from the darkness to explore their feelings for one another. They were like two islands merging into one new landform upon which they could learn the language of love.

This growing affection for each other convinced Peter to commit himself to booking the cottage for a further six months and to look for local work to help him pay the bills. He needed this regular source of income as his savings were running out.

Sylvia was delighted when Peter booked the cottage for another long spell. She had deliberating kept it free from other bookings in the hope that he would extend his stay; she was also quietly pleased that he was `dating` her daughter and was hoping that this might one-day lead to marriage.

Peter soon got a permanent job working as a chef in the Foundry. He worked every weekday lunchtime and evening, when they were at their busiest, assisting the Head

Chef who had found it hard to cope by himself. He excelled in his new role and had many ideas on how to improve the service and the menu, but only mentioned a few of them to the Head Chef, so as not to offend his large ego. The Foundry had gained an excellent reputation as one of Dorset's public houses for food. It was very popular and had many covers, which meant the landlord could afford to pay him a good wage.

However, after several more weeks of dating, he noticed a change in Alice's demeanor; it was barely perceptible at first. Nonetheless, as he had grown to know her so well, he knew something was on her mind. Then, one night, after their usual Saturday date together, she said to him.

"Peter, there is something I have to do tomorrow which is very important to me personally. I'm afraid, I can't tell you what it is, but I will tell you later. Please don't be offended, it's just that I don't want you to worry."

"But, by not telling me, you will only make me worry all the more!" Peter responded with concern.

Alice, however, was insistent that it was something she had to do by herself. She added that she was concerned that if she told him what she intended to do, he might try to dissuade her from going ahead with it. She finished by saying.

"This is something that has been on my mind for a long time. My continued recovery is dependent upon me going through with it."

Peter accepted this and didn't bring up the subject anymore, even though he was even more anxious now that she had elaborated on the context of her intention.

Sylvia was sitting in the small study at the back of the house, where she would often relax. It was ten o'clock on Sunday morning and she had just finished having breakfast with her daughter. Alice had been summing up the courage to talk with her about something that had been bothering her for some time.

"Mum could I have a word with you about dad?"

"By all means, darling. What's on your mind? You look worried."

"Mum, do you remember how I was a happy, bubbly young girl up until I turned thirteen and how I suddenly changed afterwards?"

"You didn't change that much darling."

"Oh yes I did and you know I did mum."

"Why are you dwelling on things in the distant past my dear?"

Alice did not respond directly to her question but instead added.

"My becoming extremely introverted at thirteen coincided with us staying sometimes in the Estate cottages. You remember, because dad and you wanted a break from the stresses of living in Llanmaes."

"Yes, it was a bit of a topsy-turvy lifestyle but your dad and I were very happy-we loved staying in the Cottages, especially the `Owl. ` Didn't you?"

"Well, I wasn't happy mum-in fact I was deeply upset."

"Why darling?... I never realised that... Why was this?"

"It was because of dad."

She caught her mother's reaction at the precise moment she said this. Her bemused expression suddenly froze as if she was incapable of moving her facial muscles and reacting to what her daughter had said. She seemed shell-shocked.

Alice braced herself to say the hardest thing she had ever said to anyone before. She could feel her heart bursting in her chest and feared that she couldn't go through with it, but her time with Peter had given her the inner strength to let it out.

"Mum, between the ages of 13 to 16, dad sexually abused me in the cottages."

Her mum jumped out of the armchair with a violent energy belying her years.

"How dare you say that about your father. *How dare you!* Especially now that he is dead and cannot speak for himself!"

Alice acted swiftly to regain control of the situation by saying with uncharacteristic authority, "Sit down mum and shut up and listen, for once!"

Her mother did as she was told. She was terrified of what her daughter was about to say.

Alice then repeated her earlier statement.

"Mum, between the ages of 13 to 16, dad sexually abused me in the cottages," and then adding, "that was why I changed."

Sylvia said nothing.

Alice then proceeded to outline the details of what had taken place; when, where and what Lord Traherne did, each time firmly scolding her mother when she tried to intervene. Her final words were, "Mum I have told you, if God himself be my witness, the *absolute truth.*"

There followed complete silence for a minute or two. Her mother, despite now having the opportunity to now speak, remained quiet.

Alice continued. "I need you to tell me the truth about something mum…did you know? Did you know what dad was doing to me?"

Her mother remained comatose.

"*Did you know?*" Alice shouted. "You owe it to me to tell me the truth… *Did you know* dad was abusing me?"

An infinity of time seemed to have elapsed before her mother broke her silence. It was as if the opposing forces of truth and falsehood were battling with each other in her mind.

"Yes, I did know Alice. I am *so sorry.*" Her mum muffled these words as she broke down and cried uncontrollably. Her mother's cries were those of someone who, having dreamt they had committed an evil deed, suddenly awoke to find they had actually carried it out.

Alice stood over her mother, stunned, as she tried to take in what she had just admitted to. She hadn't expected her to answer in the affirmative. She had wondered whether she knew but thought it highly unlikely that she did. But now that the truth was out, she found it impossible to digest.

"But mum why? How could you have known and did nothing to protect me? How could you!" She blurted out these words with an anger born out of the deepest feelings of betrayal.

Her mother managed to gather herself together enough to reply.

"Alice…Alice…you don't understand. I didn't find out until you were nearly sixteen. I had no idea until you just told me that it started so much earlier."

"How did you find out?" Alice demanded to know.

"One afternoon, I came back earlier than expected to the `Owl. `I went upstairs and through a gap in the bedroom door, saw him doing things to you. He caught me watching him. I then ran away, devastated. My heart was broken. I packed my bags and went to stay at my sisters, telling her that we were having marriage difficulties. I made up my mind to tell her about what I had witnessed, but your father soon arrived. I was terrified when I saw him. Your father had a fearsome temper, you know. He insisted that I accompany him to his car for a drive to `sort things out. ` Reluctantly, I agreed-I did not want to create a scene in front of my sister."

"He begged me to forgive him for what he had done; saying that he only did it that once. He said he was frustrated because we no longer had a sex life together. He begged me to forgive him and said that he would never do it again. He implored me not to speak to you about it because the thought of you knowing that I knew, might push you over the edge."

"So, I said nothing… nothing to my sister and nothing to you. I believed him when he said he would stop."

"How could you forgive him so easily? He destroyed me! He destroyed my life!"

"I didn't know. I believed your father when he said it only happened that once."

"Mum! It went on for three years!"

Alice gathered her thoughts for a moment before saying.

"Even if you didn't know it went on for so long, how could have forgiven him so easily?"

Alice then delivered her devastating verdict to her mother.

"Mum, I have made up my mind. I never want to see, or speak to, you again. I'm leaving."

"Please don't say that Alice…I am so sorry…please forgive me…I really love you."

"I'm sorry mother…I cannot forgive you…*ever.*" Sylvia bowed her head and broke down once more; it was a deep, heart wrenching, guttural, bellowing cry.

Alice calmly walked out of the study and the mansion. She would never go back there to live again. She would miss her mother terribly but could never excuse her for her inaction; only God could deal with the consequences of this.

God who was, as usual, watching them, felt a deep sadness for both of them.

Petra, who was by his side, was deeply troubled by what she had witnessed. It was very difficult for her to collect their psychic energies but she knew that it was for the greater purpose of creating a more loving and forgiving future universe.

Alice left the house grief stricken and angry. She wandered along country lanes and then into some paddocks in a state of confusion. The normally shy horses sensed that something was wrong with her and didn't run off; one even came up to her as she lay on the grass. She tenderly stroked its long face and maim. But her inner rage could have moved mountains; her sadness would have stirred the most hardened heart. Alice ended up sitting in an abandoned barn, feeling utterly alone. She remained there for several hours. All the old wounds of self-hate and powerlessness returned. She felt abandoned and vulnerable. Her life felt hopeless once more. She lay on the dry straw and retreated once more to her imaginary childhood world, where she played with her friends in a beautiful flower meadow.

God was hurting for her, but sadly could do nothing. He knew she had done the right thing to find out the truth from her mother and that it would be catastrophic.

`I still have Peter, ` she thought. ` I'm sure he'll understand what just happened between mum and myself. I hope he will not be too angry with me for not telling him I was going to see her. I hope he still likes me? ` she asked herself pitifully, like a wounded child.

She then headed across the blackened fields. Only the occasional car headlights helped guide her towards the circuitous country lane which led to Peter's cottage. She walked for three miles, dazed and disorientated, until she eventually knocked on the horseshoe shaped doorknocker, which she normally never used. It was one o'clock in the morning. Peter had been worrying about her all evening and this only escalated the later it got. He wondered who could be calling at such an hour? It couldn't be Alice, he thought, because she either lets herself in or taps the window. Therefore, he was very surprised to see her when he opened the door. "Come in...come in," he said. She stood there motionless and expressionless, but obviously in state of distress. He then put his arm around her and led her to the comfort of the sofa in the living room. She sat staring blankly into space without uttering a word. Peter was worried that she may have had a breakdown.

"Peter…my mum knew!" She said in a quiet voice.

"My mum knew!" She repeated.

Peter knew exactly what she was referring to. But before he could say anything, she told him everything that had just transpired between her mother and herself. Her last words to him were, "I hope you don't hate me?"

"No, I don't hate you Alice...I love you." That was the first time he had used these words.

Alice, emotionally and physically exhausted, fell asleep in his arms with these words resounding in her heart.

She awoke on the couch late in the morning with a warm blanket around her and a pillow under her head. Peter came into the room with a breakfast of poached egg on toast and a mug of coffee for her. Alice thanked him and hungrily consumed the lot, for she had not eaten or drank for almost a day.

Peter was the first to speak, telling Alice that he had heard everything that she had said about her mother. It was then that she broke down in tears for the first time, as the reality of her mother's deceit finally sunk home.

"Let it all out Alice…don't hold anything back."

When she had recovered, she said.

"The main reason for speaking to her was to tell her about what dad did to me, not to find out that she knew what was going on."

"I will never stay there again. I will never speak to her again."

Peter, feeling deeply upset and concerned for her, then said.

"Please stay with me in the cottage. I will give you your own space. No strings attached. We could live like two independent people. I will soon find another cottage to rent away from the Estate and you could come and live there with me as well. I will seek a full refund for the remaining time I have paid in advance for the `Owl` and will use this to go towards the rent in the new place."

Alice thanked him and said that, if it wasn't too much trouble, she would be pleased to accept his kind offer.

In the afternoon, Peter rang the Estate office and told them that Alice was off sick with depression. He said that she would be off work for the rest of the week. He then drove her to Llanmaes to pick up her things and collect her car. They waited, out of sight. for a while until they saw her mother drive off. She seemed lost, her expression vacant. Alice then quickly gathered some of her essential possessions, carefully avoiding being seen by any of the staff in the house. She then loaded them into the boot of her black VW Polo, which she had left in the driveway when she had wandered off in a daze the previous day. She then drove away from Llanmaes for the very last time.

On Tuesday, Peter managed to find a smaller two bed roomed cottage to rent not far from the Jurassic Coast, near Charmouth. It was cheaper than the `Owl` as well.

The following day, Peter received a full refund from the Estate Office without having talked to Sylvia, who had avoided his phone calls. The money was transferred straight away into his online bank account. Sylvia clearly had no objections to his request, no doubt because of the guilt she was harbouring, following her explosive meeting with Alice.

On the Friday, Alice posted her letter of resignation; she could not bear the thought of working for the Estate again.

They moved into their new cottage the following day. The last thing Alice did was to remove her secret belongings from the behind the panel at the back of the summerhouse.

Other than sharing a house in Exeter with other students at University and her parent's short stays in the Estate cottages, Alice had never lived away from the `Great

House` before. However, she soon took to her new home. She liked its quaintness, especially its aged thatched roof, little windows and low exposed oak beams. She loved to get lost in its wild garden which was overgrown with uncut wild grasses and the lilting stems of last summer's flowers. She also marvelled at a beautiful wooded valley near to the cottage with its enchanted little brook.

They quickly settled into their new home. Both had separate bedrooms and lived largely autonomous lives, each giving the other their own space. Never once did they hold hands, kiss or talk with passion to each other inside the cottage. Alice, in particular, needed this fear-free and attachment-free space, to liberate herself. She feared that closer emotional ties in their new home would hinder this. Yet they still craved a loving relationship with each other, so they carried on with their Saturday night dates. Therefore, their courtship continued outside the cottage but when they stepped back inside, they reverted to just being non-romantic friends.

Alice soon found a job as a cleaner in the Council Office in Lyme Regis; she cherished her new financial independence, for she never really had any before, because she was reliant on her mother as her main source of income.

They had an idyllic time in the cottage and loved one another's company. They had many a fun time together, not least with Alice's attempts at cooking. No matter how hard she tried, the end product was quite often a burnt offering that resembled the charcoal burial remains recently found in a Bronze Age barrow on a nearby hillside. Peter ate many an unpalatable meal without saying a word of complaint. Likewise, she never commented on of his botched attempts at DIY, like his repeated efforts to put up a bookshelf, which were something to behold!

Alice's confidence continued to grow. She found an evening job for a tuition agency, teaching GCSE and A level English to students living in the local area. She now always dressed well and looked beautiful. She walked with an upright posture and looked people in the eye more than ever before.

Peter made a great success working as a chef in the Foundry; even the Head Chef insisted they share this title because of his outstanding contribution to the menu and the dishes cooked. The landlord willingly agreed to this proposal which meant a substantial wage increase.

Nevertheless, something was increasingly troubling him, but he could not comprehend what it was. Alice, aware of his unease, was concerned for him. One day, whilst they were visiting the marshland nature reserve at Studland, the problem then dawned upon him. It came to him whilst he was observing the beautiful dance of a swarm of gnat's above a willow tree, which moved like a murmuration of miniature starlings. He then realised that it was his unfinished theory which was unsettling him, for the swarm moved like an ever-changing field, a fundamental characteristic of the God Field. From that moment onwards, thoughts of his theory kept on pestering him. It felt as if some mysterious source was nudging his brilliant mind into finally uncovering the deeper meaning of the God Field. His intuition was right of course, for Sonny had been connecting to him via the very Field itself.

Peter then worked through the substantial collection of notes relating to his theory. However, he failed to make the all-important breakthrough. He wasn't able to tap into the rich vein of creation that inspired him to develop his theory in Imperial. He therefore chose to abandon his search for a while, vowing to return to it in the near future with a fresh mind.

However, he did find inspiration in one important area-he was consumed by his passion for Alice, as she was for him. They were deeply in love. They especially looked forward to their dates together. Now neither of them took their own cars but shared a taxi instead. They would often go to nearby Lyme Regis for a meal and see a film. However, now and then, they would travel further afield to Exeter and Salisbury to visit the theatre, a comedy club or attend a lecture.

Peter continued to act the perfect gentleman; he couldn't stop himself for something within him wanted to court and woe Alice in this courteous way. She loved being treated like this as well. They would often hold hands, and when they found a private space outside, he would softly stroke her hair and kiss her gently on the lips. But when they returned home and he opened the door for her, their passionate ways would come to an end and they would resume their other life as just close friends.

They also continued their regular Saturday afternoon walks and would often explore new picturesque locations in more distant parts of the region, such as Chesil Beach, Lulworth Cove, the Avon valley, or Salisbury plain. This involved driving there first and following a circular walk back to the car. It was whilst on one such outing to a beautiful river valley, where a terrifying incident took place. It was a warm and sunny, `Indian Summer's, day in mid-October. Alice took Peter to a beautiful secluded valley she knew, where they had a picnic. Feeling emboldened. she suggested they go skinny dipping in the river, confessing to Peter that she had done so several times there in the past. "It makes me feel pure again." He found it impossible to resist her innocent exuberance and they were soon walking naked into the pure waters of the river.

The water was not as cold as he had imagined and after the initial chill, Peter found that he could immerse himself up to his shoulders without too much discomfort. Alice walked straight into the deepest pool without any hesitation. They swam, played and splashed each other like two children. Peter at one stage ducked her head under water and, as she arose, pulled her gently towards him. They looked directly into each other's eyes without fear and self-loathing. He lifted up her cheek and kissed her passionately on the lips. They both felt aroused but before Peter could continue, she said "No Peter. I can't, not now, I'm sorry… soon," she said. As they stood embracing one another, they suddenly heard a loud `bang` and saw a big splash in the water only ten feet away from them. They looked up towards the top of a field overlooking the valley to see a man with a shotgun in his hands, some two hundred feet away. He shouted, "Get off my land you fucking perverts." Terrified, they were unable to move. The man ran down the steep slope towards them and stood over the riverbank. He was a short, middle-aged, round-faced fellow, with longish, jet-black hair. He wore a heavy brown trench coat with the extra lapel on the shoulders. He had tormented features. He looked directly at Alice's face, who was being protected by Peter's body and shouted out to her, "I knew it was you- I've seen you swimming here naked before. You're Traherne's daughter, aren't you? I only wish it was your father swimming there so that I could have shot him for real, right though his *fucking head*."

Peter, fearing for their lives, attempted to appease the situation by saying, "Look, we are very sorry. We didn't know this was private property. It won't happen again, I promise you. We'll just get changed, leave and never come back. That is once you have put down your gun and turned away from us, so that we can dress in private."

The hostile man, suddenly realising the seriousness of what he had just done, became embarrassed and fearful of getting in trouble again with the local police, with whom he already had a bad reputation. He duly put his gun down and turned his back to them, before calling out.

"I'm sorry for scaring you, I didn't mean to fire the gun, it just went off by accident. I only wanted to get you off my land." He was lying of course, for he meant to fire at the water to frighten them because he wanted to scare Lord Traherne`s daughter. But he had no real intention of shooting them and the risk of him doing so was negligible, for he used to be a marksman in the Second Parachute Regiment.

Alice and Peter then ran out of the water, grabbed their clothes and headed for the safe cover of some oak trees further up the valley side opposite to the shooter's. Only then did they get dressed.

Their blissful moment together had been destroyed by a nasty act of intimidation, which was totally out of proportion to their innocent `crime` of swimming naked in a river on someone else's land. They could not understand why he had fired the gun at them, other than the hatred he seemed to be carrying for her late father. They also concluded that such a life-threatening action could only stem from someone of unsound mind.

Peter insisted they drive to the police station straight away and tell them about what happened.

"We could have been killed." He said.

Alice was reluctant to go, mainly out of embarrassment for having swam naked in the river.

"We did not commit a crime, Alice." Peter added.

She then told Peter that she thought she knew who the shooter was and that he may have once been a tenant farmer on one of the Estate farms.

Alice eventually relented and later that day they went to Bridport Police Station to report the incident. The Duty Officer immediately knew who the man was and he was soon arrested. Eventually, after some heavy police questioning, he admitted to firing the gun deliberately to terrify them. He later acknowledged that he was really angry with Alice's father over something that happened years previously and was taking his rage out on his daughter by frightening her. Fearing a heavy charge from the police, he finally told the truth about his grudge with

Alice's father. He explained how he found out from his daughter that Lord Traherne had sexually abused her when she was young girl, but she only told him about this after he had died and there was nothing he could do about it. "Have you seen her now-she is completely messed up in her head because of this?"

Having listened to his full story and feeling compassion for him, the police wrote in their report that he had fired the gun by accident. They charged him with the less severe charge of the careless use of a registered firearm, not for shooting at someone deliberately. When the police returned his shotgun to him some months later, he went straight away to the river and chucked it into a deep pool. He feared that, if he kept it, he might one-day shoot someone on purpose.

After this unpleasant incident, Peter was very concerned about Alice's phobia towards sex. He was worried for her. She, herself felt remorse for having refrained from closer intimacy whilst they embraced in the river; she so much wanted them to take this next step in their relationship. Peter had hoped that they would both be ready to consummate their romance. Up to now, he had never rushed her into a closer liaison; they didn't even have their first kiss until well into their courtship. He wondered how he could help her to overcome this problem, but its source ran much deeper than he thought.

Chapter 21

Peter delayed bringing up his concerns with Alice about their lack of intimacy. The upsetting shooting event had clearly disturbed her and made her more reserved. He was worried that the great progress she had made in coming out of herself had stalled and she may even have gone backwards. Then one Sunday morning, three weeks after the incident, just as he was about to broach his worries about their lack of closeness, Alice asked Peter an odd question.

"Have you heard of a sweat lodge ceremony, Peter?"

"Is it something to do with the North American Indians?"

"Yes-it is one of their sacred rituals."

"Why do you ask?"

"Well, I have read about it a few times; apparently they have a powerful healing effect. I noticed on the internet that there is a ceremony taking place this Saturday in a field near Sherborne, about thirty miles away."

"Do you want to go?"

"Yes, I'd like to. I have wanted to attend a sweat lodge for several few years but have always been too shy to go by myself. Its healing powers are meant to help those who have suffered from serious emotional trauma. The ceremony helps a person to find and reclaim their lost soul. Doesn't that describe us? Doesn't it feel as if we have lost contact with our true spirit?"

"You're right Alice; it feels like a disease of the soul."

"I know you have already gone a long way to healing yourself Peter, but I still feel the wound inside me. This is holding myself and our relationship back."

"Perhaps it may be good for us to go Alice? Shall we? Are there any places left; we're leaving it a bit late?"

"I'll give them a call straight away to find out." Alice quickly looked through the *Sacred Hoop* website to find a contact telephone number.

Whilst on the phone to the Sweat Lodge organisers, she told Peter that, "there are only two places out of twenty-five left. The cost is forty pounds per person. Shall I book them?"

"Yes, book them now in case someone else does," Peter replied excitedly.

After making the booking, she said, "What have we done?"

"I'm not sure Alice, but we'll find out in two days' time."

Alice then added, "I think it might help me to overcome my fear of sex. I so much want us to fulfill ourselves in this way. I know it has been worrying you as well, especially since that time in the river."

"I am glad that you mentioned it because, as you guessed, it has been on mind a lot. I want to take the relationship further but I know you have this obstacle."

The days leading up to the ceremony were full of eager anticipation for them both. Their interest grew all the more when they found out that Wallace Black Elk, a famous Lakota Sioux shaman, was to lead the `sweat. `

The sky was virtually cloudless when they arrived at the farmland where the event was to take place. There was a slight chill in the air. It was late October and autumn was in full swing. Great swathes of wind-blown leaves scurried across the road, reminding Peter of his strange experience with the spiralling leaves on the road to Cambridge to receive the Feynman Medal.

They had great difficulty finding the site, for it lay hidden in the bottom of a sheltered valley, in a meadow of overgrown tussocky grasses and flowers. Small flocks of linnets, goldfinches, siskins, were busily feasting upon the rich bounty of seed heads. The birds scattered as the car made its way across the field, negotiating its bumpy terrain. The abundant birdlife gave then a good feeling about the forthcoming ceremony.

Peter parked his car next to about a dozen others in one corner of the small rectangular shaped field, which ran alongside a small river. There were fifteen or so tents in another corner. About fifty yards away from these was a small wooden framed structure with steps, which they later found out was a compost toilet. The field on all sides, except for the river, was surrounded by dense deciduous woodland. Below, near the river, was a large teepee with smoke rising gently from its pinnacle before disappearing into the deep blue above. Twenty or so people were sitting around a blazing fire near its entrance. There was no sign of the sweat lodge.

As they neared the group, a young lady came over and warmly greeted them. She introduced herself as Eka, Black Elk's god daughter, although she had no recognisably American Indian features, for she was white skinned with blond hair. She also wore western clothes. A young man walking in bare feet, then joined them. He introduced himself as Four Feathers, Black Elk's grandson. In contrast to Eka, he looked typically American Indian with his dark red-skinned face, hawk like eyes and angular features. His hair was tied back in a ponytail and had four long feathers hanging from it. He wore denim jeans and a bead embroidered leather waist jacket over his bronze torso. Once he made them feel welcome, he took them over to join the rest of the group. On their way, Eka said that everyone else was already there, most having arrived the night before.

Alice and Peter sat down behind the others, as they felt self-conscious and did not wish to be noticed. Black Elk sat opposite them on an old plastic milk bottle crate. He was very old. The lines on his face, carved by experience and the elements, showed a person of great character. Although he seemed weary and tired looking, his eyes still shone like an eagle's. He had a battered old brown leather cowboy-like hat on his head, wore denim jeans, a dirty old checked shirt, a ragged brown jumper and a blue Confederate soldier-style jacket. He was also in bare feet, like his grandson. An ancient pair of mud coated hobnail boots were by his side. He looked quite an odd sight. Nevertheless, he had registered the presence of the new comers with a subtle glance of his sharp eyes and liked them immediately, even though they had not yet spoken. However, he seemed more interested in the fire than the assembled crowd.

Eka came over with two bowls of hot porridge for Alice and Peter, which helped to relieve the cold nip in the air.

Black Elk's goddaughter then welcomed everyone and told them of some domestic arrangements, such as meal times, washing facilities and how to use the compost toilet.

"Don't forget to chuck a handful of sawdust down the hole when you have finished, but it's probably not a good idea to look down afterwards!" This caused some embarrassed laughter from the mainly city folk who were gathered there.

Four Feathers then informed the crowd that most of the day would involve collecting materials to help make the lodge, as well as gathering firewood and stones, in readiness for the start of the ceremony at sunset.

Black Elk then spoke for the first time. He told everyone about the importance of the sweat lodge to the Lakota Sioux and other native North American tribes. It was sometimes difficult to understand what he was saying because he talked in a low voice and had a poor command of English. On a few occasions, his grandson intervened to clarify what he was saying. However, two phrases in particular struck a chord with Alice and Peter: "Each brave would hope to receive a vision from Wakan Tanka, the Great Spirit." And "For some of you, your old self will die and your new self will be re-born."

As he spoke, a young man interrupted him and said, "Look at that, isn't that amazing!" Everyone looked up to where he was pointing. The bright red tail of a comet, illuminated by the rays from the rising sun, was clearly visible just above the trees.

"What a wonderful sight," a middle-aged woman called out, "it must be a good omen."

The comet had recently become visible during the daytime over Britain, but Black Elk seemed unaware or impressed by it, judging by his joking reply.

"I thought it was an aircraft trail." This response seemed to deflate the spirits of the onlookers. Black Elk seemed to be deliberately debunking its mystical significance, perhaps with the aim of bringing the audience back down to Earth. However, his cheeky style endeared him even more to Alice and Peter.

When Black Elk had finished speaking, Four Feather's asked everyone to take a short break before gathering again to prepare the lodge. When the group reformed, Four Feathers took them to a nearby woodland where they gathered dried sticks and logs for the fire, which they placed in a large pile next to the river near where the sweat lodge was to be constructed. Several more trips were needed before enough firewood had been collected. Their next task was to collect several long thin branches from the willow trees growing alongside the river. Four Feathers fearlessly climbed to the top of a tall tree overhanging the river to harvest some excellent branches growing there.

They also collected some large stones from the river bed and placed these next to the wood pile.

Four Feathers then called everyone together and instructed them to dig a pit about three feet in diameter and two feet deep. He then gave them guidance on how to make a dome shaped frame around the pit using the firmly embedded willow branches tied together with cord. When this was completed, they pulled a very large sheet of tarpaulin over the frame to make it waterproof, leaving a flap for the entrance, which pointed towards the west. Four Feathers then placed a few large stones on the huge woodpile before igniting it.

With the preparations complete, they all had dinner in the teepee, which was deceptively spacious inside. They sat facing each other around an open wood fire and introduced themselves using a talking stick where only the person holding it could speak. Peter wondered why each of them was there; perhaps they were ill at ease with themselves or the dying world around them, he wondered.

Four Feathers said that they would only need the minimum amount of clothing for the lodge, as it would be very hot and steamy; he suggested a towel or shorts to cover the "embarrassing bits". After dinner, they retired to their tents to get ready. Peter and Alice used this time to set up their own tent near to the others.

As the time for sunset approached, Four Feathers gathered everyone near the entrance to the lodge. Black Elk then came out of the teepee wearing just a towel around his waist. He had a headband with several large eagle feathers attached to it. He was also carrying a sacred pipe. He looked towards the falling sun and blessed the lodge by thanking Wakan Tanka. He then went inside, followed by his grandson and goddaughter. Four Feathers then beckoned the rest of the group to follow and sit in circles around the pit. He then cleared a narrow pathway between the pit and the entrance. Black Elk said some more words in his native tongue and lit the sacred pipe before passing it around for everyone to inhale. Four Feathers then left the lodge to collect a large hot stone from the fire with a long-handled metal scoop and carefully placed it in the central pit. When he had collected four more stones, he closed the flap by the entrance. Everything was in complete darkness, except for the glowing rocks. They were so hot it seemed as if one could see right through them. Waves of pulsating red, yellow and white heat moved across its translucent surface. Tiny specks of light sparkled randomly; `the stars are once again here to greet me, ` Peter thought.

Four Feathers began chanting and banging loudly on his drum. The sound filled the confined space with a great intensity. Black Elk then started chanting as well. After a few moments, Black Elk drew a ladle of water from a bucket and poured it onto the hot stones, which hissed like a disturbed viper, sending a dense cloud of hot steam upwards to the roof which then travelled downwards along the inside of the tarpaulin until it `fell over` the anxious gathering.

When the steam reached Alice and Peter, it felt as if a wall of hot energy had hit them; it `threw` them and disturbed them, for its power was immense. It burned them, it hurt them, they could not think. They felt abject panic and wanted to run away, but they could not. Black Elk then poured another ladle of water onto the stones, sending forth a further wave of hot steam. The stifling heat hit them again, incapacitating them once more. The heat, along with the chanting and sound of beating drums, created a hallucinatory and intoxicating atmosphere.

As more water was poured onto the stones, one woman started to cry; she was soon joined by two others. The cries became louder and turned into an unearthly whaling sound. This was very unsettling for the others. Alice then started to cry. Soon she was making the most ungodly like sound. It came from a dark place within, where it had lain for a very long time. She was letting go of a stain, a canker, an evil energy.

Black Elk then poured a further ladle of water onto the hot rocks. The hot steam was now at its most oppressive. Alice and Peter felt as if they were about to die a physical death. 'I must go out, I'm going to die... Why is no one leaving? ' He thought. At that point, first one man, then another left the lodge, closely followed by two women. Peter and Alice made a conscious decision to themselves to remain, even if it meant their own death. Peter, concerned that Alice might be suffering like him, squeezed her hand; reassuringly, she pressed his in return. But in reality, her anguish was as great as his. However, they were incapable of speaking to one another. Eventually, Four Feathers stood up, walked over to the entrance, opened the flap, then asked everyone to go outside and recover. The first of four rounds was over.

Alice and Peter collapsed onto the damp grass. After a short break, Four Feathers asked everyone to go back inside, but to remain outside if they found the first experience too much to cope with. Three people chose not to go back. Peter feared that, if the first session was so traumatic, what would the next three be like?

For each of the subsequent rounds, the cooler rocks were replaced with hot ones from the blazing fire outside. The second round was thankfully not as harrowing as the first and the last two were much more bearable.

When it was all over, they all lay, or crouched down, on the moist, cool grass outside. Peter and Alice hugged one another. It was pitch black except for the light from the fire outside the sweat lodge. The only other light came from the dense canopy of stars overhead and the thin light of a crescent moon floating just above the horizon.

Alice then headed for the compost toilet in the corner of the field. As she did so, she could hear the footsteps of someone walking on the grass close behind her. They were not heavy steps but were more like those of a woman. She speeded up to give herself more space between them, yet the footsteps now seemed closer than before. `How dare somebody crowd my personal space after what I have just been through, `she thought. She then turned around to confront the `rude` individual, but no one was there. Shocked, it took her a few moments for this to sink in. She couldn't fathom out why no one was there and then wondered if the invisible person was her spirit guide.

Most of the others went to the teepee afterwards to sit around the warm fire and recover. Some, however, were too exhausted or sensitised to face human company and retired to their tents; Peter and Alice were amongst them. They said very little to each other and slept as soon as they had climbed into their sleeping bags.

Alice dreamt that she was living in the ancient city of Kish in ancient Mesopotamia. Her name was Nezret. Her parents had banished her from the family home when she was thirteen years old. Her only hope of survival was to wait by the central square for the chance that a person from a good household might take her as a slave. Whilst she was waiting, she was joined by another boy, Zocrat, who had also been forced to leave his parent's home. He was fifteen years old. They waited for several days and nights, living off scraps of food they found on the streets and drinking from the waters of the great reed banked river that wound its way through the city. Eventually, a mean looking man said that he would take them both as long as they did not cause him any trouble. Both agreed to go with him, as they were so desperate. However, just as they were about to leave with him, a beautiful woman, called Petra, arrived. She then proceeded to barter with the slave owner as she tried to take his two new purchases off his hands. She had to pay ten minas for each of them, before he would change his mind. Petra then took them back to her home where she lovingly brought them up as if they were her own children, just as she had done for several other `strays` who also lived with her. Nezret and Zocrat later went on to get married and have a beautiful daughter together.

Just then, Alice was disturbed from her dream by a deafening screeching sound from above the tent. Peter remained fast asleep in his sleeping bag. Alice opened her eyes and climbed outside to see a white barn owl perched on top of the tent, before it flew away. She then vividly recalled the dream she was just having and of the lovely lady who had saved her and the boy. Then as she looked up at the magical tapestry of stars, they all, bizarrely, seemed to be moving in one direction - towards the northeast. She blinked her eyes thinking that she must be hallucinating, but the stars continued to move in a procession towards the northeast, before sinking over the horizon.

Alice excitedly shook Peter to stir him from his deep sleep. "Did you hear that owl calling outside tent Peter?" she asked breathlessly. Peter said that he hadn't. He looked at her; the yellow light from glow of the fire beside the sweat lodge radiated her beautiful face. She then lay down beside him. They kissed and made love for the first time. They loved one another with a tenderness, which comes from the freedom from suffering. Their passion consumed them. When they climaxed, they felt the ecstasy that only the wounded innocent can feel when they experience true love for the first time.

They fell asleep in each other's arms. The white owl remained silently watching over them from the branch of a nearby oak tree.

After a communal breakfast, Peter and Alice gathered their things. Before they left, they nervously approached Black Elk, who was sitting by a fire outside the teepee. They warmly thanked him for the magical ceremony he allowed them be part of the previous night. Peter then gave Black Elk a wild boar's tusk he found on the riverbank that morning. He thanked them for his gift and then asked Alice if she was alright, because he noticed her suffering during the ceremony. She replied that she found the experience to be very traumatic but felt that a dark shadow had lifted from her. Black Elk then said, "I know. You will now leave here a different person, or rather I should say, you will be leaving as your true self."

Peter and Alice then drove a few miles to the market town of Sherborne, where they hung round for the rest of the day. They both needed time away from the cottage to assimilate the moving experience of the sweat lodge. They returned home later in the evening.

Chapter 22

The following morning, they were disturbed from their restful sleep by the sound of a mouse scurrying along the bedroom floorboards. The likelihood was that it was heading for its winter home in the thatched roof, having just moved in from the garden.

Peter tenderly stroked Alice's hair; she loved the feeling of his fingers exploring its smooth surface. He then went down to the kitchen to make her a hearty breakfast, the full greasy spoon works, including black pudding and fried bread. It had enough cholesterol to block a tube tunnel. He then served it to her on a tray in bed.

On seeing this mountain of `fat, ` she comically exclaimed.

"Are you trying to take a year of my life by giving me this gut buster to eat? I've just lost twenty-five of them already and I don't particularly want to lose any more!"

"Look Alice, I have figured out a way of killing someone that even the best CSI forensic detectives in the world can't prove- slow death by greasy spoon!"

"I knew it- you mass murderer. Pol Pot has got nothing on you!"

Over the following weeks, they lived as a couple in the cottage for the first time, rather than as two autonomous people sharing the same household. They also shared the same bed. They still retained a healthy independence, but now they were true lovers embarking on a new life together, far removed from their damaged pasts.

Alice was a changed person after her experience in the sweat lodge. The all-conquering black forest of fear she carried had retreated and was replaced by the seedling of self-love.

She eventually told Peter about the strange experiences she had after the ceremony. He listened carefully as she recounted the invisible presence walking behind her, her dream of Petra saving the young girl and boy and the stars moving in a north easterly direction. Peter said he was certain that she was the same Petra who had saved him and taken him to meet God. He also thought the young girl and boy she rescued might represent themselves. He also wondered whether Petra was the invisible spirit guide who walked behind her. But neither had any idea about the meaning of the moving stars.

However, two weeks later, Alice rushed out to Peter, who was putting out some bird food in the garden. She excitedly told him about a passage she had just read in a book on native American spirituality, in which a vision of the stars moving in a north-easterly direction signifies the death of the old self. She now understood that the stars represented the death of her old wounded self and the birth of her true self, just as Black Elk had said.

They went on to live happily together and cherished each other's company. They redecorated the house and worked on creating a wildlife garden in its extensive grounds. They still carried on their regular dates, but this would quite often mean having a romantic evening at home. He loved to make her feel good about herself and he never let go of his gentlemanly ways.

Alice began writing again. She wrote short stories at first and then a novel called "The Ether." It was about a young woman who was trapped in a parallel dimension, called the Ether. She was unable to communicate with the world outside, which she could see through a transparent membrane. One day, she caught sight of a handsome young man across the screen, through which he could also see her. They fell in love at first sight. Unable to hear or touch one another, they communicated by writing letters, which they pressed against the thin film between them. But as the years went by, their separation became unbearable and they were both close to dying of a broken heart. Then, one day, on the brink of death, a blinding light flooded their worlds, melting the membrane, thereby freeing them to embrace one another for the first time.

She loved the experience of writing and letting her imagination roam where it will. Alice gave up her jobs as a cleaner and tutor in order to concentrate more on her writing. She found a part time job teaching English literature in a comprehensive school on a rough council estate in Exeter. This paid more than her other previous combined jobs and the hours were much less. She became a brilliant teacher who inspired many young lives. The pupils were drawn to her warm and loving nature. She treated them with the same care and tenderness Petra had shown to her `strays. `

Alice felt a growing inner strength, which gave her belief in herself for the first time. She could now communicate normally with other people, rather than shut herself off from them as she had done in the past.

One Saturday morning, whilst shopping in a farmer's market in Dorchester, she caught sight of her mother for the first time in several months. She was in the process of buying some meat from one of its stalls. Alice, momentarily shaken and confused, composed herself, then went over and spoke to her.

"Hello," she said in a formal manner. Sylvia, quickly turned around to this familiar voice but became poleaxed with shock when she saw her daughter again.

"Alice, it is lovely to see you. Oh my God…I can't believe it's you…you look so well."

"Mum, I have something to say to you…I have forgiven you for knowing about the abuse and doing nothing… but I cannot forget." Her mother was unable to form any words in her mouth. Her face revealed the language of submission. She wanted to tell Alice that she loved her and would like her to come back home to Llanmaes, but she was unable speak.

"I have to be leaving now mother. I hope you have a nice day shopping; try the cheese store, it's very good."

With this gesture, Alice calmly walked away, leaving her mother stupefied.

Peter found a part time job working for three days a week with the theoretical cosmology team of the Physics Department of Exeter University. He also continued to cook in the pub on the weekday evenings.

Much of his remaining free time was taken up working on his God Field theory again. He was now in the right mental and spiritual frame of mind to focus on it once more. Having first tightened up the constructs of its main equation, he addressed the all-important mystery underlying the God Field. He had known for some time that the answer lay in coming to terms with his disturbed past. Uncovering Alice's secret trauma allowed him to face his own for the first time. Furthermore, Biko's, the Eskimo vagrant's and Sterling Reed's guidance that the only way to save himself was to open his heart, led to his forgiveness of Max. His subsequent meeting with God, meant that he finally let `Him` into his heart. He was then finally able to let go of the childhood wounding which had so blighted his life. This gave him the freedom to love, as symbolised in Biko's `Love` story. Meeting Alice again, allowed him to open his heart to love her and receive her love in return.

Even though Peter had brought `closure` on his troubled past and had received confirmation of the God Field from none other than God `Himself, ` it's deeper mystery still eluded him. He continued to work on this solution for several months without making the breakthrough he so desperately desired. Eventually, he gave up his search for he was becoming unhealthily obsessive in his quest to find the answer.

Peter carried on working part-time in the University. However, he had to give up his job as a chef in the pub, for his energies were now required elsewhere. Alice continued to teach with great success. She also managed to find a publisher for her book which was very well a received for first novel. Following this, she was commissioned to write a screenplay based on her book. However, she had to put this on hold for a while, for her energies were also needed elsewhere, for she had recently given birth to a beautiful baby daughter. She was six pounds eleven ounces, with black hair and wide green eyes. They named her Petra. She was conceived on November 3, 2012, exactly nine months after they made love for the first time in the tent after the sweat lodge ceremony.

One chilly winter's night, two months after his daughter's birth, Peter was disturbed from his sleep by his daughter`s crying. Alice remained fast asleep. As he opened his eyes, he saw God, for one brief moment, looking down upon Petra in her cot. By the time Peter had finished rubbing his eyes, He had disappeared. Peter got out of bed, walked over to the cot and picked her up in his arms. She soon stopped crying and looked up at him with her beautiful innocent eyes. Then, all of sudden, he understood the secret that lay at the heart of the God Field, for he felt it. The mysterious energy that is the driving force of creation through the God Field is *God's love* and a newborn child is an expression *of `His` pure love.* The unfolding of the God Field creates the conditions for God's love to express itself.

God cried tears of joy when he witnessed Peter, with his baby daughter in his arms, finally understanding `His` mystery. `His` Beautiful Collector Petra, who also observed what transpired, was so emotional that she struggled to collect the precious psychic energies from this encounter.

Acknowledgements

I would like to express my deep appreciation to my wife, Kathy Kinch, for her continual encouragement and support during the writing and publication of this book. I am also very grateful to my daughter, Tané Kinch, for all of her help in designing the front cover. Furthermore, I would also like to thank my brother Alec Kinch and my friend John Leahy, for helping me see the book through to its completion.

26533485R00195

Printed in Poland
by Amazon Fulfillment
Poland Sp. z o.o., Wrocław